The Soul Hunters

Also by Christopher Torockio

The Truth at Daybreak
Floating Holidays
Presence

The Soul Hunters

a novel

Christopher Torockio

Black
Lawrence
Press

Black
Lawrence
Press

www.blacklawrence.com

Executive Editor: Diane Goettel
Book and cover design: Amy Freels
Cover image: *Red Edge* / Girts Gailans

Copyright © Christopher Torockio 2015
ISBN: 978-1-62557-936-2

Published 2016 by Black Lawrence Press.
Printed in the United States.

Portions of this novel previously appeared in *Ploughshares* and *Colorado Review*.

For Halle
and for Giovanni

*"No one leaves the lights on
in a house where nobody lives anymore."*

—Ryan Adams, "When Will You Come Back Home"

Part One

The Table

Prologue: Abigail

They should have let the ExerCycle go for fifteen. It was a more-than-generous offer—Abigail knew this. But Sydney had sworn up and down to the contraption's "nostalgic value" as a "collector's item," and deemed it worth twenty. (*Twenty?* Please. The thing wasn't nostalgic, it was *archaic!* Nick and Abigail had bought it for his parents as a Christmas present back when the first rumors began circulating across the country that exercise might actually be *good* for you, when jogging was cutting-edge. The eighties, maybe? Seventies? Good lord, a *long* time ago.) In any case, Sydney had slapped a hand-scribbled $20 sticker on the handlebars and then held firm when an elderly gentleman in coveralls and complicated-looking trifocals was willing to take it off their hands for fifteen. Unexpectedly rebuffed, the man had shrugged, slid his hands into his pockets, and sauntered off down the driveway. Before he got to the street he turned, orange sun setting behind him.

"Knew your dad," he said, though Abigail could not place him, nor could she remember him being at the service. "Good man, Carmelo," he added. "Tough S.O.B., that's for sure." He considered his own words, staring up into the telephone wires connecting to the apex of the roof, as if reminiscing on a particular incident neither fondly nor remorsefully. Abigail had an urge to call out to him as he continued on down the driveway and turned at the mailbox. But she didn't. She'd never see him again anyway.

The ExerCycle was one of only a few remaining items scattered across the side lawn. Abigail was surprised the set of three hubcaps didn't go—they were mismatched, but perfectly usable. Some of the things, though—she wasn't even sure what they were *for*. Nick's father had a way of adapting ordinary household items to his own quirky personal use. Lidless cigar boxes had been placed in kitchen drawers to hold the silverware. They found rosemary, amazingly, planted in a Drambuie bottle, the panicked stalks somehow pushing their way out through the tiny opening at the top. A cedar trunk/coffee table had been transformed into a rather roomy doghouse for Brownie the Beagle.

(The question of Brownie herself had yet to be addressed. She bounded around the yard all afternoon like an inmate released on bail. People occasionally bent down and tapped her head, but nobody looked her in the eyes.)

In the end, though, most everything in the yard had sold. People actually stopped by looking for particular items: "Your dad still got that old weed-whacker he built from the blender motor layin' around?" (Yes, but it didn't work, and even when it *had* worked you had to plug it into an outlet, which seemed to Abigail a significant drawback for a weedwhacker. They took $4 for it.) One neighbor bought the entire collection of snowglobes from all of the campsites and trailer parks Nick's parents had visited over the years; another bought the water-warped, two-stringed banjo. What didn't sell, Nick and his brothers were now pitching into the dumpster—for which their cousin Raymond, who worked for the Township, had arranged—off to the side of the driveway. Most everything that remained was on the smaller side—knickknacks and utensils and various bits and pieces from the bottoms of closets and drawers—and could be tossed into the dumpster from considerable distance. Soon, a contest started up—fifty-something-year-old men challenging each other to see who could throw their father's old, unwanted belongings into the dumpster from the greatest distance.

Watching them, Abigail climbed onto the ExerCycle and began pedaling. The chain stuck at first, emitted a grinding, zipper-like sound. Soon, though, the chain smoothed out and settled into a crackling rhythm. Abigail rested her elbows on the handlebars. The sun was nearly gone now; a crisp, glassy coolness had settled over the yard. Abigail peddled harder. The ExerCycle's dust-covered speedometer didn't work; she had no idea how fast she was going.

"Yo! Check this out," Lawrence, the oldest son, called from behind a birdbath in the neighbor's yard, then reared back and flung a tattered rubber welcome mat like a Frisbee, which twisted and fluttered through the air and finally slapped off the side of the dumpster and fell to the ground.

"Ha!" said Stuart, the youngest. "Watch *this*!" He turned his back to the dumpster and heaved a threadbare carry-on sized suitcase over his head. The suitcase came unclasped in mid-air and dropped like a stone, nearly plunking Nick on the head and causing him to duck frantically out of the way, arms waving. The men laughed for a moment then abruptly stopped, as if remembering themselves, and continued with their work. A minute later, though, Cousin Raymond heaved a bald blue-wall tire, Olympic hammer-throw style, across the yard, and the games resumed.

From the woods beyond the house, across the adjacent street, Abigail heard the chirrup of a hoot owl.

"You should just take it." Sydney appeared at her shoulder.

"What?"

Sydney nodded at the ExerCycle, touched her recently protruding belly with the flat of her palm. "You were right. Shoulda backed off at fifteen. My bad. You should just take it."

Abigail caught herself staring dumbly at that belly; she blinked and focused on the gas grill over Sydney's shoulder. Before anything was hauled out to the yard, the brothers had divvied up everything they wanted from the house. There were few disagreements. Things that had once belonged to, or had been gifts from a particular brother, simply reverted back. Everything else of modest value was spread around in what Abigail thought was an amazingly judicious and friendly manner, and what remained became part of today's yard sale. As for the grill, years ago cement had been poured around its base, rendering it a permanent fixture that would transfer to the new owners of the house. (It was absolutely amazing how many people Raymond knew, from one end of the county to the other: the house was already sold, without a real estate agent, a handshake agreement.) Abigail wanted to say to Sydney that, seeing as how she and Nick bought the ExerCycle in the first place, she didn't need her ridiculously pregnant sister-in-law's permission to take it now. But Sydney had no way of knowing this; she was young, thirty-eight last month, and had only been married to Stuart for a couple of years—Stu's third wife; Abigail's second-favorite. So instead she said, "I think we're going to end up taking the dog."

Sydney nodded. A breeze swept past them and Abigail could smell the compost heap out behind the grape arbor. *A baby*, she thought. *Some people don't know when to call it quits.*

She kept pedaling, feeling her blood thicken and warm.

"Whoa-oh-*oh!*" Lawrence called out. "Hold up." He approached the dumpster with his arms outspread in a hold-everything gesture. Then, bad back and all, he climbed up the side of the dumpster and disappeared inside headfirst. A moment later his head popped back up; his glasses hung from one ear. "I *wanted* this," he said, and held up what looked to Abigail like a dented metal cash box.

"We *asked* you last night if you wanted it," Nick pointed out. He reached across his chest and rubbed is left shoulder; apparently he'd aggravated his old high-school football injury—an injury he rarely talked about, even to Abigail.

"The hell you did."

"The hell we *didn't*," Stuart said.

"Whatever," Lawrence said and reaffixed his glasses. "Jag-offs. Come on and help me out of here. I think I pulled something."

1. Nick

He'd surprised himself last night by claiming his father's old nickel-finish Colt revolver. There was no battle to be fought here—no one else wanted the thing; no one wanted any of the guns that were lined up in the cabinet (they couldn't sell them, a legal issue, something about permits, which everyone agreed, though annoying, sounded reasonable)—yet the force of Nick's insistence that he assume ownership of the pistol had taken the family aback. They'd blinked at him around the kitchen table until Celina asked if anyone wanted more coffee, then got up to retrieve the pot.

The sun was completely down now. Nick's shoulder pulsed. Dazzling layers of pink and purple streaked against a backdrop of gauzy black cirrus clouds to the west, in the direction of McTighe's dairy farm. Nick had worked there after school and during his summers home from college in Johnstown and then Pittsburgh—milking, feeding, spreading hay, using pitchforks to shovel liquidy globs of God-knew-what that the owners cryptically called "salage." The money he'd made over the years from the job had paid for his books, his meals, his dormitory room, and a portion of his tuition. The remaining balance on the tuition was supplemented by his father's savings, which had been depleted somewhat by Lawrence's college years, and would have to last through Stuart's. Many years later, prior to every semester, when Nick wrote the check out to Justin's pricey, private, out-of-state university—for the whole shebang:

tuition, room, board, books, fees—he felt his chest heave and his breath catch, a joyous sort of absolute satisfaction and amazement.

The feeling was familiar, but was much more welcome than the first time he'd experienced such a curious emotional mix. This would have been July 1967, and his draft notice had recently arrived. He'd only been eighteen for a matter of weeks; the notice was mixed into the day's mail along with three or four graduation cards. People joked, when they could find a way to tiptoe around the reality behind it all, about how incredibly *fast* his draft board had gotten to him. How maybe that "luck" would carry over into other things. Maybe he should play the horses. Empty his bank account and take it all down to the V.F.W. on Bingo Night and let it ride. Occasionally people would talk about deferments for college, but Nick hadn't yet enrolled for the fall; and besides, there was talk that the Selective Service would begin granting deferments only to those college students with good grades. Nick didn't know exactly how "good grades" might be defined, but he hadn't taken any classes yet anyway and therefore *had* no grades. He figured he'd just take his physical and see what happened.

Because the truth was Nick wasn't all that sure he *wanted* to avoid serving. The idea of going off to war scared him, yes. Terrified him. For one thing, he wanted a life outside of this tiny, dead-end Westmoreland County town, and he nearly brought himself to tears with the thought of dying before he got that chance. And he didn't want to die, plain and simple, but especially not on the other side of the world, alone, his parents, his family, unaware of the fact that he was in the process of dying, and then dead, until a man in a uniform showed up at their door, *his* door, the door of his home. There would be a period of time—two days, a week, three weeks; who knew how long these things took?—when his parents wouldn't know he was dead; they'd go about their days and nights thinking he was alive, or at least still *hoping* he was. Then, after receiving the news, they'd be forced to go back in their minds and revise those seemingly hopeful days and imagine their son's last moments, and…Nick would lie in bed at night, into the wee hours, his bowels constricting as his mind went crazy with the horrifying possibilities, one scenario layering on top of another and branching out into still more.

But he also couldn't get away from the knowledge that if he did somehow manage to avoid this, he'd regret it. *What* he'd regret, he wasn't quite sure, and maybe "regret" wasn't even the right word, but when the day of his physical came around Nick had his mother drop him off at the designated location, a makeshift processing station and examining room set up inside the army recruiting office in New Alexandria. It was a Saturday. She'd go do her grocery shopping at the A&P down the street and pick him up on the way back. As he reached for the Buick's door handle she touched his cheek with the back of her hand, and Nick experienced a passing jolt of feeling like a man.

But, inside, the sight of the officer sitting behind a desk and wearing a heavy, starched green uniform, hat sitting on a pile of manila folders, wiped that feeling right away. He'd expected to find a line of boys waiting to get their physicals, but it seemed he was the only one there. The man took Nick's name, examined his driver's license, had him sign some forms, without explaining them, without allowing Nick time to read them, then stood and led Nick over to another door. Nick stepped inside and a line of faces turned to him. Here were the other boys he'd been expecting, ten or twelve of them, sitting side by side on a long bench, hunched forward. One turned to him and Nick recognized the boy—a kid from Bentlee Area High, but a year ahead. Their eyes met and Nick had an urge to go to the boy, but then the boy turned away and his face blended in with the others. The look of pure fear on those faces sucked the breath from Nick's lungs. It took a moment to get it back in rhythm.

"Okay, son," the man in the green uniform said. "Have a seat. You'll be getting started in a minute."

The boy on the end, a lanky Hispanic kid with a mustache-in-progress, scooted over one ass-cheek so Nick could sit down. It was warm in the room and Nick wondered what it was ordinarily used for. The floor was tile, the ceiling was low, the walls were cinderblock. The bench on which they sat reminded him of a high school locker room, but with no showers or lockers. In one corner was a stack of empty cardboard boxes and in the air Nick could hear the faint buzzing of what sounded like an electric razor. When that sound was broken by the squeaky nervous fart of a boy at the other end of the bench, nobody acknowledged it.

The man in the green uniform entered again from the front room. He looked older this time, even a little decrepit, standing before them. "All right, men, on your feet." Everyone glanced at each other, then stood. "Strip down to your undershorts." When no one moved he clapped his hands together twice. "Let's go, let's go, come on, people. Everything but the skivvies."

Nick and the other boys began pulling off shirts, removing their shoes heel-to-toe, stumbling. They avoided eye contact with at each other. Nick realized, oddly, that his feet were cold. When everyone was down to his underwear another man entered, the doctor apparently. He held a clipboard and wore a white lab coat with a stethoscope dangling from one pocket. He was eating an apple rather noisily.

"Two steps forward," said the man in green, then he moved off against the far wall.

The doctor held the apple between his teeth and wandered around the line of boys, slowly, appraising, as if he might purchase one of them. Nick, though trying to keep his gaze forward, couldn't help noticing that the doctor looked vaguely familiar. He was fortyish, black thinning hair but fat bushy eyebrows. He struck Nick as serious but a little bored. He kept taking deep breaths, as if he were trying to keep from nodding off. After he'd circled around everyone he looked over at the man in green and blinked.

"Okay, men, now drop the Jockeys."

As one, they turned and looked at him. He took a quick step in their direction, as if waiting for an excuse to attack.

"You boys *deaf*? I said drop 'em. Down to the ankles. Then spread your feet shoulder-width apart and bend over and grab on. Now."

They did as they were told, moving slowly. It was as if nobody really believed it would actually come to this, that at any moment a friendly smiling man would jump out and say, Just joshin', fellas. Pull your pants up. Just trying to lighten the mood here a little.

Nick bent over and grabbed onto the rope of underwear stretched between his ankles. He could hear the doctor moving around behind them, and he braced himself for… What? Good lord, for *what*? A wave of titters moved through him and he was afraid he might burst out laughing; then that feeling shrunk away and he could feel tears building up behind his eyes. He blinked and watched two or three fat drops fall and splatter on the floor below.

If I can just make it through this…

"That'll do, boys. Shorts up."

They were instructed to sit back on the bench, and then the man in green took a sheet of paper from the doctor and began calling names one at a time and directing each boy through a door in the adjacent wall that Nick hadn't noticed. That boy remained in this hidden room for about ten minutes, then emerged fully dressed, holding a sheet of onionskin paper, at which point another name would be called. Upon exiting, some stared at his sheet of paper dumbly; others strutted, as if proven right about something. One boy's face was twisted into an expression of such pain Nick wondered if some medieval torturing devices hadn't been affixed somewhere on the kid's body. But when his own name was called and Nick entered the back room he found the whole set-up to be rather ordinary. An examining table; a cabinet that held tongue depressors,

Q-Tips, pamphlets, a metal waste can. The doctor never glanced up from his clipboard, just nodded for Nick to hop up onto the unpadded metal table. He flipped a page over the clipboard and then consulted the page beneath it. He seemed to pause for a moment, glanced up at Nick, then back down at the clipboard. "Okay," he said finally, placing the clipboard aside, "let's see what we can find here."

He attached the blood pressure cuff and pumped, knocked on Nick's knees, listened to his heart, ran his fingers along his spine. "Follow the tip of my pen with your eyes," he said, and Nick did. "Okay, now hop down off the table." The doctor pulled on some rubber gloves and once again Nick's shorts were around his knees and he was told to cough, then again, and then a third time. When that was over the doctor told Nick to dip into a squat, then rise; he told him to bend his elbows. He told him to hold his arms straight out in front of him and then raise them over his head, and when Nick couldn't get his left arm all the way up, because of his injured shoulder, the doctor said, "Hmm…" and went for his clipboard.

"What is it?" Nick said, the first words he'd spoken since giving the green-clad man his name.

"Shoulder needs to elevate beyond ninety degrees."

"Oh. What's that mean?"

"It means," the doctor said, "you're off the hook." He scribbled some notes and tore off an onionskin page and handed it to Nick. "Get dressed, then give this to Sergeant Voss on your way out."

Nick took the sheet and headed for the door. Something held him there, though, and when he turned back to the doctor he found the man watching him, clipboard cradled in against his chest, a stray flip of black hair hanging across his eyebrows. "It's okay," he said. "Off you go now."

Once the door was closed behind him, the three remaining boys staring up from their seats on the bench, Nick allowed himself to look at the onionskin paper. It was signed by a Dr. W. Musgrave. Toward the bottom, two boxes were checked: "Shoulder—Forward Abduction to 90°" and "IV-F—Unfit for Duty."

In the outer room the man in green, Sergeant Voss, twitched and sat up in his chair when Nick entered. He touched some items on his desk, as if to make sure they were still there, and took the paper from Nick. "Let's see what's what here, soldier," he said, reaching for a pen, but took a clear double- and then triple-take at the words on Nick's form. "Huh," he said finally. He leaned back in his chair and studied Nick, who wondered if maybe this man had the authority to reverse the doctor's judgment, a possibility that struck Nick with simultaneous hope and dread.

"Shoulder, eh?" Sergeant Voss glanced at the paper again, in case, Nick supposed, he might have read it wrong.

"Yes, sir."

"'S'matter with it?"

"Hurt it playing football last year. Rotator cuff, they think. But I kept playing the rest of the season—"

Sergeant Voss waved this away. "Which arm?"

"Left."

"So what's the problem? That your jerkin' off arm?"

Nick avoided the man's eyes. There were curtains in the front windows of the room, like an insurance office. Through the window he could see his parents' Buick parked across the street, his mother sitting behind the wheel, her eyes closed. Voss' question had sounded like a challenge but Nick wasn't sure how he might respond to it.

When Nick turned back to Voss he found the man still watching him. Finally he took a breath, and—almost imperceptibly—nodded. Then Voss filled out yet another form—a form he had to dig out of one of the lower desk drawers—and, without meeting his eyes, handed it across to Nick.

"Shoulder," Sergeant Voss spat. "All right then. Head on home and tell whoever it is that their influence paid off. Coulda come up with something more original than a shoulder, though. My opinion."

"But—" Nick began, and again Voss cut him off.

"That'll be all, son. Enjoy your life."

....

He swung the Buick's door closed behind him and just sat. A truck carrying hogs clattered past. Nick could see curly tails squirting out through the wooden slats. The radio, turned low, gave off the faint murmurings of human voices.

"So?" his mother finally said.

"So nothing," he said. "So tomorrow I'll send away for an application to Pitt. And that'll be that."

She closed her eyes, just for a second, and opened them. "Try Duquesne, too. If you're dead-set on Pittsburgh. Okay? Just 'cause they're Catholic. For me."

"Fine," he said, and let out a breath that felt and sounded much closer to annoyed exhaustion than he'd anticipated.

"Just try."

"Okay, Mom," he said.

....

When they pulled into the driveway his father was out behind the grape arbor, in the garden. He was using a hose to spray down a section of green beans.

His mother took the key from the ignition and reached for her purse on the bench seat between them. "You should go tell him," she said.

Nick nodded. He could hear the Buick's engine ticking, cooling down. His father had fought in World War Two, in Guadalcanal, one of the earliest American offensives. He'd returned home with his own injuries, shrapnel that tore through a knee preventing him from ever being able to straighten it all the way, and two toes missing, the result of an accident he didn't like to talk about. Nick wasn't sure how he was supposed to feel about any of this. Of all the scenes he'd rehearsed in his mind, lying in bed all those nights, this wasn't one of them. And so he felt nothing.

He and his mother headed up the walk together to the side porch, and she put a hand on his shoulder. *The* shoulder, which, at the moment, didn't hurt at all. When they got to the porch she let her hand slide off and went on in the house, letting the storm door clatter shut behind her.

The faint smell of grass clippings and chicken manure (Nick had long ago learned to differentiate between varieties) drifted on the air. Over the years Nick's father had increased the size of his garden to about that of half a football field. He grew a few rows each of corn, beans, carrots, green peppers, head lettuce, cabbage, zucchini, snap peas. A few herb plants, basil and rosemary. Plus each year he'd toss in a wildcard or two: radishes, watermelon, Brussels sprouts. A couple of summers back he'd nursed a pumpkin to forty pounds.

A convertible blasting The Who rambled past on State Route 33 and Nick's father lifted his head to watch it, then noticed Nick standing there between the grape arbor and back porch. He stared for a moment, squinted, the lenses of his glasses reflecting the sunlight, then turned the hose back on. Nick lifted a hand to wave—a gesture he couldn't possibly have explained—but his father had already gone back to what he was doing.

Again, Nick was at a loss. So strange, he thought, not to know how to proceed, to not have the slightest clue, at a moment such as this. So he walked through a row of summer squash, one of this year's wildcards, pulling out the stray weeds he saw. There weren't many. He wondered where Stuart was. Inside reading, probably. He was on a Jack London kick this week. Last week was Hemingway.

Lawrence wasn't around either. He'd stayed back in State College for the summer, having landed a job on campus, cleaning out a laboratory or something—Nick wasn't entirely sure—that would pay for a big chunk of tuition in the fall, his junior year. If nothing else, going into the army would have enabled Nick, assuming he returned from Vietnam alive, to go to school on the G.I. Bill, which would have made things a lot easier. Now... well, more struggles. For everyone.

He worked his way down the row of squash then skirted the perimeter by the road. He tossed the weeds he'd picked onto the gravel shoulder. At some point his father had shut off the hose and was now bent over, examining something, pushing leaves aside. He was an imposing figure, with long arms and big hands and wide, square shoulders, all of which made him look taller than he actually was. He wore Dickies and a plaid cowboy shirt, unbuttoned, over his undershirt. They were no more than fifty feet away from each other, but, oddly, operating within their own galaxies. It reminded Nick of those *Wild Kingdom* episodes where two bears would wander into the same meadow and ignore each other, each waiting for the other to move on and find another meadow. When neither did, inevitably, a vicious clash erupted, which would settle the issue. Such face-offs typically ended with one bear limping off, angry and humiliated. It was all a simple matter of instinct, the voiceover would explain.

Why he and his father should experience a similar impulse, now of all times, Nick couldn't have fathomed. But there it was. He felt it.

He was ready to be the shamed one, ready to lower his head and trudge into the house, sit at the kitchen table and allow his mother to comfort him with some hard salami and cheese, maybe a couple of left-over ravioli from the night before, when he heard, "Hey, come on over here a minute. Wanna show you something."

Nick's father was still bent over whatever plant he'd been examining, glasses slipping down his nose. A breeze had blown his hair straight down across his forehead, and Nick could make out the outline of thinning patches where his father would go soon bald. He didn't look old, but for the first time Nick saw in him the potential to one day *be* old. The realization made Nick feel a little clobbered.

Nick stepped over a row of cabbage and weaved between earthy clumps of something his father had just recently planted.

"Look-it."

Nick rose up onto his toes and peered over his father's shoulder. A big, dirt-caked hand was pushing aside a tangle of zucchini blossoms, beneath which Nick could see the tattered carcass of some small, furry, previously living creature. The fur was gray, about the size of a playing card, and looked as if it'd been run through a blender. Nick could make out part of a leg, a bit of what might have been spine trailing out of what was left of the blood-crusted torso. No head to speak of.

"Ew," was all Nick could manage.

"You know what this means, don't you?" his father said.

"That animals are getting into your garden."

"Well, yeah." His father released the zucchini plant which, thankfully, sprung back in front of the furry remains, covering them. He lowered himself onto both knees then, plucked a tuft of stray grass from the soil. "Rabbit, looks like. I can deal with rabbits. But how do you suppose it came to be in the condition this one is in now?"

Nick felt one foot sinking slightly into the soft earth and shifted his weight. *How did it come to be in this condition?* His mind went blank. Land mine? Chainsaw? Atom bomb? "Don't know," he said.

His father brushed his hands together. "My guess? Coyote."

"Oh. Hey, uh, Dad…"

"Probably come from over there." He gestured towards the woods that bordered Route 33 and went on for miles, where he often hunted small game. "Might need to put up a fence, keep my .32 handy. And keep an eye on that dog of yours, too. Coyotes don't view dogs as cousins. They view 'em as supper."

"Okay, I will. But, listen, Dad…"

"Yeah?" He looked up at Nick and squinted. The tinkle of wind chimes carried from the back porch.

"So I, um," Nick said, "I went for my physical today."

"Uh-huh." He leaned back on his heels. "How'd it go?"

"Well, I…I kinda failed."

And his father's gaze left him for just a moment, a brief scan of the sky above the grape arbor, then returned. "You did, huh?"

"Yeah."

"Your shoulder."

Nick nodded. He sensed a pulling in his chest. He was ashamed; he was insanely happy. He had the distinct understanding that he was safe, yet this safety made him sick with fear.

His father rose, nodded almost imperceptibly. "That's good," he said, and let out a breath of unmistakable relief. Nick felt a cry rise up in him but he choked it back, expelling a sound like a goose honking.

"Get a shovel, would you?" his father said. "Let's take care of this thing."

....

Nick didn't get into Pitt's main campus, in the city—even with rolling admissions he'd applied too late and the incoming freshmen class was filled—but he was invited to attend the Pitt-Johnstown branch and, after a year or two, depending on availability and his grades, he could then transfer to the Oakland campus. For the rest of the summer he worked as many hours as he could at McTighe's, putting all but a few bucks a week—for a movie or a six-pack to bring with him when he went over to his buddy Midge's house—into his savings account. Midge was stocking shelves part time at the Red & White and running errands he didn't understand for a bookie who worked out of the Elks Club. His draft notice hadn't come yet, but he expected it any time—and he didn't expect any sort of deferment, medical or otherwise, either.

Since the day of his physical Nick had been receiving hesitant nods accompanied by perplexed smiles and slightly furrowed brows in response to the news that he'd failed because of a bum shoulder. Wow, they'd say. What a stroke of luck, huh? Must've had a *really* thorough doctor. Because the fact was, this was war time. The army wasn't turning anyone away. *Any* movement in a limb was good enough. The only relevant questions were: Can you walk? Can you hold a rifle? Yeah? You're in.

Nick sensed a certain amount of snickering and mild gossip around town, but he had to admit that the knowledge of having the next four years more or less set was comforting. It was just that he couldn't get the familiarity of that doctor's face out of his mind. At odd times the image would assemble before his eyes, as if the channel he'd been watching was suddenly switched—he'd be rinsing off in the shower, or pitch-forking a mound of salage into a heifer's stall, focused on whatever task was at hand—and there it'd be: that eyebrow, that wisp of black hair, the double-take he'd given to Nick's form: *Dr. W. Musgrave.*

He took to carrying his onionskin physical form around with him, folded in his wallet.

Later, he'd tell himself he was grateful. He'd also tell himself he was angry, insulted. Most of all, though, he'd tell himself he should have known. Yet he didn't *really* know until he happened upon the scribbles on the notebook paper on his father's bedside table. The paper was folded into sixteenths but was open, lying like an overturned turtle. Nick had gone into his parents' bedroom one Friday afternoon in August. He'd just gotten home from work and needed a pair of black dress socks for his date that night with Rachel Mechanowitz. He was digging in the drawer there when the scribbles caught his attention. He unfolded the paper and revealed the drawing: building plans, Nick knew right away. His father worked in the coal mines near Keystone when the work was good, but he was an electrician by trade; he was always building something, for himself or others. He and his brother, Nick's Uncle Vince, ran an under-the-table construction business on the side. They built porch steps, doghouses, fences, backyard sheds. They painted. They roofed. They sheetrocked. Once they built an addition onto the Knutsen's house so that Mrs. Knutsen's ancient mother could live in it. They charged for materials (which Nick's father could get cheap) plus what everyone in town agreed was a reasonable fee, Carmelo's cut of which went straight into the boys' college savings account.

The plans lying on the bedside table were elaborate, though, and that's why Nick's attention lingered on it longer than it might otherwise have. At least that's what he would later tell himself. He flattened the paper and after a few moments recognized the drawing as that of a patio. Two levels, with built-in benches and flower boxes. Sixteen-by-twenty-four. At the top of the page his father had written *Bill M*. And next to it the notation *N/C*. Nick dropped the paper back on the table and left without the black socks.

He considered following his father the next day, tailing him like a private eye and seeing what evidence he could dig up. But he didn't. He couldn't foresee any semblance of a positive outcome in such an act, and anyway the truth was not difficult figure out: Dr. William Musgrave, M.D., was in the local phone book. He had a private practice in Greensburg but would be shutting down for an undisclosed period of time to serve as a medical officer in Vietnam. He graduated from the same high school as his parents, a couple years behind them, was married to a woman from DuBois, and had a daughter who went to Greensburg Central Catholic. Apparently Nick's father had never cared for the man—at least according to Uncle Vince, who, sitting at the kitchen table early one August morning, sipping coffee and waiting for Nick's father to come downstairs so they could start the day, volunteered information in alarming abundance. He was helping out on the patio job—as a favor, sure, but not for *free*. Nick's father was kicking a little something his way. "'Cept he won't tell me why we're doin' this," said Uncle Vince. "They're makin' money hand over balls down the mines this time a year." He leaned back in his chair, feet stretched out in front of him, boots unlaced. He was a chronically dirty man—it always looked to Nick as if he'd been ink-smudged by a giant thumb—who, legend had it, suffered some residual effects from having been hit in the head by a cinderblock when he was a kid. "I mean, your old man never even *liked* the guy. Beat the fucker up once in high school, as I recall." He shrugged, went to take a slug of coffee, saw that the cup was empty, and set it back on the table.

Nick muttered something about having no idea about any of that, then headed out the door for work himself. He didn't want to be late, and he didn't want to be there, in the kitchen with Uncle Vince, when his father came downstairs.

....

Once the reality of what his father had done sunk in, the anger and shame he'd felt, while never disappearing entirely, began to give way to gratitude, and love—or at least an acknowledgment of the fact that his father surely must love him to have finagled such a deal. Not that he'd ever truly doubted it, but the man who Nick, Lawrence, and Stuart called Dad had never been one to flaunt affection. He was honest, though, and if Nick were simply to ask him about the course of events that led to his avoiding military service, his father would have sighed and cracked a can of Rolling Rock and told him the truth. But then Nick would have wanted to fall into his father's arms, to press his face to his father's chest and let the tears come; to confess the fear he'd felt at the prospect of going off to fight, and his shame at having avoided that fight, at missing the opportunity to face down the fear, to return home having accomplished something. He'd want to thank him, to let his father know how much he appreciated the sacrifice, and that he understood how *much* he'd sacrificed—the willingness to approach a man he obviously didn't like (why, Nick would never learn) and ask him for such a favor, then to repay that favor by working like a servant for that same man, all with the knowledge that the sacrifices would only beget sacrifices: thousands upon thousands of dollars he didn't have for more college tuition.

Then again, Nick thought, maybe he'd done it not for Nick but for Nick's mother? He could see that. He could see them laying in bed in the dark, his mother's whisper filling the room: *Don't let them take my son.* And his father's nod, not seen but felt.

The only other possibility, which occurred to Nick several times a day, nearly zapping the balance from his knees, was that Nick's father did what he'd done not for Nick, and not for Nick's mother, but for himself. *He* didn't want to lose his son, and he did what he had to do, *whatever* he had to do, to make sure that didn't happen.

How did you thank a person for something like that? Even if that person's your dad.

Especially if that person's your dad.

....

For days after the physical, then a week, then two weeks, both Nick and his father got up in the morning and went to "work"—Nick to McTighe's, his father, presumably, to Musgrave's house. One afternoon Nick walked up the driveway, stinking and tired from a day of tying and stacking hay bales (apparently old man McTighe had no problem with the abduction levels of Nick's shoulder) and found his father in the garden again, crouched with his hands on his knees.

"Damn coyote again," he said when Nick was close enough.

The evidence was plain: the area around the beets and cabbage was strewn with big patches of brown fur and chunks of what Nick figured must be meat and bone. Strips of hide hung in the beet plants like Christmas ornaments. The soil was stirred up and several of the plants were shredded. Whatever the animal was, it had not just been killed but devoured. Nick's first thought was that it looked like a battlefield after a heavy shelling. But that wasn't quite right. It looked like a crime scene, a murder. A gruesome one, some sort of ritualistic serial killing.

"How do you know it's a coyote?" Nick asked.

His father shrugged. "What else could it be?"

When Nick didn't respond his father pointed vaguely at the mess in front of them. "A groundhog, this one. Or a gopher. Pretty big one."

"You don't want them in your garden, though, right? Gophers and rabbits and stuff, I mean."

"Well, I don't want no coyotes around, neither. This one's getting a bit too comfortable, seems to me. Found itself a steady feeding ground."

They put on gloves and got shovels and a garbage bag and cleaned up what was left of the groundhog/gopher, which, even when all the pieces were collected, didn't add up to much. And as they worked in silence it struck Nick what he needed to do. So that night, when the house seemed quiet enough, Nick got out of bed and switched on the lamp on the nightstand. Ordinarily he and Stuart shared a room, but with Lawrence in State College for the summer Nick had moved into the empty one for the time being. He pulled on a pair of jeans and a sweatshirt and stepped out into the hallway where he saw light spilling from Stuart's cracked-open bedroom door. There was no hallway upstairs, just a landing surrounded by the three bedrooms and bathroom, and Nick tried to move quickly to the first step but before he could start down Stuart appeared in his doorway, blinking, his reddish hair wild, thumb marking the page of a fat paperback.

"Where're you sneaking off to?" he wanted to know.

"Nowhere," Nick whispered. "Keep your voice down. And what're you doing up anyway? It's like…"

"One o'clock." He held up the book. It was Ayn Rand. "This stinks."

"Then quit reading it."

"Can't." Then an impish smile formed on his face. "Oh, *I* know where you're going," he said, and nodded knowingly. "Rachel Mechanowitz."

Nick moved gently toward the stairs. "Just keep it to yourself," he said.

"I knew it!" Stuart slapped the book against his thigh.

"Shhh," Nick hissed. "Go back to bed."

Stuart smiled, reached his free hand down inside the waistband of his pajama bottoms and scratched, then turned back into his room.

Downstairs, in the far corner of the dining room, Nick shined a flashlight into his father's gun cabinet. He thought he remembered his father saying something about the .32. This was good. He was a better shot with the rifles but Nick was more comfortable loading and operating the Colt. He shoved it barrel-first into the back pocket of his jeans then rummaged around for the box of ammunition, which he found in just a few seconds but promptly dropped, bullets clattering across the hardwood floor like ball bearings.

He picked up as many as he could, crawling around on his knees and elbows, flashlight shoved under his arm, and he hoped he'd gotten them all. If not, it wouldn't be so outrageous for the rest of the family to assume that his father had dropped the bullets and neglected to pick them all up. But then, as he moved down the hallway toward the kitchen door, it occurred to Nick that he *wanted* his father to know what he was doing—that was the whole point, wasn't it? Or was it?

Flashlight still in his armpit, he slid six bullets into the cylinder as he backed out the kitchen door, then flicked the cylinder shut, exactly as his father had taught him. It must have been tough on his father, how none of his sons took to his love of hunting. They didn't even like to fish, though they tolerated that activity a bit more often. Lawrence, being the oldest and therefore, Nick supposed, feeling the most responsibility, stuck with it the longest. But as each year of high school ticked away he'd found more and more reasons to have some other obligation on the first day of deer season. Nick is certain that's why Lawrence went out for the basketball team. Lawrence didn't even *like* basketball, rode the bench his entire career.

Stuart never even made a token effort.

Now Nick hefted the gun in front of him, in both hands, barrel skyward, like he'd seen on *Gunsmoke*, James Arness tracking an outlaw. He moved across the porch toward the grape arbor. It was tough to see. No stars, no moon. He could make out Route 33 running along the side yard, like a dark river, the woods beyond, and the wide black emptiness of the garden before him. The tall grass brushed his shins as he walked—he couldn't remember if it was his turn to mow it or Stuart's. God forbid his little brother should be forced to put down a book and *work* around the house.

There was no wind, the smell of coming rain. What Nick needed was for his eyes to adjust to the darkness. He paused in the grass and stared, tried to make out his father's neat rows of vegetables. He could smell the compost. The air was warm on the backs of his hands, the back of his neck, but he found he was shivering. He felt exposed, vulnerable. He'd been out in his backyard like this, at far more absurd hours than this, a million times—last year he'd unclasped Mary Gentry's bra on the bench-swing beneath the grape arbor at four in the morning—and never had he been afraid. The fact that Mary Gentry had *let him do it* shocked him a bit, true. But the idea of his father's garden, Nick's own backyard, serving as some demented creature's "feeding ground" shot Nick through with a bona fide, icy fear.

It could be anywhere.

The cornstalks loomed.

Nick pulled back the hammer and felt the cylinder turn and lock a round into the chamber.

His eyes were beginning to adjust now. Objects were beginning to acquire depth, edges, dimension. He approached the near perimeter of the garden and knelt down next to the plum tree. The grass was warm but oddly, almost imperceptibly, damp. Nick imagined microscopic critters hatching and burrowing and teeming beneath the blades of grass all around him. His hands were sweating, his palms slick against the nickel-plated grip. What was he looking for exactly? What would he see? Eyes? A shadow moving across Route 33 from the woods? What if a car drove by and saw *him*, crouched with a gun beneath the plum tree?

Didn't matter. He was going to do this.

But maybe he should have come up with more of a plan first.

He wondered if maybe he should walk around, up and down the rows, gun poised, like a badass corrections officer. No. The thing to do was to stay hidden. Stay sharp. Retain the element of surprise. But, then again, maybe the coyote could smell him. Maybe it knew he was here even before crossing the road.

And he shouldn't have worn this bright red sweatshirt.

Still, he waited. After a time his knees began to ache so he lay down on this chest, like a sniper, but he couldn't see over the nearest row. He tried sitting on his butt, cross-legged, then thought about climbing a couple of branches up into the plum tree. That worked for a while—leaning back slightly into the trunk, one foot up on the next branch, the other wedged into the crotch for support—until a couple of sharp nubs in the bark began pressing into his ribs. When he dropped the five or six feet to the ground the gun slipped from his hand and clunked in the grass. He picked it up, wiped the grip off with his sweatshirt. His vision was beginning to get screwy; the world around him was almost *too* vivid now. He felt like he was wandering inside a painting. And, like a trigonometry problem suddenly clicking into focus, it struck Nick that no coyote was going to wander into this painting tonight.

He walked over to the grape arbor and sat down on the swing. His hips ached. His shoulder throbbed, but he figured that was probably psychological. He let his mind drift back to that night with Mary Gentry on this very swing. It had not, given the circumstances, been a very good night. They were going through the motions. She'd let him unhook her bra for the simple sake of letting him do it. They'd liked each other once but the feelings had for some reason faded. They were wearing shorts but the night air was cool—every few seconds Nick could feel her teeth chattering—and the aluminum slats of the two-person swing were pressing into their backs and bare thighs. Plus, speaking of aluminum, her father had gotten a job with Alcoa—a managerial position of some sort, a big deal around town—and her family would be moving to Knoxville, Tennessee, at the end of the summer. Which they did. He hadn't heard from her since.

He aimed the pistol in the general direction of the garden, then zeroed in on the scarecrow his father had built out of two wood posts tied together like a crucifix and draped in his old clothes—a flannel shirt and mesh-backed baseball cap emblazoned with a rocket ship and the words *Cape Canaveral Florida*. His hand was steady; he felt sure if he squeezed the trigger he could pick the cap right off of the stick. His shoulder was fine.

A light sprang on in his parents' bedroom window. He lowered the gun, waited for a shadow to pass behind the shade, but none did. It was as if he were waiting for nothing. He toed the ground making the swing drift leisurely back and forth, squeaking. He took his physical form—his IV-F—from his wallet. He scooted his butt forward on the swing. The form was folded into sixteenths, the size of a matchbook, and over the past two weeks had molded solid; it had heft and heaviness. Nick aimed the pistol at the black treetops across the road then tossed the square of paper up and out in front of him, like a skeet. When it sailed into the area he'd sighted—his father had taught him how to sight a moving object back when he'd still held out hopes at least one of his sons might grow to enjoy hunting—Nick squeezed the trigger.

It wasn't until the harmless *click* registered in his mind that Nick realized he'd at some point closed his eyes. The square of physical form lay in the grass about ten feet in front of him, halfway between the grape arbor and the near edge of the garden. He knew he'd loaded six bullets, but he broke open the cylinder just to make sure. Some kind of misfire was the only explanation. He had no idea what might've caused this or what it might entail, but he'd heard his father use the word before: *misfire*. He snapped the cylinder back into place. Suddenly the gun, in its impotence, seemed horribly lethal to Nick. He stood and took a long, slow look around. No cars, no critters, no coyotes. The light in his parents' room had gone out. He picked up the physical form, placed it back in his wallet, and headed for the porch. He'd go back into the house, unload the gun and replace it in the cabinet. The coyote would never return, tonight or ever again. Nick would go upstairs and get back into to bed, try to get a couple of hours sleep. He'd get up in the morning and go to work at McTighe's; he'd do that every morning for the next six weeks, then go off to Pitt-Johnstown for two years and Pitt's main campus for two more. He'd find a way to help pay for it all, to repay it all. He'd find a way to get on with his life. And some day, by god, when the time came, he'd keep this Colt revolver.

2. Celina

By nightfall they had the yard pretty well cleared of debris. A sad word to use for what was left of her in-laws' earthly possessions, yes, but it was the only word that seemed remotely appropriate to Celina, given the circumstances. She sat on the porch step smoking a cigarette—no one would come near her at such times; it was as if she had contagious polio—and watched as her husband banged twice with the heel of his hand on the truck's tailgate and then the truck, carrying the dumpster and everything else that hadn't sold or wasn't wanted, pulled out of the driveway, made a right onto State Route 33, and disappeared, the sound of its engine fading like the end of a record album.

Lawrence stood with Nick at the mouth of the driveway. Nick was pointing down the hill, in the direction of the old dairy farm, which wasn't there anymore, and Lawrence laughed at something his brother said. Lawrence always put on a show of familial goodwill when they visited, reverting to regional vernacular and laughing at ridiculous memories, but in truth he hated visiting as much as she did. The house, since her mother-in-law's death eight years earlier, had begun to deteriorate—not structurally, but in livability. It was filled with all sorts of unsanitary smells: mildew in the carpets, mold in the refrigerator, bacteria in the bathroom, plus animal shit in the yard. Visiting meant more than the inconvenience of a 4½-hour drive from D.C. It meant packing their own sheets, pillows, towels, soap, shampoo. It meant a three-hundred-dollar trip to the supermarket. It meant washing every pot and pan and fork before anything could be cooked. It meant scrubbing down the kitchen floor, the counters, the inside of the microwave, the table and chairs, the bathroom. It meant renting a wet-vac for the carpets. It wasn't that Celina didn't want to do these things for her father-in-law—wasn't that a child's only adult responsibility to their parents, to take care of them in old age?—it was just so damn depressing. They came as often as they could the first year or two after Lawrence's mother passed away. But then...at some point they began to view the prospect of an upcoming visit with dread. They found a way to avoid visiting one summer—an obligation, an illness, a miscalculation—then one Christmas. She'd been elected to the school board some years ago, and as her seniority rose the hours kept increasing. Her weekends became full. The kids were grown; it was hard to synchronize schedules. Eventually visiting Lawrence's father became an afterthought. It simply disappeared as a part of their lives.

Now there was nothing left but the house itself. Celina flicked her cigarette butt into the grass. Immediately she wanted another one, but resisted. For the past week, ever since receiving the call from the hospital that his father's passing was imminent, Lawrence had been harping on her smoking more than usual. *You've got to knock that off,* he kept saying. *We're next, you know.* But she'd quit once before, about a dozen years ago, and had ballooned. Put on fifty pounds, seemingly overnight. She wasn't going back there again—and she knew Lawrence, if he were being honest with himself, didn't want her to either.

He and Nick were still down by the road, talking in hushed voices with Raymond. Every now and then a car would glide past and illuminate their frozen faces and stark white legs below the cuffs of their golf shorts. Stuart and Sydney were off picking up a pizza. Nobody knew where anyone was staying tonight—probably just grab a room at the

Hampton Inn in Greensburg. Then ... well, then, that was it, she supposed. There'd really be no reason for her and Lawrence to ever visit this town again. Lawrence didn't attend high school reunions. There were no more local nieces or nephews to marry off. It'd be nice to see Raymond every now and again, but she couldn't fathom how *not* seeing him would in any way detract from their lives.

Her breath stuck. She needed a drink.

"Seen Abigail?" It was Nick. He and Lawrence and Raymond were walking up the driveway toward her.

Celina stood. "No, I haven't. Maybe she went along on the pizza run."

"Settle a bet for us," said Nick.

"Ah, hell," said Lawrence, "she won't know."

"Just shut up and let her answer."

"Lemme have a cigarette, dear," Raymond said. He'd quit a few years ago and, infuriatingly, didn't gain an ounce. He also somehow maintained the willpower to enjoy a smoke every now and again without falling headlong back into the habit. But, then again, Raymond had always been an anomaly: he had the thickest, fullest head of hair on any man over fifty this side of Mick Jagger. And he was sticking with the earring, despite the fact that even Celina, in her limited knowledge of what was "in" at any given time, knew that these days earrings on men clearly were out. She bent down for the pack on the porch step and tapped one out for him. "*Grazie,*" he said.

"Fine, ask her then." Lawrence lifted his glasses from his nose and placed them atop his forehead, a recent, annoying tendency of his. "What do *I* care?"

Nick stared at his brother for a moment, turned toward Celina, then back to Lawrence. "Hundred bucks says she *does* remember."

The spark of Raymond's match lit up everyone's face. "Ooo," he said. "Now we're talking. I want in on that action."

"Get the hell outta here," said Lawrence.

"No, wait. How 'bout *this*." Nick tapped a finger into Lawrence's chest. "Loser has to take Skippy. And display him, proudly, in the house."

Raymond, still in the process of lighting his cigarette, choked on a laugh, then burned his finger on the match before dropping it in the grass and giving a little two-steppish hop.

Skippy was the boys' childhood dog, a shorthaired mutt with a vaguely Rat Terrier appearance about him. When Lawrence was nine—which would have put Nick at around seven or eight—their father ran Skippy over while pulling the Plymouth into the driveway. He felt so bad, apparently, that in an impulsive attempt at atonement he took the remains down to Butchie Spaar's taxidermist shop in New Bentlee, where he got his deer heads done, and had Skippy stuffed. The result was more jarring to the boys than Skippy's bloody, twitching death in the driveway. The dog had been set in a pose of shoulder-hunched caution, glass eyes wide, a look of naked alarm on his face, as if every moment until the end of time he were forced to see that Plymouth, an instant before impact, closing in on him. He smelled like old shoes, and at this moment was glued to his original wooden base, cracked glass eyeballs dusty, on a basement shelf.

"Yes!" said Raymond.

"Abigail said you guys were probably going to take Brownie," Celina pointed out.

"Oh. She did? Huh." Nick tugged on his earlobe. "Well, doesn't matter. I'm not going to lose." He turned back to Lawrence. "So?"

"Sure, sure. Whatever."

"Exactly. Whatever. Okay…" He took Celina by the hand, as if he were about to propose. It spooked her briefly. "Celina. Sweetheart. Darling honey-pie. This is important. Tell us: When, ballpark, did this husband of yours shave off his mustache?"

"No way," said Lawrence. "Not ballpark. It has to be ex—"

"May fourteenth, nineteen-ninety-one," Celina blurted, before it could occur to her that maybe it was in her best interest to throw this bet. *She* didn't want Skippy in their house either.

"Ninety-*one*!" Nick shouted. "See? I *told* you. Didn't I tell him, Ray?"

"You sure as shit did," Ray said. "How the hell did you know that?" His voice was full of awed suspicion.

"'Cause. It was after the whole Tom Selleck craze. *Magnum P.I.* and all that. A *couple* of years after, at least. Then we all came into town for Uncle Sam's seventy-fifth. Remember? Over at the Elks? Lawrence walks in and—*pow*! No more Magnum. He'd had that mustache for—what? Twenty years?"

"At least," Raymond agreed.

Nick turned to Celina. "I figured you'd know," he said. "I knew you would. But how'd you nail it so *exactly*? You must've hated that thing."

"It wasn't exactly my favorite look," she admitted.

"That thing looked like a titmouse under your nose," said Ray, smoke exploding from his nostrils with each laugh.

They kept at it, Lawrence beginning to look a bit hangdog, kicking a toe at the ground, as he always did when he took a ribbing. It was an ability he'd never mastered. Odd, Celina always thought, for an oldest brother.

"I want Skippy on your *mantle*!"

Celina had heard enough. She really did need a drink. She turned and headed for the kitchen door. Inside she found Abigail, sitting alone in one of the six kitchen chairs. It wouldn't have been such a strange sight except that the table was missing. The chairs were the only objects remaining in the kitchen, arranged in a ragged oval. The sight was oddly disconcerting.

Abigail looked up at her. She might have been crying, though her face was dry. "I forgot," she said. "We sold the table."

Celina nodded. Then it occurred to her to ask, "What'd we get for it?"

"Twenty-five, I think."

Celina pulled out an adjacent chair and sat facing her sister-in-law. "They didn't want the chairs?"

"Said he had chairs he could use. Then I forgot about these. To sell them, I mean."

They were plain, wood, straight-back chairs. Pine, Celina would have guessed, though she had no real idea. The rectangular table had matched. She blinked away from the empty space where the table would have been and saw that the lower half of the exposed wall across from her had two stark white rectangles where the washer and dryer units had been. They got forty for the set—Celina'd brokered that deal herself.

"Sad," Abigail said, and sighed.

"Oh, please, not *you*, too." Celina had spoken a bit harsher than she'd meant to. But still. "You're not going to start this how-tragic stuff, are you?"

Abigail turned to her. "I sat in this very chair when Nick and I told them we were getting married. I sat in that one—" she pointed at Celina's—"when we told them I was pregnant with Justin. I sat here again when we told them about the first miscarriage. And I stood by the stove while Nick sat in that one over there and told them about the second. So, yeah, I'm going to do this, I think."

What Abigail had meant, surely, was that she had sat in these various *locations* in the kitchen. Not the precise chair. She had no way of knowing where each chair had been arranged at all of these given moments. But Celina figured she wouldn't bring this up. "Okay," she said.

"Sorry."

"No. I'm sorry. And I need a drink."

"I think there's still some wine in the basement."

"What? The homemade stuff?"

Abigail flicked her eyebrows. "What? Too much nostalgia for you?"

Just then Nick clomped through the kitchen door, followed by Law-rence. They both stopped abruptly, taking in the strange, cluttered emp-tiness of the room. Raymond came next, but got stuck behind them in the tiny entryway. He peered over their shoulders. "What?"

"Jesus," said Nick. Again he tugged on his earlobe. "The hell hap-pened here?"

"Seems we forgot to sell the chairs," Abigail said.

"Yup. That'd be it. Thank you. And it's hot as hell in here, too."

Now that Celina thought about it, the house *was* rather warm. Her father-in-law had never gotten around to installing the central air he'd talked about for the last twenty years of his life. The window above the sink was open and a warm breeze kicked the curtains around.

The rest of them filed in; Lawrence went straight for the downstairs bathroom as Nick and Raymond pulled up chairs and sat. They looked around at each other. There was a weird formality to it all, as if they'd all been gathered together for some sort of focus group, or therapy session.

"So," said Raymond, once they were settled.

"Maybe we should've kept the table, too," said Nick. "I don't like being able to see everyone's knees."

Abigail crossed her legs, then reconsidered and put her feet back on the floor, knees together. "We were just thinking about some of that wine down in the basement."

"I'll get it," said Raymond. He stood, which placed him in the center of the circle. Then slid his chair aside and moved toward the cellar door.

"Do we even have any glasses?" Abigail wondered.

"I think there might be a few," said Celina. She remembered selling mostly coffee mugs with the names of resort locations and clever mottoes on them. "Old Fart" sold right away, for fifty-cents.

"Eh, forget it," Nick said. "We don't have a table to set them on any-way. Just pass around the bottle."

Abigail stiffened, cocked her head to the side. "Where's Brownie?"

"The question is," said Nick nearly shouted, directing his voice down the hallway, "Where's *Skippy*?"

"That'll do," Lawrence's muffled voice called from inside the bathroom. "It's getting tiring, little brother."

"Oh, *is* it? That's a shame. Doesn't change a thing, though. I want photos of him on your mantle e-mailed to me within the week."

"Yeah, I'll get right on that."

"Hey, don't gimme that. Can't blame this one on the president. Celina—" Nick pointed across at her—"I'm holding you responsible."

"Don't drag me into this."

"Seriously," said Abigail. "Where's Brownie."

"Where's *Ray*?" Nick wondered. "He get lost down there? There isn't even anything left."

Celina wondered how long they had to play along with this charade. She just wanted to go check in to the hotel and relax before their drive home in the morning; change into her pajamas and read a magazine. Fall asleep to David Letterman. Except that the little Podunk hotel wouldn't have a bar and she really, really, really wanted a drink.

The toilet flushed and Lawrence emerged from the bathroom, tightening his belt. "Do you remember," he said, and Celina's butt muscles clenched, "when Dad put the table out in the backyard?"

Nick snorted, a sort of half-laugh. "Uh-huh."

"Really?" said Abigail. She was playing along with all of this a little too whole-heartedly for Celina's taste. "How come?"

"We were...early teens? Something like that?" Lawrence sat in the chair Raymond had been sitting in, looking at Nick for confirmation. Nick shrugged, gave a little nod. "Dad and Uncle Vince were redoing the cabinets or something in the kitchen, treating the wood maybe." Again the need for facial confirmation from Nick—where was this *coming* from all of a sudden?—who was staring at the floor, smiling. "Anyway, there was dust or fumes and we couldn't be in there for a couple days. And Mom was all worried that we wouldn't be able to eat as a family during that time. We all were like, Sure we can, what about the living room? Or the dining room. Isn't that what it's for? *Dining*? But Mom said it wasn't the same. Dining rooms were for formal occasions. We should all be at the kitchen table. That's just how it should be." He took his glasses from his forehead, made like to set them down and for the first time appeared to truly notice that there was no table in front of him. He slid the glasses back onto his forehead. "Well, this was all news to us. To me at least. I'd never heard her say this stuff before. But then when I thought about it I realized we did eat at the kitchen table every night. Even weekends. The five of us."

"I thought about that, too," Nick said. "At the time."

"Right. Yeah. So, Dad thinks about it and says, 'Boys, grab a corner.'"

"And poor Stu is, like, eight or nine years old. Lucky he made it through alive. We had to flip the thing up and turn it on its side to get it out the door. Almost took his head off."

They both seemed to be talking to Abigail, and to each other, not to Celina. Now Lawrence leaned into the ring of chairs, and Abigail leaned forward, too, toward him, charmed nearly to blushing.

"It was only supposed to stay out there for a day or two," Lawrence went on. "Until the cabinets were done. But we all kinda liked it, plus none of us wanted to carry the thing back inside. So no one ever suggested bringing it in, and the table stayed out there for the rest of the summer."

"Which was only a couple of weeks, as I recall," Nick pointed out. "But still."

"What about when it rained?" Celina said, feeling like a buzz-kill.

Nick shrugged. "I don't remember. I think we just let it get rained on. Mom'd put like a plastic tablecloth over it."

"We ate dinner out there every night," Lawrence went on. "It got to the point where we all kind of looked forward to it." Again a nod to Nick for confirmation.

"Mm-hmm," Nick said. "We'd have eating contests, the three of us. When we were full we'd run laps around the house to make ourselves hungry again."

"Didn't you guys have a picnic table?" Abigail asked. "Your dad could've *made* one in about five minutes."

"Well, yeah," Lawrence said. "But it wasn't about that. We had to be at the *kitchen table*."

"Why haven't I ever seen pictures of this?"

"No idea. I don't remember seeing pictures either. Maybe we never took any. Didn't seem important at the time, I guess."

Nick took a breath. "We shouldn't have sold that fucking thing."

Everyone looked at him. Celina, for one, had never heard Nick use that particular curse word before. It was more shocking than she would have thought.

"Found it!" Ray shouted, emerging through the cellar door. In one hand he held up a plastic gallon milk jug, covered in dust, three-quarters filled with a blood-purple liquid; and in the other a green-tinted glass bottle, corked. "Ta-da!"

"Good God, how long have those been down there?" Celina said. Raymond shrugged.

"The last batch Dad made was…" Nick scrunched up his face, thinking.

"Five years ago?" Lawrence offered. "Seven?"

"At least."

"So?" Raymond tramped over and sat in the empty chair next to Celina, then leaned forward and slammed the bottles down heavily on the linoleum. "I worked *hard* for these bastards."

"Where were they?" Nick asked. "I thought we'd cleaned everything out down there."

Raymond picked up the green bottle and uncorked it, sniffed, jerked his head back. "That little alcove he built into the wall down there?"

"I thought he sealed that up."

"He did. I pried it back open. He must not have known these were in there."

"Jeez," said Abigail. "Are they okay to drink?"

"Damn straight," Raymond assured her. "These here are relics. Historical artifacts." He held the bottle out toward the center of the circle. "Who's first?"

"At least, you know, wipe it off or something," Abigail suggested.

Raymond put the opening under his arm and twisted.

"Aww." Abigail made a face. "Not exactly what I had in mind."

Lawrence rose. "I gotta hit the head."

Raymond shifted to Celina and pointed the neck of the bottle at her like a microphone, waiting.

3. Carmelo

Their father, Carmelo, known to friends and family as Mel, pretty much built the house himself—along with his brothers and father and father-in-law (at the time *future* father-in-law) and various other neighbors and family members—starting in 1940. He was twenty-one and would not let himself believe that war in Europe was a possibility. He was moving ahead with his life. He'd bought the land, a good-sized parcel at the intersection of the only two paved roads in Bentlee—a community of coal miners and dairy farmers, but a community willing to give deeds and loans to the sons of immigrants. The loan went toward the land and materials. Two other sons of immigrants in town—boys Mel had grown up with—had started a contracting company, Pavlovik Bros. Builders, which would remain in that family into the third generation, through the nineties, when it became clear that people had completely stopped building things in the area. Then the Pavloviks sold to a company out of Monroeville, which was owned by a developer based in Charlotte. In 1940, though, the Pavloviks helped Carmelo out with cement mixers and good, cheap lumber, insulation at cost. Over the years, before he and Vince started out on their own under-the-table operation, Carmelo did electrical work for Pavlovik Bros. when the mines were shut down because of weather or worse.

The style was a loose adaptation of classic farmhouse, irregularly shaped and positioned—the back porch and door, which was used as the main entrance, was really on the side; windows were cut wherever the space between the reinforced beams and studs were most accommodating. There were very few accoutrements: the house was intended to be sturdy and unpretentious. He already had one of the best locations in town, no need to get greedy. Besides, he didn't need his neighbors talking behind his back about Carmelo trying to one-up everyone with his gaudy new house. He wasn't even married yet, he could imagine them saying. But he would be, soon, to Anne David, whose father was rumored to be Jewish. Nobody could be positive on this count, "David" being a rather ambiguous surname, ethnically. Either way, it didn't really matter—she'd be Anne Padula soon, and Carmelo was willing to overlook such technicalities, as long as it didn't call attention to itself. Which was his general philosophy regarding the house design, too. There were no true "hallways" to speak of: the interior layout was vaguely circular, one room bending into the next. Three bedrooms, one bathroom upstairs (the second, downstairs bathroom would be added later, at the end of what would in fact *become* a hallway); a half-attic accessible by pull-down ladder.

He allowed himself one indulgence and regretted one omission.

On the basement, Carmelo went all-out, making use of the entire area of the house, and then some. He wanted a place to store his tools, his fishing gear; an area to bleed any game he'd killed. And he wanted the place to be orderly. To this end he built small, eight-by-ten or so, rooms— "secret rooms" his sons would call them—into the walls, as well as several medicine cabinet-sized storage spaces. Two of the rooms would eventually contain his oak barrels and other winemaking equipment. His own father, who spoke almost no English, taught him how to make it.

But the basement was more challenging to dig than Mel or anyone else had anticipated. It all had to be dug by hand—spades and picks, the earth lifted out via a bucket-and-pulley system—and when the winter of 1940 arrived, work could be done only following warm stretches when the ground softened a bit. The slow work set the project lingering into '41.

Carmelo continued to live in his family's house in town. Weekdays, he'd work the mines with his father in the morning, get off at three, then he and whatever helpers he could assemble that day would start on the house. When summer came he'd work three straight sixteen-hour days at the mines, then have four off in a row. Things picked up. But if they were going to finish by the time the weather turned again, they'd have to forego the fireplace Carmelo had planned for the dining room. No one in the crew had ever built a fireplace before; plus, enough brick for the job was proving difficult to locate, even with the Pavlovik's contacts. The whole endeavor made Carmelo nervous. So they drywalled over the space and kept going, an act Carmelo recalled every frigid January evening as he shoveled more and more coal into the furnace, every Christmas when the boys pinned their stockings around the painting of a pair of bucks, every time he cut down a tree and gave the split logs away to someone with a fireplace.

By mid-October of '41 the house was ready enough to show to Anne. Thus far, he'd only let her see the outside. Though the interior was nothing extravagant or remarkable, he wanted to maintain some semblance of surprise, of unveiling, when everything was finished. Anne had been working as a check-out girl at Mauch's Market, which later became the Red & White food store, just to occupy her time. On that day in October when he felt his labors were finally worth revealing, he waited for Anne on the sidewalk outside the market. It was late afternoon. He'd gotten off his shift at the mines, took a last walk through the house, then had gone back to his childhood home and bathed, put on a fresh white dress shirt and corduroy trousers. The day was bright and shimmering, the smell of burning leaves drifted by on the air and dissipated. He rolled a cigarette as he waited.

When Anne stepped out the door of the market, in her blue smock and nametag, lovely powder-blue skirt, and saw Carmelo standing there, her face registered surprise—he'd never met her this way after work; in fact, for an engaged couple, they hardly saw each other, except for Saturday nights, their schedules being so unsynchronized—then understanding. Her hair was in curls and pulled back from her face with barrettes. "It's ready?" she said.

He nodded, tossed his butt to the sidewalk. "Ready enough. Finally."

She threw her arms around his neck, right there in the middle of town. "I wouldn't care if it took ten days or if it took a thousand years," she said.

He had no idea what that meant.

Her arm hooked through his, they walked the mile and a half out of town to the intersection of Tremont Avenue and what would become State Route 33. The yard was rutted and muddy. There was no driveway yet. After his walk-through earlier in the day, Mel had arranged a series of plywood planks leading up from the road. Still, he scooped Anne up, careful to make sure her skirt didn't skim the ground, and carried her, bride-style, to the front/side door.

In the kitchen he set her down. She stood for a moment, then turned around slowly, as if the room were too much for her to take in all at once. "Oh, it's lovely, Mel," she breathed.

"We'll have to get a stove," he said. "Gas lines for it'll go right there. And an icebox."

She nodded, barely, and set off drifting from room to room, her mouth squeezed into an unforced smile. She liked the natural light the living room received (a complete accident) and the amount of space in the pantry. The burst of pride Carmelo felt at her unconditional approval surprised him. He'd been living with this structure for nearly two years, was so acutely aware of its flaws, its compromises, its oversights, that it hadn't really occurred to him that he'd done it: he'd built the damn thing.

"I'm going to put a grape arbor out back," he told her. "And make my own wine."

"That's a wonderful idea. I'll be able to see it from the kitchen window, above the sink." She headed for the stairs, then paused and reached back for his hand. "Let's see the bedrooms."

She'd maintained, nearly from day one of their courtship, that she intended to "preserve herself" until they were married. At the time Mel was fine with this pronouncement. He just hadn't expected their courtship to go on so long. Most engagements lasted a couple of months, or however long it took to book the church and the hall. Theirs had dragged on to the point where sex in the abstract, let alone the literal, had disappeared as a possibility in his mind. So he was caught off-guard.

"But…" he said. "There aren't any beds yet."

"That's okay."

"We have to buy that stuff."

"I know, I know."

The stairs didn't creak on their way up. Carmelo registered this fact. They went into what would eventually become Nick and Stuart's room. It was chilly; the furnace hadn't even been tested yet. A part of Carmelo wanted to stop this—he wasn't comfortable, wasn't ready; it wasn't the time or place or circumstance. But, then again, sure it was. Anne was smiling, her cheeks were flushed, so he didn't suggest they stop. There were a couple of drop-cloths in the corner and he spread them out on the wood floor, double-layered. He stood there looking at them, speechless. A shaft of late-afternoon sun streaming through the window illuminated a hazy wall of dust.

"Perfect," Anne said, and seemed to believe it.

It struck Mel then that she'd had this planned for some time, and now was simply playing things out, whether the circumstances were "perfect" or not.

In the end, it was awkward at best—cold and quick and periodically painful. Mel would be pulling splinters from various body parts for the next few months. They said all the right things: they loved each other, it was wonderful, special, who'd have thought, huh? But when they quickly positioned themselves to get up, Anne rolled over on a stray nail. Mel pulled it out but it'd dug in pretty deep and Anne had to get a tetanus shot. Explaining to her family and doctor how she came to get a nail stuck in her thigh was no easy sell, and Mel never asked what excuse she eventually came up with.

This was in October.

In December the United States would be forced into the war, beginning in southwest Asia. By the following summer Carmelo was there, too.

The house sold for sixty-six grand, his sons' original asking price.

4. Lawrence

He stared down into the commode, waiting for something to happen. He'd been doing a lot of that lately: staring into various toilet bowls as time passed around him. This one was white porcelain, low water level ringed with a thin layer of dark grime. Lawrence knew it well, was there when his father installed it, listened while his parents fought over the door that would conceal it—his mother wanted a regular wooden door, with a knob, that swung open and closed and could be locked, if necessary, like doors possessed by civilized human beings; but his father countered that there wasn't enough room at the end of the tiny hallway onto which the new bathroom would be added, and insisted on a flimsy closet-style door that folded open like an accordion. She'd renew the argument periodically, for the rest of her life: "You can hear *every*thing through that lousy door. It's like you're going to the bathroom right in the *kitchen*."

Lawrence took a breath and let his head drop back. Near the ceiling, the wallpaper border—mixed fruit, chosen by his mother—was cracked and peeling. There was a faint smell of Listerine and mothballs. He thought he felt something happening at the base of his torso, but it was a false alarm. He shifted his weight to his other foot. It could be a while yet. Oftentimes that was the case.

"Oh, bullshit," he heard Nick's voice from the kitchen. "What should he have done? Tell me that. You wanna be attacked *again*? Huh? Do you?"

And Raymond's feeble, mumbled, unintelligible response.

Lawrence didn't want to partake in any of this, didn't want to hear his brother's practiced, Fox-Newsey rationale as to why the current war was good and the president was on the right track, even if the goddamn liberals were trying to cut his legs out from under him. Lawrence had no idea where any of this came from: his brother was a good man, generous, kind-hearted, smart. Arguing with him about these matters made Lawrence feel small and weak, made him question his own values and beliefs. So he'd keep them to himself and just let Nick go on and on and on. Then, once they'd parted, Lawrence would lie in bed berating himself for not defending more aggressively what was in his heart.

"Well then what would *you* have done?" Nick demanded of Ray, his customary refrain. "If you liberals have all the answers…"

The last time Lawrence and Celina visited, he'd sat at the table with Nick, late at night, poking with plastic forks at slices of store-bought cheesecake. Celina and Abigail were in the dining room, talking, killing time; Stu and Sydney had already left. Who knew where Dad was—puttering around in the basement? Sleeping in the recliner in the living room? They were talking about their kids, then about housing prices in their respective towns, and as usual Nick tied these topics to politics, to taxes (didn't his brother understand that his salary, his livelihood, *depended* on taxes?), then to the war. He pushed some chunks of pie crust around on his plate. Then he said, "You know, if I were I little younger, I'd enlist. I would. I still might. Seriously. I mean, what the hell, I can drive a truck, right? I can unload boxes. I can…shit, I can mop up. They must need *some* things done over there that a healthy fifty-six-year-old man can help out with."

Lawrence was about to let out a chuckle, to tell Nick, good-naturedly, to get the hell out of here. But when Nick looked up from his plate Lawrence saw immediately that his brother wasn't joking.

"You would think," was all Lawrence could manage.

It was a brief, tender respite from the veiled accusations of naïveté Nick typically hurled at Lawrence like screwballs, seemingly easy to swat back at him, yet time and again Lawrence found himself flailing blindly. And when Nick began nodding—not in agreement but as if Lawrence's inane statements simply confirmed Nick's expectations—and allowed a press-lipped smile of pity to ease across his face, Lawrence felt about ten years old. *You poor, poor misguided sap,* Nick seemed to be implying, *relying on mere facts to help you form your opinions. Such a shame.*

But Lawrence was *not* naïve. Couldn't be. And the insinuation left him bristling. He'd lived, goddamn it, he'd suffered, he knew what it meant to work for a living. He knew what it meant to put three daughters through college at a time when the number of Pell grants was declining every year and interest rates for education loans were rising. He knew what it was like to get his $600 tax rebate check in the mail on one day and the very next receive word that, as a result of these rebates, his salary would be reduced by two-and-a-half percent, as would the salaries of every other faculty member in the Wade-Ridgefield School District. He knew what it was like to play it a little too close to the vest, to try and push through the rough patches as if nothing had changed, and wind up filing for bankruptcy at fifty—something he'd never told his brother, the financial wizard—to look your wife in the eye and admit to each other that your lives hadn't gone the way you'd planned, that in fact they'd taken a terrible turn. He knew what it was like to stare at a bottle of Valium in the medicine cabinet and wonder what it would be like to swallow the whole goddamn thing.

But he also knew what it was like to get past it. After the bankruptcy hearings, he had known what he had to do, knew that in order to get their life back he had to work summers, two and three sessions each, advise the yearbook club, coach the lacrosse team, take on tutoring clients from other districts. And he did: they got their life back, avoided foreclosure, bought themselves a Saab 9-5 exactly like the one they'd lost—same color, same year.

He knew never to get too comfortable. Once his and Celina's life appeared to be back on track, he knew the numbing anger of discovering that his youngest daughter's boyfriend had been hitting her, knew the fear of confronting this boy on the front step of his apartment, of threatening the boy's life, and meaning it.

And Lawrence knew how to keep a secret, like the one he was keeping now. He closed his eyes, tried to relax, to block out the sound of his brother's rehearsed rationale. He took a breath, opened his eyes. On the back of the toilet tank was a magazine, turned upside-down—the back cover featured a full-page ad for Copenhagen snuff. Lawrence reached out, retaining his position in front of the bowl, in case any developments should suddenly occur, and flipped the magazine over. It was an *American Sportsman*, December 1998. The year their mother had died. Most likely their father never renewed the subscription afterwards. On the cover was a smiling man in camouflage kneeling over a felled buck, his hand gripped around the antlers, lifting the deer's wobbly head off the ground. Weaving around the buck's antlers was a string of illuminated green, red, and white Christmas lights. Some of the stories inside included "Why You Miss Ducks," "Gun Dog Training Resolutions for '99," "Beginner Tips for Coyote Hunting," "Catch Coldwater Bass on Spinner Baits," "The Truth About Kentucky's Whitetail Population." And what appeared to be the holiday feature: "Deer Hunting is Good for the Soul."

Lawrence wondered what the truth about Kentucky's whitetail population could possibly be, but not enough to open the magazine to find out. Probably it depended on who you asked. One truth that could never be challenged was which brother had tried the hardest to follow in their father's footsteps as a hunter. Stu was useless in the woods, never even bothered to fake an interest. Nick, who admittedly was the most accurate shot of the brothers and therefore received the most marksmanship-related praise from their father, went on two deer-hunting trips, maybe three, before beginning to come up with fake excuses. But Lawrence, though technically not as good a shot as Nick, stuck it out the longest, tagging along with his dad and his buddies, learning the best spots, the ins and outs of tracking, when to be patient, when to fire, where to aim for the kill shot. He took no pleasure in any of it, but he was the oldest, and he was willing to make sacrifices if it meant achieving a level of his father's approval beyond what Nick enjoyed.

Lawrence recalled clearly the day he stopped trying. He was sixteen, a Sunday afternoon, autumn. That summer, Duquesne Light had begun clearing a section of the wooded area across SR 33 for the construction of a remote transporter station. Only a half-dozen or so trees had been cut down and hauled away by this point, but there was one particular stump, its wide, flat surface about three feet off the ground, on which their father and his buddy Cal had taken to placing random items—old milk jugs, coffee cans, spent oil filters—for target practices. They'd stand in the side yard, between the house and garden, on the slight incline alongside SR 33, and fire across the street. Illegal: most likely; monitored: never. But 33 was rarely traveled, and Carmelo and Cal, whether drunk or sober, usually were careful to check for cars before sighting their weapons. After a while adjustments and modifications were made to the activity: Cal wanted more of a challenge so he began tying a three-foot-long length of fishing line to the low branch of a half-felled oak, and hanging items from it. The target would swing casually in the breeze, thereby increasing the level of difficulty.

Cal had been their father's tightest companion for as long as Lawrence could remember. He was short and beefy, with a completely shaved head, and he emitted a faint but constant aroma of stuffed cabbage. Cal never

married, and as they grew older—particularly after Anne passed—he
and Carmelo took to bickering like an old married couple. Recently, Cal
had gone through chemo half a dozen times; had his spleen, a kidney, an
eye, and parts of a lung removed; but, competitor that he was, he showed
up at their father's funeral in a bathrobe and an eye patch, dragging an
oxygen tank on wheels behind him. His scalp looked like the plucked
skin of a raw chicken.

Back in the day, though, his competitiveness could be insufferable. He
was a bit of an exaggerator, too: one of those guys who, if you happened
to mention the pesky splinter in your thumb, would snort and tell you
that wasn't nothin', that he once nearly had his arm lopped clean *off* by a
rogue pine shaving while trying to clamp his enormous Christmas tree
into its base. And once, at a Fourth of July picnic, he cornered Lawrence
off to the side of the charcoal grill and explained to him that a human
being farts an average of fourteen times a day, but that he, Cal, operated
on a level that was *way* above that average, sometimes pushing his daily
output into the triple digits. There was an edge in his voice that seemed
to add, *So if you're harboring any delusions of someday topping my performance, just forget about that right now, little man, 'cause it can't be done.*

Carmelo wasn't one to back down from a challenge either, real or
manufactured, and though the target-practice sessions typically were
impromptu, starting with just a quick couple of rounds for the hell of
it, without fail things would turn into marathons and grow borderline-
belligerent. The target, whether placed on the stump or hanging from
the branch, was a hundred and fifty or so feet away. From that distance,
of course, rifles were the firearm of choice. No scopes were allowed, but
they made things interesting by continually reducing the size of the target—Cal once took aim at a shot glass, fired, and though the glass did
not move, did not have a mark on it, Cal claimed that he skimmed the
side so delicately, kissed it almost, that the glass spun ninety-degrees

on the stump, which was exactly what he was trying to do. "Look," he demanded, "I put it here with the wolf head picture facing right *at* us. Now, look, it's facing the whole other way. I spun the fucker right around."

"Your ass, you did," Carmelo said.

"My ass? *My ass*? Then *you* explain it, wise guy."

"Well, Christ, how the hell do *I* know what direction the goddamn picture was facing? I didn't see you put it there. I was way the hell over here. And I wouldn't've given a fat holy shit if I *had* seen you put it there."

"Well, I *did* put it there."

"Then why didn't you say so beforehand, dipshit? 'Hey, watch this, I'm gonna kiss the side and spin it around.' All you had to say. But oh no, not you, you gotta be all secretive. What the goddamn shit-ass sense does *that* make?"

"That was all part of it," Cal explained, a roguish grin snaking across his face now.

"A part of *what*? Jay-zuss. Okay, fine, whatever. You spun it right around. Wyatt fuckin' Earp over here."

"You didn't hear that *plink* sound when the bullet nicked the glass?"

"Oh, right, right, the *plink* sound." Carmelo smacked the heel of his hand to his forehead. "Sorry. My mistake. The hell was I thinking?"

Cal shrugged. "Shoulda been paying better attention. Missed the shot of a lifetime."

"Horseshit of a lifetime's more like it," Carmelo said. Cal saved his most absurd excuses for whenever one of Carmelo's boys managed to show him up—picking off a flashlight battery that Cal clearly had missed ("Goddamn gnat flew right in my eyeball!"), answering Cal's feat of plugging an old baby doll with a gutshot by blowing its head clean off ("Well, yeah, but that ain't the proper place to aim at a human"). Usually the culprit was Nick, which Lawrence found maddening.

So on that autumn Sunday afternoon, 1964, Nick came to Lawrence with a plan. The objective was a practical joke of sorts played on Cal and their father. As the two men stood bickering in the yard along SR 33, Lawrence walked out of the house carrying the Colt .32 revolver and a box of 40-watt light bulbs. Cal fired off a shot that sent bits of the stump flying, then he and Carmelo turned to see Lawrence approaching.

"Go put that thing away before you shoot your leg off," he said.

Lawrence paused; there was a moment when he considered doing what he'd been told. Then he regained his pace. "I won't," he told his father. "I wanna show you something. Been working on it."

"Working on what?"

"Just watch." He stutter-stepped down the little incline and crossed the road. When he reached the stump he placed the revolver there, then took a light bulb from the box and began tying the end of fishing line around the bulb's neck. As he did this, according to the plan, Nick should have been removing a deer rifle and box of shells, along with their father's best scope, from the cabinet. He then would have to maneuver past their mother and make his way upstairs, where he would crawl quietly out their parents' bedroom window and onto the roof of the back porch.

Lawrence struggled with the knot; his hands were shaking for some reason.

"Are those good bulbs?" his father called. "We need those."

But Lawrence kept on. About twelve inches above the bulb he tied a second, then began tying a third above that, like a string of fish. He had to stand on the stump for the highest bulb. "The hell's he doing?" he could hear Cal asking, and his father said, "Hanging light bulbs, apparently. Jesus, Cal, how the hell should *I* know?" When he was finished he picked up the Colt and headed back across the road. As discreetly as he could, he glanced upwards and spotted part of Nick's face and the top of his head. He was lying flat on his stomach, butt of the rifle pressed to his shoulder, sighting the string of light bulbs through the scope.

"Something on your mind?" his father asked Lawrence once he'd ascended from the road to where the men stood.

"Just watch," he said, and snapped open the Colt's cylinder. He dug three bullets from his jeans pocket and pushed them one at a time into the chambers.

"Whoa, boy," said Cal, a slight whine in his voice. "Just...ho—hold on there." He turned and appealed to Lawrence's father. "Mel, I mean, come on. What's he...come on."

"Shut up, Cal," said Carmelo. He spit into the grass. "So what'cha planning to do, son?"

Lawrence snapped shut the cylinder. "Shoot out those targets I just hung there."

"Mel," said Cal, "Mel, this is..." He turned and began pacing around the lawn in a tight circle.

"Son," Lawrence's father said calmly. "You can't hit a target like that, from this distance, with a handgun. You just can't. No one can."

"I can," said Lawrence.

"You wanna shoot," his father said, "that's fine. Here, try the twenty-two." He handed a rifle to Lawrence.

But Lawrence raised the Colt with his right hand, let his left hang casually at his side. He steadied the gun, closed his left eye and sighted down the barrel. In the distance he could see the string of light bulbs hanging perfectly still in the breezeless summer air. On the stump was the empty box—he'd forgotten it there. A prematurely orange leaf drifted down through his field of vision.

Cal made an odd strangled noise. "What's he—"

"One," Lawrence said, loudly. "Two...three!"

He squeezed the trigger; Lawrence's arm snapped upwards, violently, and across the road the bottom light bulb exploded. It all happened so fast Lawrence had to blink the world back to life. Only then did he realize how loud the gunshot had been; he could still hear it echoing beyond the house and over the trees. His hand and wrist vibrated.

"Holy…" Cal began.

Carmelo stepped forward and squinted at the string of what now was two light bulbs. Then he turned and regarded Lawrence. "How did you do that?" he asked.

Lawrence swallowed. "Just aimed and shot," he said.

"Can you do it again?"

"Sure," Lawrence said. "Maybe."

"No way," said Cal. "*No*body gets that lucky twice."

"Go ahead," Carmelo said to Lawrence. There was a touch of encouragement in his voice that Lawrence had never heard before—at least directed toward him.

"Okay." Again Lawrence raised the Colt. Again, for the sake of authenticity, or perhaps just for the hell of it, he aimed at what had been the middle light bulb. "One…two…three!"

He was ready for the kickback this time, and this allowed him to focus on the gunshot, which was as loud as a thunderclap and contained an infinitesimal second beat: *b-bang!* The light bulb disappeared with a splash.

"Good god," Carmelo said after a moment. "Son. That's amazing."

Lawrence felt his throat close up a little bit.

"Why's he saying one-two-three?" Cal wanted to know. "The hell's *that* all about, huh?"

Carmelo scratched his bald spot. "Why *are* you saying that?"

"I just…" Lawrence started. It struck him that he should have anticipated this question and prepared a credible response. "Because, I don't know, 'cause that's how I practiced. It gets me into kind of a rhythm and, sort of, relaxes me." He waited a moment and then said simply, "I don't really know why I do that."

Cal sharpened his gaze at Lawrence. "Do it again. But without the one-two-three."

Lawrence felt his heart stumble and trip inside of him. "I don't know," he said. "I didn't practice…"

"Oh, for shit's sake, Cal," his father said. "You really care if the kid counts to three? Are you shitting me? For real? Aren't you the same guy who can't raise a bet without tapping his cards on his nuts first? Sheesh." He clapped Lawrence on the back. "Go ahead, son. Get that last one. If you wanna count, go right ahead and count."

Lawrence felt tears percolating inside him. His eyes burned. Something awful was about to happen and he felt powerless to stop it. He raised the Colt once more, quickly shouted, "One-two-three," and fired. The shot rang out and the last bulb shattered; the shot's echo crackled across the afternoon.

Lawrence looked at his father, who was smiling, arms folded over his chest.

"Dad…" Lawrence's voice cracked.

His father turned to Cal, who was staring dumbly across the road. "Any questions, dumb-ass?"

Cal farted, reflexively; it had two pitches to it—low and guttural, and then an octave higher, like a foghorn in reverse. It went unacknowledged. Cal's lips moved but no words came out.

"That's what I thought." Again Lawrence's father clapped him on the back, kept his hand there this time.

"Dad…"

And that's when Nick giggled, just a quick muffled bleat with a squeaky lilting tail at the end. Cal and Carmelo flinched and began glancing around them, arms held out as if groping for balance. Lawrence didn't look but he could hear his brother scurrying across the shingles; he heard the rifle stock clatter against the window frame as Nick hurried back inside.

"What the...Hey!" Cal pointed up at the porch roof. He knew something was afoul—the wrinkled expression on his face said as much—yet he didn't know exactly what. He looked at Carmelo, who was still glancing upwards, blinking, allowing his mind to adjust to the events that had transpired. The bedroom window was still wide open; the sheer curtains trailed outside.

"Mel," said Cal. "I think..." He considered his next words for a moment then decided to just be honest. "What just *happened*?"

Lawrence realized he was still aiming the revolver at the fishing line across the road. He lowered the gun, but it felt awkward in his hand. Something deflated inside of him and he held the gun out to his father, butt-first.

His father took it. "Good one," he said. "Tell your brother. Had me completely fooled." He chuckled, but it was forced, almost painful-sounding. He held the Colt in his palm and considered it. "Yup. Plum flummoxed. How 'bout you, Cal?"

Cal was squinting across the road. Sweat beaded on his bald head. It was clear he still didn't know what had happened. "Huh?"

"Never mind. I'll explain it all later."

Suddenly Lawrence had to go to the bathroom. "Dad..."

"It's all right," his father said.

But it wasn't really.

He didn't, at the time know why it wasn't all right—he just *knew* it wasn't, and never would be—but it occurred to him now, standing and waiting at the foot of the toilet bowl, that maybe he *was* naïve, and had been all along. Maybe this unacknowledged truth was at the root of all his problems.

There seemed to be no relief forthcoming, and for the first time Lawrence admitted to himself that he'd better see a doctor, that something most definitely was wrong, that he couldn't keep his condition a secret— from Celina, from himself—any longer. He flipped the *American Sportsman* back over and zipped up. He flushed, as he'd done on his last trip to the bathroom, for appearances' sake.

The Colt's kickback had resulted in a sprained wrist for Lawrence, which he discovered the next day and tried to blame on slipping in the shower, which his father never came close to buying. And after that day, no son ever was invited on another hunting trip. Carmelo continued to go with buddies, and, later, his buddies' sons. When he'd get a deer he'd always give his boys and their families a good bit of the meat, which, at Lawrence and Celina's house, would sit in its white masking-taped butcher paper in the back of the freezer until it grew frosty with freezer-burn, at which time it would all get thrown in the trash.

Lawrence washed his hands with the cake of decade-old Ivory soap and dried them on the pleats of his shorts. Then the pressure returned, rising from his knees, it seemed—and he spun around, unzipping, ready to resume his vigil.

5. Sydney

Why did it seem like Sydney, after just two years of marriage, knew her husband's hometown better than *he* did? The drive from his father's house to Joey O's Pizza in Latrobe was a twelve-minute haul, tops, one that Stuart had made hundreds, thousands of times in his life. Yet on the way back, there she was, Sydney, calling out the turns. Something must not have felt right, though, when she instructed him to make the hard left onto Harkner. He entered the turn cautiously, then pulled out of it, his feet slipping between gas and brake on his father's—now their—Ford pickup, before swinging back onto the two-lane they'd been on.

"Are you sure?" he said, as they headed now in the direction of Blairsville.

She touched her forehead. "Yes, Stuart. I'm sure. I was sure then, and I'm sure now."

"Doesn't look right." He glanced in the rearview mirror, as if he expected an answer to appear behind him.

"Well, I don't know what to tell you."

The pizzas were getting cold. She could feel the temperature diminishing on her thighs. When they arrived in the center of Blairsville he said he thought he knew where he was now and turned onto an unmarked road that Sydney truly *didn't* recognize. Since then they'd been winding through blackness and rolling countryside, an occasional stretch of low, barbed-wire fence, an occasional farmhouse in the distance with a lit window or two.

Since the pregnancy she'd been prone to motion-sickness, and now, with all these winding, uneven roads, she felt that familiar queasiness behind her eyes and an aluminum tang in the back of her throat. Her stomach heaved. The night was so dark beyond the car, it was like moving inside of nothing.

"Stuart," she said.

"I think we might be circling back around."

"Let's call your brothers," she said, though she didn't reach for her cell phone. Any movement exacerbated the condition.

"You'll never get a signal out here."

She could tell this was going to be an extended bout. Oftentimes she didn't even vomit, though she had a constant sensation that she would at any moment. She'd on occasion have to go directly from the car to her bed and lie down for the rest of the day or night, eyes closed, head still, but even then the nausea didn't subside, seeming to have settled into her bloodstream, a total physiological takeover of her being. The following day she'd still feel a slight heaving behind the eyes.

"Pull over," she said. "Let me drive."

He looked across the seat at her. "What?"

"Pull over. Seriously. Now."

He did so, slowly, as if waiting for traffic to clear. Gravel crunched beneath the truck's tires as they came to a stop along the shoulder. Out of the corner of her eye Sydney saw an orange light pop on next to the speedometer and stay illuminated. Check Engine? Abandon Ship? She took a deep breath through her nose and let it out, unbuckled her seatbelt and sat for another moment.

"You okay?" Stuart asked.

"Just give me a second."

The engine rumbled like a motorboat. There was a faint squeak coming from somewhere beneath them. She held the pizzas across to Stuart, who accepted them as if he'd never seen such things before. Sydney imagined them exploding in his hands, the puzzled look on his face the moment before he disappeared.

She dropped from the cab and slammed shut the creaking door. So they had a pickup truck now. Lovely. What they'd do with it, she wasn't sure. Parking within twenty blocks of their current apartment in Ft. Greene was a nightmare. And to secure a garage space would cost more than their rent, had their credit been good enough to secure one in the first place. Probably Stuart would sell the truck, they'd pocket the cash, and it'd be gone within the month.

A metallic warmth collected in her skull and seeped downward to the back of her throat. The baby kicked, seemingly upwards, as if trying to help her puke. She hadn't even gotten this sick at the beginning of her pregnancy, as everyone told her she would. Each time was different, though, as woman after woman reminded her. Everyone but Abigail, who offered no guidance, support, or even criticism whatsoever. Sydney knew her sister-in-law considered the pregnancy to be irresponsible, frivolous, even mean-spirited. But the accusations were unfair: Sydney hadn't even been in the picture yet when Abigail underwent her surgery and chemo. That was years ago (a decade?). And it certainly wasn't *her* fault that Abigail's doctors had advised her not to have any more children; she and Nick simply would have to be grateful for the son they had. She felt bad for them, sure, but if Abigail was looking to pin her frustrations over not being able to have a second child on someone, she'd have to look elsewhere. Sydney would not shoulder that guilt: She was thirty-eight years old and had been presented with an unexpected gift. Should she apologize? Well, maybe, sure. Okay. But not to *her*.

Jealousy, that's all it was.

Her stomach had settled, but the nausea remained, pulsing through her capillaries.

The dome light flashed on in the cab of the truck and Stuart leaned over, rustling through the glove compartment. Looking for a map? Or just killing time, seeing what was in there? Here on the side of this deserted road, with the truck's dome light casting a fuzzy halo over them, Sydney felt as if she were standing on a movie set, or an Epcot Center recreation of what rural Pennsylvania might look like in the dead of night. The dark expanse of field grass receded into a high wall of black trees. A little ways back, just before darkness enveloped it, was a small billboard that looked to Sydney as if it'd been there forever, and very well might have been. The ad was for a lawyer, Ernest O. (Ernie) Wasmundt. The paper was peeling from the wood, big chunks of it hung like parched tongues. "Arrested?" the billboard asked. "Injured? Don't take it lying down! I'll fight for YOU!!" and listed a contact number with a 4-1-2 area code, even though the entire county had been switched to 7-2-4 years ago. In the center, Ernie Wasmundt sat in a jacket and tie, as if posing for a senior class portrait, and smiled through his mustache out into the night and into Sydney's eyes.

She leaned over and vomited, abruptly, unexpectedly. Afterward she felt the need to confirm what she'd done, locate the evidence: there across the top of the high field grass lay a gray broken trail, like a passing lane extending into the distance and vanishing. She wiped her chin—further verification. The baby settled. Sydney took a deep, cleansing breath that pushed her belly tight against the elastic waistband of her maternity pants, then circled around behind the truck and opened the driver's side door.

Stuart was snapping shut his cell phone. "That was Nick," he said. "I got directions. We have to turn around, go back the way we came."

"Okay," she said. "Scootch over."

"Syd…"

She nodded impatiently and when he didn't move she shooed him with the back of her hand. Finally he undid his seatbelt and slid across to the passenger seat, placed the pizzas on his lap.

"Thought you said you'd never get service out here," she said.

"One bar."

Sydney swung back onto the road, the truck's wide turning radius carrying them partly onto the opposite shoulder before she had them heading back in the direction from which they'd come. She pressed down on the accelerator creating a gurgle in the engine and a sensation of sheer power pushing through a paper bag. Insects ticked against the windshield; she hadn't noticed that when she wasn't driving.

"So, my dad's dead," Stuart said, quietly, his face reflected back at them in his glass. "He took the 'turn for the worse' we'd all been expecting. We got the call in the middle of the night, all that. We sold the house, cleaned it out. We're through it. It's over." He stared straight ahead, into the bright cone of the truck's high beams. "So are you going to tell me now?"

She unintentionally kegeled. The steering wheel vibrated in her hands and she squeezed it.

"I know I've been busy. Distracted. There's been a lot of bullshit in my life, I know that. You know that. But I'm not an idiot. I can do the math."

"I know you're not an idiot," she managed.

"Well…?" It sounded as if he were speaking over long distance.

"Well, what can I say? I've done the math, too, Stuart."

"Holy—" his tone sharpened abruptly. "*You've* done the math, too? What're you saying? So I'm *right*?"

"I don't know," she said.

"Holy Christ."

The conversation felt imaginary—an occurring premonition. She'd been driving as if in a dream, completely unaware of the gentle curves in the road she'd been negotiating, unaware of her speed, so the sudden appearance of the intersection at Blairsville caught her off-guard. She hit the brakes as if a person had leapt in front of them. The seatbelts locked and their heads snapped back.

"Make a left," Stuart said. He reached forward and pressed in the lighter knob. The truck also had the old non-digital radio that had to be manually tuned. It was on, glowing, but the volume was turned all the way down. "So when were you planning on telling me?"

Apparently never, thought Sydney and continued through the turn.

"When was it?" he said. "Never mind. I know when it was—ballpark anyway. *Where* was I? How about that? Where were *you*?"

"Stuart, I don't want to."

"Well, okay, let's back up. *Who* was it? Certainly I'm entitled to know who the father of my kid is. Wouldn't you agree?"

Sydney wasn't sure. She had to admit now that she'd hoped, over time, to convince herself that her one foray into unfaithfulness had never actually occurred, that she'd *dreamt* it and could shake the vision from her mind and take a deep breath and go back to sleep. But this was not the case. There was no way to blink herself back to familiarity, and the sudden awareness struck like a match in her stomach. The baby flexed.

"I don't know," she said.

"You don't—wait." He turned his entire body to her, slid his ankle beneath him, like a child. The pizzas fell from his lap onto the floor. "Jesus, how many *were* there?"

"No, I mean, just one. I mean, no, that's not what I meant."

The lighter popped out and Stuart leaned forward and removed it. He held it up near his face, orange coils glowing. It seemed to calm him. He closed his eyes, opened them.

"Sydney, you'll have to forgive me. But this has been on my mind for a while now, and my imagination is going fucking crazy."

She hadn't considered this. He'd given her no sign of knowing, which, perhaps, had contributed to her pretending it hadn't happened. She wished she were the sort of person who got out in front of problems, confronted them head-on, nipped them in the bud, all those clichés of preparedness. But she wasn't. She just kept on with life until the problem caught her, then promised herself she'd never let that happen again.

"Who was it?"

His face flashed before her, hovering just beyond the truck's hood ornament: espresso skin, receding hairline, graying goatee, dark eyes absorbing the headlights' beam. If she spoke his name, it would make it real.

"You won't tell me." There was disappointment in his voice. The lighter coils had lost their glow and he replaced the knob back in the dash. "You know, I can't do this," he said. "I mean, I'm fifty-four years old. I can't just take these sorts of things on the fly anymore. It's bad enough it took me this long to figure out what I wanted to do with my life, and who I thought I wanted to spend it with. But I don't have *time* to get over things like this, to make it work, to get used to the idea, to ever get to a point where I'm able to look back on it and see it in a different light. Do you see what I'm saying?"

She felt an air bubble expand in her lower abdomen, beneath the baby. "Bruce," she said. "It was … it's … Bruce."

He glanced at her, looked away, then back. "Lambert?"

She hadn't been aware of her face's reflection in the windshield until she saw it nod back at them, and now she wished the faces—hers, Stuarts, even Bruce's—would just go away.

"Jesus."

"I'm so sorry."

He gripped the door handle. "Could you pull over, please."

Now it was his turn to be sick. Though she kept her eyes closed she could hear him through the closed windows. Between heaves he would cry, trying to catch his breath, and she was momentarily afraid he might choke and asphyxiate himself. She opened her eyes. Up ahead was a railroad trestle spanning the road. Sydney recognized it. They weren't more than ten minutes from the house now.

A car approached from behind, slowed, then gave a wide cautious berth around the pickup before continuing on beneath the trestle.

The door creaked when Stuart swung it open. He dropped heavily, as though exhausted, and sat for a moment, breathing. Then he reached out and heaved shut the door. He did not bother with his seatbelt.

"Okay," he said. "Tell me."

She put the truck in gear.

"No. Just sit." He put his hand on hers and together they slid the gear shift to Park. When both of his own hands were safely back in his lap he said, "Bruce Lambert."

"Stuart... God." She let herself slump back into the seat.

"Here." Stuart reached down beneath his feet and emerged with one of the pizza boxes. He flipped open the lid. "Eating for two and all, you know. Gotta keep your strength up."

She searched his words for tones of irony and, finding none, took a slice of pizza. He took one for himself and flipped shut the lid.

Joey O's used an odd crust for its pizza—more like crackers than conventional pizza dough. Everyone in the family loved it—they just *had* to have Joey O's pizza whenever they all visited; it was a must—but Sydney couldn't get past the weirdness factor: the crust was too sweet, too crispy, too... odd. She never voiced this opinion, though, as doing so would only peg her as the newcomer and outsider she truly was.

But tonight—maybe it was the pregnancy—tonight the Joey O's pizza, even lukewarm, tasted delicious. The cheese, the sweet crispiness, just the right combination of basil and oregano in the sauce—she ate one down and flipped the box lid open for another.

"We should have gotten some beer, too," she said, then caught herself. "Soda, I mean."

"Yeah."

"Look, Stuart," she began, and once she did she understood that there was no turning back. "Bruce—" she swallowed—"Bruce came by the office one night right as we were closing up. You'd just called and said you were staying late again. I was kind of upset I guess—"

"Syd, jeez, how many times do I have to tell you, I had to—"

"I know, I know. I'm not saying... I'm not blaming you. I understand, you were going through stuff. It's just, well, at the time, I was upset. I couldn't help you and you were shutting me out, it felt like. I was frustrated—"

"So, oh man, so this was *revenge?*"

"No! Stuart. God. No."

"I didn't even know you had a thing for black guys."

"I don't—I mean, that has nothing to do with anything. Would you let me finish?" She took a bite of pizza, then wished she hadn't; she forced herself to chew and swallow. Stuart turned away and tapped on the window with his fingernail. Beyond, situated between the truck and the railroad trestle, was an abandoned gas and service station, crumbling and overgrown with weeds. The windows had been shot out; what looked like a filthy tattered bra fluttered from the ancient gas pump. In front was a hand-lettered sign that practically pleaded FOR SALE OR RENT. Sydney felt her stomach collapse. She tossed her partially eaten slice of pizza back into the box.

As if reading her thoughts Stuart said, "My cousin used to own that place."

"Really?" Her throat caught and she cleared it. "Which cousin?"

"On my mother's side. Tommy. Everybody called him Toenail. I don't remember why. We always used to take our cars to him when they broke down. He's in a home now, I think. Completely blind. I bought my first car from him. A 1960 Valiant. Fifty bucks. My dad never thought he was a very good mechanic, but..." He let his thoughts trail off. Then he turned back to Sydney. "So Bruce came into the office..."

"Stuart, please."

"What? Was he in the market or something? For an *apartment*, I mean."

Sydney realized she'd been holding her breath; she had to gasp a couple of times to settle it. Air caught in her throat and she burped. "Oh. Excuse me." She settled back against the seat; she could feel the truck's engine vibrating against her. "He said he was, yeah. He was kind of frantic. Said he couldn't take his landlord for another day. I guess the guy was making him get rid of all his pottery equipment or something. Said it was an electrical hazard. Plus the dust from his sculpting wouldn't come out and the cleaning wouldn't be covered by Bruce's deposit. He was really mad. Bruce was, I mean. He had his lease with him and wanted me to look it over. So, well, I mean...there was nothing in there that specifically said he couldn't make his own pottery in the apartment. And he could probably fight it if he wanted to. Discrimination, or whatever, though Bruce didn't mention that. Not specifically. But he did suggest that the landlord would just find *something else*, and was the effort worth it and...God, I was tired and frustrated. I've said that. Anyway. He wanted to know if I had anything he could afford. I wanted to go home but I did have this place on Adelphi Street. The previous tenant had just moved out and I had the key, like, right there on my desk. So...Oh, Christ."

She was thinking about Bruce's outrage, his unapologetic sense of having been wronged, and his willingness to fight the persecutors—or to leave. She couldn't help herself. Bruce was just a guy from the neighborhood, an aging artist who everyone she knew agreed was crazy-talented, but he kept changing mediums and therefore could never get on any of the requisite art world radars. He was running out of time. Stuart had been friends with him before she and Stuart had begun dating, and they sometimes still bumped into him at the occasional opening or reading around Brooklyn; Stuart was interested in Bruce's latest project: a series of sculptures reinterpreting Delillo's depictions of New York City in his novels. Or something like that. He was thin and wiry, wore jeans and western shirts but gave them an urban flair by adding Chuck Taylor sneakers and the occasional skull necklace. The nickel-size tattoo on the back of his hand, between his thumb and forefinger, she found oddly sexy, like a well-earned bruise. He grew his hair out into a stylishly unkempt yet compact Afro, and on the whole he struck her as a bad boy who nonetheless needed to be taken care of, needed to be mothered.

She'd found herself wanting to help him. Because he'd asked.

"So we walked over there," she went on. "It was snowing. He was just wearing a denim jacket." In her efforts to stall, to avoid this story's inevitable destination, she found herself recalling details she hadn't known she'd stored away.

"Did he like the place?" Stuart asked. "I mean, I guess not, since he hasn't moved. Or has he?"

"No, he didn't like the place," Sydney said. "There wasn't enough studio space. Which I'd known beforehand. Plus the owner was going to be an asshole about credit references. I don't know why I even took him over there."

Stuart blinked at his reflection in the windshield. "Oh." She sensed a shrug in his voice, though his body didn't move. "So, once he decided he didn't like the place you two were overcome by passion and just attacked each other on the parquet floor. Jungle Fever. Or what? You went across the bridge, to the Tribeca Grand? A little stop-off at Agent Provocateur along the way. Did it up right."

"Stop it, Stuart," she snapped, but her disgust was toward herself. She hadn't allowed herself to see the situation in this light—but what other light was there? Though she hadn't admitted as much, she'd let it happen; in fact, in a way, she supposed she'd wanted it to happen.

"That's not an answer."

He wiped his palms across the thighs of his shorts. She wiped away a tear she hadn't known was there.

"Yes," she said. "In the apartment. I'd started crying. Out of nowhere. I was thinking about you and your situation at work and how miserable you were and how unfair it all was, it all is, and how helpless I felt and there I was at six in the evening standing in this vacant apartment trying to get a couple hundred bucks commission and I was crying, and I think it spooked him because he put his arms around me at some point and...I swear, Stuart, I made him stop. I did. And he *did* stop. Just...not in time."

"Not in—" Stuart lifted his butt from the seat and let it drop. He writhed as if trying to pass a kidney stone. It was obvious he wanted to hit something. "Not in fucking *time*? Well there certainly must have been enough time for...for...*Christ*!"

"There was. I mean, look, I'm not saying I didn't mess up here. I'm not saying I don't *regret* this. All of it. I mean..." She thought for a moment. "Yeah, yes, I regret it all. Even...And I'm sorry. Oh, God, am I sorry." She leaned toward him but did not reach out. "And I *did* make him stop—"

"Okay, okay, Jesus, that's enough." He waved his hands around his head, like a child: *La-la-la-la-I-can't-hear-you.*

"You wanted me to—"

"I know, I know. And thanks for your...honesty."

"Stuart." Now she did reach out for him, but of course he shrugged away. He leaned down and took the two pizza boxes back up onto his lap. He closed his eyes and his jaw went slack and suddenly Sydney saw what Stuart would look like when he was dead.

"Does he know?" he asked, eyes still closed.

His voice caught her off-guard and she honestly had no idea what he was asking her. "Who?"

"*Who.*" He spat out a nasty laugh.

"Oh. No. I mean, I have no idea. I haven't talked to him. I don't *want* to talk to him. There's no ... Stuart, please, let's just—"

"Pretend?"

Yes, she wanted to say. *Can't we? Why not?*

"Well, Jesus, Syd. I'm pretty sure he'll *know.* He can do the math as well as we can."

A shiver, like having swallowed too much ice cream, pushed through Sydney, from her jaw down her spine to her tailbone. Of course: Of course Bruce would know. Everyone would. She'd considered this. Right? Hadn't she? How could she *not* have? How could she have been so obtuse, so avoidant? Her mind emptied and then filled with a silent howl, and then Stuart's cell phone went off, the silly cucaracha ring tone he'd chosen a disturbing contrast to the mood inside Carmelo's old pickup truck. He pulled it from his pocket and glanced at the caller ID screen, but didn't answer. "We better get back," he said. "Pizza's probably cold."

6. Stuart

Actually, he knew exactly where he'd been that evening Sydney showed the apartment on Adelphi Street to Bruce Lambert. He'd just taught a three-hour class on *The Mayor of Casterbridge*—struggled through, would be the more accurate depiction—and was in the office he shared with two other untenured instructors, on the campus of B——College, assembling his annual contract renewal support materials. He'd been teaching there for five years, as a "generalist," and each spring the English department chair would approach him with the information that he'd once again petitioned the appropriate administrative agencies to convert Stuart's position to tenure-track in the area of 19th and 20th Century British and American Literature. It hadn't happened yet, and Stuart was beginning to think it never would. He taught five classes each semester, at least 175 students in all, plus two summer sessions, which was fine, he could handle it, he didn't mind working, but the waiting was starting to get to him. He was in his fifties now, on his third wife, and he didn't know how much longer he could afford to bide his time. Part of the problem, he knew—*much* of it, in fact—was that it had taken him way too long to go ahead and pursue the life he'd wanted for himself in the first place. Growing up, he'd managed, like his two brothers before him, to avoid the draft. He enrolled at St. Vincent College in Latrobe a week before graduating high school, but by the time fall rolled around his heart wasn't in it. He commuted from his parents' house, made no friends, listened to his father complain about how all Stuart did was lie around reading, and ended up taking three Incompletes and a C in Introduction to Information Arts, the contents and purposes of which he wouldn't be able to recall on a bet. He sat out the spring semester and managed, somehow, not to get called up, then went back to St. Vincent the following fall.

During the next six years—years that featured some of Vietnam's most bloody fighting—Stuart attended four different colleges or community colleges; between stints he held jobs as a grocery bagger, photographer's assistant (holding rubber squeaky toys up behind the photographer's head for children to laugh at), ice cream truck driver (he was the ice cream man! which was pretty cool, in theory, for about three weeks, until "I'm a Yankee Doodle Dandy" began to drive him bat-shit and he experienced that first troubling impulse to run over a charging kid), and shoe store clerk, which was the worst of all: feet, feet, and more feet. The jobs were all secured for him by his father—the employers were people he'd known forever. The job at McTighe's dairy farm, the one his brother Nick had abandoned, was periodically available, but mucking stalls was something Stuart told himself, and his father, he'd rather avoid. It was fine for Nick— he'd used it as a means of escape. Stuart would be using it as a means of *existence*. And there was something unfathomably sad about that.

He felt as if he'd been drifting. At twenty-three he was still living in the house his father *built* when he was twenty-one. He'd never fired one of his father's guns—didn't care who's feelings he might hurt when, even if he had absolutely nothing else to do, he steadfastly declined hunting trips. But there were times when he'd wake up—or was *still* up—at four in the morning, before his father was stirring, hours before he had to be in at the supermarket, or shoe store, or when he'd roll over in bed to once again skip his class in introductory statistics, and he'd think about walking downstairs, going to the gun cabinet and taking out one of the pistols he'd heard his father talk about as being easy to use—like the Colt his brother claimed last night—and using it to end it all. Problem was, his father didn't keep them loaded; Stuart would have to figure that out on his own. And the prospect of bungling the venture due to the fact that he'd refused all of his father's offers to learn how to operate a firearm was simply too shameful. He kept on living in the house, taking terrible nowhere jobs, and skipping his classes.

But he kept reading. Not books for any of his classes; just stuff he found himself picking up and checking out while in the library researching something else. He started with the usual suspects: Hemingway and Fitzgerald and London, then went backwards, to Dickens and Melville and then pushed forward again, discovering Richard Wright and Kerouac (though Kerouac frustrated him and he gave up after *The Subterraneans*) and Richard Yates. It had never occurred to him to major in English literature. College was for the purpose of obtaining a job—a good job, a job that, unlike his father and everyone else he knew on the face of the earth, didn't entail punching in at the start of the day and scrubbing down with pumice soap at the end. That's why his father was willing to dish out the tuition money in the first place. Besides, he admitted to himself later, he didn't want his enjoyment of what he'd read, the worlds he'd created in his mind, the truth and beauty each book had engendered in him, ruined by having to study it, by being told what the author *really* meant. His most pleasurable moments were when he finished the last page of a story or novel that had moved him, that had come to feel as if the people in it were a part of his life. He'd close the book and think, *Holy shit!* Just that: *Holy shit.* No analysis. No exploration. In fact, his favorite stories made him speechless, literally and mentally, and he didn't want this revealed in a classroom.

It wasn't until Stuart was on his fourth school, Indiana University of Pennsylvania, that it occurred to him that he himself might want to make people go *Holy shit.* Maybe it was because writing stories was not something anybody he'd ever known had ever done. Just *reading* them made him feel like an alien around the house and his hometown. Besides, he wasn't creative; he had no imagination, no *ideas*.

Yet at some point, during that first term at IUP, it struck him that ever since the first story he'd read and had been affected by, in the third grade, a Hardy Boys mystery, *The Secret Panel*, he'd been subconsciously assembling in his mind all the various methods an author might use to bring a world to life. Though he hadn't realized he was doing it, Stuart took note of the dialogue—the cadence and tempos, the progression, the music; he took note of how a character developed a personality in his mind, how some of them, like Joe and Frank Hardy, could walk in through his bedroom door and he'd *recognize* them. How was this possible? How did Franklin W. Dixon (later he'd hear rumors that such a man never existed; that in fact the Hardy Boys books were written by a stable of staff writers for some shadowy syndicate that used *Franklin W. Dixon* as a pen name for all of them) do it? He even, upon reflection, understood that he'd always been aware of the "writer": he liked Dylan because he wrote his own songs, preferred Brian Wilson to Mike Love because he wrote the Beach Boys' stuff; Jefferson was his favorite founding father because he wrote the Declaration of Independence; when he saw a movie he liked he, of course, paid attention to the rhythm and flow of the dialogue, but he also stuck around for the credits to see who wrote the thing. Upon seeing *Butch Cassidy and the Sundance Kid* he figured he was the only seventeen-year-old in Pennsylvania who knew the name William Goldman.

He attempted his first story at the age of 21, in his bedroom in his parents' house, two in the morning, while he was supposed to be studying for a philosophy of religion exam he had to take just twelve hours later. He wrote it out by hand in a composition book—a story about two high school buddies, now in their twenties, who have boring jobs, nagging wives, and bratty kids, and decide, for a little excitement and extra dough, to go on a drug run to Florida; they'll pick up the drugs—marijuana of a made-up quantity—from their contact in Cedar Key (a spot he picked out on a map) and return it to the dealer up north who had mysteriously and unaccountably propositioned one of the buddies off-page prior to the story's opening. On the drive down, the buddies have some misgivings, begin to think their lives might not be that awful after all; the deal goes bad, with the contact, a guy named Conroy, handing over two wrapped bricks of what turn out to be oregano in exchange for the duffle bag of banded hundred-dollar bills presented to him by the two protagonists. The final image is of the buddies on a dock, bending over the just-opened packages, and discovering their folly at the moment the boat carrying Conroy and their money pulls out to sea against the setting sun.

The story was titled "The Sun Also Sets," which Stuart at first thought was clever, then stupid, then perhaps ironic, then good enough.

He worked on it all night. He sat sweating over the final page as the morning's first light spilled through his bedroom window. When he heard his father leave for work he got out his typewriter and typed up the story. It was 13 pages long. He snapped the last page from the typewriter's roller and laid it on the stack, squared off the edges then re-read the story, his stomach fluttering behind his ribcage. When he finished he pushed the pages aside on his desk and sat back in his chair. What he experienced then was a simultaneous exhilaration and embarrassment.

In any case, now that he'd written the thing, he had no idea what to do with it. So, after flying out of the house and speeding off in his Valiant to Indiana to miserably fail the philosophy of religion exam he hadn't studied for, he went straight to the library and wrote another; and then, the next night, another. After a half-dozen or so it began to dawn on him that he'd begun, unintentionally, to write stories about sons not living up to what they believed to be the expectations of their fathers. Nothing specific to his own life—Stuart didn't have much of a relationship with his father and had very little sense of what expectations the man might actually have for him—but the insinuations, it seemed, were clear enough: stories about fathers bailing sons out of jail after having committed numbskull crimes, about sons making patently unwise life decisions simply to rub the fathers' noses in it, misunderstandings aplenty.

The stories piled up in his desk drawer. As he wrote them he discovered his feelings for things in his life he hadn't known he'd had feelings about. He realized that his opposition to the war in Vietnam was much stronger than he'd thought, and that if his current deferment were to be revoked, he would bolt for Canada. If he did, his father would hate him, truly, as would his brothers—or, at least one of them would. (Luckily, though, the draft was ended later that year.) He found he was angry and disappointed with himself for not having gotten more involved with the civil rights movement. Stuart was 16 when Martin Luther King was assassinated—young, yes, but old enough to do *something*, to get involved somehow, at least locally. He'd heard King's speeches on TV and the radio, read the transcripts in the Pittsburgh newspaper—paying attention, as always, to the lyricism, the tempo, the imagery, the subtext, the nuance. He was a fan. But he was afraid of his father's reaction to any involvement he might have in such a movement. His father was sorry about King's death ("damn shame"), but wasn't it his own damn fault? If it weren't for all the ruckus he was making in the first place nobody would've felt compelled to shoot him. It just made the country *look bad* all-around, brought out wounds that could've just as easily remained buried. And he couldn't forgive the blacks (he spat the word as if it were a curse) for the rioting that ensued. "I tried," he said once, sitting in his chair in the living room watching footage of a burning car in Baltimore, "I really did. But they're showing their true colors now."

For a time, when he was at Pitt-Greensburg, the third of the four colleges he'd attended in his twenties, Stuart dated a black girl who waited tables at a coffee shop just off campus. Her name was Alicia. She was two years older than he was and lived with her mother in an apartment above a bakery in town. They started seeing each other after a most ordinary sequence of events: he came into the diner a few times with a book or stack of notes and would fret over what was before him while nursing a soda or a plate of fries. They started talking. His complaints about his studies seemed to resonate with her. She took to sitting down in the booth across from him when business was slow. He didn't remember ever technically asking her out, but at some point it was assumed that they should get together, see a movie sometime when she was off and he didn't have class. They'd make plans at the diner to meet and he'd pull up at the curb in his Valiant and toot the horn. A few seconds later she'd emerge from the street-level door next to the bakery's entrance.

They talked easily: it was as if they both knew the relationship could never actually go any further, anywhere approaching permanence, so there was no reason to hold back. He was interested in her family. She told him her mother never talked about her father—Alicia had never even seen a picture of him—but Alicia suspected he was white, not only because her mother refused to acknowledge him but because of her own eyes, which were light brown with an ethereal greenish tint, and her hair, which was curly, yes, but lacked the conventional tight kink possessed by her mother. She figured some white guy knocked her mother up and, upon learning what he'd done, fled the scene. Subsequently her mother erased the guy from their existence. Stuart didn't know what to make of this; it all seemed reasonable, even plausible. But Carmelo wouldn't have given two shits about the logistics—he wouldn't have approved of his son dating her. And Stuart couldn't get past his own suspicions that he was dating Alicia simply *because* his father wouldn't have approved of it.

But Stuart *did* like her; when he'd look back on the experience he'd tell himself he might even have loved her.

They'd never exchanged phone numbers. So when Stuart decided (was asked) not to return to Greensburg at the end of the spring 1970 semester, he quit going to the diner, quit pulling up in front of the bakery. And that was that.

Though he eventually stopped writing stories, he never quit reading them, loving them, and finally finished at IUP with a B.A. in English. He was twenty-seven. He worked at a print shop and wrote obits for the *Latrobe Bulletin* for a time, then managed to get himself accepted, provisionally and completely unfunded, into the Master's program at the University of Scranton. For this Stuart took out loans he was still paying off. His father had no idea what he was up to. "The hell you still doin' in school?" he wanted to know, often. "You're a thirty-year-old man."

Surprising everyone, he finished, got his M.A., started accepting gigs at community colleges across the state. In DuBois he met Linda—they got married in Williamsport, her hometown, and divorced in Harrisburg, where he was teaching at Capitol Community College and where he met Susan, with whom he lasted five years.

He'd been through two marriages, had two step-children he never saw anymore, and was in his mid-forties when he decided to take a shot at a Ph.D. Even through all of the part-time assignments, Stuart to this point had resisted teaching as a *career*, probably because that's what his brother Lawrence was doing—teaching high school history—and had been doing, well, for many years. But Rutgers offered partial funding, so the accepted the offer. He focused on the Modernists, wrote his dissertation on Dos Passos. B—— hired him A.B.D. as an instructor, promising to convert the position to tenure-track once Stuart's dissertation was defended and the degree was in-hand, a promise they were still making, and not keeping, to this day.

He wondered, now, if, should the baby be a girl, Sydney would object to naming her Alicia.

....

Assembling this year's contract renewal materials had been particularly taxing for Stuart. The package was supposed to convey to the department evaluation committee a (fully documented) sense of the candidate's worth to the department: narratives of his teaching approach and philosophies, a list and descriptions of courses taught, classroom materials, peer and student evaluations; research in-progress, completed, under contract, published; conferences attended, papers presented; service to the department, to the students, to the college—every claim supported by letters, e-mails, agendas, sample syllabi, class notes, manuscripts, a scribbled note from the editor of *The Faulkner Review* in response to Stuart's submitted article on *The Reivers* saying, "Not this time, but an interesting premise. Try us again next reading period?"—everything tabulated and indexed and appendixed and arranged according to the college's bylaws in a series of enormous three-ring binders.

The process had always been grueling, and vaguely degrading, and took forever—days and nights of not only writing and arranging, but photocopying and collating and hole-punching, printing out the little labels for the index tabs. The tenure-track folks who were not yet tenured had to go through the same bullshit, but there was an unspoken understanding that for them the procedure was merely a formality. Stuart knew that most of them utilized the department's secretaries and student workers to help construct their materials. Whether or not the two or three other non-tenure-track instructors—recent post-docs twenty years his junior—took advantage of the same perk, Stuart didn't know, but he didn't want to call attention to himself. So he set up shop in his shared office after hours, papers strewn around him, feeling sick and irrelevant and directionless, trying to convince himself that his life so far was worth it all, that there was still reason to push forward, to give it one more year.

And this is where he was that snowy night in February—in that shared windowless office, surrounded by reminders of his unfulfilled life—when his wife showed an inferior apartment on Adelphia Street to a struggling but talented middle-aged artist.

He wasn't even sure how he'd managed to wheedle a Ph.D. in the first place. Whenever he looked back on the years leading up to where he was now, it seemed like an accident, like at any moment the fraud police would knock on his door and say, *Sorry, but we figured you out, pal. Pack up your stuff and get on back to where you came from.* This year, though, was particularly frustrating. The previous fall he was given the opportunity to teach a 300-level course called "Aspects of Fiction." The chair had made it seem like a gift, something Stuart should appreciate, which he did. The catalog description for the course threw terminology around like "realist," "regionalist," and "naturalist," but the chair said Stuart could pretty much do whatever he wanted to do, so Stuart took it as an opportunity to teach some of his heroes, some of the novels that helped form his love of stories in the first place. And it went well: the kids seemed to like it, dropped by his office to talk about the readings, evaluated him well, and Stuart had the most fun he'd ever had in a classroom.

But in the December department meeting, the last one of the semester, as they were about to adjourn, everyone gathering their notebooks and dayplanners from the conference table, wishing each other safe travels and a restful break, Professor Floyd Reese, scholar in African American literature who twenty years ago had published a handful of poems in journals Stuart had never heard of, several of which didn't exist anymore (Stuart had Googled), which apparently gave him some additional rights, piped up and said, "Before we go, I think we need to attend as a department to a few concerns I have regarding the level of diversity as it's being addressed in our classes."

Everyone froze, half-standing. It was four o'clock, mid-December. "Oh. Okay," said the chair, a prematurely white-haired medievalist named Tinkler, who was clearly afraid of Professor Reese. He looked at his watch. "I guess we have a few more minutes. Everyone..."

"I've taken it upon myself," said Professor Reese, "to examine the syllabi from every literature course taught in the department over the past two years. And it was staggering, and, quite frankly, appalling how underrepresented minority writers are in our courses, time and time again. Writers of color, women, writers of alternative sexual orientations and other historically overlooked cultures, simply do not show up enough in our syllabi. This is true regardless, but particularly for a premiere campus of higher learning in a major American city like New York. Professor Padula's class, for example—" he slid a sheet of paper from a folder and examined it—"Aspects of Fiction. Just one woman and one writer of color on the reading list. And those are O'Connor and Baldwin. *Hardly* stretching to the outer reaches of the cannon."

Stuart had felt his throat close up.

Nobody glanced at Stuart, though it was agreed that the issue of diversity in the curriculum was important to everyone and certainly warranted looking into and addressed accordingly. Perhaps some sort of sensitivity training was in order, it was suggested. An ad hoc committee? Those who didn't speak nodded with gusto. Would Professor Reese like to assemble one and report its findings and recommendations back to the department some time in the spring? Take your time. He would, but he wanted it known that he was doing so under protest. It was shameful that he, a man of color himself, and a relatively new colleague (rumor had it he he'd been denied tenure at Lehigh and threatened lawsuits the whole time he was being pushed out the door, though he claimed to the hiring committee at B—— that he'd chosen to leave for the opportunity to teach at a more culturally diverse campus) should be forced to bring this to the department's attention, and then be asked to research it further. "What this has come down to," he said, "is an outright case of White Privilege, and as an unfortunate consequence I simply have refused, and will continue to refuse, to teach any white guys in any of my classes." What remained unsaid was the implied coda, *And what's anyone going to do about it?*

The meeting broke up, quietly and awkwardly, after that. There were a few mumbled *Have-a-good-break*'s and *Good-luck-with-grading*'s, and one or two colleagues offered Stuart a quick *Take it easy*, as if his judgment and racial sensitivity (White Privilege?) hadn't just publically been called into question.

Stuart didn't sleep that night. And he didn't mention anything to Sydney. How could he? What would he say? To defend his actions seemed only to try to justify his racial biases. The whole thing seemed so surreal. In another context—if he'd just *heard* about the situation, or read about it in on someone's blog—he'd have probably backed Reese. Of course he would have. So what dumbfounded Stuart most of all was how he hadn't seen this coming from a mile away. How was it possible that he'd put his syllabus together—and so many others—printed the fucking thing out, looked it over, made copies, and didn't notice the preponderance of white men on the reading list? Shouldn't he have *known*? It made him think that, after all, he really wasn't meant for this job.

The day after the meeting Stuart wandered the English department halls skittishly, as if being stalked. He still had one last class to teach, take-home finals to hand out, student evaluations to solicit. On his way into the department offices to grab a stack of the evaluation questionnaires, he nearly slammed chest-first into Professor Reese.

"Pardon me," Reese said automatically.

"Oh, Professor Reese?" said Stuart before he could help himself. "Do you have a quick second?" He wasn't sure what he wanted to say.

Reese turned in the doorway. He had a big, square head, close-cropped hair, gray at the sides. His body was wide and square, too, though he was not tall: Stuart was caught off guard in recognizing he had a couple of inches on the man—such a possibility had never occurred to him. Despite his wide frame, though, Professor Reese's clothes—tweed jacket, wool trousers, untucked oxford—appeared to hang off the man, draped, as if he'd bought the clothes a size or two too big in preparation for future weight gain. He sniffled, squinched his nose like a rabbit, fixed his attention on a spot just above and to the side of Stuart's face. "Yeah," he said. "A second. What's up, Stu?"

"Well, I just—" Stuart began, thinking how he wanted to proceed, what he really wanted to know from Reese, and what came out was, "You're not mad at me, are you, Floyd?" He even tapped the man on the shoulder, buddy-style, further horrifying himself.

"Nah, Stu, man, I ain't mad at 'cha." He took a step past Stuart into the hallway. "But you better start thinking about the way you go about things here. It's time this place started moving forward. I've made it a priority to do all I can to recruit more students of color into the English department—if we want to be a top-tier liberal arts college we have to teach our English majors more than just dead white guys. And we'll take along those educators who are pushing forward with us."

"Right," said Stuart, "I understand, sure."

"Meet Annabeth Stern," Reese said, indicating a young woman next to him. She had a beauty mark on her chin, thick-framed but stylish glasses, her hair pulled back in a ponytail—the standard arty/sexy look so many of the girls seemed to be going for these days. Stuart hadn't seen her and wondered how long she'd been standing there. "One of our stars around here. Doing graduate-level work in my Harlem Renaissance seminar."

"Hi," said Stuart.

"Hey," said the girl.

It wasn't until after they walked off together and disappeared into Floyd Reese's office that Stuart realized his colleague had managed to not *truly* introduce them: Annabeth Stern had no idea what Stuart's name was, and likely never would.

....

And so the terror set in, the paranoia. Stuart dreamt nightly of that question—*You aren't mad at me, are you, Floyd?*—and the cringe-inducing shoulder-clap that accompanied it. Winter break was hell. He made an excuse—his health? Sydney's? he couldn't remember—to avoid traveling to Pennsylvania for the holidays, what would turn out to be his father's last. At some point during those bleak January weeks it occurred to Stuart that this was it, he was out of chances, out of time; if B—— got rid of him, it was all over.

What he kept coming back to in his mind, though, were the racial undertones (*under*tones, hell! the tones were right out there in front of the pack, leading the way!). He wasn't *intentionally* not teaching writers of color. Was he? He loved Richard Wright, Baldwin, John Edgar Wideman, Alice Walker, Charles Johnson, he could go on, past and present, and, in his mind, he often did, mostly to avoid facing the question that truly plagued him: Did the people he worked with, the people he wanted so badly to be permanently associated with, think he was a *racist*? The word, even in his mind, made him gasp. Maybe, he thought, there was an icky film of Bentlee on him that wouldn't wash off, and never would. Is this really what all of the silent rejecting and blind challenging of his father's uninformed insularity had gotten him? The possibility made him sad. No other word: just sad.

If he were twenty, even ten, years younger he'd just find another job, wherever and *what*ever it might be. But there wasn't much demand for fifty-three-year-old college instructors who'd never been tenured, never even held a tenure-track position. Maybe Lawrence could help him land a high-school gig somewhere, but his skepticism of doing so without secondary teaching certification was nearly as strong as that of his tolerating sixteen-year-olds. So he put all of his efforts into his renewal binder, intending to show, through this medium, the man he truly was. The narrative of his teaching philosophy would showcase his spirit of diversity, of inclusion, his passion for literature, regardless of the author's ethnic or cultural background. Maybe he'd talk about his own modest background and how it shaped his literary passions and cultural awareness. He'd get student endorsements, letters from past mentors. He'd point out projects he had in the works (at least he *planned* to have them in the works) that echoed these philosophies. He'd remake himself, in this binder, into the teacher he always believed he was.

....

The night Sydney showed the apartment to Bruce Lambert, Stuart was in his shared office working on the narrative of his Research and Creative Activity section. The office was chilly; Stuart had left his door open to try to attract some of the heat from the hallway. It was just after seven and the halls were empty. He also had the little (illegal) space heater turned on in the corner. It occurred to him that the heat generated by the space heater might drift right out his open door, but he sat there and let it happen. He was tired and frustrated, but determined: he was trying to relate a planned article on Baldwin's earliest short stories, which he'd had in his head for some time though he hadn't written a word of it, to his larger goals as a scholar—which he was also trying to clarify in his mind—when he heard, through his open door, the metal stairwell door around the corner clang open and Floyd Reese's magnetic voice carry down the hall.

"He looked me right in the eye and said, 'You're not *mad at me*, are ya, Floyd?'" He cackled sarcastically. "Like a child. A damn *child.*"

"Wow," said another voice, a woman's. Stuart couldn't place it.

"Amazing, ain't it? A damn fifty-whatever-year-old man. Boo-hoo."

Then the voices receded down the hall.

Stuart's blood froze, stopped. He felt something rise in his chest then hold there, halfway up.

His first thought was: *They've been talking about me. What have they been saying?* And then he knew what they'd been saying. He looked around him, at the pages and plastic sheet covers covering his desk and the desks of his office-mates, and his sorrow was pure and absolute, a soul-sickness. He didn't move for a long time.

. . . .

The truck made a clacking noise from somewhere under the dash on the right side, and the left turn signal didn't blink but simply lit up, glowing constantly. "How much do you think we can get for it?" Sydney asked, her eyes set on the headlights' cone in front of her, the first words she'd spoken since her revelation. They were on the home stretch now, Route 33, a minute or two from the house; she'd driven the rest of the way without a single direction from Stuart.

"I don't know," he said. "Few hundred maybe. I might keep it, though."

She tucked a few strands of stray hair behind her ear. "A pickup truck in Brooklyn. Okay."

"I just . . . Never mind."

"It's fine," she said. "Honest."

"Don't be all agreeable with me now just so you can . . ."

"So I can what?"

He blinked, held it, felt his eyeballs pulsing behind the lids. "I don't know."

He'd have to start over, he figured. Again. He actually had managed to get his contract renewed at B—— for the upcoming academic year, his sixth there, but with reservations: The Department Evaluation Committee wanted to strongly encourage Stuart to diversify the reading lists in his courses, and to place an increased, focused emphasis on research and scholarly activity in his field (translation: publish something). The recommendations were seconded by the dean and further confirmed by the academic vice president. By the time the renewal ordeal had played itself out, Stuart finally was able to sit back and admit to himself that, even in his fifties, with an uncertain, perhaps never-fully-blossoming career, and despite the fact that he hadn't planned it, he was looking forward to having a child of his own. And he loved Sydney. He'd been distant lately, he knew that, but he was ready to pull himself together and get on with the things that really matter. Briefly, for the first time in many, many years, he'd felt encouraged.

But there was the nagging problem of the math, which Stuart should have been more aware of. Occasionally the thought would drift into his mind and he'd swiftly push it back out: He and Sydney hadn't slept together in . . . Christ, a long, long time. Months. How, he wondered, could he have let such a thing happen?

In a way, he supposed he'd suspected for some time. Why he chose now, the night after burying his father, to know for sure, he couldn't have said. But he had a feeling that this setback, this latest *failure*, might turn out to be more than he could bear.

Then again, maybe he could cite the half-black baby as scholarly evidence in next year's renewal materials?

Never, *never* had he so badly wanted to simultaneously laugh and cry. His insides squeezed so hard it tickled.

They pulled down past the remnants of his father's garden and Sydney made the right-hand turn (*that* signal worked fine) in front of the house. When they reached the driveway she turned in, slowed, then stopped, still halfway in the road.

"Look, Stu," she said. "Don't hate me, okay? Just . . . not yet. I know it'll be hard. And weird. And awful. I *know*. But . . . give it some time. Please? Give me a chance?"

What he thought was: *You're not mad at me, are you?*

"But what if I can't look at you?" he said, his voice so lacking inflection it chilled even himself. He'd been seeing, without realizing it, his current wife and Bruce Lambert, in an unfurnished apartment, up against the built-in shelves, moving in unison. "What if I can't look at...you know..."

Staring out through the windshield at the garage and the grape arbor beyond, the tears came quickly. She blinked and wiped them away and put the truck in gear and as she stepped on the gas a splotch of brown and gold flashed in the headlights and a dull thud followed from underneath. She hit the brakes and the truck lurched and rocked to a stop.

"What was that?" Sydney said.

"No idea."

"Was it... Oh my god, was it the dog?"

"What dog? Brownie?"

"Oh, God."

Stuart got out of the truck and walked around front, gingerly, bent at the waist, as if anticipating a booby trap. He saw nothing in the splash of headlights, just gravel and sand, stray blades of grass poking up through cracks in the driveway's cement, and, oddly, a giant binder paperclip reflecting the light like a diamond. Then he heard the rustling and jumped back as Brownie came shooting out from beneath the truck's grill. She was yelping and moving fast—flailing really—moving in tight curlicues around the driveway, and then Stuart noticed that the dog was dragging her hindquarters, as if orchestrating a sort of frenetic crabwalk. Stuart froze, mesmerized. The dog kept yapping—a high-pitched, pulsing car-alarm sound—kept dragging itself around the driveway in spastic bursts. A moment later Stuart noticed the dark trail Brownie was leaving across the concrete in her wake. "Ah, shit," he said out loud.

Sydney cracked open the driver side door and poked her head out. Behind the glare of headlights she was only a shadow. "It's the dog, isn't it?"

Stuart didn't answer. Brownie crossed through the path of light again and Sydney dropped from the truck, which she'd left running. "I can't believe this," she said. "I can't believe this."

"Where've you been?" came a voice from the porch: Nick. "We're starv—" He squinted into the light. "What's going on?"

"I hit the dog," said Sydney. "I did it; it was me," as if identifying the culprit as quickly as possible were of any value.

"What dog?" Nick stepped down off the porch and moved toward the driveway. Lawrence appeared behind him.

"Dad's dog," said Stuart. "Brownie."

"*Hit* it? With the *truck*? You're shitting me, right? "

As if in response Brownie scuttled back through the cone of light, still dragging her hindquarters. This time, when she got to the grass she collapsed on her side. Stuart and his wife and brothers closed in cautiously. When they'd encircled the dog they watched it for a moment.

"Someone get a blanket," said Sydney. "We have to take her to the vet."

"Where exactly would that be?" Nick said. "Aren't many twenty-four-hour doggie ERs around here that I know of."

Sydney was making a noise as if shivering from the cold. "I'm *so* sorry," she said. "Jesus."

"It's okay." Stuart put an arm around her. He patted her shoulder.

The dog panted, then raised her head and seemed to glance one by one at the faces staring down. Streaks of blood were smeared across its fur but the location of the actual wound, or wounds, was unclear. Its hip, however, had a funny contour, was dented; it might have even been crushed completely. She lay her head back down in the grass.

"Oh, Brownie," Sydney sobbed.

"Hang in there, girl," added Lawrence. "What do you guys think?" He turned from Stuart to Nick.

"I'll be right back," said Nick. He headed to the porch and disappeared inside the kitchen. "What was—" they heard Abigail begin to say, but her voice was cut off by the slamming of the door.

"This is the worst day of my life," said Sydney.

"Oh, come on now, sweetie," Lawrence said. "It's okay. Don't blame yourself. It was an accident. We'd been *wondering* where the dog was. The crazy thing'd been running around out here all night. Nothing you could've done."

Sydney stared. The dog's breathing was steady but quick, its side almost fluttering, eyes half-open, as if she were merely tired. Stuart glanced up just as Nick came out through the porch door holding the Colt revolver down by his thigh. As he walked he flicked his wrist snapping open the gun's cylinder.

"Whoa, whoa, whoa there, cowboy," said Stuart, stepping towards his brother.

"Nick, no!" Sydney cried. She grabbed Stuart's arm and squeezed it, as if holding him back from something. "Absolutely not!"

Lawrence glanced at Sydney with alarm, then turned to Nick. When he saw the gun he said, "Christ, Nick! You're joking, right?"

"It's the best thing," Nick said, sliding loose bullets from his left hand into the cylinder—one, then another. When the gun was loaded he flicked shut the cylinder.

"I swear, Nick," Sydney said, nearly whispering, "if you shoot this dog…"

"It probably is the best thing," Stuart heard himself say. But what he meant, clearly, was it's the *easiest* thing.

Sydney turned to him

"Let's just settle down here for a minute," Lawrence said. "Get a grip on ourselves."

"Trust me," said Nick, and pulled back on the hammer. But when they looked back down they saw that the dog, Brownie the beagle, was no longer breathing. Her mouth was open slightly, gums pulled back in a passive, almost apologetic snarl. A breeze blew across her fur. Nick un-cocked the gun with his thumb just as the truck, from lack of gas or stamina, shut off.

7. Abigail

After just three slugs of the red wine Abigail was starting to feel it. The first sip was weirdly thin and metallic, with an ungodly vinegar aftertaste. There also were tiny solid particles floating around in it, like pulp in orange juice, only grittier: it reminded Abigail of silt in a lake. Lawrence had spit his first mouthful in the sink; Nick didn't even try any and suggested Abigail pass as well. ("Christ knows *how* that crap'll react with your medication".) So Abigail passed the bottle back and forth with Celina and Raymond. Each had a different reaction after every swallow: Abigail giggled; Celina shook her head sadly, as if her life had finally and definitively clunked bottom; and Raymond nodded pensively, lips pushed out in a suggestion of someone trying to kiss the past. Soon Abigail felt as if she were settling in. She was about to offer what she knew would be greeted as an absurd suggestion—that they all forego the hotel and just crash here (she planned to use that word: "crash"), pick a spot on the carpet and nod out; or just stay up all night, see how much of this mutant wine they could gag down—when they heard Stuart and Sydney pull into the driveway.

"Finally," said Nick.

Lawrence stood, grabbed his ankle and pulled upwards toward his butt, stretching his quad. Then he sat back down. "He never did know his way around here. He was always getting lost. Remember the time he couldn't find his way home from Ligonier on a date? The girl's father had the police out scouring the county for him and he ends up *calling* the police from some farmhouse in a panic: *I'm lost, come get me!*"

Raymond passed the bottle to Abigail for swig number four. "Keep it going," he said. "Once you get your stomach coated with this stuff it gets easier. I'd say six snorts oughtta do the trick."

"The hell are they *doing* out there?" Nick moved to the door and pushed it open. "Where've you been?" he called. "We're starv—" Then he went outside.

Snort four did go down easier, Abigail had to admit. She didn't understand why, when Mel was still alive, she'd never wanted to join the group of men that sat around the table with him drinking his homemade wine. This was kind of nice.

She passed the bottle to Lawrence, who passed it immediately on to Celina; they heard murmuring from out in the driveway, a disharmony of overlapping voices. Lawrence then got up and followed the voices outside.

Raymond took a long swig, held it in his mouth for a moment, his cheeks bulging out, and swallowed in three separate gulps. "I think I'm getting laid off at the end of the summer," he said, wiping his lips with the back of his hand. "Ooh, it's getting good now, huh?"

Abigail wasn't sure if he'd meant the wine or conversation—the fact that he might lose his job. "What makes you think so? Did they tell you?" To be honest she wasn't entirely sure what Raymond did at the township. Something administrative involving ordinances.

Raymond shrugged. He corked the green bottle and reached down between his feet for the milk jug. "I don't have enough to do for a full-time job. It's true, I don't. I admit that. I've been seeing this woman out at the Toyota dealership in New Alex. She works behind the glass in the cashier's office. I'm out on calls a lot so we synchronize our breaks. We'll sneak off into one of the cars that's just been bought and is lined up to get vacuumed and detailed and all that." He smiled, looked from Abigail to Celina to gauge their shock level.

"Raymond!" Abigail couldn't help herself. "You're a middle-aged man!"

Ray's smile grew. "Yup. A *single* middle-aged man. Say what you want but it's fun as hell."

"How old's the girl?" asked Abigail. It occurred to her that she might be a little jealous, though she wasn't sure of whom.

Raymond unscrewed the top of the milk jug, gave an expressionless sniff while he appeared to think this over. "Twenty-four, something like that?"

"Good god, Ray!" Now it was Celina's turn to feign disgust. Apparently what Raymond had been doing during his breaks wasn't as offensive to her as the age of the woman he was doing it with.

He waved this off. "Nah, it's fine. I did the formula."

"Oh, jeez." Celina pinched the bridge of her nose and squinted. "I can't wait for this."

"You take the guy's age, halve it, then add one. And that's the minimum acceptable dating age. So, I'm forty-eight. Half of that is twenty-four. I made it with a year to spare."

"No, Raymond," Abigail said, "you *missed* it by a year."

"Wait. Oh…shit."

"Where'd you even hear this anyway?" Celina wondered.

"Read it in a magazine while I was on the can."

"Lovely," Abigail said.

The door flew open in the hallway and Nick stepped into the kitchen. He didn't glance at them as he turned and disappeared toward the dining room.

"Honey?" Abigail called.

"What time is it?" Celina asked.

Raymond checked his watch. "Almost ten." He sniffed the milk jug's opening again. "I think this one might be a rosé." Then a giggle morphed into a bout of uncontrolled laughter. When he finally collected himself he sniffled and said, "Nah, I'm just kidding."

Abigail wasn't entirely sure what the joke was.

Nick clomped back into the kitchen and went straight back outside.

"Um, was that the *gun* he was carrying?" Celina said.

"Yup," said Raymond.

"What?" Abigail found herself a little confused. Her lips were tingling and the backs of her hands were itchy. "The one...his *dad's*?"

"Ray, go out and see what's going on," Celina said.

"Nope." Placing two fingers through the handle and the other hand underneath, Raymond lifted the milk jug to his mouth and drank. When he lowered it some of the wine slopped over the lip and onto the linoleum. "They're fine. I like it better in here with my girls." He handed the jug over to Abigail. She waved it away but he held it there so she took it.

She wondered what Justin was up to. He, and the other grandchildren—those who were able to make it in—had stayed for the funeral but left soon afterwards. He'd never been comfortable in crowds, or when particular reactions were required of him; plus she could tell—from the hunch in his thin shoulders; the way, when someone talked to him, he stared just past the person's ear—that something wasn't right, that he was struggling with something other than the death of his last grandparent. But he wouldn't let on, wouldn't let whatever it was become an issue, even when Abigail had asked.

She hefted the jug and drank. This one tasted like white zinfandel had been mixed with cheap whiskey and Windex. She coughed.

"I'm guessing this was from a different batch," said Raymond.

The voices outside grew louder. Abigail thought she heard shouting, perhaps even crying. She clearly heard Lawrence say, "Christ, Nick! You're joking, right?"

"I don't like this," Abigail said.

"You'll get used to it," Raymond assured her. "Just like the last one."

"No. I mean, what's going on outside. Something's wrong."

"Okay, fine." Raymond stood slowly. So did Abigail. Celina took out her pack of cigarettes and tapped it on her knee. Abigail turned and started for the door but when she got there it flew open and Sydney rushed inside, brushed past. She shoved a chair aside on her way to the back stairs and stumbled up.

"Think she knows there's no furniture up there?" Celina said.

Lawrence, Stuart, and Nick came in next, one right after the other. Lawrence went straight to the sink and washed his hands.

"Did we sell all of the shovels?" Nick asked.

Celina lit a match. "Damn straight," she said, cigarette dangling.

"I have shovels," said Ray. "We can stop by my place."

Everyone waited.

"It's the dog," said Stuart. "Little accident involving Brownie."

"Gotcha," said Ray.

Abigail felt totally confused; she was about to ask what in the world was going on when it hit her suddenly. She saw it in her husband's face, a steely mix of frustration and purpose: enough's enough. What appalled her most, though, was the next thought that pulsed through her: *Pfew. At least we don't have to keep the dog now.*

"So where's the pizza?" Celina asked.

"Oh. It's out—" Stuart began and then the lights—every one of them, inside and out, flashed once, twice, and then went out.

For a moment, nobody breathed. Then, as if it were some sort of reflex, everyone began reaching out. Abigail felt hands, elbows, shoulders, wrists. Somebody bumped into a chair and said, "Oof." Lawrence.

"Did Dad forget to pay the electric bill?" Stuart's voice.

"No," came Nick's. "I did. I mean, they're supposed to shut it off tomorrow. Maybe it takes effect at midnight. What time is it?"

"Not midnight," said Raymond. "Somebody jumped the gun."

"Damn Republicans," said Nick. It was apropos of nothing but drew some mild laughter, which felt good moving through the dark room.

Abigail was beginning to make out shapes and variations of light. Moonlight was spilling through the window above the sink. She could see the milk jug on the floor, gleaming.

Footsteps pounded down the stairs.

"Stuart?"

"Right here, baby."

Shadows moved and converged. A couple of people stumbled into chairs.

"Now what?" Lawrence wondered. Abigail could see his glasses twinkling.

"First thing's first," said Nick and, remarkably, reached out and pulled Abigail into his arms. She had forgotten he was standing next to her. He held her there, touched his forehead to hers, gently. "Ray, where're those shovels of yours?"

Part Two

Out of Season

8. Abigail

The only candles in the house were Glade air fresheners—lilac, pine forest, and sweet summer breeze—which Lawrence found under the sink in the upstairs bathroom. He stumbled back down the stairs in the dark, shouting "Got 'em!" Toward the bottom he lost his footing and slammed into the adjacent wall. He came limping into the kitchen, cradling the candles in his forearm, the clear plastic holders clanking against each other.

"Sprained something," he groaned and dropped into a chair.

They lit the candles with the blue flame from the gas stove, then turned all four burners on for more light. The bluish shadows playing across the walls and glinting off the window above the sink made Abigail feel as if she were underwater, in a swimming pool at night, dimly lit from above the surface. It was not an unpleasant sensation: it filled her with a sense of dreamy *occasion*, like an illicit but ultimately harmless moment that you know will be a memory forever.

Nick put the candles on the counter. "Let's go," he said. "We've got a dog that need's burying."

"It's my wrist *and* my ankle," Lawrence said.

"Um, I might be drunk," said Raymond. He hadn't gotten up from his chair—not when the commotion began outside, not when the lights went out, not when everyone started looking for the candles. "I haven't been drunk in…" He moved his tongue around. "This wine puts a coating inside the walls of your mouth like shellac." In the pale blue light, his face looked like that of a psychotic but pranksterish villain in a superhero movie.

"Why don't we just go to the hotel," Celina offered. "We're all tired. And some of us have a long drive in the morning."

"Shake it off, Lawrence," said Nick. "Rub some dirt on it or something."

"You're not going to shoot me, are you?"

"Depends." Nick turned and regarded Ray, who sat with his knees apart, the bottle and the milk jug each balanced on a thigh. "And you—put that shit down. Come on, Ray. We need those shovels."

"You know," said Raymond, "I can have that dumpster back here in about two shakes."

Sydney let out a gasp with a little squeak at the end of it, like a surprise hiccup. Abigail had forgotten she was in the room: she and Stuart leaned against the wall where the washer and dryer used to be, hidden in a flickering shadow, clinging together like their plane was going down.

"Fine," said Raymond, and plunked the bottles down at his feet. "But you know, Uncle Mel didn't even *like* that dog. He said a million times that dog was gonna get flattened one of these days. Couldn't control it. Used to go around telling everyone the dog was retarded. 'Got the only mungaloid dog in the world,' he used to say. I don't know but I think it was pretty old, too."

Everyone stared. Even Sydney pulled her puffy face away from Stuart's chest and turned to stare. She looked awful, her face bloated and purple-tinged. Yet Abigail, shamefully, couldn't muster up any sympathy for her. She had to fight back the giggles.

"Finished?" Nick asked.

Raymond leaned forward, rested his elbows on his knees, gathering himself. Then he raised his face and met each set of eyes in the room, one by one. "So we're burying a dog now."

"You catch on quick," said Nick. "You're no fool. I don't care what everyone says about you." He clapped his hands together. "Come on, Stu, Lawrence. Let's go. We got some manly work to do."

They seemed to shrug collectively—Stuart embraced Sydney as if he were going off to war—then moved slowly toward the door. Nick had been using his positive attitude, why-all-the-long-faces, let's-go-get-'em-it'll-be-fun-you'll-see voice. It was a voice he often used with Justin when trying to convince him that mowing the lawn or cleaning out the garage would only take ten minutes, and would be fun to boot; or with Abigail when it was time to go for one of her treatments.

"Well…wait, hold the phone." Celina stood up from her chair and it toppled over behind her. "What about the hotel? How long are you guys going to be?"

"Oh, you'll get there," Nick said, his tone registering feigned disappointment that Celina would feel the need to even ask such a question. "Just relax. Night's young."

"Have some wine, dear," Raymond suggested. "Nicky's on one of his missions." Then he stood, tripped into the hallway and crashed up against the door, righted himself, and disappeared outside with the rest of them.

Abigail had never seen him drunk before. He hadn't been drunk, he claimed, in nearly four decades, since the night when he ran off and got married to a stripper from McKeesport ten years his senior, and even then Abigail hadn't technically *seen* it. Abigail and Nick were still just dating, having met a few months earlier at Pitt when his fraternity was matched up against her dorm during a charity volleyball tournament. Later in the spring, just before final exams, they'd made the ninety-minute trip from Pittsburgh for a Sunday dinner. Abigail liked Nick's family, but they made her a little uncomfortable. She wanted to be liked, of course, accepted, but with this group there was almost *too much* familiarity. She'd felt welcomed immediately, which was nice, but she wasn't sure how to proceed: She wasn't used to the instant closeness, the family-style dining—everyone eating out of the same giant salad bowl, four (or five or six) forks clinking against the side—the way nobody had any shame, confessing embarrassing gaffes and oversights, revelations of skin rashes in inopportune bodily regions. It was as if they'd skipped the getting-to-know-each-other phase.

They had been sitting around the kitchen table, which, even on this, only her second visit, already felt like de rigueur—she and Nick and his parents, Mel and Anne; an aunt or uncle or three; Stuart might have been there, too. The dishes had been cleared away and Nick's mother was breaking out the store-bought ladyfingers when Aunt Marjorie, Anne's sister, whom Abigail had met briefly on the previous visit—came barreling in through the kitchen door wailing, "He did it, he did it! Oh my God help him!" Her graying hair was falling out of rollers and her face was ashen and red-splotched, though she was smartly dressed in a silky spring turtleneck, lavender, and tasteful slacks. Then the look fell apart again at the bottom, as her feet were wedged into a pair of silver-tone, single-strap bedroom slippers.

"Hold on," said Mel, palms flat on the table on either side of where his plate had been. "Who? *Who* did *what*?"

Aunt Marjorie paced over to the refrigerator, loose curlers bobbing. "*Raymond*. He did it. He went off and married that...that *whore*."

Nick's mother, standing behind Aunt Marjorie at the counter, gasped and the box of ladyfingers fell to the floor. "No!"

"He did, he did, he did!" Aunt Marjorie traced a path back and forth from the stove to the fridge, fingertips pressed to her forehead. But Abigail couldn't stop staring at the woman's feet, which were wedged so far into the slippers that her toes overlapped onto the floor while her heels slid halfway up the slippers' surface, like snowshoes. Abigail felt oddly embarrassed, but couldn't look away.

Nick and his father both stood and led Aunt Marjorie to a chair. Once seated, a juice glass of Johnnie Walker before her on the table, she exploded into tears. She buried her face in her hands; a curler uncoiled and fell to the table, then rolled off and onto the floor. Nick's father patted her shoulder.

"She came to see me," Aunt Marjorie wailed. "She came to my *house*. To rub it in my face. That...that...that..."

"Where is he?" Nick asked her. In his voice was a confident mix of *Let's just relax and take this one step at a time* and *I'll kill the bastard when I get my hands on him*.

"He's..." She was staring across the table at the wall, on which a giant wooden fork and spoon were hung. "What?"

"Where *is* he?"

"Oh. I...I don't know. Hiding, I guess, from us. Joe's out looking for him." She picked up the glass of whiskey and sipped from it, made a face, set the glass back down.

Nick's Uncle Joe was a celebrity of sorts around town, having been elected to two terms as mayor; he currently was serving as chairman of the town board of commissioners. If he needed answers, there weren't many people in a five-zip-code radius that he couldn't call. For reasons nobody completely understood, Nick's father and Uncle Joe never got along.

"When did this *happen*?" asked Nick's mother. Mel stood and allowed his wife to ease down into his chair. She'd re-assembled the ladyfingers onto a plate and set them down gingerly. Nobody but Abigail looked at them.

"Last night, apparently. He didn't come home. Then this morning *she* shows up. Knocks on the door. 'Aren't you going to invite me in?' she says. So I do. I *do*! And she sits at my kitchen table, this piece of *trash*, and says, all professional-like, 'Well, I just thought I'd let you know that Ray and me are married. He's moving in.' She'd '*let me know*.' And—oh my God—Nick, honey, she was…there was *dirt* under her *finger*nails. Do you *know* this girl?"

"I've met her once or twice."

"I know her old man," said Mel. He was leaning back against the clothes dryer, using a toothpick on his molars. "Served three months for waving his dick at a bunch of old ladies outside the Shop and Save over in Jeanette."

Anne twisted around in her chair. "Mel!"

"Well, he did."

"She smelled like cigarettes," Marjorie said. "Her teeth were *yellow*. Like a mangy hyena."

This comment seemed to be directed at Nick, so he took a breath, nodded.

"You *have* to talk some sense into him," she said.

Nick reached across the table and patted her hands, which were clasped together on the tabletop. "I will, Aunt Marge. Don't worry. He's just rebelling. Stupid idiot."

"Rebelling against *what*?" Aunt Marjorie wanted to know.

Nick withdrew his hand, shrugged. "I couldn't say."

"Talk to him, Nick," his mother said.

"I will."

Aunt Marjorie smiled sadly. "You're a good boy."

"Raymond's a good boy, too," Anne reminded her.

"He's an ingrate."

Anne slapped her sister's wrist. "Don't you *say* that!"

"Oh, Anne, it's true!" The two leaned into each other and hugged tearfully. It reminded Abigail of pictures she'd seen of baby chimpanzees clinging to their mothers—though she couldn't remember from where. "This is because of *me*. He hates me!"

Mel went to the closet in the hallway and slipped on a jacket. "I'll go and find Joe," he said. "He's probably starting over at the Eagles. Or the Fountain. Be back after while." And he kicked open the door and left.

They stayed late that night and didn't get back to Pittsburgh until after three in the morning. Somehow, Raymond was tracked down and brought back to Nick's parents' house where he was confined to the kitchen. (Abigail and the other women retreated to the dining room.) Sense, apparently, was talked into him, tears were shed, and an agreement was reached for Ray to seek an annulment. Uncle Joe knew all the right people. Besides, all the facts pointed to the perception of an older woman taking advantage of a kid, which should be easy enough to work with. And it was. The marriage was promptly annulled. The woman (whose name Abigail never heard spoken) made some noise for a while—sent a few threatening letters to Aunt Marjorie, stalked Ray half-heartedly, took up with an imposing-looking guy from a DuBois motorcycle gang—but eventually went away. And the incident—that night—was never mentioned again.

But Nick and Raymond would grow closer and closer as the years wore on. They became each other's primary confidante. In fact, when Justin was born, Nick wanted to have Raymond stand up as the boy's godfather. Abigail had thought one of Nick's brothers should fill the role (her sister served as godmother), but Nick didn't want to choose between his brothers. He figured, instead of running the risk of bruising any feelings (at one, brief, point they flirted with the idea of *co*-godfathers) they'd go with Raymond, who was like a little brother anyway. (Actually, Abigail thought Nick was fonder of Raymond than his *own* little brother, which vaguely saddened her.) Plus, Ray would be surprised enough by the request to actually be flattered by it. (He was.) Then, the thinking went, once one of his brothers had a kid, whoever *he* chose as godfather would inform Nick and Abigail as to who should stand up for their *next* one.

Even then Abigail viewed the logic more as avoidance than anything else, but in the end she figured it didn't make all that much difference. And it worked out well: as an added (surprise) bonus, Raymond took the position seriously, to this day calling Justin every couple of weeks just to see how things were going, e-mailing all through Justin's college years. Then, more recently, texting. It made Abigail wonder, from time to time, if Raymond didn't know more about her son's life than she did.

In the end, though, their plan didn't entirely pan out. Nick was godfather to Lawrence's first; Stuart to Lawrence's second. Stuart never had any children—of his own (until now)—and, as it turned out, Abigail and Nick never had any more either.

Her sorrow over this fact would grow to embarrass her. Why, after all, should she be sad? She *had* a wonderful son. A bit difficult at times, sure, but whose kid wasn't? From two or three the boy seemed to have a chip on his shoulder. Kindergarten tested everyone's patience. Justin angered easily, argued relentlessly with any adult who dared to disagree with him, became frustrated over his inability to accomplish overly difficult, even impossible tasks: making a basket in a ten-foot hoop, convincing his dog to follow his meticulous instructions, sculpting a pack of velociraptors attacking a family of stegosauruses—to scale—out of Play-doh. He yelled a lot. When Abigail passed by his bedroom at night she'd hear him grinding his teeth in his sleep. He developed a reputation—at school, around the neighborhood—for being something of a brat.

But Abigail understood that his outbursts, his anger, were in fact ordinarily directed at *himself*—"You're so stupid!" he'd mutter under his breath, jaw clenched, upon privately admitting his failure to pile the peas on his plate into the shape of a submarine. Problem was, the frustration, the shame, eventually directed itself outward, to others. In truth he was a sweet, loving, generous, loyal little boy. And when they found the tumor in her—by accident!—and did what they had to do, it was this beautiful, sweet, eight-year-old boy who sat for hours on end in her hospital room, waited at home for her when she went off for her treatments, brought her tea and toast (which she couldn't bear to put into her mouth) as she lay in bed recovering from those treatments. Sometimes he would crawl into bed with her.

He never asked about the illness itself—at least not as a child; and once he became older he just seemed to *know*, to understand, and so there seemed no reason to talk about it. At that time she and Nick had been trying to conceive. Justin wanted a sibling (and Abigail couldn't help but hope that one might calm him a bit). Nick wanted a daughter. Okay, she thought, and figured it'd be easy. She'd become pregnant with Justin within a matter of weeks. This time, though, things weren't happening. One month, two months, a third. She'd count down the days 'til she could officially declare her period missed, then it'd show up. In the fourth month of trying she felt a painful puckered lump, like a clenched fist, in her lower left abdomen, almost her groin. She went to the doctor and laid flat on her back and was prodded and told she'd developed a hernia. *How* she'd done this was not speculated upon. She didn't even think women could *get* hernias. So she asked. Turned out that inguinal hernias, like hers, occurred twenty-five times more often in men. Had she excessively exerted herself lately? (She hadn't.) Lifted anything particularly heavy? (Not that she could think of.) Twisted suddenly? Awkwardly? (Who knew?) Or it could be the Great Hernia Secret: that most were caused by people straining too hard in the bathroom. Abigail wouldn't let herself believe this, so when anyone would ask, "How in God's name did you get a *hernia*?" she'd shrug and shake her head, as baffled as anyone.

In preparation for the surgery, to determine which kind of inguinal hernia—direct or indirect—she'd managed to develop, the doctor ordered an ultrasound (unusual at the time, but so too were hernias in women, and the doctor wanted to be sure about what he was dealing with). So Abigail showed up at the hospital lab at the appointed time and slipped into a gown and hopped up onto the table. She was wearing nothing from the waist down but the technician glanced at her only long enough to squirt the ice-cold gel and position the wand. The process itself was familiar. But whereas last time the technician had asked if she and Nick wanted to know the baby's sex (they didn't), this technician, a barrel-chested, hard-breathing, mustachioed, thirty-something man with chapped lips and hairy forearms, said, "Hmm…"

"What?" said Abigail, rising up slightly onto her elbows. She'd told Nick not to bother coming. Routine stuff. She'd be in and out in twenty minutes. Not worth a personal day.

"Nothing. There's…Hold on a sec." He repositioned the wand a couple of inches above where she'd believed the hernia to be. He pushed, a bit harder than he'd been pushing, and twisted the wand downward as if trying to pry her stomach open with a crowbar.

"What do you see?" Abigail asked.

"Not sure." He was breathing heavily through his nose, almost straining. "Kind of a funky shadow or something."

The funky shadow he saw was a cyst on her ovary, a growth. A growth that turned out to be a tumor and precipitated the ovary's removal. Of course the technician didn't tell her this, even when she pressed. He was new. In fact he was supposed to have been observed by a senior tech who hadn't shown up. Instead of waiting, instead of calling around to figure out what was what, he saw the absence as an opportunity to prove himself. In a way, he did prove himself: he probably saved Abigail's life. Having never performed a hernia ultrasound before, he began by exploring the wrong area—slightly above where an inguinal hernia would ordinarily be. (A minor controversy ensued: Should the technician be fired? He'd clearly ignored hospital protocol and could have severely jeopardized the health of a patient. But he *didn't* jeopardize the patient's health, far from it, and in the end he was placed on some sort of probation. And then Abigail lost track of the proceedings.) Discovering the cluster of cysts was an accident, a miracle, if not a little baffling (at least to Abigail), and she and Nick were told by doctor after doctor how incredibly lucky they were. Ovarian cancer was as rare in a thirty-six-year-old woman as were hernias, and incredibly tough to detect, and so usually went *un*detected until it was too late. The fatality rate was near eighty percent. Abigail had no symptoms, no reason to go looking for anything (other than her difficulty in conceiving); the discovery was a fluke—a *timely* fluke. The cancer had not yet metastasized. It could be cut right out as easily as the hernia. The two procedures would be performed consecutively: first the hernia repair, followed by ten days of recuperation; then the cancer surgery. Then the round of treatments. And then, hopefully, she'd be cancer-free.

Up to that point in her life Abigail had had her tonsils removed when she was six and the chicken pox when she was nine. Since then, not so much as a pulled muscle.

They stuck with the "lucky" angle. Thank God for the hernia. Thank God for the inept ultrasound technician. Thank God they found it *now*. More children were out of the question, of course, but thank God they already had their beautiful boy Justin. From here on out they'd just be a close little band of happy thieves. Us against the world. And that was fine with them, more than fine. Thank God.

But. As she lay in the hospital bed following the second surgery, watching Justin, alone in the chair by the window, doing his homework, hunched over a math workbook balanced on his knee, it struck her: one day, Justin, alone, is going to have to take care of them in their old age. She had a vision of her son sitting over her in forty years, fifty years, however many it took, alone, no one with whom to share the burden, to alternate shifts, no one else who would feel the same pain he was feeling, the same frustration and sorrow, the same helplessness.

And when they died, he'd have to bury them alone.

Before she knew it Abigail was crying; she clamped down, tried to hold it in, but the strain put pressure on the incision, on her I.V.'s point of entry, which *hurt*, and made the crying come in loud, irregular, gasping bursts. Justin sprang forward, his workbook slapping the tile floor, and went to her. He pressed the nurses' call button, over and over again. With his other hand he touched her forehead, rubbed the hair from her face, a little too hard. "Mom, Mom!"

She tried to tell him she was okay, it wasn't anything, don't worry. But her knowledge of the unavoidable future was knocking up against the sight of her terrified eight-year-old son, and she kept crying that horrible strangled bleat of a cry, and by the time the nurse came rushing in and injected the sedatives into her I.V., Justin was crying too, silently, and then they both fell asleep, her in the bed, propped up, Justin in his chair, tilted forward, his head in her lap. They never talked about that day. But Abigail would never forget the sight of the top of her son's head, the sprouting cowlick there, when she woke. She swore to herself then: *I will make this up to him.*

....

Some time after her surgeries, her treatments, her recovery, Justin began to sleepwalk. Occasionally he'd end up in bed with Abigail and Nick, but more often she'd find him wandering downstairs. Once she found him in the kitchen, opening and closing cabinets; when she, as gently as she could, asked what he was doing, he said he was looking for a plastic baggie. In the morning he had no memory it. Another time she awoke to the sound of scuffling and came down to find him in the darkened living room, sitting on the floor at the coffee table in his pajamas, using scissors to cut odd, random shapes out of colored construction paper. He held his elbows out like chicken wings, keeping his hands steady, slowly guiding the scissors through each meticulous cut. Moonlight streamed in through the window behind the sofa, casting his shadow across the far wall, cowlick sprouting like a geyser. He was twelve years old.

Then one night the following summer Abigail sat up in bed suddenly, overcome by the scent of burning toast. She felt herself blink, trying to gain some context of sensory dimension: Where was she? Was she dreaming? What time was it? Why did Nick never wake up? The burning toast smell moved through her again, like a cloud gathering, and she wondered: Was it possible to be awakened by a *smell*?

She checked Justin's room and of course he wasn't in his bed; then she moved downstairs where she found the toaster on the countertop, conscientiously unplugged, its metal surface cool. A shadow moved beyond the window above the sink, and her heart jumped. Abigail went to the sliding glass door, framed her face with her hands, and looked out. Justin was over by the wooden swing set Nick had built from a kit back when the boy was four, which hadn't been touched in several years. The structure recently had become a point of conflict between father and son: it saddened Nick to see this thing that he'd built by hand (kind of) for his son fall into such abysmal disrepair. The wood was beginning to warp and split; the once-sturdy plastic swing seat had snapped completely in half, each piece hanging by its chain. For a while Nick would drop subtle notes of disappointment and regret with regard to the swing set's demise. ("Kinda wish we could put a garden back there, like my dad's. Too bad the swing set takes up all that space. At least if someone *used* the thing...") Abigail understood his frustration, but facts were facts and life was life and the truth was Justin simply was too old for the swing set—had been for some time. What did her husband *expect*? Justin accepted these ribbings silently (once he'd grown out of his disobedient/ impulsive/argumentative phase, he developed, almost overnight, an uncanny maturity, able to accept disappointment and carry on un-phased, to see through people's ulterior motives and find, somewhere, their innate good intentions), even gave a shrug and guilty I-guess-you-got-me smile from time to time.

Abigail was happy to acknowledge to herself that her son had become a good kid with a good heart.

She kept the lights out in the kitchen, and she watched him, through the sliding glass door; he was barefoot and clad in a t-shirt and pajama bottoms, digging with a spade around one of the swing set's wood posts. The moonglow revealed the presence of other tools scattered around him—Abigail could make out a pick-axe and the block head of a sledgehammer. A few other metallic sparkles dotted the grass, which looked soft and black.

He pried with the spade at the post's point of entry; his movements were casual, precise. Abigail's first impulse was to go out to the yard, quietly, and retrieve him, lead him back to his bed, clean up the tools, and never speak of this moment again. But she found herself not acting. Just watching. Then she found herself going to the stove and putting water on for tea. She stood so she could see Justin out the window over the sink and removed the kettle right before it squealed. Then she took her cup back to the sliding glass door and sat down cross-legged on the linoleum.

Justin worked steadily, his back to her, almost as if he'd been programmed, trying to jimmy the post from the ground with the spade. Abigail wondered why he didn't begin with the screws, bolts, dismantle the thing piecemeal—he had the tools—instead of trying to dig the post out of the ground. Then she remembered he was sleeping and that maybe her sitting here watching him, staying out of his way, was doing more harm than good. She took a sip of tea, noticed the cup was almost empty. She also noticed she was deriving some sort of pleasure from watching her son dismantle his childhood swing set at—she checked the clock above the stove—at three-forty-eight in the morning. It…well, it just warmed her heart. She couldn't have said why. And then Justin abruptly stopped prying at the post and dropped the shovel into the grass. He turned, causing Abigail to flinch—it was the first glimpse she'd gotten of his face—and scanned the grass around him briefly. His face was damp, glistening against the moonlight, and Abigail understood, with a quick collapsing sensation in her gut, that he'd been crying silently this whole time. She stood and waited, not breathing. Never in her life, up until then or since, had she experienced a moment of such absolute certainty: *Something's wrong.* The thought—the knowledge—made her skin tingle with fear.

Finally she opened the sliding glass door and went out to him. He looked at her curiously, with an expression like, "Well…?" As if he'd been waiting for her assessment of the situation. She said nothing, and he let her guide him back upstairs, and put him into bed. He closed his eyes, and she studied him. Was he still crying? He didn't seem to be, *actively*, though his eyes and cheeks appeared to retain a lingering moist sheen. The only words he said, as she pulled the summer sheet up over his chest, was, "I didn't find it."

"No," she said.

"It's going to rain."

As she snuck back outside to retrieve the tools (in addition to the shovel, hand-sledge, and pick-axe he'd foreseen the assistance of a Phillips-head screwdriver, a level, a staple gun, two extension cords, and a hedge clipper) she felt like a murderer cleaning up the crime scene. Nightgown bunched between her knees, she crouched in the shadows and packed as much of the soil around the wood post as she could and tamped it all down with the back of the spade, then returned the tools to the shed. She didn't know where any of them belonged but she did her best to recreate a sense of natural disorder. She shut the latch on the shed, double-checked it. Back in the kitchen she washed her mug, dried it, put it back in the cupboard. The thought of changing her nightgown (was there a smudge, a spot of dirt on it that she might have missed?) but was afraid Nick would notice in the morning. She slid back into bed—Nick snorted, moved his legs under the covers—and stared at the ceiling until sunlight squirted through the gaps in their bedroom curtains.

....

Later in the summer Justin and Nick disassembled the swing set together. The following year, one day after school, she descended the basement stairs to the sound of ping-pong balls knocking against paddles and found Justin's friend Andrew returning a volley while naked but for his white socks. Justin, who was shirtless, turned to see her as Andrew's return whizzed by his head.

"Ha!" said Andrew. "Twelve-ten!" then noticed Justin's face and turned to find Abigail standing there halfway down the stairs, watching them. He jolted forward, as if punched in the stomach, and quickly scooted to the far side of the ping-pong table.

Abigail felt oddly exposed herself, and thought she should say something. "I…" she began, but then couldn't remember what she'd come down to the basement for in the first place. To tell Justin something? *Ask* him something? Did they want sandwiches? Her mind was a total blank. For years afterward she would try to recall why she'd ventured down there—if only she *hadn't* ventured down there!—but the reason never returned to her.

"Mom," Justin said, kind of a shout, "it's cool. Seriously. I mean, it's stupid, really. We were playing strip ping-pong. You know, just to make it more interesting." He shrugged. "I'm winning."

Suddenly Abigail wanted to get out of there, like drifting into a dream she'd rather not have and then trying to wake herself up. "No, no," she

said, turning away. "My fault. Sorry." She hustled back up the stairs, calling, "Just let me know if you..." and deliberately let her voice trail off.
At the top of the stairs, she shut the basement door and leaned her back
against it. She closed her eyes but couldn't get the boy Andrew's pasty
naked body out of her mind—the slightly sunken chest, the protruding
hip bones, the hairy shins above the elastic of his socks. She'd never seen
this Andrew before (Justin referred to him as "this new guy I've been
hanging around with; he's kind of a new friend"); understandably, it was
the first and only time he came to the house.

Justin was fourteen at the time. Now he was twenty-six. Abigail
eventually had managed to push the strip ping-pong memory from the
forefront of her mind. But the recent preoccupied air about him, his
uncharacteristic aloofness at the funeral, brought it all back: the hospital, the sleepwalking, the ping-pong. Everything could be explained,
of course—a child's genuine concern for his mother, anxiety, teenage
curiosity. Now, though, as she watched her oldest sister-in-law Celina
hold the jug of age-old homemade wine up to the flickering light cast
by the air freshener candles—to gauge the bottle's remainder, Abigail
supposed—Abigail was forced to make some connections she'd been
avoiding for some time: his dearth of serious girlfriends over the years
coupled with an abundance of girl "friends," an arrangement he seemed
to prefer; he always had male friends, too, throughout high school and
college but he seemed to acquire a new batch each year. "Nothing to
worry about," Nick had told her. "Isn't that what you want? Lots of different friends? Popular with everyone? Look at Toby McElroy, with his
steady girlfriend, nobody *sees* the kid anymore."

Abigail had to admit this was true. But Nick hadn't been in the basement that afternoon, and Abigail had never told him about it. Why? A
good question she'd asked herself dozens upon dozens of times since, a
question she didn't have an answer for, until Nick claimed his father's

pistol with such adamancy the night before. Her husband's views had become so conservative of late—Fox News on TV, Fox News on the car radio, anti-liberal tirades addressed to the empty kitchen, flag magnets on the backs of their cars. How would he react to—?

She'd never let herself finish the thought.

Besides, her frustrated anger/jealousy/whatever-it-was toward Sydney might have been a truer reflection of her fears. She could handle the social aspects, she felt sure of that. Her fears were selfish ones: Not having any other children meant not having any *grand*children. If they'd had another, Abigail knew she could embrace Justin's situation—whatever it might be—completely. But now... She was fifty-four years old. She'd just buried the last member of the previous generation. She needed something new. Something to protect. A purpose. She understood now that Justin's sour, preoccupied mood was the precursor to an announcement. Perhaps he figured now that the last of the oldest generation was gone, the time was right. Well, she'd support him—absolutely, willingly, lovingly. Of course she would. Fuck her conservative friends. Fuck them all. But there'd be a sadness, too. And this sadness, she knew, would privately shame her.

God only knew the depth of how he'd struggled over the years, without her.

"Let's go out," she said then, standing suddenly. The chair rocked back behind her but did not topple. "Let's go out and get a drink. A *real* drink."

Sydney, leaning back with her elbows on the counter, glanced theatrically down at her belly. The candles threw speckled shadows across her face and for a moment she looked demonic. "A drink," she said flatly.

Celina threw up her hands. "Good god," she said. "What next?" Then she said, "Oh, hell. Where?"

"I don't know." Abigail sat back down in the chair. She'd become lightheaded. "The Elks? No, they're probably closed. The Lion's Fountain?"

"Oh, perfect," said Celina, her voice so full of sarcasm it practically crackled.

"Well, I'm going," Abigail said, rising again. Her head had cleared; things felt right again. "Sydney, you can have a Coke. Have two Cokes. A little caffeine won't hurt the precious little angel. Where are the keys to the truck? I'm driving."

"Truck's out of gas," Sydney told her.

"Well—" The steam momentarily sucked from Abigail, she scanned the darkened kitchen. Where was her purse? "Fine then. I'll drive."

"But I'm blocking everybody in," Sydney pointed out.

"Oh, Jesus *Christ*, Sydney! Would you—" But she didn't know what she wanted from her.

"Oh, for the love of—" Celina carried the jug over to the sink and poured the contents down the drain. "If we're going to do this, let's just do it. Since there's obviously no way we're going to make it home tomorrow. There're a couple of jugs in the back of the garage, probably gas for Dad's lawnmowers. Which we cleared forty bucks for, by the way."

"Ew, how old is that gas?" wondered Sydney. "*If* it's gas. Couldn't that hurt the engine?"

Celina stared her down for a moment. Then she raised her hand and counted off her fingers. "One, I have no idea. And B—or, I mean, two— do you *care*?"

Sydney just stared back at her. The kitchen was beginning to smell like soap.

"Come on, ladies, let's go fill the pickup with a jug of gas so we can go the bar," Celina said and headed for the door. Then she said, as if to some new person who'd just arrived, "This is quite a life I lead."

Abigail followed. "Lighten up, Mama," she said to Sydney. "If you think that kid of yours is going to end up being *rational*, with half of its chromosomes being Stuart's, you've got another think comin', girlfriend."

She was so preoccupied by her amazement at having used the term *girl-friend*, which she'd never done, not in that context anyway, that she almost didn't register Sydney's hushed reply: "You don't know the half of it."

They found the two five-gallon gas cans in the back of the garage, behind a filthy, manure-smelling plastic tarp. Both cans were half full.

"Huh," Abigail observed. "Looks like we missed some stuff, huh? There's more left over than I thought."

"Yeah" Celina agreed. "Wine, candles, firearms, diesel fuel. All the essentials."

They took hold of one of the cans together, each grabbing on at the handle and maneuvering their way out of the dark garage. They lugged the can in halting jolts, hunched over it, the gasoline sloshing inside. Bent over as she was, in the dim light, with her graying hair hanging across her face, Celina looked to Abigail like the witch who tried to roast Hansel and Gretel.

When they got to the truck and put the can down in the grass, they straightened and Celina said, "What?"

"What-what?"

"You're staring."

"Oh," said Abigail. "Sorry."

"So...*what*?"

Abigail shrugged. "I don't know. Nothing."

Sydney was already in the truck; when they turned back to the gas can they understood why: Brownie was still lying off to the side of the driveway, in the grass. She was on her side and seemed to be smiling.

"They didn't take the thing *with* them? Goddamn morons," Celina said.

Abigail unscrewed the gas cap. They lifted the can and poured. Some of the gas ran down the side panel of the truck.

"What's this thing get, about two miles to the gallon?" Celina wondered. "Good thing the Fountain is only a couple miles away."

"Think this'll work?"

"Yeah," Celina said, sounding oddly sure of herself. "It's called karma."

And it did work: the truck started right up, roaring as if awakened prematurely from a satisfying nap. Abigail drove, Celina rode shotgun, and Sydney sat in the middle, hands resting on her belly like it was a tabletop. As they pulled out of the driveway Abigail moved to put on her seatbelt, but then didn't. No one did. No need: They were a band of carefree badass chicks, out on the town, looking for trouble.

9. Nick

They followed Raymond, who swayed slightly from the wine, up the path beneath the grape arbor and into the field behind the house. Some years ago, as a favor to Aunt Marjorie, to get Ray out of the house and living on his own, Carmelo had given Ray a parcel of land a couple hundred yards up the gentle incline from the garden. On this parcel Ray built a green-shuttered split-level with a one-car garage and an aluminum storage shed that was almost as big as the house. There were no access roads—the house essentially was in Carmelo's backyard—so additional permits and waivers had to be secured from the town to construct a gravel drive that wound its way up from Holbrook Street to the east. Where the money came from for any of this, Nick had never been sure.

"There's a little dip here," Raymond called out in the darkness and pointed at the ground to his left. "Careful." And Lawrence promptly stumbled. "Told ya."

There was no light to guide them, no streetlights, no porch lights, but the moon cast a cool white glow over the scene that seemed to be rising up from the ground. Raymond's earring glimmered.

"What'd we come up here for again?" Ray said as they cleared the rise leading to his house. "Oh, yeah. Over in the shed."

Nick went over to it. It was the size of a small barn, with two giant sliding aluminum doors, putting Nick in mind of an airplane hangar. "Isn't it locked?"

"Huh-uh." Raymond turned and headed slowly across the gravel toward his front steps.

"Aren't you afraid someone'll steal something?"

"Yeah," said Ray, without turning. "Happens all the time. Stuff usually shows up again later, though. I'm going to bed."

Nick rattled the latch on the shed's door. "Like hell you are."

"That wine," Ray said. "I shoulda known better. Live and learn, I guess." He kept going, his back to them. "I don't think I'm up for burying dogs right now. Have fun, though."

"I'm with him," said Stuart, and followed. "Call us in the morning."

"Lawrence, stop him," said Nick, and then used both hands to heave open the sliding aluminum door.

"*I'm* not stopping him."

"Stuart, stay right here. I'm not screwing around. We need you for this."

"Need me," said Stuart, "for what?" He stopped and turned; Raymond kept right on going up his front steps and in through his unlocked front door, which he did not pull all the way closed.

Nick didn't feel as though he knew how to tell his brothers what he needed them for. But he did need them "Just…come on. Or—wait. First see if you can find a porch light inside the door. I can't see a goddamn thing in here."

Stuart closed his eyes for a moment and seemed to sway. Then he climbed the front steps and disappeared inside the house, and Nick—and Lawrence, too, standing on the gravel drive with his hands plunged into his shorts' pockets—waited to see what would happen. The porch light sprang on and then Stuart came back out, pulling the door closed behind him. "How's that?"

Nick had no idea if the light would help or not. "Perfect," he said.

Stuart and Lawrence waited as Nick groped around in the shed, knocking over rakes, flagpoles, upright patio furniture, various posts and rods that toppled over with hearty metallic clanks. He wanted to wait for his eyes to adjust but was afraid of taking too long and losing Lawrence and Stu. He stepped toward the center of the shed and smacked his knee against something—a riding mower that seemed to appear like a spirit in the darkness. "Fuck," he muttered, and shuffled around it.

"Everything okay in there?" Lawrence's voice. He'd poked his head inside the shed. "Look, Nick, why don't we just bag this. And I mean that literally. I'm sure Ray's got a Hefty bag in the house that'll do the trick quite nicely."

Nick spotted a lineup of ghostly plate-size reflections along the floor of the far wall: Shovels. Had to be. He shuffled his way over to them, shards of loose metal and plastic snapping against his bare shins, and groped for the handles. "Here," he said, and held them out in Lawrence's direction.

"Yeah, okay," Lawrence said, a note of grudging resignation in his voice.

When Nick stepped back out onto the driveway he found his brothers standing there looking at him. He felt as if he'd been caught in some act that finally revealed a shortcoming that had never been proven yet everyone suspected he possessed. "What?"

"I have to pee," Lawrence said. Out in front of him he brandished a spade and a steel-toothed rake.

"Okay. Well, here, gimme that." Nick indicated the rake. Lawrence handed it back to him and Nick replaced it in the shed, then slid shut the door. "Pee anywhere you want on the way back."

"Nope. Can't. I need…I mean, it's a whole production. I gotta carve out a window of time for it. A few minutes at least."

Now Nick and Stuart stared at Lawrence.

"I don't wanna talk about it right now."

"Fine with me." Nick ducked back inside the shed. He remembered Raymond commandeering one of his father's old battery-powered spotlights, which they might at some point tonight find some use for. Unlike the shovels, the spotlight was easy to find: in the near corner, leaning on its side between a sawhorse and the wall. Now, as long as the battery wasn't dead…

....

They headed back down toward their father's house. The uncut grass folded over on itself and occasionally grasped their feet and ankles. Lawrence carried the shovel, Nick the spotlight. The breeze had shifted and now there was a smell in the air like moldy mushrooms. Fifty yards short of the garden they passed by a crabapple tree and Stuart's legs flung straight out in front of him and he seemed to hang in mid-air, in a sitting position, hands still in his pockets, then dropped, hard, onto his backside.

A sound escaped from him like, "*Oof*," then he lay back and writhed from side to side, just a shadow moving across more shadows. "Ah, Jesus Christ," he moaned.

Nick couldn't get his mind around what he'd just seen. "The hell *happened*?" He looked at Lawrence, whose face was blank, and back to Stu.

"I think… Holy shit… I tripped or something. On a crabapple."

"You… tripped… ?"

"Yes, goddamn it. Like, I stepped *on* it. Like a marble or something. And my feet… and then I… oh, fuck… then I fell *on* one, too… and… Jesus, right up my *ass*."

Stu appeared to be lying on his back, feet flat, lifting his hips off of the ground like some sort of yoga exercise. "You're kidding," Nick said flatly.

"Hell no, I'm not fucking kidding!"

"How could it… wait, I'm missing something here." He looked at Lawrence again for help.

"People," said Lawrence, uninterested. "Remember: Urinary emergency?"

"It didn't go *up* my ass," Stuart said. "You prick. But I think…I mean, it *would* have—" he took a breath, as though gathering air to inflate a blow-up toy—"if it weren't for…the pressure is…Ah, fuck you and him both."

"Well, shake it off," Nick said. Then he said, "Hey, remember—" and stopped.

"Remember what?" said Lawrence. He handed the shovel to Nick then turned his back to them and unzipped his shorts.

"Remember when Stu fell off the roof?"

"If I hadn't been wearing pants, we'd be heading to the Emergency Room right now," Stuart said.

"If you hadn't been wearing pants," Lawrence said into the darkness, "we'd have dumped you somewhere long before this, Professor."

Nick leaned on the shovel, adjusted the spotlight in his other arm, as if cradling a baby. "I thought you were dead," he said.

"Me, too," said Stuart, rising up onto his elbows. His voice seemed to be steadying. "How embarrassing would *that* be? Death by crabapple in the asshole."

"No. I mean when you fell off the roof."

"I was *sure* he was dead." Lawrence still stood with his back to them, hands poised. "In fact, my first thought was: *How are we going to cover this up?*"

A small, abrupt chuckle escaped from Nick.

They'd sent him up there to retrieve a tennis ball, a wiffle ball, a lawn dart, something, under the pretence of inclusion: Whenever an article of their after-school play got stuck on the front porch's roof (which was often) Lawrence or Nick or one of their similarly aged friends would go up to get it. At the time, Lawrence was twelve, Nick eleven; Stuart was nine and frustrated at still being made to feel like he was tagging along. Why was *he* the only one not allowed on the roof? It wasn't fair. And if they wouldn't let him, then he'd tell Dad—a formidable threat, as the fact was that *no one* was allowed on the roof, ever, to collect stray balls or for any other reason.

Stuart had drawn a line in the sand—the first such stand he'd ever taken—and the others couldn't afford to call his bluff. Nick and Lawrence had looked at each other, then searched the faces of their buddies, three or four of them, who where scattered around the side yard. Fine then, someone (not Nick) had said. Go up and get it.

To get to the porch roof in the middle of the day you had to go into the house and sneak upstairs, past their mother, who usually was in the kitchen but could be anywhere, then go out through the bathroom window. The roof had a slight pitch and the shingles could be sticky in the summer heat. Lawrence, Nick, and the other neighborhood boys their age had mastered the intricacies, but Stuart, who had a reputation for clumsiness to go along with his overzealousness, hadn't. Later, Lawrence and Nick would admit to each other that as they silently watched their brother disappear through the kitchen door they knew this wouldn't end well.

While they all waited for Stuart to emerge through the bathroom window nobody spoke. A kid named Sonny Wheeler sniffed his own armpit and went, "Ugh." Jimmy Mertz sat down in a patch of shady grass near the cellar doors. A minute later, up above them, a sneakered foot appeared, then a leg, then Stuart's head and torso. He stood with his knees slightly bent and gauged his balance, looked down at everyone. The expression on his face was one of petrified exuberance.

"*Careful!*" Lawrence hissed, though Stuart had barely moved. "You fall and that's it; you're a goner."

The ensuing sequence of events was so predictable it didn't feel quite real.

Stuart took a cautious half-step to his right, in the direction of the boys below. Upon reflection, it always appeared to Nick as if Stuart then *decided* to fall off of the porch roof: He took one more step toward the edge, his knee buckled faintly, then he seemed to tuck his shoulder as if attempting a flip into a swimming pool and leaned out over the edge. The next instant he was airborne, the fall itself slow and horrifying: in the moments before he hit the ground Nick actually had time to prepare for his brother's death, accept it, grieve, and move on.

This is what it feels like to see someone die, he thought.

Looking back, Nick would have to admit that Stuart's shoulder tuck was rather impressive, rotating his body as he fell just enough so that Stuart landed flat on his back. The sound was like a sack of grain dropped on a barn floor.

He landed alongside the house, behind a gold-blooming forsythia bush.

Nobody ran to him immediately—everyone most likely pressing the do-over buttons in their brains. When that didn't work the small crowd of boys converged slowly, peering around the forsythia.

"He's not breathing," someone said, almost casually.

"He's fine," said another boy. "Just get him on his feet."

They were both right, as it turned out, though nobody knew that at the time. If Nick's and Lawrence's mother hadn't come outside just then—instinct, that's all Nick could chalk it up to—there's no telling what the boys' next move would have been.

Their mother was remarkably calm. Once she leaned out from the porch, beyond the corner of the house, and saw Stuart lying there on his back, she dropped the dish towel she'd been holding and ran back inside the house. Then she was kneeling beside him with her hand flat on his chest, talking unintelligibly but gently to him, the other boys forming a tattered ring ten steps behind on the driveway, when the paramedics pulled up.

The wind had been knocked clean out of Stuart, of course. But he'd landed so perfectly flat on his back—the shoulder-tuck off the roof was the key—that no bones were broken, just some bruised ribs and tailbone (coccyx, it was actually called, a word that might have been—*should*

have been—funny but from that day forward filled Nick with shame
and dread every time he heard it), plus a concussion. They kept him in
Latrobe Hospital for two nights in case any internal bleeding should
develop. None did.

That first night, after returning from the hospital, their father called
Lawrence and Nick into the kitchen. When each brother pulled out a
chair to sit their father said, "No. Stand up."

They stood before him, between the table and sink, shoulders grazing.
On the counter was a saucer with three or four kalamata olives.

"So I guess I wanna know what you were thinking." He glanced from
Lawrence to Nick, then down at his own enormous hands, which he
rubbed as if they were arthritic.

Lawrence turned toward the window above the sink. He bulged his
cheeks out then released an airy little lip-fart. "Look…he just…I mean,
he always—"

The slap came from below, from the hip. There was a sharp clapping
sound as Lawrence's head snapped back toward the window and his
knees buckled, then Nick saw the blur coming toward his own face.
He had the urge to call time-out. Something wasn't right: let's just back
up and start this over again. But the giant hand struck him before he
could get the words out. Nick staggered backwards a couple of steps,
then dropped to his butt. He could feel his eyelids blinking, blinking,
blinking. He couldn't make them stop.

He'd hit them before, though rarely, and anyway this was different.
This wasn't a spanking, wasn't a motivating smack; this was a backhand,
meant not to punish, but to humiliate, to *hurt*. Nick felt his stomach collapse inside him. Lawrence leaned back against the refrigerator, touching
his face as if surprised to find it still there. Carmelo stood staring out
the window over the sink, rubbing is hands again, a slight embarrassed
slouch to his shoulders now.

"That's your *brother*," he said, and turned his face to them. "Your mother's little boy." His bottom lip trembled, then steadied.

Later that night, back at the hospital, they apologized to Stu, then made a show of tearfully apologizing to their mother—an apology she accepted so readily and unquestioningly, punctuated by hugs and slobbery kisses, that it was a little uncomfortable.

....

Still kneeling, Stuart spread his knees a few inches, put his hands backwards on his hips and bent forward at the waist. "I think I may come away from this night with some internal issues," he said.

Lawrence hadn't moved, hands poised in the ready position, elbows out, glasses halfway down his nose. He had the air of a man with all the time in the world, and the patience to use it. Nick felt suddenly restless. He had an urge for a symbolic gesture. The thought shamed him, but the shame passed like a wave of nausea and was replaced by an empowering sense of fortitude. He needed to perform an act of tribute to his father, and he felt sure that after tonight such a tribute would no longer be possible.

"Finish up, Lawrence," he said. "Stuart, let's go, on your feet. We're going hunting."

Their faces snapped to him simultaneously. "Come again?" Lawrence said.

"Before the night's over, we're going to hunt something down, kill it, clean it, cook it, and eat it. Maybe mount its head, but no need to cross that bridge just yet."

Stuart laughed, pure amusement, and for a moment they were twelve again.

"Christ, Nick," said Lawrence, "why can't we just get *done* with this? Dad's buried. The house is sold. Now you have us burying a dog. I wanna wrap this shit up and go *home*."

"That's just the point," Nick said, though in the instant it had taken him to speak the words he'd lost the thread of what the point actually was. He took a step toward Lawrence, then was afraid his brother would finally start peeing and turned away again. "Don't you see? That's the way we do *everything*. I mean, Dad *built* that house we just sold. He served in a goddamn World War—"

"Oh, here we go," said Stuart, pushing finally to his feet. "Good holy goddamn god, Nick, when are you gonna get over that? War is bad. I don't *care* what Rush Limbaugh says." He shrugged theatrically. "Accept it and move on."

"Wait, hear me out. It's not just that. I mean, Dad—" Nick thought for a moment—"he could take apart a coal furnace and convert it to oil. He could fly-fish, start a fire with stones. Build a patio from scratch—two levels. Some guy at the wake told me Dad beat him nearly to death and it was the best thing that ever happened to him. Saved his life, the guy said. Whatever *that* meant." Nick rested the shovel on his shoulder like a rifle, let the spotlight dangle from his other hand. He felt a cool electricity moving through him. "What have *we* done?" he said. "We have nice houses, a couple of cars."

"Speak for yourselves," said Stuart.

"Well, yeah, okay. Except for Stu. But, I mean, look—a couple weeks ago I was watching this reality show. I forget what the object was, except to make me feel like the oldest person on Earth, but people were being matched up together—couples—they were, like, I don't know, in their twenties. Goddamn *kids*. I remember thinking they were Justin's age, younger even, and then being appalled. Anyway, they had to spend the day together. The first half of the day doing something one person liked to do, the second part spent doing what the other liked to do. I guess the point was to share a part of their lives with each other. And at the end they decided if they were a good match…"

"The hell were you doing *watching* that show?" Lawrence said over his shoulder.

"No idea. Couldn't even tell you the name of it. But, anyway, one girl taught this guy how to make sushi. They're slicing it and rolling it and wrapping it in…whatever they wrap it in—seaweed. A guy taught a girl how to play chess. They went to this big park at the beach, in California I think, where the chess pieces were, like, life-size. Another guy took a girl surfing. A girl taught a guy how to make a knapsack out of—whaddaya call that stuff—hemp. And as I'm watching this, do you know what I'm thinking?"

"Kill me now?" Stuart offered.

"Kind of. But no. I'm thinking, I'm fifty-six years old, and if I were on this program now, what could *I* show someone about my life? Honestly. How to balance a checkbook? How to jog a ten-and-a-half minute mile? How to go to the movies and be content with popcorn without butter and then have no opinion whatsoever about the movie? I mean, *Jesus.*" He turned sharply to Lawrence. "Are you gonna fucking *piss*, or what?"

Lawrence's shoulders rose and fell. "I think I have a prostate thing going on," he said. The voice was quiet, flat, as if he were talking to himself.

"Jesus *Christ.*" Nick felt like he'd been punched in the heart. He took a breath. "Okay, look, I'm going hunting. I'm going to kill something. Tonight. And I want my brothers with me."

"I'm not killing anything," said Stuart. He rose gingerly to his feet and stood as if testing his balance.

"Fine," Nick said. "You can spot. Here." He held the spotlight out to Stuart, who stared at it. Nick sensed the arrival of a pivotal moment, and he held his breath. When Stuart reached out and took it Nick was so happy he was afraid he might squeal.

"Where's Dad's?" Stu asked, hefting the spotlight. "Didn't we buy him a fancy new one just a couple Christmases ago—rechargeable and shit?"

"Sold," said Lawrence. "Eight bucks."

"This is Dad's old one," Nick pointed out. "Must've given it to Ray. But it's *better* than the new one. It's *perfect*." He nudged Lawrence's shoulder blade with the handle-end of the shovel. "Any chance you can put that business on hold for a while?"

"Sadly," said Lawrence, zipping up, "yes."

10. Celina

Since going back to work and assuming her responsibilities on the school board, Celina had become somewhat of a drinker. She'd admit that to anyone. She liked to have a glass of red wine in the evenings—a glass that often turned into half a bottle—and on the weekends she made vodka martinis for herself, straight up, with a couple of olives she didn't bother to spear with toothpicks but just left float free in the glass. Lawrence didn't drink. Any alcohol at all made him fall asleep on the spot. Last Fourth of July, at their neighbors' party, he had half a beer and conked out on a patio chair, hands clasped in his lap, chin tucked into his neck, mouth open, face sunken like a corpse, his snores audible between blasts of fireworks.

Maybe it was the repeated act of drinking alone, but Celina, in addition to gaining twenty pounds in the past twelve months, had built up a fairly impressive tolerance for the alcohol she consumed. She couldn't remember the last time she felt drunk—or, perhaps more accurately, "high". (She'd been drunk and *depressed* many, many times.) In Verona, maybe, after the opera (the title of which had immediately vanished from her memory)—the quiet café in the piazza, the cobblestones, the lit coliseum in the distance, the feeling of trying to stay in love with Lawrence: the wine had gone straight to her head.

Or maybe it was at her daughter's rehearsal dinner. All those toasts.

Whatever the case, she decided, as Abigail parked their father-in-law's (now, apparently, brother-in-law's) pickup truck nose-first at the curb out in front of The Lion's Fountain Tavern in deserted, downtown Bentlee, she would goddamn well get good and drunk tonight.

An Iron City Beer sign flickered in the front window. Celina's ass-cheeks clenched.

"Let's go, ladies," Abigail said brightly, jamming the truck's gearshift into Park and flicking off the ignition. "I didn't bring my purse," she said. "Here," and she tossed the keys to Celina. "Buck up. This is gonna be fun." Then she giggled. "*Buck up*! I've never said that before."

Celina's butt seized. This had been happening to her all day and it struck her that this reflexive response was becoming a habit she didn't want to have. She took a breath, tried a different tone: "Oh, dear," she said, opening her purse and dropping in the keys. Then she pushed open the squeaky passenger door. "Someone's giddy."

And so they entered The Lion's Fountain—a place Celina had heard about for decades and must have driven by a thousand times but had never been inside of—to find a half-dozen sleepy-eyed men hunched over the slightly curved oak bar. A few turned and inspected the women in the doorway, eyes drifting up and down, then went back to their hushed conversations. The place smelled of yeast and urinal cakes. Behind the bar, on a shelf surrounded by half-filled bottles of Jim Beam and dusty, age-old, never-opened crème de cacaos, a nineteen-inch television sound-lessly projected the flickering images of a nature show: a khaki-clad man barreled splashing into what looked like an Amazonian swamp and for no apparent reason began wrestling an enormous snake.

"Fuck *me*," said one of the men at the bar, evidently impressed.

On the opposite wall was a dartboard cabinet, one door hanging by its hinges. An unseen jukebox, which clearly hadn't been updated in decades, played a song Celina, remarkably, remembered as "Shadow Dancing" by the Bee Gees, or maybe one of the Gibb brothers. Alex? Andy?

Abruptly, Celina was afraid she might start weeping.

"Okay, come on," said Abigail and headed for a table along the far wall. There were only two chairs so she slid over another. They were metal folding chairs, and Celina felt as if she could see the bacteria glowing on them, like toxic waste in cartoons. She and Sydney stood in the doorway, watching Abigail arrange the furniture. When she finished she looked up at them. "Well?" she said.

"They're *smoking* in here," Sydney said in a whispered hiss.

"Oh, please," Celina heard herself say. Now she was annoyed at Sydney, which made her *want* to stay at The Lion's Fountain. Her allegiances seemed to be shifting so fast she couldn't keep up with them. "A little nicotine's good for the fetus," she said. "Toughens it up."

"But, is it even *legal* to smoke in here?"

Celina shrugged. "Call a cop." She headed over to the table Abigail had commandeered but along the way the bottom of her sandal stuck to the floor, causing it to catch for a moment and snap loudly against her heel as she lifted up. Again faces turned, surveyed, lost interest, turned away. "Jesus Christ," Celina muttered.

One leg of the table was shorter than the other three, so they switched to another whose legs seemed to have *three* different height variations. They went back to the original table. Once settled Abigail announced, "First round's on me. *I* am having a boilermaker."

Sydney rattled the table back and forth, from one leg to another. "Ew," she said. "What's *in* that?"

"Dunno," Abigail admitted, "but it just *sounds* like the right drink for a place like this, huh?"

"Just what, exactly," said Celina, "are you trying to accomplish here?"

"Accomplish?" Abigail leaned forward, thumped her elbows down on the table, which shifted toward her, hard. "Who's trying to *accomplish* anything, Celina? We just buried our father-in-law. I'm feeling mortal and goofy right now and wanted to have a drink. A boilermaker, because... because, well, because why the fuck not? You've got somewhere to *be* right now?" She stood and dug the keys from her pocket and dropped them on the tabletop. "Be my guest." Her eyes grew wide then and she blinked several times in rapid succession. She glanced down at Sydney. "Coke?"

"Well," Sydney said, "uh, the caffeine..."

"Oy-vay." She turned back to Celina. "So?"

"Dewar's rocks," said Celina.

Abigail shuffled sideways between tables to the bar where she again leaned forward on her elbows, speaking to the bartender—a potbellied man of indeterminate age (graying hair, black mustache), with a barbed wire tattoo around his neck—as if they were old friends. Apparently she was determined to plaster a sincerely nostalgic face on this evening, and this knowledge, oddly, released a wave of calm that poured down over Celina, softening her jaw, her shoulders, stomach, her ass. She folded her purse strap in half, and into thirds, then bent over and tucked the folded strap under the shortened table leg. She sat up and tested the table's stability. "*Perfetto*," she said, and—Jesus!—she winked at Sydney.

The Andy/Alex Gibb song ended and the room went silent. Then some murmurs, vague and imprecise, as if leaking from the walls. From over by the bar Celina could hear Abigail saying, "Yes, but what's *in* it?"

"I think Mel liked you," Celina said to Sydney. "He never liked me. Neither one of them did."

"Well, that's comforting," Sydney said. She slid her ass forward a few inches and leaned back in her chair, let her arms fall to the sides. "Good to know I've got that going for me. Happy day."

"I think it's because he never thought Stu would end up with anyone. The writing was on the wall with those other two. You were his last shot—according to them. And plus, you're just so darn cute and perky. Ain't'cha?"

"How sweet of you to say," Sydney said flatly. She was staring off toward the far corner of the room, where a bunch of old boxes were stacked, top flaps splayed like wings.

"Hey, come on now. Don't get snippy. I'm just making chitchat."

Actually, Celina's words were truer than she had intended them to be. She always felt as if Mel *didn't* like her. Nor did Anne. Especially Anne. She'd always assumed it was an oldest son thing—that ancient belief that no woman will ever be good enough. Perhaps. But that only applied to Anne. As for Mel, it was simple: She'd always felt like a fraud around him.

Mel was nothing if not authentic. And Celina, well, she didn't even know what she wanted anymore.

"They liked you fine," Sydney said. "Get over it."

"On the surface maybe. But—"

"Okay, so here's the thing," announced Abigail, approaching the table with a manhole-sized brown tray, on top of which were several glasses containing liquids of varying depths and colors. She looked, to Celina, every bit like the middle-aged waitress that might actually work in a place like this. Apart from the rose-pink capris. "Turns out a boiler-maker isn't really a *drink*, per se. I got one anyway, though." She placed the glasses on the table one at a time. "Ginger ale for the little mother."

"So what is it?" Sydney asked.

"Well…" Abigail sat and flicked her bangs across her forehead. In front of her were a draft beer and a shot of what appeared to be whiskey. "It's just, you know, a beer and this shot of…well, I forgot to ask. Apparently I'm supposed to drop the shot glass into the beer glass then drink the whole thing." She used her index finger to point out the sequence. "Which, if that happens, will pretty much kill me dead on the spot."

"Nah," Celina put in, "you can do it. We'll all do it." She motioned for the bartender but then realized that no one, ever, would be approaching their table to take orders. So she stood. "Be right back. Hold on one sec."

"Um," said Sydney, "not all of us will be doing that."

"Right. Check. Don't worry; I'll come up with something."

She worked her way to the bar, her body, for some reason, feeling heavy and cumbersome, and took a seat on a stool between two men. Simultaneously, she realized that she had no money (her purse was still jammed under the short leg of the table) and that the two men she'd sat between had been in conversation with each other. "Whoops," she said, "sorry. I didn't—"

"No, no," said the man to her left. He was old, eighty-ish, with a thick, lumpy nose which supported thick trifocal lenses that absorbed the multi-colored light in the room. Celina couldn't see his eyes. "It's fine, hon. Sit." He patted her wrist.

"Oh. Okay." She eased herself down. Where was that bartender?

"You're one of Carmelo's girls, ain't ya?"

"I am," Celina said. A quick, ridiculous jolt of feeling like a celebrity ran through her.

"Mmm, thought so. Junie—" He craned his neck around Celina to the man sitting on her right—"One of Mel Padula's girls."

The man to her right nodded, grunted.

"Celina," she felt compelled to say.

"Right," said the man called Junie. "How ya spell that."

She told him.

"Huh. Polish?"

She nodded. "On my mother's side." But Junie had lost interest. She tuned back to the other man, the one on her left, who was staring at her.

"Those your sisters?" He nodded behind him. He had a solid two-day stubble of beard, but each whisker seemed excessively spaced from the others—not patchy, just a wide scattering—and Celina found she was transfixed.

"In law," she said.

"Mm. Right, right. That's what I meant." He took a sip of what was before him, a yellowish liquid in a cordial glass. "Milo'll be back in a minute. He goes into the stockroom to take naps. Usually doesn't last too long. Nice service, by the way," he said. "Tasteful."

"Oh. Thank you. You were there? I'm sorry, I don't remember."

He shrugged. "That's okay. I just stopped in real quick, to pay respects. Carmelo was a stand-up guy, for sure. Real tough S.O.B. But it was Anne who I . . . well, I was more familiar with her. With Anne, I mean. Never mind." He glanced up and suddenly gave the TV his attention. More animals. Celina knew the show: *Meerkat Manor.*

Celina didn't recognize this man from her mother-in-law's funeral three years earlier either. Over the years she thought she'd met just about every one of Lawrence or her in-laws' Bentlee acquaintances. Apparently not. The man was still staring up at the meerkats, his glasses reflecting their furious activity. Curiously, the air between Celina and this man had taken on that of a silently feuding couple locked in a small room: aware of each other, ignoring each other, each waiting for the other to speak next, to apologize. "I'm Celina," she decided to say. "Lawrence's wife."

The man turned to her. "Lawrence is the oldest."

Right, thought Celina. *And the next*—she cut herself off. "Mm-hmm."

He held out his hand. "Andy Mooney."

His hand was big and hairy and hung limp at the wrist, like a chimp that'd been taught to shake hands. Celina took it. "Hey, feel like playing some darts?" she heard herself suggest. Was it simply for something to say? Something to do? Was it so she didn't have to talk directly with anyone—her sisters-in-law or Andy Mooney?

Whatever the case, he said, "Well . . . sure. That'd be fine." He turned toward the dangling cabinet. "I mean, I dunno if all the pieces are there. I never seen nobody play it before."

"Or…oh, I'm sorry. I didn't mean to take you away from…" She motioned to the man on her right.

"Oh, him? Fuck him." Mooney leaned past Celina and met the other man's eyes. "Hey, fuck you." To which the man seemed unmoved one way or another.

Andy Mooney pushed out his stool and stood, wiped his palms across his thighs—he wore jeans and a denim shirt, tucked in. A slight paunch hung out over his belt but otherwise Andy Mooney was in the shape of a man half his age. Heads swiveled and immediately Celina regretted her darts offer: it was obvious that the dartboard was an accoutrement at best; darts was not played at The Lion's Fountain, and now they would attract attention, much to Andy Mooney's chagrin. Plus, Celina didn't know *how* to play darts.

"Except," she said, "I promised drinks for the table."

"Goddamn Milo," said Mooney and craned his neck to see down the length of the bar toward the back room. "Hold on." He rose and moved along behind the row of balding heads to the hinged section of bar top and swung it upwards and open, slipped behind the bar and looked around—overhead, underneath, as if taking inventory. "Okay," he said. "What'cha need?"

"Scotch," said a stoop-shouldered man at the other end.

Andy Mooney opened his mouth to speak, then sighed, took down a bottle, checked the label, and refilled the man's glass.

"Top this off for me, wouldya Moon?" said another man two or three stools down.

"That ain't Scotch in your glass," Andy Mooney pointed out.

The man shrugged. Mooney topped him off. More voices called out for drinks.

"Now everybody settle down. Gimme a goddamn minute." Andy Mooney turned to Celina. "Now what was it you needed, hon?"

"Well, I need a...a boilermaker, I guess it's called..."

"A boiler—Are you sure that's what you want?"

"Big glass of beer? Shot of something whiskey-ish alongside?"

"Well, that'd be it, yeah."

"Okay. And something *like* a boilermaker. A glass of something, with a shot of something alongside to drop in. But none of it can have alcohol. Or caffeine."

Andy Mooney squinched his face together and his glasses slid down his nose an inch. He scratched his cheek. Then he nodded, took a beer mug, squirted something into it with the soda gun, took out a bottle of grenadine, poured some into a shotglass. He looked across the bar at her for confirmation.

She shrugged, nodded.

As they made their way over to the table, Andy Mooney carrying their tray of drinks, Abigail glanced up and shouted, "Hey, Mr. ExerCycle!" and pointed at Mooney as if she'd spotted a rare white elk.

He smiled, unsurprised. "Woulda paid the twenty," he said, setting down the drinks. "Truth be told. Didn't have it on me, though."

"I'd've *bet* that twenty I'd never see you again," said Abigail. "Have a seat."

Celina felt suddenly disoriented, as if she'd wandered into someone else's dream. Across the table, Sydney looked mortified; she began clutching at her neck, raking her fingers along the blotchy skin there.

"Oh," Mooney said, "I, um, I don't wanna intrude..."

"Nonsense!" said Abigail. "There're plenty of extra chairs—" as if this were the only thing keeping Andy Mooney from joining their absurd little troop—and to demonstrate she dragged a chair over from a nearby table, set it next to her, and patted its metal surface playfully.

Mooney rubbed his fingers together, as if making the sign for money, *moolah*, then glanced over toward the bar. No one was watching, or seemed even mildly interested for that matter. "Okay," he said. "Sure. Why not."

"What'cha drinkin'?" Abigail asked. "You need a drink. Get yourself a boilermaker. No, wait; it's on me."

"Well, I really… I'm not sure—"

"Oh, I in*sist*!" Apparently funerals and backyard fire-sales of loved ones' earthly possessions turned Abigail into a twenty-two-year-old sorority girl. She shouted out, "Hey, another boilermaker over here!" To whom, Celina had no idea.

"Junie," Andy Mooney called, "go wake Milo up. For Christsakes."

Eventually, Milo the bartender was extracted from the back room; a drink waspoured and delivered to Andy Mooney at their table. No money changed hands. Crystal Gayle now played on the jukebox, "Don't it Make My Brown Eyes Blue," and the sound of it instantly reminded Celina of driving her kids to school, that song playing on A.M. radio, 1978. She despised the song; even then, in her late-twenties, it somehow made her feel old and irrelevant.

As Abigail raised her shot of whiskey and held it over her beer glass, calling out, "Okay, people, here we go," Celina felt a sharp pang of remorse. Her mind seemed to fizzle and gasp, expelling every last breath of oxygen, and she placed her hands flat on the table, afraid she might swoon.

What did she have to show for her life since the last time she'd heard that song, some twenty-five years ago, as she carted her kids to school?

"Celina, you, too," Abigail scolded with a playful smile.

Shot glasses were brought into position. "One," Abigail began, "two…" and Sydney's slipped from her fingers and clunked against the rim of her beer/ginger ale glass, splattering red grenadine across the table. Everyone recoiled. In the bar's dim light the tabletop looked like a murder scene.

"It's okay, it's okay," Abigail said. "Everyone else, ready—*three!*"

Then she hastily released her shot glass, as if the whole production were some sort of race; it fell into the glass of beer awkwardly, a little off-kilter, and instead of clunking straight to the bottom and sending an amber cloud fizzing upwards, the way Celina imagined it should, the shot glass floated on its side for a moment then eased down into the beer like a sinking ship. Abigail stared at it, then glanced up and blinked.

"Here," said Andy Mooney. He slid Abigail's glass over in front of himself and pushed his own over to her, then dropped his shot into the glass, perfectly, causing the mushroom-cloudburst Celina had been expecting. "Go!" he said and picked up Abigail's original, failed, flat-looking boilermaker, and began calmly to chug it down, his old man's Adam's apple bobbing rhythmically.

Abigail picked up the other one and started drinking, first with her eyes wide, then squeezed shut; her lips were pushed out, as if kissing. Mooney watched her over his glass, the meniscus receding steadily. Every few sips Abigail would gasp, a sucking sound punctuated with a "*huh-uh.*" Celina found herself caught in a weird kind of No Man's Land as it occurred to her that she should be drinking *her* boilermaker, too. Wasn't that the point—to do them together? She scooped up her shot and dropped it in the beer glass and began drinking. It tasted tangy and murky, like flat, aged, overly fermented champagne, and she was reminded again of Verona, the opera at the arena: *Carmen,* that's what they saw. How could she have forgotten *that*?

Then again, who was she kidding? She'd forgotten the opera because of what had happened afterwards—when they'd returned to their hotel just off Piazza Brà and began readying for bed. The room was charming but small, even by European standards, which made Lawrence oddly trepidant. They'd just come through the other end of their bankruptcy, a process that had allowed them to keep their house and their daughters' college educations, but had decimated their credit rating and self-esteem. They'd filed for the bankruptcy in secret: they told none of their friends, no family. As far as anyone knew, they sold their Saab in a belt-tightening move, made a few seemingly frugal lifestyle changes. Outwardly, their reputations were safe. But they couldn't look each other in the eye without feeling the shame. How in God's name could they have so patently neglected their daughters' college funds? Had they thought the money would just magically *appear*? How could they have not seen it coming, especially given Lawrence's own tenuously funded college years? Maybe they *had* seen it coming, but couldn't bring themselves to act; maybe they froze, as they'd frozen on the TrenItalia platform in Bologna just as the last train of the night pulled away for Florence, where their hotel room was for that night, leaving them stranded without a change of underwear, their cholesterol medications, without a toothbrush:

Is this the right train?

I think so. Hold on, where's the monitor?

Should we get on?

Yeah, probably. Well…wait, yes, this has to be the one, I think…

Lawrence…

Yes, yes, get on… as the doors hissed shut.

So, too, was the ridiculous ass-dragging they'd exhibited in establishing those goddamn college tuition funds. *We need to do this*, they kept telling themselves. Well, of *course* they needed to do it. And they *did* do it. Just far, far too late.

They sat through meetings with admissions counselors, listening to the costs of tuition and books, dorm rooms and meal plans, and nodded like confident shitheads, all the while privately thinking, *How are we gonna pay for this?*

Their W2s revealed too much income to qualify for much in the way of financial aid; each daughter earned a meager thousand or two a year in scholarships. How they paid for the rest was with loans, and credit cards—and then another loan for graduate school. They refinanced the mortgage that was five years from being paid in full, with cash out, so that they'd be paying for their house all over again. One daughter got into Bucknell; the other was even willing to stay nearer to home and had committed to William and Mary. How could they be denied such opportunities? Well, their girls would *not* be denied those opportunities. Celina and Lawrence ended up with a physical therapist, an environmental engineer, and a Chapter 11 in the family to show for it all. A trade-off they told each other they were more than willing to make.

They were proud. They were ashamed.

Italy was the first gift they gave to themselves after emerging from the bankruptcy. Lawrence picked up summer courses, took over as coach of the lacrosse team, even became an assistant girls' volleyball coach and took on a faction of kids from neighboring districts and area private schools to tutor out of the house for $45 an hour. Celina, reluctantly, went back to work for the county, placing halfway house "graduates" into the local workforce, then was elected to the school board. In seven years they had their credit rating back, and by extension their life; they bought back the Saab, paid off every debt that was in collections, and were able to take the trip they'd been saving for all through the recovery process. Three weeks: Rome, Florence, Venice; plus side trips to Pisa, Siena, Bologna, Lucca. They'd shoot the works, for no other reason than they could *afford* it. They didn't have to feel guilty.

But, despite Lawrence's enthusiasm, from the moment they checked their bags at the airport Celina couldn't shake the feeling that they'd worked like dogs for the past seven years and had finally arrived...back to exactly where they'd been ten years ago. This wasn't the way things were supposed to go. She sat on the plane heading to Italy, looking out the window at the black clouds in the night sky, feeling cheated. Her husband, reclining next to her, was sleeping, mask over his eyes, mouth slightly open, flimsy airline blanket pulled up to mid-chest. The plane's engine hummed. She checked to make sure her seatback had an airsick bag in the pocket, just in case.

They worked their way north from Rome by train. The heat was more oppressive than she'd anticipated. Venice was overcrowded and over-priced—the only Italian city where they felt nickel-and-dimed. And on those occasions when she'd experience a moment of true pleasure, her breath fluttering in the awe of it all—lunching in a Trastevere café, walking in the evening along Lucca's outer wall, dinner on Via del Pratello in Bologna, standing on the Ponte Santa Trinità in Florence, looking east past Palazzo Vecchio—she'd catch herself and ask, What in the world are we *doing*?

She was the one who'd insisted on Verona—the opera at the Arena—even though it wasn't part of their original plans. For the most part, she'd been letting Lawrence set each day's itinerary. When she offered the sugges-tion he nearly lunged at it, relief clearly visible in his eyes. He jumped on the laptop right away, at the little desk in their Florence hotel room, and began checking out hotel options and train schedules. They left the next day.

Maybe it was because she'd chosen the destination, but she loved Verona. She did. Something about the picture-postcard exterior con-structed around the surreal honesty at its center. Unlike some of the pretty little Tuscan towns they'd traveled to that struck Celina as Epcot Center recreations of what a renaissance-era Italian village should look like, Verona had an inner *life* to it. People living, working, loving, griev-ing, probably even lying. People paying their taxes and taking their pets to the vet and not calling their parents back—she could sense it all. They just did all their living on cobblestones, within winding medieval alley-ways. Standing in the enclosed piazza, looking up at Juliet's balcony—*the* Juliet's balcony—Celina understood that it was probably a crock. Who knew if "Juliet" even ever existed, let alone whether or not this had really been her house. But Celina didn't care; she was captivated. She stood on those cobblestones and gazed up at that pink-tinged limestone façade and its little marble balcony. She'd been expecting a palace, but the building reminded her of an ancient replication of the condos or townhouses on some tree-lined back street in the Federal Hill section of Baltimore, where some young professional might take a lease on a one-bedroom flat in celebration of her first real job out of college. But Celina was no fool: of course nobody lived here now. Now it was a museum. People *used* to live here, had lived here for five hundred years. But no more. A shadow moved behind the window of the balcony, just above her, and Celina's heart shifted. She felt an absence she couldn't express.

Lawrence wanted to know if she was interested in going inside. There was a fee, of course. But the view from outside was fine with Celina.

She wished she'd have felt the same about the opera. The two-thousand-year-old Arena was an imposing sight during the day; at night it was otherworldly. It reminded her of the Coliseum in Rome but smaller, and in better condition—working condition. Crumbling, yet functional—like so much of Verona. When they stepped out through the doors of the trattoria and made their way, in the new suit and dress they'd bought that afternoon, across Piazza Brà, they found the Arena, a sea of yellow-white light spilling through the arches, pulsing as if radioactive.

This stopped Celina. She'd felt heavy from the meal they'd just eaten. Her new dress—a lavender, knee-length, silk and lace number with a sash tie at the high waist—didn't seem any *tighter*, but she felt markedly bulkier beneath the fabric. She sucked in air, held it, then exhaled when the piazza's sudden liveliness struck her. The glow around the Arena, the shadows, the startling brightness, yet with a lack of primary colors, put Celina in mind of what it must look and feel like on the surface of the moon.

She froze. "I don't think I want to go inside," she said to Lawrence.

He laughed softly, self-consciously—of course she must be joking. Right? He'd paid 250 euros for these tickets. He guided her by the elbow toward one of the entrances.

As they handed over their tickets and were led to their seats, Celina felt as if she were traveling deeper and deeper into a dream. Who *were* these people, and what were she and her husband doing among them?

The orchestra started up, the brightness inside the Arena shifted, pushing outward from the stage in a convex wall of light, like an aneurysm must look, only beautiful. And as the performance progressed, the evening grew even more surreal: the black sky above, the full moon, the sweet breezeless air on her skin. The acoustics were so flawless and crisp Celina would swear she could hear the music inside her fillings. She sat in her seat, stage left, and watched, and she felt a dull heaviness even as her soul lifted. Odd: the evening could in no earthly way be any more perfect—a script she would never have dared to imagine. And so she found herself unable to imagine it, even as she lived it. Perhaps the problem was that she—and Lawrence— didn't deserve it. They were *bankrupt* just seven years ago, for christsake. Friends their age were beginning to shop for second homes—Scottsdale or Naples or Las Vegas. The dollar-euro exchange rates were abysmal to begin with, and she and Lawrence couldn't rent a car in Florence because the rental company wouldn't take a debit card—*actual* credit cards only. The expressions on the faces of hotel clerks when Lawrence counted out and signed over his archaic traveler's checks made Celina's insides twist.

The stage, the sky, the marble pillars—it was all too much for her, too beautiful. Above them, the red lights of an airplane blinked across the night sky.

She cried during the ovations, which Lawrence took to be a good sign. He smiled compassionately, gave her a handkerchief and pressed his hand to the small of her back. They filed out in silence.

And they stayed more or less silent for the rest of the evening: wandering back to the hotel through the alleyways off Piazza Brà, folding their new clothes into suitcases and dressing for bed; Lawrence seemed to be smiling to himself in the mirror as he brushed his teeth. She could tell he was feeling reverent, savoring the moment. But Celina was frightened. Of where they were now; of where they might go next.

Lawrence took his Xanax and his Mevacor and flossed his teeth and then promptly fell asleep with his arm across Celina's chest. She lay on her back, with the bedside light still on, and listened to the occasional motorbike buzzing by on the street below their window. When she heard an excited voice—*"Rimanere alzato per me!"*—Celina carefully took hold of Lawrence's wrist and lifted his arm. Then she swung her legs out of bed and sat for a moment before rising and putting her new lavender dress back on.

Her makeup was still intact; her hair needed a brush pulled through. The hotel room's door was from a previous century: no hydraulics, no metal reinforcements. It closed nearly silently—a tiny click at the latch. Downstairs, the girl behind the front desk glanced up from her magazine as Celina dropped the oversized room key into the dish for safe keeping—which apparently was how things were done here. The girl offered a close-lipped smile, but did not make eye contact.

What does that mean, exactly?

Outside again, this time alone, Celina turned left on the narrow street, in the opposite direction of the Arena, a new direction. She felt energized. She could feel the oxygen moving through her capillaries when she breathed.

She wandered along, looking up at the flat surfaces of the buildings, clothes hanging on lines strung between windows. The street was too narrow for cars, but plenty of people were still out. Occasionally Celina would nod at a passerby and mumble a *"Buon giorno,"* until it dawned on her that *buon giorno* was for the daytime and that "good evening" was *buona...noche*? No, that was Spanish. Or at least part of it was.

Sera—that was it. *Buona Sera.*

But the realization was too late. She'd hoped to feel like a native, a local, to feel *natural*, strolling the back streets and alleyways of Verona. Instead she felt like a dope.

The street curved and twisted and converged with others and then finally emptied onto a small piazza where a café appeared to still be open. Three or four of the tables, which were arranged right out in the piazza, were occupied by couples and small parties in the obvious processes of finishing up, lingering, sipping at empty glasses, and Celina headed over and settled at one of the unoccupied tables on the outer edge.

Turned out the café *was* open. A waitress in black pants, a slightly cropped, tight white shirt, and hair the color of Halloween—black with orange streaks—approached and said something in Italian Celina didn't follow. So she smiled knowingly and said, *"Vino rosso di casa?"* which was one of the few things she'd learned to order.

The waitress nodded with approval. *"Un bicchiere?"*

"Sí," said Celina, though she wasn't entirely sure what she was agreeing to. A glass or a carafe or a bottle. She supposed she'd just take her chances.

The air had turned cooler. Celina's skin tightened; she could feel the heft and stiffness of her bones, and this awareness made her feel unusually thin, skeletal. She leaned forward on her elbows. The couple to her right was talking intently—politics or betrayal—faces doused in shadow from the candle between them. Across the way a party of four whooped it up in English. One of the men called for another round of *limoncello*s but there was no one from the wait staff around to hear.

"Martin, I was talking about her *ankles*," said one of the women—a skinny, lollipop-shaped little thing in sexy-librarian glasses—and everyone laughed.

"So was *I*!" said Martin, which caused even more raucous laughter, and the other man, the one who'd ordered the *limoncellos*, laughed so hard he slapped the table, rattling the candleholder and bread dishes.

Celina turned away. She noticed for the first time an old man seated up against an adjacent building across the piazza, only a few steps away from where she sat, just before the opening to a narrow street a few yards beyond. The man had long, curly white hair beneath a blue floppy hat emblazoned with the word VOLVO. His white beard hung to mid-chest, and he sat atop and among a stack of boxes and crates, some of which over-spilled with books, notepads, record album sleeves, photographs, and loose sheets of aged paper. To his right, an unframed watercolor painting, wrapped in clear plastic, of what looked to be the man himself, was propped on one of the boxes, leaning on the wall behind. To his left a coffee-table book was propped in the same way: on the cover, again, was a painting of this man, who at the moment stared off—gazed, as Celina would later recall—across the alleyway, toward the corner of the building the café shared. He chewed thoughtfully, almost indistinctly (*was* he chewing? Celina wondered), fore-arms resting on his spread knees, lit cigarette burning between his fingers.

His eyes were deep-set; his nose wide and lumpy and pink. He could have been sixty, could have been a hundred and six. When his gaze suddenly shifted, just his eyes, toward Celina, her breath stuck; she turned away, down at her tabletop, but then regained enough composure to glance back at him, smile sheepishly, and offer a mumbled "*Buona sera.*"

The man returned her smile and nodded, almost bowed with just his head. "*Buona sera, signora.*"

Celina touched her necklace, raked her fingers across her collarbones.

"Are you American?" he said, in perfect Midwestern English. Where was it, she tried to recall, where the people were said to have no accent, no hint of regional dialect whatsoever? Iowa? Indiana? She wasn't sure, but wherever it was, this man could've been from there.

"Yes," she said, then, noticing the jump in pitch of her own voice added, "*Sí*."

He smiled again, wrinkles spreading from the outside corners of his eyes. His forearms never left his knees, cigarette continuing to smolder.

"Maryland," she offered.

"Ah. Poe."

Her mind blanked for a moment. "Oh. Right. Yes. That's right," she said, unable to keep the surprise from her voice. "He was born in Baltimore, I think. I think there's a museum there. We live... closer to D.C."

Again the smile, and when he smiled his face softened and pinched inward; the upper edge of his beard seemed to rise a half-inch on his face. He struck Celina as part Santa Claus and part... well, God.

The waitress arrived with Celina's wine—it was just a glass—and set it before her. The glass was stemless and filled nearly to the top, which Celina liked—seemed more *ethnic*. She hated those goldfish-bowl-sized wineglasses that some so-called fancy restaurants used, as if they were overcompensating for something.

"*Grazie*," Celina said, and the word came out surprisingly natural, even the little lilting *ay* at the end. It felt good.

"*Prego*," said the waitress, and began to move away.

"Excuse me," said Celina. "*Scusi*," and motioned the waitress back. "Um," she began, "*parla Inglese?*"

"*Piccolo*," the waitress said, holding her thumb and forefinger a couple of inches apart.

"Okay, uh... *vino*—" she'd already forgotten the word for *glass*: Something with a B. She lifted her own as a visual aid. "Un glass di vino," she said, and cringed. "For—" and she pointed as inconspicuously as she could toward the man seated among the boxes—"*il signore*."

The waitress smiled knowingly. "Ah, yes. Signore Mario. He prefer the, how do you say? *Rosato*. The pink."

"Oh. Okay," said Celina. "*Per favore*. From me."

The waitress nodded and moved off. When Celina turned back to the man on the boxes—Mario—she saw that he had already reaffixed his gaze across the alleyway, to the corner of the building again. It occurred to Celina that she had hoped to somehow form a relationship with this man. Why, she couldn't have said exactly. But the disappointment at having apparently failed was palpable.

She sipped the wine and was the taste comforted her: Tuscan, Veneto, it all tasted the same to Celina. Her chest warmed and when she glanced back over to Mario she saw that he had closed his eyes—head still held high, back straight, cigarette still burning above his knee. When the waitress stepped across the alleyway to deliver his glass of wine he opened his eyes and accepted the glass with a smile that registered through the eyes. The waitress pointed to Celina; the man lifted his glass to her and then sipped. And that appeared to be that.

But Celina wanted more from this man. She felt he had the ability to reach into her chest and rearrange her heart. She stood and took up her glass, gripped the chair-back with her free hand and began to drag it into the piazza. The chair was cast-iron, much heavier than she had anticipated, and the cobblestones meant she had to lift slightly as she dragged. The result was clanging and bouncing and scraping that caused the few people left at the tables to stop all conversation and watch as she bent over in her dress and tried to keep her wine from splashing all over herself. For a moment she was horrified that the old man would stand and help her, then was surprised and a little put off that he didn't. When she finally wrenched the chair over and arranged it next to him, Mario still sat calmly—forearms on knees, cigarette in one hand, the wine she'd bought him in the other.

"Very nice initiative," he said, apparently pleased, as she tried to catch her breath.

"Well, thanks," she said. "A lot. And for the help, too."

"Yes, please forgive me." He nodded downward toward his hands. "My knees aren't what they used to be. Of course most Italian men would jump at the chance to help a lady drag a chair across a piazza." He flicked his chin toward the café. "Evidently none of them are Italians."

"And what about you? You're not…?"

"I'm Swiss by birth. But I've lived in Verona for forty years now."

"Oh." She sat in the chair and crossed her legs.

"Thank you for the wine," he said and raised the glass slightly. "Perfect timing. I can't have any until after nine or so—once the sun is down completely. Just one glass turns my cheeks too rosy."

"Yes. Mine, too," said Celina, just for something to say, but as she spoke the words, the context of *his* struck her: He's a…*model*, of sorts. Artists must come around and pay him to pose for their paintings: *Ethnic-looking Grizzled Old Italian Man*. "How many paintings have been done of you?" she asked.

He shooed this question away with a wave of his hand that held the cigarette, its red tip dancing in the space between them; he inhaled one last time as its long ash crumbled and fell, then crushed it out on the wall behind him. Celina had the urge to ask him for one, but then thought the request might come across as rather uncouth. "Over the years, at least one thousand five hundred. I used to keep a tally, but then I…" He sipped his wine, swished it thoughtfully in his mouth, savoring, and then swallowed. Celina watched for the bounce of his Adam's apple but it was completely hidden behind the tangle of beard.

"Do you have a favorite? One that…"

"Made me glad to be who I am? Yes. All of them. Every one."

"Oh, come on," said Celina, rather harshly. "Everybody has favorites. Everybody has *least* favorites. Surely there's been some lame-o, Picasso-wanna-be hack who made you look like a polar bear or something. Right? I mean, you gotta hate that."

He turned to her and smiled. "Not at all, my dear. It's simply not worth it. We're not here for very long."

"Not here for very long? Forty years!" she said and realized that she was pleading with this man for something, though she didn't know what. "Fifteen hundred paintings!"

"I mean *here*. On this Earth. This life."

The waitress came out and looked around the piazza—the tables were all empty; Celina hadn't noticed the other parties get up and leave—and wandered over to where Celina and Mario were sitting. She bent at the waist and kissed the old man right on his wiry cheek. "*Mettere i bicchieri sulla tavola quando voi finito,*" she said to him. "*Tutto bene?*"

"Ah, *Sí. Grazie mille, Matilde.*"

The waitress returned to the café and when the back door closed behind her Celina and Mario were alone in the little piazza. Celina looked at him.

"She just asked us to put our glasses on one of the tables when we're finished," he told her.

"Oh," said Celina. It seemed to her a suggestion to leave. She straightened. "Okay. Do you need...I mean, how will you get all of this stuff home?"

"Ha-ha!" Mario bellowed. It was a fully enunciated laugh, like someone trying to teach a Martian how it was done. "My dear, I *am* home."

Celina felt herself blink. For some reason she'd pictured this man setting up his wares each morning and dragging everything back to some two-room basement apartment across the river, in a section of town tourists didn't know about. He seemed to Celina as just a peg or two above penniless, but he hadn't struck her as homeless. Perhaps she'd overestimated him—or underestimated him; she wasn't sure which. Either way, she felt utterly stupid.

"Oh," she said. "I didn't mean..."

"It's perfectly all right, my dear." He leaned forward and touched her knee. *I'll have to have this dress cleaned now*, she thought. "It's a life I've chosen, and would choose again, if truth be known."

"We're bankrupt," said Celina. "Or, we were."

The man nodded. "In the end, all will be well."

"I know. But we shouldn't be here. Not now. Don't you think? It's wrong, and it's made things worse. But my *husband* doesn't know this and I'm starting to wonder if I love him anymore." She finished her last swallow of wine and wanted another. A sadness pulsed through her with a totality she'd never experienced before. "I don't want to go back to the hotel room, let's put it that way."

"Then don't go back," the man said.

She looked at him. "That's a hell of a thing to say."

"So go back. There are always options, my dear. Even *my* life, this existence I lead, such as it is, was a choice. I could have taught literature at the University of Lausanne for the rest of my days. The Russians make my heart spin with joy. But that will always be the case, whether I'm in the classroom or not. And I like that my face inspires artists to create that which pleases them. Once my face is on their canvas, it's not my face anymore. But that's all right. I like that. I like being that agent of transformation."

"Well, can't you be an 'agent of transformation' while…living, you know, *inside* something? A physical *structure* of some sort?"

"This is true, yes. But things have fallen as they have. And perhaps it's for the best. You have a home and then you need a telephone and a bank account, and then pretty soon you want a television and a video machine and a microwave oven." He blinked and held his eyes closed and for a moment Celina thought he'd fallen asleep. Then the eyes sprang open. "I don't like the anxiety of trying to have everything I want and need in life. Where does that truly get us? I don't like cluttering my existence with worries imposed upon me by others. I made that first big choice forty years ago, and have made fewer and fewer ever since, to the point where the biggest decision I made today was when to brush out my beard, a pleasure I saved until the early afternoon." He chuckled at this, took his free hand and squeezed the bulk of his whiskers beneath his chin, then released. "All that matters is peace."

He smiled at her.

"To be completely truthful, I suppose a family would have been nice," he said. "That is true. I cannot deny that."

"I have to get back," said Celina abruptly.

"Of course you do. I appreciate the wine very much." He lifted the glass to her, as if in a toast. "I will try to make it last throughout the night." He swirled the wine that was left in his glass, but did not drink.

"Can I buy one of the paintings of you?" Celina asked then. "Or are they just..."

"I would love for you to have one." Mario set his glass down at his feet and turned away, rifling through the stacks and boxes to his left. "I have just the very one; it is around here someplace. Ah..." He shifted back around and in his lap held a rolled canvas, about twenty-four inches wide. He unrolled it slowly; it was a little frayed at the edges and, from what Celina could see in the dim light, yellowed with age. He fingered its surface briefly and then held it up for Celina to see. "A lovely young Hungarian woman named Zigana painted this. Some years ago. I've always liked it quite a lot. Here—" and he handed it towards her.

"Oh, no, I couldn't possibly—"

"Nonsense. Please. I will insist that you to have it."

"But it's obviously very special to you."

"Quite true. And it will still be special. What difference if it is in your home in Maryland or here in Verona? *Per favore*. Please."

She accepted the painting from him. Until this moment she hadn't really even *seen* it. But now she took it in. It was just a charcoal sketch of

Mario, a much younger version, in profile, from the shoulders up. The
beard was still just as long, hanging down beyond the bottom of his
bust, which faded out like an inky horizon; it was just as white, just as
shaggy, but somehow more kempt, less spastic—as was his hair, which
was combed back damply over his head, creating little shadowed creases,
like troughs carved through the whiteness. It reminded Celina of snow
in April, piled along sidewalks. He gazed off into the distance, and there
was the hint of a close-lipped smile playing across his face: not quite
Mona Lisa-esque ambiguity, but definitely muted and mysterious and
contented. The crow's feet at the eyes were deep, over-pronounced probably, but served to give this younger version of Mario the appropriate
suggestion of experience he would acquire later in life. Now.

"It's lovely," Celina said. "Thank you." She caught herself and smiled.
"*Grazie.*"

Mario's eyes softened. "*Prego*, my dear. Enjoy it in good health and
happiness."

She rolled it back up like a baton and stood. She had a sudden urge to
slap it against her thigh—an emphatic gesture—but resisted.

"Leave the chair, if you don't mind. I'll put my feet up on it." He
reached down for the glass he'd set on the cobblestones.

They stayed in Verona for two more days, doing little more than walking around town aimlessly. They passed through the little piazza twice
and each time Mario was in his usual spot, sitting spread-kneed, cigarette
burning, and each time he offered Celina and Lawrence a friendly *Buon
giorno* and a smile, but no more familiarity was alluded to. On the flight
home, somewhere over the Atlantic, the painting (which she later would
frame and display on the stairway landing in their home) safely stowed
overhead, Celina bolted awake as it occurred to her that she'd never
actually *paid* for Mario's wine—or her own.

....

"Galveston"—Glen Campbell—was playing on the jukebox now, and Celina felt as if she'd been sucked into a movie, some sort of bleak, Sally-Fieldish film about middle-America, meant to teach the viewer a lesson about the struggles of the lumpenproletariat. Or maybe yet another dream: Abigail's, most likely, this time. Her sister-in-law couldn't seem to shut up, blathering on and on to Andy Mooney in a steady chirp. It was true that she'd had a lot to drink—for Abigail. The boilermakers weren't working for her—she'd choked down a couple of swallows of the one then abandoned it—but she then moved on to vodka cranberries and now was working on her third, by Celina's count. Celina, on the other hand, had stuck with the boilermakers, after Andy Mooney expressed how impressed he was at her handling of the first one. So they'd done a second together, toasting to the meerkats that were still on the TV screen above the bar. Her belly felt full, but a tingling warmth radiated from her face and ears.

"Anne never liked me," Abigail said, apropos of nothing. It was the first hint of regret to tinge her voice all day.

"People thought that a lot," said Andy Mooney. "It's a ... whaddaya-call, misconception, though. People didn't get her. Never did. Well, ever since..." He looked back up at the TV: a commercial for dog food.

"Since what?" Celina asked.

"Nah," said Mooney. "Don't matter."

"What doesn't matter?" Celina pressed. "And, by the way—" she turned to Abigail—"Anne liked you fine. It was *me* she didn't like."

"See?" Mooney said. "This is what I'm talking about."

"How many gay people do you think are in this bar right now?" Abigail wondered.

"Abigail!" Sydney nearly spat her ginger ale. Celina had nearly forgotten this other sister-in-law was still with them.

"My guess?" Abigail went on. "Zilch. Zippo." She held up her hand in a goose-egg gesture. "*Na*-freakin-*da*. Any takers for a friendly wager? We'll poll the room." She moved to get up but when nobody reached out to stop her she sat back down on her own.

Celina swirled the last of her second boilermaker around in the bottom of her mug, then threw it back and swallowed, careful not to let the shot glass clack against her teeth. "I think I'd like to hear more about our mother-in-law's reputation about town, and how you seem to know so much about it. Mister... Mooney, is it? Funny how we've never even *heard* of you until tonight." She stared across the table at Abigail for some show of support, but Abigail only blinked expectantly.

"Granted," Mooney agreed. "I can't argue there."

"Ah, well, that's a relief." Celina had no idea where her allegiance to her mother-in-law, to *any* of this, was coming from. But it was bubbling up in her and she couldn't force it back down. She wanted to leave this life; she wanted to move on. But she wanted to leave it clean, unmuddled, declare a sort of historical bankruptcy, clearing the slate in preparation of whatever came next. "Funny you should all of a sudden be in the market for a slightly used eighties-era exercise bike at this particular point in time, too, huh?"

Mooney shrugged. "Just trying to..."

"Trying to *what*?" Celina demanded.

Sydney put her forearms on her stomach, as if protecting it. "Celina."

"Shut up, Sydney. I want to know where the hell this guy came from all of a sudden."

"Fair enough," said Andy Mooney.

"How about tequila shots?" Abigail suggested. "Who's in? Huh?"

"They don't got no lemons here," Mooney said. "Sorry, dear. Unless you wanna have 'em straight up."

The blank expression on Abigail's face revealed that she had no idea what he was talking about. "Fine," she said. "Line them up. Let's do this if we're gonna do it."

Mooney went to the bar for the tequila shots. The music had switched to something twangy with a female voice Celina didn't recognize. It seemed more in the background than it had been; the room had grown livelier, even though not a soul had entered or exited since they'd arrived.

"This kid's gonna have emphysema for sure," Sydney said and coughed.

Abigail glared at her, then licked her lips and smiled. "I'm fairly certain that one night of second-hand smoke won't give a fetus full-blown emphysema. But if you'd rather leave…" she closed her eyes and for a moment Celina thought maybe she'd fallen asleep. Then her eyes opened. "I understand."

"It's an exaggeration," Sydney pointed out. "Relax, Ab. God."

"One more drink," Celina said. "Sydney, if you want to leave, just take the truck. We'll get home. Or one of the guys can come and pick us up later."

Sydney's back straightened. Sweat beads had formed at her upper lip and forehead. A strand of hair was stuck to the corner of her mouth and she pulled it away. "I'm fine," she said. "We're all super-fucking fine, aren't we?"

Andy Mooney was chatting it up with a couple of men at the bar while the bartender poured healthy shots of clear tequila into three cocktail glasses. Celina intended to let Andy Mooney pay for all of them.

"How drunk are you?" she asked Abigail.

"Huh?" She stiffened. "Why?"

"Just hang in there with me. I need you. Something's up."

"What? What's happening?" She turned and cased the room as if checking for spies.

"Nothing. Stop that. It's just this Mooney guy."

"Oh, he's fine," Abigail said.

"Fine. Well, of course he's fine. But where's he *been*? How come we don't know him?"

Abigail leaned forward onto her elbows. "Maybe because you and Lawrence have been *gone* for twenty years now. Maybe because you've gone out of your *way* to avoid this place and to forget this place. Maybe…" She huffed, a near-growl. "Never mind."

Celina opened her mouth then realized she didn't have anything to say.

Andy Mooney returned to the table with a tray of tequila glasses. He seemed puzzled now as to what to do with them.

"Sit down," said Celina, "and tell us about yourself, Mr. Mooney."

Mooney blinked, licked his lips. "Yes, okay, sure." He set the tray down in the center of the table and then sat across from Celina. "Who wants one?" he asked.

"Me," Abigail said. "Right here. Please."

He passed them around. "I apologize," he said to Sydney. "I forgot another ginger ale for you."

"You know what?" Sydney flipped her hair out of her eyes and sat back in her chair. "I'm really, really okay with that."

Mooney eyed her for a moment, as if trying to mentally translate the words into Arabic. Then he turned back to Celina. "What would you like to know, dear?"

"Well… You tell me. Something tells me you know *exactly* what I need to know." She hadn't planned the response, and now, hearing it, it sounded to her like a cop-out, if not completely indecipherable.

But Andy Mooney nodded and sipped thoughtfully at his tequila. Then he set the glass down and moved it around between his heavy fingers. "I never wanted to interrupt their lives," he said. "That was never my intent, and, by God, I stuck to it. I never *did* interrupt their lives. But Anne and me, we—we shared a...common suffering."

"This is none of our business," Abigail said. She appeared to be speaking more to Celina than to Andy Mooney.

"No, no," the old man said. "It's all right. I've been...I always knew I'd tell you—one of you, or the sons—one day."

"Well, I don't want to hear it." Abigail took a quick shot of her tequila, tossing about half of it back, then began coughing like a consumptive.

"Wait, let him talk," said Sydney.

Mooney waited for Abigail to settle down. "Don't worry. It ain't nothing too...ah, hell, I don't know the word for it."

"Disturbing," Celina offered.

"All right."

"Illicit."

"No," said Mooney. "The first one."

"I'm leaving," said Abigail, though she did not move to get up.

"Look, it's...I lost a son in Vietnam—my only son—and I guess we sort of had that in common, Anne and me."

"Actually, you had *none* of that in common with Anne," said Celina sharply, then caught herself. "But, you know, I'm sorry to hear it."

"It's okay."

"She had three sons, and lost none of them, in Vietnam or anywhere else." Her indignation was back up again. "None of them even *went* to Vietnam."

"Yes, yes. I understand that. I do. Maybe 'in common' wasn't the right way to put it. I mean, we knew each other, from before." He closed his eyes and sniffed the air. "But when she heard about my boy she came to *me*." He opened his eyes again, as if awakening suddenly. "I didn't understand at first either, but I was glad for it. I admit. My wife had been gone five years by then—pneumonia took her. It was just my boy and me when

he got his notice. I didn't want him to go. I mean, I didn't agree with—
you know, I just didn't think…" Andy Mooney took a breath, rolled his
glass between his palms and stared into it. "He was all I had. I thought
about taking him to Canada. Woulda gone with him. Shoulda, too. I
shoulda done that. Shoulda clubbed him over the head and *took* him.
Even if he hated me for it. What did I have to keep me…" He looked
square into Celina's eyes then, as if he expected an answer from her, and
an explanation. Then he shrugged, sniffed again. "But he went off. Who
knows why. Probably to get out of this goddamn town. And then, when
I got word, then it was just me… and Anne, she…."

Celina and her sisters-in-law waited for the rest, but Andy Mooney
seemed to be finished. He took off his glasses and set them on the table,
pinched the bridge of his nose. After a moment he downed the rest of
the tequila.

"Seriously," said Abigail. "How many gay people do you think are in
this bar right now? I read someplace that one in ten people are gay in
this country. That would mean…" She turned in her chair and used her
index finger to commence a head-count.

"Where'd you read *that*?" Sydney asked.

"I don't know. Someplace."

"Yeah, well, I think you made it up. And, anyway, it's a sliding scale.
I don't think it's one in ten in Bentlee, Pennsylvania."

"Oh, I wouldn't be so sure," Andy Mooney said.

Abigail stopped counting and regarded the old man. "Really?"

He shrugged. "Never know."

Suddenly, Celina felt drunk.

"I have to use the little girls' room," Sydney announced.

Abigail pushed out her chair. "I'll go with you."

"I think there's only one, you know… facility," Mooney informed
them.

"We'll make do," said Abigail and she reached out for Sydney's hand. "Let's go."

And then they were gone, and Celina sat staring across the table at Andy Mooney, who lifted his eyes to her and offered a timid smile. He put his glasses back on.

"So," she said. "You sticking around, or what?"

Andy Mooney cleared his throat and shifted in his chair, and Celina understood that he'd taken her question as an invitation to scram.

"Oh, relax, Romeo," she told him. "Next round's mine."

11. Anne

The man had collapsed in aisle 3, across from the bath tissue, as he reached for a box of fancy drinking straws. Anne David was the lone clerk in the store, punching into the register the prices of the basketful of items placed there by a young man in a windbreaker and thick-framed glasses, like those she imagined an FBI agent might wear.

The man in aisle 3 made a sound like, "Eh," then fell forward—Anne happened to be half-watching the man in the magnifying mirror at the end of the aisle—bringing a clatter of boxes and jars to the floor along with him. The FBI agent went to investigate, and Anne followed, untying the apron string at her lower back. They found the man splayed on his chest, his legs spread and bent, like a still-frame of someone running.

"Hey, pal," said the FBI agent. "You all right?"

It was clear that he was not, an assessment confirmed when the man, who wore blue dress pants that rode up his lower legs, revealing white socks and hairy calves, began to twitch, his hips pulsating against the tile floor—a vision that struck Anne as oddly, frighteningly, lewd. She jumped back a step.

"Ah, hell." The FBI agent stripped off his windbreaker; he knelt and tried to wedge it under the man's head, which now was smacking temple-first against the floor. "Call Leo down at the station house!" he barked over his shoulder.

Then, in 1940, the town maintained one emergency vehicle—a Chevy pickup loaded with sandbags, rock salt, shovels, tow rope, and a first-aid kit—out of the municipal garage. Merle Horning, who now owned Mauch's Market and would soon turn it into a Red & White, made Anne memorize the phone number. But her mind went blank.

"Hang on there, partner," the FBI agent was saying as Anne backed away. "It's gonna be okay." She heard a staccato clicking sound and realized that the man's teeth were rattling together. It occurred to her that this man was going to die on the floor in front of her, and Anne didn't know why, and she didn't know what to do. She didn't even know who he was. She saw now that his thin graying hair was matted down in a circumferential line, indicating that he'd been recently wearing a hat. And there it was, over by the dog food display: a dark green mesh trucker's hat, lying upside-down.

"Go!" the FBI agent screamed at her. But then the man's flopping ceased. Anne waited, guiltily anxious for it to begin again. The man gave one last heave upwards with his hips, gasped, eyes and mouth opening fully, like a fish, then collapsed and lay still.

FBI agent put his hand on the man's back, paused, and said, "Holy Christ. Guy's...guy's *dead*." He turned to Anne. "Did you know this guy?"

Anne stood back and stared at the dead man, her hands twisting her apron strings. The man's forearms were hairy, too, but even the hairs looked suddenly dead. The middle fingernail of his right hand was a deep purplish-black.

"Leo here yet?"

Anne shook her head.

"Maybe we should..." He pointed at the man's rear-end area, where his coat flaps had flipped over his lower back revealing the bump of a wallet.

"Maybe we should wait," Anne managed.

"Probably right."

"I never called the station house," Anne blurted.

The FBI agent stood and slapped his thighs, as if brushing dust away. "Yeah, well. Wouldn'ta made any difference. Jesus." He adjusted his glasses frames and glanced down at the man on the floor. She noticed now that his eyes were heavy-lidded, like a sleepy person's. It made his movements seem slower than they actually were. "We should probably call now, though."

Once Leo arrived with his first-aid kit, a chewed cigar dangling from his mouth, and saw what was up, they had to put a call in to Greensburg for the paramedics. Mr. Horning was summoned and the store shut down. Phil Stuzik, the police officer on duty that day, asked Anne and the FBI agent—who of course was not an FBI agent but a livestock feed and supplements salesman named Andy Mooney—some questions while standing a few steps off to the side of the body:

So, jeez, the hell happened here?

Guy just fell over, huh?

The hell he want straws for?

Anne didn't know the answers to any of the questions. People were peeking in through the front windows. All she could think was how later she'd have to explain all of this to Carmelo. He'd been working on the house—obsessed with it really—after his shifts at the mine, and was becoming short on patience for any topics of conversation not at least tangentially pertaining to the house itself or their plans for after they moved in. But she didn't know what she'd tell him anyway; suddenly she couldn't remember any of the specifics. The dead guy's name was... They'd told her, but she couldn't recall it. The guy had a white sheet thrown over him now—the sheet was old and stained and smelled vaguely of citrus, but at least it covered the dead man completely.

The dead man. From that day on, this is how she would remember him. As if he had never been alive. As if he'd walked *into* the place already dead.

The paramedics finally came and lifted him onto a stretcher. Anne didn't watch. She imagined limp arms hanging and untied shoelaces, but already the dead man's face was beginning to fade from her memory. His name, as they would later discover, was John Gurnack, passing through town on a week-long sales trip. Apparently John Gurnack, the dead man, sold high-pressure water hoses, manufactured in Clarion, to farms and small factories across the Mid-Atlantic States. His truck, parked around the corner, was loaded down with the stuff.

What he needed straws for was anybody's guess.

Once the dead man had been loaded into the ambulance and driven away, Mr. Horning said he'd be bringing a cleaning crew in to disinfect aisle 3. Anne should just go home, take the rest of the day off, start back fresh tomorrow. Which was fine with her, except that Carmelo wouldn't be by for hours to pick her up, and there was no way to reach him. Her parents' house was about a mile and a half away. She could walk, but how would *that* look—young woman walking down Prospect Street by herself? She had a sudden feeling of being stranded.

"I'll see that she gets home," the FBI agent, Andy Mooney, said to Mr. Horning.

He drove her to her parents' house in his maroon Plymouth sedan. The vinyl bench seats were cracked and the floorboards were worn, but otherwise the interior was spotless. She could tell he was quietly meticulous about maintaining the car. The only talk between them was when she gave him directions. Anne caught glimpses of his face from time to time, in profile, as he steered the car, and she realized that he was considerably younger than she had thought—not more than a couple of years older than she was. It was the glasses, perhaps, that were misleading—the chunky style was way too old for him. When they stopped in front of the house he put his forearms on the steering wheel and said he hoped she'd be okay.

Anne didn't realize until now that she'd been hoping he'd try to make her laugh. There was nothing *funny* about what had just happened at Mauch's, of course, though it certainly had been absurd—ninety minutes ago everything had been fine; now she had the experience of having watched a man die to carry with her forever. And the absurdity needed, Anne thought, to be remarked upon.

This man, Andy Mooney, was incapable of such a remark, though. Which was not a bad thing.

"I'll be fine, thank you," she said, reaching for the door handle. "I just wish I would have *done* something."

"Nothing you coulda done," Andy Mooney said. "Either of us." He stared off through the windshield at the stop sign up the block, at the intersection of Prospect and Montross. The top screw had fallen out years ago and the sign had been hanging upside-down ever since. It was a warm summer day and children were playing in the yards. "Didn't do a whole hell of a lot myself. Maybe next time... next time we'll know what to do."

....

"Next time?"

"Well, hopefully there won't be one," he said. "But if there is."

....

For a time, then, Andy Mooney dropped off the face of the Earth. Anne remembered hearing that he lived in New Bentlee, but knew nothing else about him. She found herself watching the streets for his maroon Plymouth, lifting her eyes from her register every time the doors swung open at Mauch's. And then one day, a couple of weeks after the man had died in aisle 3, he did come into the market. He offered a sad smile in Anne's direction as he entered, then got in line behind the two or three customers patiently waiting with their items. Her fingers shook as she punched in the keys, and she hoped she wasn't making any mistakes. Mr. Horning was not a screamer, and he was not prone to fire people in anger. But he checked the register every night and was a stickler for details, and if things did not add up he had a way of squinching his lips and affecting a disappointed air, as if you'd just told him you no longer wanted to be his friend.

Anne finished bagging a woman's groceries and handed out her change—the woman said "Afternoon, Anne," but Anne didn't recognize the voice and hadn't made eye contact—and then Andy Mooney stepped up to the register. She tucked a curl of hair behind her ear but it flipped right back.

"How're things around here?" he asked her.

"Fine."

"Just…uh, stoppin' by. See how you were holding up, I guess." He placed his hands flat on the counter. She looked down at them. The left pinkie was bent slightly outward.

"Yes," she said to his fingers. "I'm fine."

A customer slipped in line behind him. Andy Mooney tapped his pockets, as if searching for his keys, then reached out and took a pack of Pall Malls off the rack, thought better of it, and put it back. "Well," he said. "Okay, then. Take care of yourself." And he left.

After that, he stopped in every couple of weeks or so. Sometimes he'd buy something small, a banana or a box of matches, sometimes he didn't, but he always waited in line, if there was one, to speak with her. One time he wore a dress shirt and striped necktie. And on one visit he told her that the dead man's cause of death had never been determined. Andy

Mooney himself suspected a stroke. Or an epileptic seizure that *caused* a stroke—though of course they'd never know for sure. After the third or fourth drop-in, Anne began to wonder if there weren't some sort of pattern to his visits, but she couldn't come up with one.

....

She began to dream about the dead man. Sometimes, in her dreams, it was Anne herself who killed him. Sometimes, the man would collapse, just as he'd done, bringing boxes and packages from shelves along with him, thousands of drinking straws scattered in aisle 3. And, just as he'd done, he would begin to twitch and flop and rattle his head against the tiles. But sometimes, in the dream, the man wouldn't *die*—refused to: the twitching and knocking just goes on and on, then grows to violent spasms, accompanied by a strange, inhuman whining sound, like squeezing the lips of a balloon to let the air slowly escape, with Anne and Andy Mooney standing back, watching helplessly. In this dream, the desire to make it all stop is unbearable. The flopping continues, the sound grows louder, screechier, and Andy Mooney turns to Anne and looks at her like, *Well?* And the next thing she knows Anne has the dead man by the throat and is squeezing. But he twitches out of her grip and then Anne is using both hands to beat the dead man with a fireplace andiron, which has appeared out of nowhere but which Anne understands they evidently now sell at Mauch's. She delivers blows, the ferocity and sheer power of which astounds her, to the dead man's head, throat, midsection—but mostly head. The sound, on impact, is like a dribbled basketball. She is horrified at herself, even as she pulls the andiron back and cocks her shoulders, DiMaggio-style (she'd seen pictures in the newspaper), in quick preparation for yet another swing, yet she can't stop. In fact, a small fiery coal burning in the pit of her stomach forces her to swing *harder*, to inflict more damage, to make the dead man die.

But just when it all seems to be ending—the relief that pours through Anne stops her breath; it's like diving into ice-cold water that suddenly turns warm—the dead man begins his flopping all over again, even more intense now, and the andiron turns soft in Anne's grasp, waggling unsteadily. She screams, but the sound is muted, and then she is aware of the fact that she is dreaming, but she can't wake herself up, which makes her want to kill the dead man, a desire somehow altogether different than simply wanting to make him to die, and she begins kicking him—her shoes, her feet, are very heavy, like bricks. She never sees the dead man's face, but, as her foot drives into him, she becomes acutely aware of his bulk, and his flesh which encases it; soon the man is giving off a smell like roasted almonds mixed with sweat. She keeps kicking at him with everything she has.

She does not awaken; the dream does not end, it just tapers off until it is gone.

....

What did end, eventually, were Andy Mooney's visits to Mauch's. For this, Anne blamed herself. She obviously had not been appreciative enough of Andy Mooney's sympathies. If, for all his efforts, all he was going to get in return was noncommittal, monosyllabic affirmations, then why bother? Frankly, she was impressed he'd hung in there with her as long as he did.

Problem was, she missed him. Maybe *missed* wasn't the right word for it. Or maybe what she missed wasn't necessarily *him*, but the possibility of his next visit. In any case, when he stopped coming by the store, when it became clear to her that there was no longer any chance of Andy Mooney taking his place at the rear of the check-out line and patiently waiting his turn, just to talk to her, Anne was sad.

She took to reading the obituaries.

Carmelo finished the house. They got married and moved in. Carmelo went away for a while—which they, ignorantly, it seemed to her, hadn't anticipated—but he came back, a couple of toes lighter, but alive; and, though he didn't talk about the experience much, they moved on, together. It took Carmelo some time to settle in, to reacquaint himself to life in Bentlee, to feel a part of things. As a result she was pushing thirty by the time they had Lawrence, which necessitated their having Nick and Stuart in quick succession. But that was fine. The boys grew. She lived her life. She was happy, or at least not *un*happy. Still, whenever she'd see a maroon sedan, Plymouth or otherwise, on the street, parked in a lot, up on blocks at a service station, her thoughts would stop for a moment, as if the world had blinked.

And she couldn't shake a vague droning apprehension that had settled inside of her, had become a part of her basic physiology, something she'd just learned to live with, like 20/40 vision, or arthritis. She wasn't so much afraid of dying as she was afraid of *death*. The dream had decreased in frequency but had not left her altogether. It became a dream of frustration, a dream telling her to *do something*. And her inability to grasp what needed to be done left her lying in the dark next to Carmelo feeling spent and discouraged.

One of those nights, shortly after Nick had received his draft notice, she drifted from the dream into wakefulness; she lay still for a moment, trying to gauge the time of night and feeling the sweat slide down her temple and onto the pillowcase. Then she got up, went to the bathroom and splashed water on her face, returned to the bedroom, sat at the edge of the mattress and clicked on the bedside lamp.

Carmelo opened his eyes and sat up casually, as if he'd been expecting this. In the dim light he found her with his eyes and waited.

"We have to stop this," she said.

"Okay."

"Whatever needs to be done. I'm ready."

"So am I," he said. "Just waiting to hear you say it."

She felt like there should be more, but the matter appeared to be settled. So she flicked off the light and slipped back under the sheets next to him. As sleep overtook her, quickly, beautifully, she waited for the pangs of guilt borne of this plain case of maternal meddling. But none came.

After, Nick would be unable to rectify what had happened. Anne could tell. At odd moments, shoveling snow from the driveway or putting on his jacket in the back hall, she would catch him gazing off into some middle distance, eyes glazy and unblinking. He developed an apologetic air about him—less confident, it seemed. And thankful. Routinely, he'd thank Anne each morning for the breakfast of oatmeal and bacon; he'd get out of the car to thank the station attendant for washing the windshield; he went out of his way to thank his *brother*, Stuart, for the novel he'd recommended. At no one's suggestion, he hand-wrote thank-you notes to everyone he felt helped him get into college—teachers, coaches, Mr. McTighe down at the dairy farm, even his own father—and walked them over to the post office on Upper Broad Street.

Somehow, Anne knew, her son had come to consider himself unworthy of his life.

Anne didn't care; she felt only relief.

....

March, 1968. Mid-morning, alone in the house, bars of sunlight stamped across the kitchen floor. Intending to leaf through the previous day's edition of the *Latrobe Bulletin*, Anne unfolds the paper and flattens it across the kitchen table. Immediately, her attention catches on the headline above the fold, "Township Man Killed in Sniper Attack Near Cambodian Border."

Her usual routine would be to skip such stories: she'd close her eyes, offer up a silent thought, sort of a prayer but not really, and turn the page. But

Township Man was a little—okay, a *lot*—closer to home than headlines of past days. She'd seen *Greensburg Man*. She'd seen *Former County Baseball Star*. And frequently there were reports of *Pittsburgh Soldiers* or *County Marines*, which she all but ignored. So that word, *Township*, made her eyes linger a moment, just long enough for her to notice the photograph.

The boy—he was not a man—was in dress uniform, hat brim level and low across his forehead, coat squared through the shoulders, as if held in place by a wooden hanger. The photo was in black and white, of course, and a little grainy; the boy's gaze was fixed just off to the left of the camera—if he were in the kitchen with Anne he'd have been looking over her right shoulder. His smile was close-lipped and flat.

And he looked—Anne squinted down into the picture—sleepy.

Which is what made her scan the first paragraph for a name: Andrew Carl Mooney, Jr.

Anne leaned back in the kitchen chair. Suddenly exhausted, she looked around her, as if expecting another person to be there. She heard a rough vibrating sound above the sink and she jumped. At the window, a hummingbird fluttered against the outside of the glass. Startled, she put a hand to her chest, expecting to feel her heart racing. But it wasn't; it was just beating along as is should be.

....

If someone had asked, Anne wouldn't have been able to explain why she went looking for Andy Mooney, nearly thirty years after they'd lost contact. And she certainly couldn't have said why she kept the search a secret from her husband—kept it a secret from everyone. What was she hiding, exactly? She didn't know the reason herself.

At odd times—and some predictable ones, too—throughout the day, Anne caught herself seeing the young Andy Mooney in his thick-frame glasses bending over the dead man in Mauch's Market, trying to help but unsure of precisely how, and so doing whatever he can think of, touching the dead man's back, shouting for Anne to call for help.

And then she'd see that man today: he's wearing the same glasses, but there are wrinkles around the eyes; the stubble on his cheek is a mix of brown and grey. And there's another dead man, but this time, the dead man is not just "a dead man," and there's nothing Andy Mooney can do, not even place his hand on the man's back and tell him everything's going to be okay.

There was sorrow, yes—she was purely sad for Andy Mooney. Or, sad that this had happened to him. There seemed to be a difference. She kept picturing him in the years since they'd lost contact: getting a promotion, or getting fired; going on the first date with his wife; his wedding day; the birth of his son, Andy Jr.; some catastrophe, or scandal—a friend's disloyalty, a sister's drinking problem; then a bases-clearing double by Andy Jr. in the pony league championships, Andy Sr.'s cheeks warming with pride.

But how was it that they'd never crossed paths—at one of these games, or the PTA, or someplace, anyplace, else? Maybe Andy Jr. didn't play sports. Maybe he liked sailboats. Or guns. Origami. Maybe he had a learning disability. Maybe he was pigeon-toed. Diabetic. Had depth perception problems. No, that would have kept him out of the service later. Maybe—maybe he was just shy. Or scared, scared of life, a frightened kid by nature. Which would have made going off to war even more terrible. For the boy, for the parents. For Anne.

What she'd been fighting to admit to herself was that she at last felt guilty. Sad, yes. Heartbroken. But relieved, too, because her son was home, or at least in Johnstown, in college, safe. She felt as if she and Nick had avoided more than the draft; she felt as if they'd avoided their lives being blown to pieces, they'd avoided death. Surely no more than one boy from Bentlee, Pennsylvania could possibly die in this war—the odds were crazy—and, since Nick wasn't there, Andy Jr. was that boy.

She'd try to rationalize, tell herself to be reasonable, but her thoughts always came back to the certainty that Andy Jr. took her son's place among the dead, and the guilt was unbearable, pressing into her ribcage and causing weird twitches that she could feel internally, among her organs. She had to find Andy Mooney. She had to talk to him.

....

It wasn't as difficult a task as she thought it would be. His address was listed in the local phone book. She'd anticipated the search taking longer, so when she saw the name—Mooney A, Cedar Swamp Rd (no house number), New Bentlee Twp—it spooked her. Now the task was figuring out how to approach him, and what to say once she did.

She waited a week, then another. The original guilt always was there, squeezing her heart up against her spine, but now a new source of shame moved in on her, subtly, like a shadow hovering over her shoulder: She should have gone to the boy's funeral. They all should have gone. But Carmelo said they didn't know the family and shouldn't intrude on what might be intended as private. She'd supposed he was right—no specifics regarding any services had circulated, and no one seemed to know the boy or his parents personally—but Carmelo also didn't know of Anne's connection to Andy Sr. Twenty-eight years ago she'd related the tragic event at Mauch's to Carmelo, perhaps dropping the name Andy (she couldn't remember); but she'd never told him of Andy Mooney's subsequent visits, and she didn't connect any of the dots for her husband when he read the article in the *Bulletin* twenty-eight years later. To do so now seemed like admitting to lies she hadn't told.

She was on her own in this venture. Whatever happened, she would not share it with Carmelo, with anyone, ever. This realization both chilled and exhilarated her.

Her guilt over not attending the funeral faded, but still she did not go to visit Andy Mooney. She'd lie in bed at night thinking, *Tomorrow*, then not go, and when she'd get into bed the next night she'd berate herself for not having gone, and she'd think, *Tomorrow*.

The problem was logistical. When should she go? And under what pretense? What was Andy Mooney's work schedule? When would she be most likely to find him home? What if she went and knocked on his door and his wife answered? (The almost certain existence of a wife was a point Anne rarely considered, and when she did, the sudden, brute awareness made her feel silly and a little mean.) A wife was one thing, but what if another *child* answered, another son or daughter? How would Anne explain herself to these people? The *Bulletin*, oddly, had not mentioned by whom Andy Jr. was survived. She felt as if she were embarking upon this mission of hers completely blind.

Except she did know the destination, knew exactly where Andy Mooney's house was. She often had access to the car when Carmelo got home from work at around 3:30, if he didn't have a side job planned, and she used a few of these afternoons, claiming errands, to zero in on the Mooney house. She took the Buick over the suspension bridge spanning the stockyards and crossed into and then out of New Bentlee on Route 933. She'd never turned *off* of 933, which led to Blairsville in one direction and Ligonier in another, not in her life, there'd never been a reason to; but on these exploratory journeys she'd swing the Buick onto the occasional lonely-looking county road, so narrow that if another car happened by, Anne and the other driver would have to nearly stop and carefully maneuver past each other, side mirrors missing by mere inches. And for some reason the asphalt of these roads was a lighter shade of grey, and seemed extraordinarily convex, the rounded peak at the center falling away on either side, so that it felt as if she constantly were driving on the right two wheels. Her window open, she'd travel each strange county road, until the barbed-wire fences lining the road began to sag and fall away, or she detected a new ghastly fungal smell wafting on the air that told her she'd gone far enough. Bentlee was tiny. The town of New Bentlee was tinier. But New Bentlee Township, land-area-wise, was enormous, stretching into the hills toward Johnstown. There were a few farms, dairy and mushroom; a hog slaughtering plant; and a surface mine that had a reputation as a death trap and, for all Anne knew, had probably been shut down by now. Lots of Germans. For Anne, and people she knew, "The Township" was a place to look down upon. She squeezed the wheel; being there made her jumpy.

Then one afternoon, late spring, the whole world smelling of mud, she zipped around a curve on Rod and Gun Club Road, past what looked like an ancient Singer sewing machine lying half in the weeds and half on the gravel shoulder, and saw the sign, such that it was, on her left: a wooden four-by-four post at the entrance to a single-lane unpaved road. Anne blew right by it and only after she'd passed did it register to her that *Cedar Swamp Rd* was hand-written in black paint down the length of the post itself. She hit the brakes and skidded. She looked around her—as if expecting to find someone standing at the side of the road, observing—then backed up the few yards, applied the emergency brake, and studied the post, the road, which was rutted and slanted from right to left and led up a slight rise before disappearing through a wall of high tan grass.

She pulled in. The car bounced and twisted around her; the crucifix hanging from the rearview mirror smacked the windshield. She was moving too slowly for the incline and she grinded the gears and stalled out, thought about turning back, then restarted the engine and kept on. As the front end of the car cleared the rise she could see a red-painted cabin-style house a couple of hundred yards off. She stopped, the car angled as if set to take flight. The dirt road ended at the house in a little square patch of packed earth, adjacent to a net-less, slightly leaning basketball hoop. Against the far side of the house was an impressive stack of firewood, expertly split; there were no curtains in the windows, no smoke rising from the chimney. There was a doghouse just off the tiny front porch, but

no dog. The grass was high and unruly. None of the land—and there was
a lot of it, a good eighth of a mile to the road and several hundred yards to
the dense woods in back—appeared to be used for anything.

And where was the swamp? Anne wondered. There was no *swamp*.

Then Anne's awareness locked onto the brown patch of earth at the
end of the road, what amounted to the driveway. And what struck her
now was: No car. Her heart thumped and her ears seemed to fill with
air. She'd been expecting a maroon car (why? that was twenty-eight years
ago!) and when she didn't see it her brain didn't make the next possible
leap: that nobody was home, and someone might be *coming* home at
any moment. The hard facts rushed in on her and she let her foot off the
brake and eased the Buick back down the narrow road in reverse, twisted
at the waist and praying, praying that she didn't drift off into the weeds
and get the car stuck.

Somehow, she made it back onto Rod and Gun Club Road, evened
out the turn, and took off for home as if fleeing a crime. She'd come back,
she told herself, her throat tight and her cheeks damp. She knew where
it was now; she'd come back.

....

Another week passed, then a month. School let out. Nick, looking
a little stunned and disheveled if otherwise healthy, came home from
Johnstown for the summer to work at McTighe's. Out of nowhere Stuart began breaking out in hives; they went away with an allergy pill, but
kept coming back. Anne changed soaps and detergents and when that
didn't work finally took Stuart (who was seventeen and embarrassed to
be *taken*) to the doctor, who told them he couldn't see any medical reason
for the sudden appearance of hives and that they probably were caused
by anxiety. Lawrence had met a girl at school—Celina, with whom he
appeared to be rather serious. Worried about a recent drop-off in con-

struction work at Pavlovik Bros., Carmelo was sleeping about ninety minutes a night, off and on. Anne would wake and hear him downstairs in the kitchen, the soft murmur of the radio, the metallic clack of him cleaning his rifles, and it was at these moments that she'd think of Andy Mooney and his red house. *I have to get back there*, she'd tell herself; but by the time she woke in the morning some more convincing part of her figured, *What difference does it make now? I'll get there when I get there. My boys need me. I have my life.*

Yet she knew she wouldn't be able to move on with any real comfort, any optimism—she'd always feel that percolating guilty torment, like a fugitive looking over her shoulder. She figured when the boys went back to school, then she'd see to her own peace of mind. But, for now— Stuart carried a tube of topical ointment around with him wherever he went; Nick never suggested not returning to school, but there was a programmed aspect to his movements of late, almost robotic in the way he drifted from one activity, one responsibility, to the next, seemingly unaware of the world around him. It was like eating without chewing, without tasting. Lawrence phoned regularly, and spent the Fourth of July weekend at the house with his girlfriend, Celina. Anne didn't care for her. She *wanted* to like her. For several days before Lawrence and Celina's arrival she *prepared* herself to like her. But over the course of the weekend Anne found the young lady to be rather aloof and sarcastic—when she was present at all. She spent much of her time wandering empty rooms of the house, disappearing to the bedroom, taking baths at odd times of the day. It was as if she were avoiding them, and Anne finally said as much to Carmelo at the conclusion of the weekend, after the kids had left.

"She don't mean nothing by it. It's just her way," he said to her. They were sitting at the table. "She'll grow on you, I bet, if it comes to that." And he touched her hand. "Perfectly natural for you to be … doubtful."

"I think it's more than that," she said, though she wasn't sure how.

They visited again for Labor Day weekend, but little had changed. Except that Celina kissed Anne on the cheek when they arrived, which was nice, if a tad rehearsed. And Lawrence had started doting on the girl a bit too much for Anne's liking. On Monday Carmelo barbecued for everyone—ribs, chops, and venison steaks they'd frozen from the buck he'd gotten the previous fall—and Lawrence followed the girl around the yard like a servant, whispered into her ear in calming, encouraging tones. "Can I get you another can of pop?" he asked as she sat at the picnic table, looking bored. "If you don't like the deer meat, it's okay, you don't have to eat it." The girl smiled blankly, noncommittal, and put the back of her hand to her nose, causing Anne to wonder if this weren't a response to the scent from the dog pen behind the garage wafting in her direction.

Two mornings later Anne woke to the first frost of the year shimmering on the grass and she thought, *Today. I'm going today.*

And it felt nice to be certain. When Carmelo arrived home from work she took the car, under pretence of stopping by the pharmacy, the fabric shop, and her sister's, and drove out Route 933, to Rod and Gun Club Road. Again, she was particularly conscious of the smells in the air, blowing through the car's vent—burning leaves, compost, fungus, cow shit, all drifted in and out of her awareness. When she arrived at the bend in the road where the wooden post was driven into the ground and the packed dirt met the blacktop, it was just past 3:45. As far from home as she felt, it'd taken her less than fifteen minutes to get here.

She took the hill quicker this time, with confidence, but as she approached the crest she suddenly found herself hoping not to see a car at the end of the dirt drive—and then, when she cleared the rise and *didn't* see a car next to the red house, she was disappointed—a disappointment so severe she felt her stomach bottom out.

After a moment, she continued down to the house anyway, switched off the ignition, and sat listening to the silence emerging from the absence of the engine. From this close up, the house looked unlived-in. No curtains—she'd confirmed that on her last visit. The red paint was chipping badly. A wooden chair on the porch was missing one leg and leaned over in a crippled sort of pose. When she shifted her gaze to the side yard she saw a groundhog wander out of the rotting doghouse. But it was more than a lack of upkeep that made the house look abandoned: A numbness emanated from the place. It felt stagnant. There might be people inside, but there was no life. Anne thought of a turned-off television.

Then, for the first time, the possibility occurred to her that, following the death of their son, the Mooneys simply had left town.

A chill shot through her and she reached for the key and then the front door of the red house pushed open and a man in a ball cap stepped out onto the porch. She recognized him immediately, yet Anne's stupefying first thought was, *How odd: that guy looks just like Andy Mooney.* The man squinted through his glasses (they were similarly thick- and dark-framed if slightly less severe) and held up a cautious palm in greeting. He was thin—thinner than she remembered—and his denim button-down hung from his shoulders. The tails were tucked into his work pants but bulges sprung out around his waist. She could see the tendons in his neck.

Anne pushed the car door open and stepped out slowly, trying for grace in her movements but hoping for a simple lack of clumsiness. When she swung the door shut and turned to him she saw the recognition on his face. She smiled.

"Well…" he said and shoved his hands in his pockets. "I'll be. Hello there."

"I hope I'm not intruding."

He shrugged. "Nothing to intrude on."

She stood before him on the packed dirt. She was wearing a pink and green dress that came to mid-calf, just one of her simple everyday dresses, but she suddenly felt absurdly overdone, like a gaudy figurine atop a wedding cake. She clasped her hands in front of her and wondered if he'd rather she left.

"I…" she began. "I was just…"

"Look at you," he said. "You come out good."

She felt herself blush.

"Are you okay?" he asked. "Is everything all right?"

"No. I mean, yes. I'm fine. I was just thinking…thinking about…about your…" Abruptly, her being there felt wrong and she had the urge to flee. "I'm sorry," she said and lunged for the door handle. "I'm going to go. I was thinking…before…" She pulled the door open but the handle slipped from her fingers.

"No, wait." Andy Mooney stepped down off the porch and pushed the car door shut again. It didn't latch securely. "I apologize. I'm not used to visitors. And I ain't equipped for seeing people here at the house." He scratched his cheek, which was clean-shaven. His hair on the sides winged upwards from beneath his cap and glasses' arms, a sort of charming schoolboy quality. "But, we could go for a drive. Would that be all right? To go for a drive? Like to hear how you've been."

How *she's* been. The words illuminated what clearly, Anne now saw, were selfish motives on her part. Her coming here had been self-serving, to relieve those burdens of guilt, and she was ashamed.

"That'd be lovely," she said. "Would you like to drive—" and she remembered the absence of any vehicle on the property—"or should I?"

....

They struck a compromise whereby Andy Mooney drove the Buick, taking her farther out Rod and Gun Club Road until it switched to County Road 10, heading north. The terrain took on an undulating quality that for some reason reminded Anne of Europe, or what she imagined Europe to be like, since she'd never been. Andy Mooney gripped the wheel firmly. He was trying to project a picture of dependability, of safety personified. They rounded a bend and saw a giant turtle, the size of a car battery, making its way across the road. Andy Mooney pumped the brakes and downshifted, took a wide arc around it, and continued on.

"I don't know where I am," Anne said.

"We're up Loyalhanna way," he said. "Or generally anyhow."

"Well, I'm lost."

"Used to be a farm up around here raised alpacas. Ever seen one? Strange looking beasts, those things. Kind of like if you bred a camel with a sheep. I sold these folks the feed. Had to special order it from... well, I forget where. Down south someplace. Don't know what they *did* with the things. Musn't have been any money in it, though, 'cause the farm's gone now. Burned to the ground a few years back, the main house and the barn and a couple sheds. Place was deserted, though. Had been for a while. No one got hurt but some rats and owls, I suspect. Probably wasn't as much of an accident as people thought. And right over there—" he pointed over the dashboard toward a stand of pines—"I was accosted by a man because he'd heard I called him a coward for smacking his wife at the VFW. He came at me and I ended up beating the man pretty bad. Busted up his, you know, his nasals. From that day on whenever he breathed it sounded like a cough." He touched the bridge of his nose, adjusted his glasses, then returned his hand to the wheel. "Only fight I've ever been in in my life."

"I'm so sorry about your boy." Anne hadn't been sure she was going to say anything, after all. In fact, she'd been starting to think that maybe she wouldn't. But there it was. "When I heard... I just, I can't imagine how you... how the both of you..."

"Yes." He glanced down at his speed, eased off the gas. "Well. Yes, I do appreciate that." And then, as if the need to talk had been percolating inside of him forever and the story he'd just told was the first opening twist of the floodgates, he began telling Anne about the death of his wife five years before his son got called overseas (he'd loved the woman more than life, though he feared he had failed to daily and adequately exhibit this to her), how he and his son sat with her at her bedside as she passed. He told her about the day Andy Jr.'s draft notice arrived, how his first thought was, *Canada,* which shamed him, the very fact of the thought itself, but only so much because in his heart he knew that if his son went off to the war in Vietnam, he would not come back. Yet he never even suggested Canada, not out loud. He'd drop hints—*Are you* sure *you're up for doing this? There are ways…* —but he never said the words he needed to say. He was waiting, he supposed, for Andy Jr. to say it, or at least to ask, *Dad, what do* you *think I should do?* If he *had*…well, but he didn't. And the physical came and went, and he received his assignment, and the night before he left for Fort Dix, Andy Mooney went to bed per his usual routine and slept soundly and dreamlessly, as he still believed that moment would come when he and his son looked at each other and one of them said the words, *This is crazy; we can't do this. Let's help each other.* But then he was gone, and Andy Mooney stood on his porch, a chill on his bare arms, looking out at the tall grass waving in the breeze and listening to a crow cawing and cawing and cawing from somewhere behind the house.

Soon, letters arrived from Fort Dix—chatty, informative, very little complaining. Andy Mooney wrote back, trying to subtly convey to his son that he was doing fine here at home, though Andy Jr. hadn't really asked.

"Look," he said now, "I knew the drill. I was in Italy in forty-three. I'm not anti-…" He dropped a hand to his lap; it lay there as if he'd lost feeling in it. Outside, the sunlight had dimmed, casting the world in a coppery light. They'd been driving a long time, all in the same direction—north, it seemed to Anne—and she was beginning to worry about how late she might arrive home. "But this was different. And I knew that. We're not talking about—whatever ya call it—hindsight, here. I knew *at the time* that that war was a goddamn mess, just like this one now. And I did nothing. Just let it happen."

Anne found that she was shivering. She wasn't cold, yet she sensed her muscles constrict and she had to clench her jaw to keep her teeth from chattering.

"Once he shipped out, I waited for the news to come. I knew it would. Maybe I jinxed him, I don't know, but I couldn't help myself. I just knew, goddamn it, like you know winter's coming, like you know your own name." For the first time, he turned to her. "You know?"

She didn't. And she felt to lie to him now would be a colossal disservice. "I can't imagine," she said. He sighed and then she placed her hand on his, the one lying limp in his lap. He glanced down at this and the Buick drifted; he had to jerk it back onto the road.

"Maybe we should head back," she said.

He lifted his hand back to the wheel. "Yeah, I guess you're right. We're pretty near to Clarion already as it is." Then he swung the car around and drove back down CR 10, the sun setting behind the hills off to their right, and Anne trying to come up with something to tell Carmelo upon her return, something as close to the truth as she dared to get.

....

She never apologized to Andy Mooney—simply because she could never put her finger on exactly what she was sorry *for*. But she began making regular stops to the red house out in the Township. Once a week or so, maybe every ten days. On her first return visit Andy Mooney suggested they go for another ride, but Anne made him let her into the house, despite his protests. She didn't know what she was expecting—some sort of hedonistic bachelor pad she supposed, empty beer cans, dirty sweat socks hanging from bookshelves, weird musky smells. But that's not what she found when she entered. Not entirely. The house was cluttered, yes; like someone moving either in or out. Yet there was something else: As soon as she stepped through the front door she felt the frozen, echoey quiet of desertion.

"Sit," she told him, and pointed at the kitchen table, strewn with yellowed newspapers, half-empty jars of canned tomatoes, record album sleeves, a goldfish bowl with a goldfish hovering in six inches of what looked like dishwater. On the far side of the table was a typewriter, a blank sheet of paper rolled into it.

He sat and looked up at her. The lenses of his glasses were caked with dust. "I'm embarrassed."

"Nonsense." She went to the refrigerator. Her plan was to cook something for him, but now she feared there would be no food in the house to cook, thereby embarrassing him further. Luckily, she found some eggs, some bread, a jar of instant coffee. Four in the afternoon, yes, but no matter: she could work with this. After washing out the pan (a good sign, she thought; meant he'd been using it) she set to work. He watched her for a moment, then began shuffling items around on the table. Anne put the fried eggs and toast on a plate, which she also felt compelled to wash, and turned to find that Andy Mooney had cleared two places at the table.

"Oh," he said. "Aren't you…"

"Just eat." She set the plate down in front of him. "Now, where do you keep the cleaning supplies?"

"Please. You don't have to—"

"Don't argue, mister. Just eat. And for Pete's sake, take your hat off at the table."

By her third visit she had the downstairs pretty much cleaned and organized. It wasn't that the house was *dirty* so much as projected an air of being unused. Static. She did a lot of dusting, picking up and rearranging. She tossed some things, like board games with missing or mismatched pieces, and an old margarine tin filled with years-expired coupons. One day she brought the vacuum from home, offhandedly telling Carmelo it needed to be repaired.

There were times, driving to or from the red house in the Township, when Anne feared that Andy Mooney would fall in love with her. Or her with him.

But their relationship fell into a condition of easy, appreciative companionship. She cleaned and cooked—sometimes she'd make casseroles or trays of rigatoni that he could freeze and have throughout the week. Sometimes she'd give him what he called "homework assignments" (*Clean out that washtub so I can use it next week*) and he'd do them. And they talked. Andy Mooney told her how he had quit his job after his son's funeral, how he couldn't bear the thought of slogging through a day trying to sell feed to well-meaning but unaware farmers in Uniontown. At first he thought he'd welcome the distraction, but that wasn't the case. It was pure torment. He was okay for money, though: in addition to some savings, he'd received a lump sum payout from Westmoreland Life when his wife died; and now he was getting his son's death benefits from the government as well. And he had no real debts to speak of. Still, he hated himself for living day-to-day on what seemed to him a windfall from his wife's and son's deaths. He drank, but not *too* much, he didn't think; thought about leaving town but didn't know where he'd go. It occurred to Anne that Andy Mooney was depressed, maybe even suicidal. There were guns in the house—she'd seen two rifles while tidying the hall closet, and there was a loaded pistol in his night table drawer (which she'd found simply by snooping).

There was a part of Anne that couldn't blame him. But that part was overwhelmed by the knowledge that if Andy Mooney were to take his own life, or even to slog through the rest of his days in absolute sorrow, with nothing to sustain him, she'd never be able to live with herself.

She upped her visitation frequency. Her being there, just being in the house, moving around, the smell of Pine Sol and Pledge in the air, injected a semblance of life inside those walls, and seemed to restore some purpose in him. Anne could feel it. In a very real way—yes, she allowed the words to form in her mind, and they did not make her cringe—she was saving him.

Carmelo asked some questions, and she begged off with excuses of errands and a nonexistent volunteering commitment at the Salvation Army in Latrobe. "With two boys gone and Stuart back in school I need to feel useful," she told him, and he nodded, lifted his eyebrows in compassionate acceptance. His absolute trust in her added a dreadful weight to her endeavors. But she would not stop, ever. She couldn't.

Though she did, one afternoon after several months, ask Andy Mooney to please keep their recent—she searched her mind for the right words—"re-acquaintance" solely between them. He'd gotten some color back in his cheeks and had put on a few pounds; he was on a regular sleep schedule; he bought a used Ford half-ton and had recently begun taking it into town, doing some food and new clothes shopping, spending some time making new friends at The Lion's Fountain Tavern in Bentlee—reintroducing himself to the world, as he put it. When she raised the issue of discretion she was worried how he would take it: She was not *embarrassed* of him or of their relationship, such as it was; it was just... she didn't think others would understand, particularly her family.

"You have to promise me," she said, "that you'll never let my family know of our... friendship. That it won't somehow get back to them."

It was summer. They were outside in the yard, raking leaves from the previous fall—from the previous *several* falls. She was afraid she'd offended him, hurt him, ruined everything.

Andy Mooney leaned on his rake. "Of course," he said. A droplet of sweat fell from his nose and he dabbed it with the back of a gloved hand. "I'm just grateful."

And so was Anne. She watched him; he smiled at her over the waist-high pile of leaves, and she considered right then telling him about Nick, about Dr. Musgrave, and acknowledging her certainty, and thankfulness, that Andy Mooney's son had been sacrificed for her own.

But she didn't. There seemed no point. He was grateful, and so was she. Perhaps more so. If he ever *did* reveal to her family the details of their secret shared healing, she and Andy Mooney would still, not in a million years, ever be anywhere close to even.

12. Lawrence

They chose a spot out back, towards the center of the garden, where the rows of green-pepper plants typically would have been. Or, rather, Nick chose the spot. It had been decided that whoever carried Brownie's body—which, upon return from Raymond's, they discovered had become dense and heavy and a little stiff, though still relatively warm—would get to choose the burial location; and since this was all Nick's morbid-ass idea...

The air had moved beyond chilly and now was approaching downright cold. Beneath the hem of his Bermuda shorts Lawrence's exposed knees felt brittle, the tendons behind them stiff and tender, capable of snapping like piano wire. He looked at his watch. In the fuzzy moonlight he could make out the hands—1:25—and his mind began calculating how far it was beyond his typical bedtime: nearly four hours. Yet he wasn't tired—or, at least, not *sleepy*; just jelly-headed, the way he felt on an airplane when it shifted altitudes.

Nick was carrying Brownie with just his forearms, trying to hold her out away from his body, and was struggling. When he got to the middle of the garden he bent forward and tried to lay her on the ground gently, but he was only using his wrists and forearms which provided no leverage, no grip, and as a result he dumped her the final two or three feet, as if from a wheelbarrow. Brownie tumbled in a heap.

"Shit. Okay." Nick straightened. His chest heaved; sweat glistened on his forehead. Lawrence hoped it wouldn't freeze. "So, who's digging?"

Stuart glanced at the shovel he was holding, then let it drop to the ground. "That's a joke," he said. He turned to Lawrence. "He's joking, right?"

"Work it out," Lawrence said. "I'm going in the house to pee."

"Good," said Nick. "Bring out the two shotguns. And some shells."

"Yeah. I'll get right on that." Lawrence turned and located the back porch, some fifty yards off, submersed in dense shadow. He then remembered that there was no electricity in the house, and the thought of standing, for god-knew-how-long, before the toilet in pitch-darkness caused a quick tremor of dread.

"Wait." Nick's breathing had returned to normal. "Don't make me give another speech. I need this . . . I'd *like* for this to be a . . . a joint effort. The three of us. I'm not keeping score or anything. Really. Okay? But, you know, I carried the fucking dog. And I'll dig, too, I don't care. Just, someone else has to—"

"Jesus Christ." Stu bent and snared the shovel handle. "Fine. Lawrence, get the guns, will ya? Let's do this already." He tapped Nick in the thigh with the backside of the spade, and Nick jumped back as if bitten by a snake. "Easy, captain. Where's the spot again?"

Lawrence wasn't sure where his little brother's sudden burst of coolness had come from, but he found himself unable to question him. He headed toward the back porch, and as he passed by the driveway, the only sound in the world the rhythmic metallic cuffs of the spade slicing through earth, he noticed that his father's pickup was gone.

. . . .

Amazing, Lawrence thought, how his body moved through the kitchen purely by memory, instinctive, a physiological extension of his being. The air freshener candles had burned out, but a bitter smell—of pine mostly, but with soapy floral undercurrents—clung to the air. It didn't matter, though; he knew where he was.

He made his way through the kitchen and into the dining room, holding his hands out for furniture that no longer was there. When he got
to the gun cabinet his vision had adjusted somewhat. Diamond-colored
speckles of light reflected off the front glass, the muted image of his own
face superimposed overtop. What it came down to, he supposed, was
his desire to avoid, or at least postpone, that inevitable private scene of
shame in the bathroom, so he reached out and opened the cabinet door.
Nick had the Colt—that much had been confirmed, *ad nauseam*—which
wasn't a hunting weapon anyway. So that left…Lawrence squinted into
the cabinet: three more rifles. Christ, how many guns did his father own?
He knew they'd given some of them away: Big Rex Pavlovitch and Uncle
Jidge took a shotgun each; cousin Willie took a crossbow. Nick said they
were going to kill an animal. Did that mean a deer? Lawrence didn't know
what season it was—small game, most likely—but knew it wasn't deer
season. Should he just take a couple of deer rifles anyway? Shotguns? Were
scopes necessary at night? Had they given those away, too? Was there really
a wrong answer? Probably not. But then why did Lawrence feel so dumb,
the import of his choice tugging at his stomach?

He could smell the gun oil—his brain seemed to absorb the scent; it
settled there, weighed down his mind, like water in a sponge. He imagined the last time his father had cleaned them, imagined his father sitting at the kitchen table holding one of the rifles across his lap. This
was not much of a stretch; the image came naturally. He'd witnessed
his father shoot and kill many an animal over the years, and Lawrence
began to catalog them: deer and more deer, some wild turkey, pheasant,
some squirrels, even a raccoon or two, until their mother announced she
would no longer cook them—their hands looked too *human*. He'd shot
and killed a bear once, too. A black bear. Lawrence had not been there
for that, hadn't seen it, though from time to time he wished he had. It
was the fall after Lawrence and Nick's sharpshooting illusion.

A buddy of their father's had suggested the bear hunt. Apparently there were concerns of overpopulation across the state, and a certain number of bears needed to be "harvested." This window of opportunity was small—the season was three days only—and there were a zillion regulations put out by the gaming commission, but Carmelo and the other guys settled on a location in Clearfield County and bought the appropriate gear and upgraded their rifles and ammo and knives to bear-hunting specifications, and on the morning of their departure Carmelo told the boys to be ready, brace yourselves, 'cause he'd be back in a couple days with his bear, maybe two of 'em, monsters. There was a smile to his voice, though, and Lawrence suspected his father didn't really believe his own words.

But he did come back with a bear—and the story of how he got it would become a staple of his from then on. He told it often, once during his last week, lying on his side, eyelids half-mast, bony knees pulled up into his torso, on his single bed in the assisted-living wing of Latrobe Hospital, sheets pulled to his hips. Typically the hospital room had functioned as a lounge, or a break room, with Lawrence and Nick and Stuart and their wives dropping in and out at all hours. Raymond, too. Sometimes they all were there, sometimes different combinations floated in and out; sometimes cousins, grandkids, nieces and nephews, neighbors. They mingled by the window or in the doorway, walked together to the soda machine down the hall, sat at the edge of the bed nudged up against Carmelo's covered feet, greeted each other with embraces right in front of Carmelo's squeezed-shut eyes. Carmelo himself, for the most part, was mere furniture, as much a part of the room as the swivel-armed food tray or vinyl sitting chair. When a nurse would excuse herself and sidle into the room with a blood pressure cuff or syringe of morphine, the disruption to the social proceedings was minimal, much like a waitress bringing more coffee or clearing dishes.

Carmelo's weight had been melting away—they knew this would happen, but that knowledge didn't make the reality any less shocking to see. One day he turned and lay on his side and stayed there; his knees began to pull in toward his chest.

But right before that—a day at the most—he'd abruptly opened his eyes and cleared his throat, a damp crackling sound, and struggled to sit up. Lawrence and Nick lunged toward the bed to help him.

"Easy, Dad," said Nick. They put their hands on him, took him by the arms and shoulders, gently, but his gown was twisted and yanked down on one side; the skin around his shoulder was cold, rubbery, and the bones beneath felt stiff and brittle. The sight of his father's protruding clavicle made Lawrence turn away.

He heard sheets rustling, bedsprings creaking, and then his father's sticky, rough voice: "Ah, hell," he looked down at himself, as if searching the sheets for loose change. "Pissed myself, I think."

His words were like an invitation to notice the smell.

"Ah, goddamn it anyhow. What's wrong with me?"

Abigail and Celina came to him; Nick went for a nurse. They eased him to a sitting position on the side of the bed and straightened his gown, and he let them. Maybe he was embarrassed, or maybe his self-awareness had gone beyond the capacity for embarrassment; but in any case, to Lawrence, his father seemed profoundly disappointed in himself. There was surrender in his movements, in his total acquiescence.

"It's fine, Dad," Abigail was saying brightly. "No worries. We'll clean this right up." She patted his shoulder.

"Yeah, just relax, Mel," Celina added. "Stay still."

Lawrence felt himself drifting, losing symmetry of his thoughts, as if he'd been hurled down some long, dark funnel. There was a humming in his ears, then they popped and a hard weight settled in his jaw. "Thank you, hon," he heard his father say, though he probably didn't know who he was speaking to.

Once the hospital staff cleaned him up he fell back to sleep, on his back this time, head titled back and mouth open to expose his gritting dentures, like photos of a mummified King Tut. A month ago the cancer had returned to Carmelo's bladder. But he'd gone without a catheter until that day, when they hooked one up to his sleeping body and hung the bag on a metal arm beside the bed. The bag filled slowly, steadily. No one paid it any attention; the visiting and mingling and conversations continued: Nick and Raymond talked Steelers and argued politics; Abigail and Celina gossiped about the kids; Stuart and Sydney huddled in a corner, whispering conspiratorially to each other.

Then Carmelo woke up that one last time. They heard a garbled, crackling voice drift in from the corner of the room, like background music at a cocktail party, and they turned to find his lips moving, talking up toward the ceiling. Everyone converged, huddled over him, as if he were a campfire in a blizzard.

It was like a radio station fading from static into clarity, and it took a moment or two of blinking confusion for Lawrence's mind to catch up: "…split up, which wasn't too smart, not too smart at all. Shouldn't a done that. Gibby's idea. Last day and losing daylight. Cold as a…." His eyes closed and everyone waited, thinking he'd fallen asleep again but just making sure. Then he licked his lips. "I's just trying to keep warm. Wasn't thinking 'bout no goddamn bear no more." He made a soft sound like a belch, then laughed to himself and his eyes opened and rotated in his skull, then settled. "It come up over a little rise. Head kinda floated on top of the brown grass. Real tall brown grass. At first I thought it was a pheasant. Dunno why. Bear's head don't look nothing like a pheasant. Thought about shooting it but pheasants was out of season. Then it got closer and I saw its shoulders and about shit m'pants." He laughed, all lungs and throat, but Lawrence's stomach twisted. "Just stood there like a numbskull. 'Cause then it hit me, you know—uh, that's a goddamn *bear*. Black bear. Could tell right off. Which was what we were here for.

All this is hitting me at once, right? So I figure I better shoot the damn thing. But before I can, he stands up on his two hind legs and gives a roar at me, like you see in those movies." He stopped there and lifted his hands a few inches from the sheets, as if to demonstrate for effect, but then just let them drop again.

A word sprang into Lawrence's mind: *Deathbed*.

"And I raised my rifle, and I'm thinkin', I'm gonna get a bear! *Heh-heh*. God damn! Which was a crazy thing to think, 'cause none of us really thought we would. Those guys'd never admit that, but it's true. So, I don't remember firing, but I did, must've, 'cause the gun went off and then a little puff of smoke bounces off the bear's fur, like, right on his, like, his chest." Again he tried to indicate with his hands but couldn't quite get them where he wanted them. "But—but the thing didn't *drop*. Just stood there, kinda pissed off; then it started steppin' towards me. Like, stumbling. That was... that was the first time I ever thought, That's it, gonna die. Right here, like this, torn to bits by a bear. Never once had I ever had that thought before. Not even in the Pacific. About dyin', not the bear-maulin' part. Somehow I managed to get off another shot. But still he kept comin'. So I tried to ready a third shot. I imagine I didn't think it'd do no good, though—even if I could get it off by the time he got to me. Figured that was it. I was a goner. But then, right in front of me, the thing goes down. Fell right over. Like a dream, the whole thing. Had to stand there and figure it all out. Wasn't cold no more. Wasn't hot neither. Wasn't anything."

They'd all heard this story before, of course, many times—except for the about-to-die elaboration. Still, everyone in the room seemed to be leaning toward the strained voice rising from the bed. Nick and Abigail were smiling sedately, Nick's hand resting on her shoulder. Celina stood at the foot of the bed, her hand on Raymond's wrist, as if holding him still. Behind them Stu and Sydney leaned against each other. Carmelo's lips twitched across his gums, like a baby settling into a nap. A thimble's worth of urine flowed through the catheter tube and into the bag.

"So I had the bear," Carmelo said, eyes closed now, "but what was I going to *do* with the damn thing? Separated from everyone, middle of nowhere, just me. Thought I was gonna have to leave the poor dead thing there." Faintly, sorrowfully, he appeared to turn his head from side to side; or maybe he was just repositioning it on the pillow. "I just set down there next to it and waited. Figured the guys'd come lookin' for me. Gus had rigged up this, I don't know what ya'd call it, a rack, kinda, and he bolted some lawnmower wheels to the bottom. And ropes. What would you call somethin' like that?"

He waited.

"A…a pulley system?" Stu offered.

"Eh."

"Um…" Nick searched the room with his eyes for help. "A…winch?"

"A wha?" Carmelo's face squeezed in on itself, as if he'd swallowed something sour. "Don't matter. We didn't know how to use it anyhow. Didn't think we'd *need* it. Other choice was to process the thing right there in the field. But none of us knew how to do *that* neither. Not exactly. Probably coulda figured it out, though, I suppose."

"Of course you could have, Dad," Nick said. But the old man ignored him. Or didn't hear him.

"I'll tell you, though. Sittin' there next to that bear, sun goin' down. It was a big bear, too. No shit about that. But, layin' there like that, kinda curled on its side, wind blowin' across its fur—he kinda looked like a great big black…dog. Made me a little bit sad, tell the truth. Dunno why I felt that way. Never felt that way about a deer. Or a turkey, or a rabbit. Even coons—Anne thought their hands looked like a person's. But that didn't make no nevermind to me. Tasty little rascals. Stopped shooting 'em, though. For her." He seemed to reflect on this for a moment. His chest

rose and fell with his breathing. "Guys showed up a while later. Callin'
my name—never woulda seen 'em otherwise. Just about all the way dark.
Real dark, way out there like that. Kept thinkin' the bear was gonna wake
up and eat me. *Heh-heh*. But we rolled him onto Gus' contraption—that's
another story, for sure, remind me to tell that one some time—and it took
us 'til noon next day to get back to the trucks. Hell of an ordeal; took some
real doing. You know—" he turned slightly toward the wall—"I never said
this before, I don't think, but I woulda rather left the bear, just got the hell
out of there and come home and had a glass a beer. Or—at least not have
killed it in the first place. But the other guys were so excited, weren't no way
they were gonna leave it. Plus, I'da felt bad leavin' it. Poor goddamn thing.
Almost killed *me*. *Woulda* killed me. Shoulda been proud of myself. Proud
as hell. But I wasn't." He turned back to the ceiling. "I wonder why that is?"

Nick's smile was still there, but it had stretched and flattened out.
Over his shoulder, Celina—Lawrence was almost sure—appeared to
wipe away a tear. Carmelo made a sound in his throat, but no clearing
resulted, just a gurgly shifting of fluid in his chest.

Lawrence coughed.

"Then we had to *eat* it." Carmelo's voice brightened, just barely, but
everyone noticed it. The room seemed to take a breath. "Wish I knew
how long *that* took. Bear steaks, bear stew, bear chili. Bear and eggs...."

"Spaghetti and bear balls," Nick offered.

Someone laughed: Abigail.

"Right. Yeah. Bear balls. Anne made 'em taste pretty damn good."

"Bear ribs," Lawrence heard himself say.

"Uh-huh." Which would be the last words, such as they were, that
Carmelo would speak.

"Those were my favorite, actually," said Stuart.

Nick agreed. "Little barbecue sauce, char 'em up real good. Can
hardly tell...."

"Did you eat the *organs*, too?" Sydney asked.

"Liver," Nick said.

Sydney made a face.

"Ooh, that sounds good," Abigail offered. "I'll bet Mom could've done wonders with some bear liver and a little garlic and olive oil."

"Dad gave a lot of it away," Stuart said. "Still took us forever to eat what he kept. It was awful, really, but it turned out to be kind of like...a quest. We had to finish it. We *all* wanted to."

"Got to where I'd try to avoid Sunday dinners at your house," Raymond said.

They all laughed. "Good choice," Nick said. The mood had turned. But Lawrence couldn't stop watching the catheter bag, seeing the level rise, one drop at a time. Every so often a slightly more significant discharge would trickle in, about a syringeful, and at these moments Lawrence would excuse himself and head for the men's room down the hall, where he would stand before the lone, rail-assisted toilet bowl and break into a panicked, chilly sweat. The prostate was not the bladder: Lawrence knew this, understood it as a logical point of fact. The prostate was easier to treat—if caught in time. So why hadn't Lawrence at least gone to see a doctor, get the thing *looked* at? Maybe it was the sense of inevitability he couldn't shake. A week earlier, before leaving for Bentlee from Maryland, Lawrence had double-checked his life insurance policy: Five hundred grand. Plus the death benefits through his school. Celina would be fine. She'd be better than fine, actually: Lawrence knew she'd been unhappy—depressed, he suspected—for some time, at least since the filings, maybe even before, when the girls went off to college. Those were dreadful, sleepless, soul-crushing years. Every day was a new humiliation. But he had expected them to suffer through it all as partners, as a team; and seven years later, once they'd gotten through it and emerged more or less intact, he realized that he had foreseen them collapsing into one another's arms, exhausted with shame and joy and love and, maybe, even hope.

But Celina had moved on, psychologically. He should have seen it once the drinking started. Or the day the final lien was removed: On that day Lawrence picked up a bottle of middle-grade champagne on the way home from work (an event for celebration that was highly questionable, Lawrence had to admit) and presented it in the kitchen from behind his back, like a bouquet, a moronic smile no doubt stamped across his face.

"Oh, please," Celina had said, unplugging the dustbuster from its charging base, "now we're celebrating *normalcy*? Jeez, come on, Lawrence; let's not beat this thing to death, huh?" Then she disappeared into the living room. A moment later he heard the dustbuster whine.

Lawrence had felt betrayed, and he was angry—at his wife's lack of emotion, at her indifference to his. But what he felt most was alone. He had nowhere to turn. What could he do? Talk to one of his friends, or his brothers, or his father, about his wife's shitty reaction to the bankruptcy he'd kept a secret from all of them for seven years?

The frustration kept bubbling in his stomach.

Italy had been his last-ditch effort, but the trip succeeded only in confirming what he'd already suspected: His wife had abandoned him. He was alone.

So silly, juvenile even, but the truth was unavoidable: Celina would be better off without him.

Was he afraid of dying? He hadn't thought so. But after watching his father shrivel and shrink, long after death mercifully should have come to him, after hearing him wheeze and moan, and seeing and smelling the awful things leaking from his father's soulless body, Lawrence could admit to himself that he was afraid of dying *like that*. The bankruptcy, and his wife's withdrawal from him, had been more humiliation than any person should be forced to endure in one lifetime. Certainly Lawrence could not fathom enduring more.

....

The rifles that remained in the cabinet apparently lacked sufficient quality or nostalgia for anyone to claim them. Lawrence was no connoisseur, but he did recognize two from way back—the stocks were worn and streaked from decades of oiling and use; in the hazy darkness the surfaces looked almost soft. One was a shotgun, a Remington .12-gauge, and the other was a Browning bolt-action, which didn't look big enough to be a deer rifle—probably for varmints. Lawrence took one in each hand and lifted them, simultaneously, from the cabinet. He examined them in the moonlight shining in through the curtain-less front window. Carefully, he broke them open: both were empty. Probably this was a good thing. He performed a quick mental scan of the house, what was left in it, where a handful of loose shells might be found. Maybe Ray had some—they were going back up there for his spotlight anyway. No: they already had that. Plus, Ray didn't hunt anymore. Any bullets in his house had probably been there for decades, or were handgun shells of mysterious caliber that Ray had bought cheap out of the back of a buddy's van, "just in case."

The basement:They didn't spend as much time cleaning down there as they probably should have. It was dank and dusty—whatever they'd left, the new owners could keep. Plus, it had an odd smell of rust and cat piss. They'd had a cat for a short time when the boys were young, and the thing would go down there to piss—the basement had stone walls which had crumbled over time, the resulting sand settling along the edges of the floor, and this cat (which didn't have a name; they just called it "Cat") thought the entire basement was the world's largest litter box. Finally Carmelo tired of its act and one day Cat was just gone. When they asked about it Carmelo shrugged and said, "Cats are strange animals—nearer to *wild* animals than pets. Might come back some day. You never know." As none of the boys had any particular allegiance to Cat, they let the subject drop.

That was more than forty years ago. Still, when you breathed in the basement air you could feel the urine-soaked bacteria flowing into your lungs.

Earlier today, Ray had found wine down there. And at one time Carmelo had set up a makeshift shooting range over in one corner, made from a three-foot-square of lumber affixed to the wall. This was years before the stump across the road. Lawrence recalled many evenings of his father's buddies congregated down there, drinking beer and telling jokes, the thunderclap of gunshots and laughter echoing up through the floorboards.

Of course only low-caliber pistols were used in the basement firing range, but you never knew what might have collected in the general vicinity over the years. Lawrence set the rifles on the kitchen floor, against the wall across from the basement door, and opened it.

He could make out the top four steps; below that the stairway melted into blackness. Lawrence remembered the air freshener candles, found one that still had a little bit of wick remaining on the kitchen counter; he turned on a stovetop burner and and lit the candle by holding it upside-down over the stove's dancing blue flame.

Now, glass-encased candle in hand, he descended the basement stairs once more. There was something sinister-feeling about the whole enterprise: the candle flickering against the darkness, the deserted house, the eerie basement with its creaky stairs, guns leaning at the top, possible shotgun shells at the bottom, dead dog being buried outside. Lawrence felt a chill split him. Why should that be? he wondered. This was his childhood home. There was nothing sinister here; never had been. There was nothing to be frightened of. Then he realized that, despite the chill moving through his blood, he *wasn't* frightened. He felt as if he were navigating through a choppy, blurred memory, like old newsreel footage. And he was curious. Anxious, even. He wanted to see what he'd find in the darkness. Perhaps, he thought, this is what it felt like to pass from life into death.

The scent of the candle wafted into his face—lilac—covering the cat piss.

He thought there was one more step than there actually was, and tripped at the bottom, stumbling into the wall. The candle sputtered but stayed lit; he could see dust from the wall drifting through the fuzzy glow. Lawrence stood for a moment, letting his eyes adjust. With no lights, the basement looked and felt like a series of catacombs, with crude doorways cut through the stone walls. He could make out the doorway that led to a back room, where the upright freezer used to be, and where, in a corner by the floor-drain, his father used to clean his fish and hang small game to bleed out. But it was in this area, to the left of the stairs, where the practice range used to be. The candle wavered—a breeze was coming from somewhere, though Lawrence couldn't feel it—and for an instant Lawrence could smell his father, a mix of fish and wet leather and mold and Ajax hand soap. Then it was gone, and he had to pee, badly. An emergency. The pressure clamped down in his groin and began climbing upwards through his hips and into his abdomen. He stood there, waiting, trying to ignore the sweat forming along his hairline, purely interested to see where the pain would go next. When it drifted up into his chest and seized there, pressing against the backside of his breastbone, Lawrence reached for his belt and the lilac-scented candle fell from his hand and shattered. Everything went dark. Lawrence unbuckled and unzipped; he tried to picture the room, where he was exactly, which direction he was pointed in. Didn't matter: he took a step forward and braced himself, then released.

He couldn't have said *what*, from inside of him, he was releasing—which muscles, which inhibitions—just an all-encompassing letting go. He heard the splatter on the concrete, like an open hydrant on a city street, felt a relief so complete, so magnificent, that a tickle of pure pleasure moved through him; he felt a subtle tugging at his stomach, like a tiny string coaxing him forward. He leaned his head back and closed his eyes. All awareness of his physical presence in the world drifted away; the sensation was wholly spiritual now, a kind of euphoria he'd never experienced before—and he began to giggle. His shoulders bounced and the splattering took on a staccato cadence that tripped him from his dreamy trance. He blinked open his eyes and was startled to see the beams crisscrossing the ceiling. He could see the knots in the stained wood, the wires and cables stapled to the undersides, cobwebs in a corner. Maybe he was still dreaming—or whatever it was he'd been doing. He blinked again. No: he could see everything, clearly, through the darkness.

The sound of his urinating against the concrete floor had receded into pleasant background noise.

He took in a deep breath, and when he released it he saw a tiny white light wink at him from among the ceiling beams, almost like a star in the night sky. There was a moment that came over him, a moment when he thought, *Oh, okay, so this is it; this is what it's like. This isn't so bad.* And the little flicker of light winked at him again. In another instant he noticed that he'd finished urinating—or at least the spattering sound had stopped. He reached for his belt and zipper and fixed himself, never taking his eyes from that sparkling pinpoint of light: it looked miles away, light-years, yet once he had himself zipped and buckled, he reached up toward it, slid his fingertips along the beam and they bumped something. The pinpoint of light went out. Lawrence rose up onto his toes and felt around. Again his hand bumped something, and this time it fell to the floor with a heavy clatter. Lawrence's heart leapt into his windpipe. He shuffled slowly to his left, toward the doorway that led to the next room, and the glimmering star appeared again, on the floor this time. He bent down for it and just happened to take the grip perfectly in his hand; his finger slipped easily around the trigger.

The frame was small, with no more than a two-inch barrel. The grip was rubber-coated. This gun, Lawrence understood, was new. It was bought for a purpose. He stared at it, moved it around in the darkness to get a clearer look. There was writing on the barrel. Lawrence brought it close to his eyes: *Smith & Wesson*. He swung the cylinder out and waited for his eyes to catch up with his brain.

A single chamber held one bullet. The other five chambers were empty.

Lawrence snapped shut the cylinder and stood hefting the gun, for some reason trying to gauge its weight. It was light. How much did this thing *cost*? he wondered. He sniffed the barrel—as if he knew what he was sniffing for—but caught only the sudden resurgence of his own urine—rivers of it most likely snaked along the uneven basement floor. He stuck the revolver down the front of his shorts and turned back up the stairs, rejuvenated.

....

"No shells," he announced as he headed back across the side lawn toward the garden, where Nick and Stuart were bent over, studying the ground. They turned to him. "Found these rifles, though."

He didn't mention the revolver.

The moon was high and bright now, casting a blue-black glow across the grass that reminded Lawrence of the ocean.

"Hell you been?" Nick called. "You missed all the work." He straightened, pushed his fists into the small of his back and arched into a stretch. "That's okay. Maybe you could say a few words for the occasion."

"I still don't think we dug it deep enough," said Stuart.

"It's fine." Nick looked around near his feet. "We need some kind of marker."

"If the new people plant here next spring they'll dig him right up."

"Her."

"Huh?"

"Dig *her* up. Brownie. She's a her."

"Whatever. I'm just saying. She's not down there very far."

"This won't even *be* a garden next spring. They'll plant grass over all of this."

"How do you know that?"

Nick shrugged. "Feeling I got from the people. How about this?" He bent down and came back up with a squat empty tin can, its lid pried open. He held it up in the moonlight and turned it in his hand. Carnation evaporated milk. Their parents always drank it in their coffee and tea. Stuart used to like it on his cereal. "I think this'll do, huh?"

"Look, guys," Lawrence said. He stepped past the plum tree and over to his brothers in the garden. "Listen—"

"I hope you're working on that eulogy," Nick said.

"I'm all eulogy'd out, I'm afraid."

"Ah, but Brownie was such a good dog."

"Saved my life in Korea once," Stuart said.

"Ha! Yeah, right!" Nick hung the Carnation can upside-down on a stick and jammed the other end into the ground "Ah. There." He brushed his hands together. "I feel good about this. You guys feel good about this?"

"I feel fairly satisfactory about this," Stuart said.

Nick looked at him.

"I couldn't find any shells for the rifles," Lawrence said.

"Yeah. 'Kay." Nick stomped on the spade-end of the shovel and the handle rose halfway to his hand. He leaned forward and snagged it, surprising himself, it seemed to Lawrence. "I think I saw some loose shells on a shelf in the garage. What rifles did you find?"

Lawrence held them up for inspection.

"That one's for small game," Nick said. "Small game's out of season. Dad never would've shot anything out of season." He shrugged, sniffled. "Guess it doesn't matter, though."

"I told you," Stuart said, "I'm not shooting anything."

Lawrence, casually, untucked his shirt to hide the butt of the revolver poking out from his shorts.

"Got it," Nick said. "No shooting for Stu. Check." He stepped over to the dangling Carnation can and looked down at it. Lawrence and Stu fell in on either side of him. A breeze swept across the garden and the can shifted slightly on its stick.

"I'm having problems with my prostate," Lawrence said.

"No shit," said Nick. "What was your first clue?"

"No. I mean, something's *really* wrong. Big-time wrong."

Nick looked over at him, then back at the grave marker. "So. Go to the doctor. These days, they can take care of those things in an afternoon."

"I know," said Lawrence. "I know."

"Go as soon as you can," Stuart said. "As soon as you get back home. Don't screw around. You just gotta catch these things early, that's all."

"Yeah, well, that's the thing." Lawrence adjusted the revolver beneath his belt. The ridges of the cylinder were pressing into his hip bone. "I've— I've kind of... well, I've been sitting on this for a while."

Nick turned to him. "How long?"

"Months."

"Jesus Christ, Lawrence."

"Yeah. I know."

"The hell're you trying to prove?"

Stuart let his chin fall to his chest. He shook his head incredulously. "Leave him alone, Nick. Believe it or not, you don't know everything about everyone."

"Well... Jeez, Stu..." Nick's eyes narrowed; he looked pained. "I just..."

"No, it's okay," said Lawrence. "He's right. I guess I was waiting for a reason—for someone to give me a reason to go. I wanted to. But I wouldn't let myself until I got, you know, that reason. But I never got it. And now..."

"Just *go*," said Nick. "What's done is done."

"I know. I will."

The coolness of the air came back at Lawrence again. He'd forgotten about it for a while, or had grown used to it, but now his exposed skin quivered, or seemed to, and he was abruptly aware of the gun against his hip, the hardness of it, like bone on bone. He could hear the telephone wires humming above them.

"Want me to go with you?" Nick said then.

Lawrence looked at him. His brother's beard had grown beyond a five o'clock shadow, and Lawrence could make out flecks of brown, black, red, grey.

"To the doctor's. I could come down for a couple days. No sweat."

Lawrence's eyes grew suddenly tired. He sat down in the grass and weeds and overturned earth in what used to be his father's garden, next to Brownie's grave marker and the two rifles. "What I need," he said, "from both of you, is to promise me you won't let me go out like Dad did. Wasting away and pissing the bed."

"Shit," said Nick. "It won't come to that."

"But if it does."

"What're we supposed to do?" Stu asked. "Pull the plug on ya? Smother you with a pillow? Rewire your car, cut the brake line so it looks like an 'accident'?"

"Shut up, Stu." Nick shifted on his heel and looked down at Lawrence, faced him straight-on. "Honest answer?"

Lawrence waited.

"Whatever we say to you now, the truth is, if God forbid it ever came to something like that, which it won't, we'd do everything we could, just like we did for Dad. All the tests, all the treatments and surgeries, all the medications. Anything, *anything* to make it last one goddamn day longer. Because he was our dad, and you're our brother, and you're some-body's husband and father, and because that's the way this shit works."

Headlights appeared from the south on SR 33. They watched as it approached and crossed over Tremont, slowed slightly, then motored away into the night.

"Got it?" Nick said.

Lawrence blinked long and slow. When he opened his eyes the world seemed to have been scrubbed smooth and dipped in shellac. "Got it."

"But it's not going to come to that."

"No," said Lawrence.

"Say it."

"It's not going to come to that."

"Good. Now let's go kill us somethin'."

"Right," said Lawrence. He was so tired. "Just help me up."

He held out his hands, and his brothers came to him.

13. Sydney

Two A.M. Yet, against her better judgment, Sydney found that she liked being in the company of Andy Mooney; she felt an odd pull toward the man, a connection she couldn't identify. So when, as everyone was in the process of being thrown out of the Fountain, he suggested another place, a place that stayed open late, a place they'd never heard of before, over the bridge in Bentlee Township, so they could continue their conversation, Sydney did not object.

Of course she knew they wouldn't actually *go* to this place out in the Township. That was just talk. Even Andy Mooney didn't really want to go. He just wanted to hold on to something. They stood on the sidewalk out in front of the bar and looked skeptically at the pickup. Sydney had moved beyond the point of exhaustion to a state of buzzed wooziness. She could feel the capillaries behind her eyeballs throbbing in her skull; her skin hummed.

"So... okay, process of elimination," Celina said. "I guess Sydney's our chauffer for the rest of the evening." She was staring at the truck's right front tire.

Abigail put a hand to her lips, as if squelching a hiccup. "I don't feel so hot, people."

"Well, look," said Andy Mooney. He shoved his hands into his pockets. The air was still and had turned rather cold, yet Sydney's blood felt warm and thick. She wondered if steam were rising from her skin. Her feet felt heavy, like bricks. "This is wrong of me," Andy Mooney continued. "I don't want to keep you good young ladies out too late. I—" He paused, apparently realizing that that ship had long since sailed. "But I…I'd like to show—to share something with you, the three of you. I never shown it to no one before. And, but, well…it's awful late." He looked at his wrist but there was no watch there. "Real late. But if you could stick it out with me for just a little while longer yet." He looked Sydney square in the face, startling her, then shifted his eyes down her torso, and Sydney was momentarily alarmed to remember that she was pregnant. Had she actually forgotten? The baby hadn't kicked in a while, but still. She touched her stomach causing Andy Mooney to turn away, and a resolve, a determination she didn't know she'd been lacking, or was in need of, bubbled up from inside of her.

"Okay," she said. "Let's go. Take us."

"It's late," Andy Mooney said again. He kicked at a double-A battery lying on the sidewalk and it skidded over the curb and into the gutter. The stoplight at Upper Broad and Bentleeville Road clicked from green to yellow and then began blinking. Sydney realized that nobody had spoken for a time; they were waiting for Andy Mooney to continue, but he appeared to have nothing more to say.

"Why don't you ride with us, Mr. Mooney," Sydney offered. We'll get you back here afterwards. Or take you home. How long will it take? I just need a little protein. Maybe we can stop at a gas station; I can get some milk." She turned to Abigail, realized she was out of breath, paused a moment. "Who has the keys?"

"Oh, crap." Abigail's arms were crossed around herself; she was bent slightly forward at the waist and her teeth were chattering. "I drove. I don't know what I did with them."

"They're in my purse," said Celina. "But—" She touched her shoulder, expecting a strap to be there. "I must've left it inside."

"I'll get it," Andy Mooney said, and he heaved open the door to the Fountain again and went inside.

After a moment Celina said, "Good god. What the hell are we doing?"

"I think I'm done now," Abigail said, unable to control her shivering. "I *seriously* don't feel so hot."

"That's fine," said Sydney; she was working to keep her voice neutral, her tone sincere—because she *was* sincere. "I'll ride with him. You guys head back to the house and make sure the boys didn't hurt themselves, burying that poor dog. Oh...oh, Jesus—" A sticky chill shot through her, like the moment before waking from a nightmare. "I nearly forgot all about that—all about what...what I did."

"Do you think these two—" Abigail pointed a thumb toward the Fountain's door—"had a, you know, a *thing*?"

"Who knows?" Celina said. With her fingertips she massaged her temples. "Probably. You never know what's going on with people. What *went* on. Whatever. And anyway, we didn't really know them, Anne and Carmelo, if you think about it; we were just daughters-in-law. And I just want to go home."

"I don't," Sydney heard herself say.

"I can *smell* that whiskey inside me," Abigail said. "Like, smell it in my *blood*. Is that possible?"

Nobody said anything. A sudden gust of wind rattled a No Littering sign, causing a sound like a groan.

"Can you imagine? A fifty-four-year-old woman vomiting on the sidewalk?" Abigail tried to laugh but it came out like a sneeze. "This could be bad."

Above them, the yellow-blinking streetlight swayed slightly—eerily, Sydney thought—forward and back.

"What's he *doing* in there?" Abigail wondered, a slight whine rising in her voice now.

"Oh...shit." Celina pressed the heel of her hand into an eye socket, hard. She looked ready to shake apart, and Sydney didn't want to see it. "I had my purse jammed under the table leg."

"He'll find it," Abigail assured her.

"Well, but he *hasn't* found it, has he?" She kept her hand squeezed into her eye socket for a long beat, and then another, then she took a breath and stomped toward the door. "Wait here."

As the door swung closed—the sliver of space inside that Sydney could see looked deserted—the baby gave a kick, the first one in quite a while. Abigail hung her head, as if having fallen asleep standing up, like a horse. Sydney wondered if Stuart was thinking about her, worrying, if there was still the capacity for concern for her in his heart. What, she wondered, were his thoughts right now?

What had she done to him?

The silence, the stillness, the dewy dampness in the air, triggered a tightening in Sydney's chest; her lungs felt small and stiff, inadequate. She wanted to say something to Abigail—she wanted to talk—but when she opened her mouth all that came out was, "Wow, it really got cold."

"I'm so angry at you," Abigail said. "I might even hate you a little."

"What?" She knew there had been some resentment building within Abigail, some awkwardness between them—how could she not have noticed?—but the abruptness of her declaration, and its unmistakable directness, was like a punch in the windpipe.

"I'm sorry. I can't help it."

"But what did I...? The exercise bike?"

"That...that *baby*." Abigail glanced up from the sidewalk and looked at Sydney's stomach, then closed her eyes slowly—a long, sad blink—and lowered her gaze again. "I'm sorry."

"I know," Sydney said, "it seems a little desperate. What am I—are we—trying to prove, right? But it's...it's complicated. It's not what you think. I wasn't try—"

"No, Sydney, it's not what *you* think. I don't *care* what you and Stuart do with your lives. I'm not judging you. I'm *jealous*."

Even as Sydney's mind felt empty, a vague recognition was moving through the void. "Of what? Of *me*?"

"Have ten babies," Abigail went on. "Have one a year 'til your business dries up. Be one of those women on TV with fifteen of them running around. I honestly couldn't care less."

"Maybe I'll give this one to you."

Abigail turned to her sharply. Her face was pale; in the muddy haze of the streetlight she looked lifeless, bloodless. Her lips were gray and chapped. "What," she said, "are you *talking* about?"

Sydney shrugged. Surprisingly, she didn't want to take her words back. Though impossible, they made sense to her. "This whole thing...it's difficult. There are circum—"

The tavern door slammed open against the brick wall and Celina stepped outside; she paused for a moment, blinked against the light and coughed, her purse dangling from the balled-up strap in her fist. Andy Mooney followed and closed the door gently behind him.

"So, okay, we have the keys," Celina announced flatly. She glanced from face to face. "What next?"

And with that Abigail turned her head and silently launched a rope of vomit that splattered against the pickup's rear fender.

....

The pregnancy was Sydney's second. The other was sixteen years ago, and had ended procedurally and, later, regretfully. She was twenty-two—old enough, she later would understand; it's not like she was some snot-nosed teenager, knocked up and oblivious. It'd have been tough, yes (what isn't?), having the baby, keeping it, but it could have been done. Of *course* it could have been done. There was nothing stopping her; nothing except… On those rare occasions when she surrendered to a quick memory of that time, and the question of what had stopped her would flash in her mind, the first word that always appeared next was *fear*: Nothing stopping her except fear. But *was* that it? Maybe it was a simple case of revisionist memory, maybe it was the benefit of sixteen year's worth of reflection, of, hopefully, a bit more maturity on her part, but there were times—more frequent these days—when she thought, *I wasn't scared, I was afraid*. There seemed to her a subtle yet palpable distinction: One was natural, the other was cowardly.

What would her parents say? Her friends? What would her life become? Had these fears made her incapable of going through with it, of having that baby?

Or did she just not want to?

And then she had to reel her thoughts back in. It was unfair of her—a thirty-eight-year-old woman pregnant with a baby that wasn't her husband's—to judge the fears, real or imagined, and decisions, selfish or prudent or otherwise, of that twenty-two-year-old girl. That girl had just graduated from Fairfield State University in Connecticut with a degree— settled on after much stalling, brooding, and then a handful of switches from one to another —in Cultural Studies, which in effect meant no degree of any practical, marketable value at all. She'd gone to Fairfield because of the half-dozen or so schools that had accepted her it was the closest to New York City. True, she'd never been to New York City, but she knew that was where she wanted to be: the idea of it struck her as the way she wanted her life to feel. Ohio depressed her. The landscape itself was aggressively banal; even the weather seemed bored with itself. As her senior year of high school wound down, she became aware of a cold, persistent ache in her chest cavity, just beneath her heart, like an ice cube slowly melting. Though she'd always had friends—she prided herself on the fact that she was not a member of any one particular clique but could move freely among several groups—by the time June rolled around she found herself curiously lacking real companionship. The phone had stopped ringing.

And then early one evening, a week or so after graduation, as Sydney was watching TV, her mother called in from the kitchen asking why there hadn't been any graduation parties. Sydney thought for a moment. Probably there *were* graduation parties. Of *course* there were graduation parties. She just, apparently, hadn't been invited to any of them. None of her three or four so-called *best* friends had hosted parties, but those best friends of Sydney's weren't friends with *each other*, and friends of *their* friends had parties. The scenario struck Sydney, at first, as extraordinarily arbitrary and unlucky and unfair. The desolate feeling of being friendless shot through her. It stung, sharply, and then lingered, the sensation warped by the belief that she *did* have friends. How could this *be*? Yet, here it was. And maybe it was all her fault; maybe she needed to confront the fact that she hadn't exactly put herself in position to be invited to any of the parties. She most likely knew the hosts, she was *acquainted*, at least, and most likely would have been invited, as a matter of courtesy (she was not *dis*liked, after all), had she made herself socially available—hanging out at the right places at the right times; just being *visible*—over the past four or five months of school. But she hadn't. She'd been gradually shutting things down, withdrawing from her life in Ohio, from Westlake High, ever since she'd torn open the acceptance package from Fairfield. Something had changed at that moment: It was like she'd already left town. Her friends felt like memories to her. Sometimes, even though they'd be standing right in front of her, she saw them as existing in the past; she missed them. But that was okay, because she also felt like she already had acquired *new* friends—not necessarily better friends, but... *truer* friends. She didn't know what she expected from Connecticut itself, from New York, from the east coast. Nothing, she guessed. She didn't want to be an actor, didn't want to be a singer, an artist, a fashion designer, an investment banker.

She wanted...what?

The absence of emptiness perhaps.

Yet her image of New York City was vague, constructed mostly from TV and dreamy, brightly lit assumptions. Though the image wasn't visual. Not really. She simply knew how she wanted life there to *feel*: she wanted to feel included. Considered. She wanted to be one of a thousand people under the same roof in an apartment building, everyone jam-packed together, bumping into each other on the elevator and deciding to go for coffee and commiserate together, community within a community. She wanted street sounds at all hours, and the feeling of being a *part* of those sounds, a part of something larger than herself—yet to remain her own person; a person with options, who had friends with plans, itineraries, futures. She wanted to move among such people, to breathe the same air. She wanted to feel what they felt.

She liked the sound of the word "colleague." The phrase "lunch date."

And so she had allowed a series of choices to transpire as she approached her graduation from Fairfield (four years that tumbled by so quickly and uneventfully she'd often wished for a do-over). In April of her senior year, through the university placement office, she was offered an interview with Starland Travel, LLC, a company with an office in Murray Hill that sold timeshare "properties." During her interview on campus, the recruiter, a bored young man named Scot, with one T, who sported a mullet haircut, two-day's worth of blond whiskers, and the pink, flaccid eye-sockets of a basset hound, talked up the company's forward-thinking methodology and its need for self-motivated, personable, young "associates," recent college graduates interested in helping to build a company—indeed an industry—from the ground up. He thought her cultural studies major was perfect, though Sydney also got the impression he found it rather hilarious. Commission was involved; Scot threw around numbers, absurdly high percentages that Sydney doubted. The payoffs, he said, for anyone willing to take the risk, to put in the time, would be "substantial." In an analogy Sydney didn't quite follow, he referenced Silicon Valley.

At one point, thirty minutes or so into the interview, after apparently having seen enough of Sydney to find her sufficiently deserving of his candor, Scot sat back in his chair and glanced around the bare-walled conference room of Naylor Hall, his arms dangling out to the sides. Suddenly it occurred to Sydney that his polka-dot tie might be a clip-on. "Look," he said, "it's a racket, what can I say. But what business that makes a ton of dough isn't? Do I sometimes feel bad for the people I convince to buy into these things? Sometimes. I mean, I *did*, at first. But you know what? Most of them buy into the programs because *they* think they're scamming *us*. So…" He shrugged. "And you *can* make a lot of money. A couple of sales and the commissions add up fast. My check last month was for eight grand. The other associates are young and pretty cool. Most of them, anyway. There're some shitty hours—sometimes we have group presentations in the evenings, so people can come after work. But then everyone goes out after—to this place on Twenty-first, sometimes we haul down to Tribeca. I won't snow you, Sydney: I'm always looking for something else; I don't see myself *retiring* from this job. But, hey, it gets you to the city. Which is key. Once you're in the city options start opening up."

With this last statement, Sydney's interest piqued; that grave, icky feeling in her stomach vaporized, replaced by something like an electrical charge. She had misgivings; something told her *Don't*. But the timeshare industry wasn't yet the punch line it soon would become. Before she left the conference room and headed back across campus to her dorm, Scot had offered her one of three paid spots in Starland's Sales Associate Training Program, beginning June first.

Sydney—terrified, thrilled—asked if she could have a few days to think about it.

Scot smiled, as if he expected this. "Take a week," he said.

Reality never matches one's fantasies. Sydney knew this. And so she tried to temper her expectations. She was conscious of this mind-act. A friend (this was a loosely affixed label for an acquaintance who briefly had been the girlfriend of a former boyfriend's friend) named Karen offered go halfsies with her on a place in New York. Karen was an elfin ex-cheerleader from Rhode Island whose father had customers and other various contacts in the city, some of which might be able to help abbreviate the apartment-search process. A heavy knot abruptly formed in Sydney's stomach and twisted, hard. Again, she said she'd think about it.

....

Thank God for Mark—for Professor Weymouth.

In the sixteen years since, but less frequently as time went on, Sydney would try to psychoanalyze herself. For her entire life, from junior-high through college, she'd dated boys her own age. A year older, max. She was not one to bring strange older boys to the senior prom—maturity was overrated; and, when it came to boys, it also was relative. To wit: How "mature" was a twenty-year-old willing to attend a high school homecoming dance anyway?

Nor was she in need of a father figure: Her dad was her dad—a dad of the classic variety: supportive and exasperating, stubborn and selfless, clueless and brilliant. Away at Fairfield she'd sometimes forget about him for long stretches—for days at a time he simply did not enter her thoughts. Then she'd bolt wake in the middle of the night—her heart thumping in her chest, her brain humming—with the sudden notion that her father had died. She'd have to blink at the shadow-washed cinder-block walls of her dorm room for a minute or two, and mentally flip through the Rolodex of her life—*I had urban anthropology this morning, aced the quiz; I'm in bed in Connecticut; Jennifer borrowed my typewriter and broke the Shift key, cried again when she told me about it; Thursday is St. Patrick's Day, I'm going to Callahan's with Maureen and Kelly and Jennifer, if Jennifer can make it that long without an emotional crisis for me to solve; my mother sent a skirt from The Limited yesterday, but it was a half-size too big at the waist and a style I've long outgrown; I'm okay; yes, I'm okay, everything's okay*—until she established with certainty that her father could not *possibly* have died, that he was in fact alive and well and asleep in her childhood home in Ohio.

No, Sydney refused to believe that anything psychosomatic had led her into a relationship with Mark Weymouth, refused not because she was *unwilling* to consider it, but because she had logically and systematically eliminated such a possibility. Mark Weymouth had taken an interest in her, sure, a *professional* interest. He was her academic advisor, a professor in her major, a specialist in media ethics and communications theory. He had tousled curly hair and wore glasses in a way that made you forget he wore them; he had a boyish charm and an intelligence that came so effortlessly he seemed bored by it. He sat in his office, in a straight-backed chair on the near-side of his cluttered desk, and was not afraid to make unorthodox suggestions to his advisees: "Ah, huh-uh, nah, you don't wanna take her, not for that class. Let's just say I've heard things. Honestly? She's a train wreck. Wait 'til the spring, when Manning teaches it. Just trust me on this." He didn't even care that his door was wide open.

And as a cultural studies major, someone who didn't know what she wanted to do with her life—not just for forever and ever, but next week—Sydney was drawn to his courses, whose descriptions in the academic catalog seemed to consciously avoid language that might suggest any practical application in the real world. Some of his courses were cross-listed with the English department, some with Philosophy, some with Communications, some with combinations of all three. During each term's first class meeting, he stood in front of his group of thirty or so puzzled but hopeful students, each of them likely wondering what the hell "the rhetoric of popular culture" could possibly *be*, but nonetheless thankful that it met one of the tougher-to-fill general ed requirements. He'd lean an elbow against the lectern, radiating a rascally confidence in his un-tucked oxford, cuffs unbuttoned and folded to just above his wrists; a smile always seemed to be brewing on one side of his mouth, though he rarely allowed it to fully form. He quickly fostered an impression that in merely teaching this class he was getting away with something, and it wasn't long before the students shared this awareness. After that first class, they emptied out into the hallway thinking, sometimes saying, "Well, I still don't know what that was, but I kinda *liked* it."

Sydney, though, felt as if she alone knew what "it" was—and why the other kids liked it. And Mark knew she knew it, and respected her for knowing it, and this mutual understanding afforded her a sense of privilege that Sydney found downright empowering. She felt like an insider, which, she realized, was all she ever really wanted out of life.

She registered for every course Professor Weymouth taught; when he called roll at the beginning of each term's first class meeting, Sydney noticed the spark of familiarity in his eyes as he came to her name on the roster, the veiled smile as he spoke the name and located her among the rows of desks. She never said "here" or "present" or "yes," only smiled back.

It was sometime during her junior year that people began to talk, as she knew they would. Somehow, though, this knowledge only increased Sydney's enjoyment of the situation. Even Jennifer, one night after half a bottle of peach schnapps, said to her, "I don't give a flip—" her caked mascara sticking together when she blinked—"honest I don't, Syd. But, you know, people can *tell* somethin's definitely up with you and super-stud-boy Marky W. It's, like, *obvious*."

Sydney shrugged—she always shrugged, a trite reflex. She wasn't hiding anything, and it surprised her to realize that she honestly didn't *care* what people thought. *Had* she cared, she could have pointed out that Mark Weymouth was a single man (which everyone knew anyway), but even *that* technicality didn't matter because there was nothing going on between them. So if the uninformed wanted to speculate on what might or might not be happening behind what suddenly appeared to be the velvet ropes of her life, Sydney had been fine with that. More than fine. Still was.

She'd done nothing wrong.

But she was unwilling to cut herself any breaks for the way she'd allowed things to progress from there. Part of it was a matter of familiarity: Mark had gotten used to having her in the classroom, semester after semester, and eventually came to lean on her a bit, turning to Sydney for assistance with clarifications and examples when students expressed confusion over Mark's hyper-complicated response-paper criteria. He'd begin to explain, then pause and suck in a breath. "Well . . . Sydney, you've been through this silly routine of mine a time or two. Can you give a sense of what everyone can expect, what they should focus on? Maybe that'd be simpler." And so she told everyone how she'd approached the response-papers in past classes. "It's not that bad," she assured everyone. "He's not looking for anything in particular, so don't just try to give him what you think he wants. Just make sure you support your statements with references from the text and you'll be fine."

At this, his smile broke through. Maybe he came to rely on her. God knew she'd been relying on him.

December of her senior year he asked if she'd be interested in being the TA for his 200-level rhetorical ethics course during the spring term. It'd give her three credits in her major that she wouldn't have to fill with some bullshit class she'd be bluffing her way through, it'd look great on her résumé, and it would be worthwhile experience if she were ever to consider teaching down the road. This is what she told her parents, and in fact all of these advantages were a hundred percent factual. The *truth*, though, was that none of those facts mattered to Sydney. The truth was she was flattered.

She graded quizzes and acted as a mediator between the students and the professor. ("You might find that some kids will feel more comfortable coming to you with questions," he told her.) He gave her responsibilities; he trusted her. In April he let her give the lecture on the rhetoric of persuasion, a subject she'd become particularly comfortable with. He looked her notes over beforehand, made some suggestions, and when the day came he watched with pride as she shared what she knew, steering the students through her logic. She made notes on the blackboard. She'd worn a tight-fitting cashmere sweater with a cowl neck—she knew the outline of her bra strap was visible through the fabric—along with a sharply pleated skirt and three-inch heels. When she turned her back and took up the chalk she could feel the eyes on her.

Her blood warmed with joy. She felt beautiful, in control.

And when she received the offer from Starland Travel, the first thing she did the following morning was drop by Mark's office, that heavy knot from the day before twisting ever tighter in her stomach. It was early and the door was closed (these weren't his office hours) but Sydney knew he sometimes came in early to work on his screenplay—a comic drama that followed a beleaguered New York City reporter struggling with the ethical and emotional tensions he confronts in a typical news day, plus a wife at home, pregnant and missing him; Sydney liked the premise and felt a very real sadness for Mark when, a couple of years later, she recognized his basic plot in a Ron Howard film called *The Paper*, starring Michael Keaton—and so she knocked and called softly, "Mark?"—his first name foreign on her lips—and he opened the door for her.

She wanted to know if she was being naïve, reckless, in even considering the job offer. Truth be told—and she'd *only* reveal this to him—she
had no real idea what this job *was*. Starland Travel? A joke, probably. She
wanted to be in New York, but, fuck, she wasn't even exactly sure *why*.
And even if she could have explained why, even if she *had* a valid reason,
a vision, what sense did it make to jump blindly at the first ambiguous
offer? Maybe she should just wait?

Mark sat across from her, nothing between them, their knees six
inches apart. "Syd," he said, calmly, that invisible smile flickering at the
corners of his mouth, "you're…how old? Twenty-one?" Somehow the
tone was absent of any trace of condescension. He was simply curious.

"Mm-hmm. Twenty-two in July."

He shrugged. (Had he picked that up from *her*?) "Look," he said, "take
this for what it's worth, which quite honestly isn't much. But the way I see
it, you have your whole life—an enormous chunk of it anyway—to settle
in on a, whatever, a *career*. What a dangerous word that is. We attach way
too much importance to our *careers*. So maybe this Starland-whatever-the-
hell gig *is* a total sham. Maybe it's a colossal load of utter horseshit. The
company won't *exist* in twelve months for all we know. So what? You can
hook yourself up with another company just as fucked up next year, and
the year after that; find yourself a new garbage company every year for the
next five, and you'll *still* only be twenty-six." He sat back in his chair and
crossed an ankle over a knee, where a hole was beginning to wear through
his jeans. "As long as they're *paying* you—make damn sure up front that
they can, and as soon as you sense they *can't*, then get the hell out. As long
as you're happy, or something like happy, and optimistic and seeing your
work for what it is…" Again the shrug, which he held for an extra beat.
"You know, I went straight from college, right to grad school, and then to
my doctoral program, boom-boom-bam. Everyone thought I was some
kind of wonder-kid or something. But I only did it because I was terrified

of becoming a marketing rep at Pfizer, like my dad. Don't get me wrong: no shame in that; it's an honest profession. But the idea scared me to death; it wasn't me. And I didn't realize you don't have to have a *career* right away, that careers can…they can happen organically. I wish I'd known that. So I kept going from school to school to school as *avoidance*, and the next thing I knew, I had a career—without ever having lived. And now—" he glanced around his cluttered office, as if scouting for spies—"god damn, I'm so freaking *bored*, Sydney. And I feel…pointless. And—and I have thirty-five more years of this shit." He blinked, kept his eyes closed for a moment, and when he opened them he was looking right at her. "What am I gonna *do*?"

....

She was twenty-one: She didn't have an answer for him. Later, years later, she would come to understand that Mark Weymouth had no earthly right to dump his life's neuroses and disappointments on to her—she was his student; she had come to *him* for advice—and that his doing so revealed an immaturity and naïveté that she herself would never know. But at the time she felt only an urgent desire to help him. And so, on that day, she left his office and walked back to her dorm room and called Scot at Starland Travel and accepted the offer. Then she called Karen. "I'm in," she announced. "Let's do this."

"Who-hoo!" said Karen.

....

The difficulty of finding a suitable apartment in a city filled with a bazillion *un*suitable ones hadn't occurred to Sydney until then. The search, which she had hoped would be a sort of adventure, was in fact soul-crushing: they were all so tiny, so expensive! But she'd known that, she kept reminding herself; this was what she'd expected, what she'd *wanted.* She gave herself mental pep-talks: *Come on, Syd! Get a grip! Suck it up! Smile!* She tried. She pushed on, and she and Karen decided on an apartment. But it was way up on 114th Street, eighty-some blocks away from Starland's block of cramped, depressing offices; plus, both Sydney's and Karen's fathers had to co-sign the lease for any landlord to even *consider* renting to them. With each new challenge Karen simply applied a fresh coat of lip gloss, flipped her blond hair back over her shoulder, and pirouetted on to whatever task or revelry came next.

Sydney's parents tried to warn her. She heard the skepticism, the bewilderment, and then finally the raw fear in their voices as she provided the details of her intentions—the 600-square-foot apartment she'd be sharing with a girl they'd never heard of before ("Harlem? It's in *Harlem*?"); the vague job that was not even guaranteed, technically, after the six weeks of training, in an industry that...that was...uh....

"Explain it to me again, Sweetheart?" her father gently pressed her over long-distance, his voice a mix of caution and doubt—more a question than a demand. "This company does, um, *what* exactly?"

Her mouth would dry up and her heart would pound: She didn't know.

"Please, honey. I'm not criticizing. Honest, I'm not. I'd just like to understand."

She soon discovered that the job was hers to lose; the training was a part of the gig, not some kind of trial period. She also discovered that the gist of Starland Travel was not exactly a pyramid scheme, not really telemarketing, yet not too terribly distant from either of those rackets. At the same time, the decision-makers at Starland were careful to keep the general workforce as ignorant as possible regarding matters of policy, a consideration—or lack thereof—that Sydney greatly appreciated. It was clear that she was indirectly responsible for ripping people off, yet she was a tad fuzzy with regard to her actual role in this act. She was schooled in the basics: How much the average family of four spends per year on vacations; the mystery of the unknown when it comes to hotels; the hidden fees and surcharges that travel agents and airlines and hotel companies funneled right into their pockets. Part of Sydney's job was to put together mailers asking rhetorical questions based on such information, and address one or two hundred of them per week to people all across the tri-state area who had been "chosen" based on "various factors," such as their travel history, income, and etc. and etc. (In truth, the mailers were sent to everyone in the tri-state area who had an address, and neither Sydney nor anyone at Starland had the first clue as to the recipients' travel history or etc.; sometimes names could not even be tracked down and the mailers were addressed to "Resident.") Of the 150 or so weekly mailers, perhaps six or eight would call with interest—or at least questions: "What *is* this thing exactly?" they'd ask, sounding like her father. "And how'd you get my name anyway?"

"Good questions," Sydney would acknowledge brightly, because she didn't know the answers to them herself, but also because it was what she'd been trained to say. Then she'd invite the caller and his or her spouse to attend an informational session later that week.

At these sessions her role was to appear upbeat, smart, yet down-to-earth. After the main session, she would meet privately with an interested couple. She'd been trained to ask questions rather than answer them.

"What would it mean to your family if you could *own* your vacation?"

"Own? What do you mean, 'own'?"

"Well, how much did your last vacation cost?"

"I…well, I don't know. I mean, that's, you know, private."

"Well, where did you go on your last vacation?"

Here the husband and wife might look at each other, as if trying to decide whether or not to lie, or at least exaggerate.

"Florida."

"Mm-hmm, mm-hmm—" Sydney practiced her smile at home. She worked on what Karen called her *That's-so-awesome-and-I-know-exactly-what-you-mean!* voice. "Sure. We have *lots* of wonderful properties all *over* Florida. Now, for a family of four, the average week-long vacation with travel from New York to Florida, estimating conservatively, departing from Newark and staying in a three-star hotel, is around fifteen hundred dollars. That's money you'll *never get back* once the vacation's over. It's like you're *renting* your vacation." She'd been jotting all of this down with a Sharpie—random figures and phrases in big, happy, girlie, curlicue script—on an unlined desk blotter between herself and the couple. "But with a Starland property, you can *own* your vacation. When you return home, what you spent is not gone, it's still working for you."

The husband and wife then would look at each other again. The husband might run a hand across his five-o'clock shadow. Then, if they hadn't walked out on her by then, Scot or another member of the senior sales team would take over, tossing around possible deposit amounts and interest rates and payment plans. According to the statistics, by the end of each session 1.5 couples put down a deposit, either by check or credit card, ten percent of which Sydney received as commission.

There were free gifts involved—vouchers for two nights in New Orleans or Myrtle Beach, sometimes a round-trip domestic flight—this is how they got people to come to the sessions in the first place. But Sydney had no idea how these "vouchers" worked, and every day she fielded calls from angry ex-potential customers complaining about the complexity or veracity of the vouchers, calls which she passed along to one of the resolution reps on duty. These creepily congenial people were known to drink during the day.

And yet Sydney did not hate herself as much as she'd thought she would. The apartment she shared with Karen was small, but everything worked, the super was reachable, her neighbors were friendly, and with a 6-train stop right around the corner, an eighty-block commute wasn't that big of a deal. Karen herself turned out to be an excellent roommate: she was pleasant and optimistic, and since she had no job, yet, she had plenty of time to decorate the walls with funky hand-painted accents and to keep the place clean and organized, and she was always available to meet for happy hour or to run an errand for Sydney in the middle of the day. Plus, along with Karen came a fine array of furniture and appliances that Karen had immediately referred to as "ours."

Sydney was having fun. She had some money in the bank. She'd made a couple of friends at work, who had become Karen's friends as well, and who thought of them when things came up on Friday nights and gave a call. She wasn't changing the world, but damn if she hadn't begun to feel like she was a part of it.

So.

Mark's advice, self-pitying as it might have been, had been dead-on. She called to tell him. She figured he'd be glad to hear she was getting along well.

He was. And two weeks later he called to say he was going to be in town: he had some grant money left and it would go away if he didn't use it, and he wanted to finish up some research he was doing at NYU before the fall term got going. She met him that Friday after work at Max Fish on the Lower East Side, for drinks. But it was awfully loud so Mark suggested they get a bite at I Truli, an Italian place he liked on Twenty-seventh, just a short cab ride uptown.

She had thought when she saw him again that he would look ancient—like, well, like an older man. But in fact he seemed to have somehow grown *younger* over the past three months. Oddly, though, this apparent age-regression made him more attractive to her—no, not *more* attractive: attractive for the first time. She'd always admired him, of course—his intellect, his achievements; but now these qualities struck her as even more impressive, now that he was no longer her professor.

He paid for everything, with his credit card; when he took it from his wallet she could see that there were not many bills inside. He was becoming more human, more readable, to her by the moment. They talked about her job, her day-to-day life in New York, of which Sydney detected in his warm smile a touch of envy; he revealed to her which faculty members in Cultural Studies and Communications and English were assholes. He joked with the waitress. They talked about TV and music and the O.J. trial. They talked about their parents—Professor Weymouth's parents!—and how in their eyes, and therefore in your own, you never grew up; you didn't know shit about the real world. If you let it get to you, the shame could be crippling.

They didn't go back to her apartment. He'd taken a room at the Gramercy, just a few blocks away. They could walk.

....

Like most tragedies, the one that followed might not have been avoidable, but certainly, in retrospect, Sydney knew she should have seen it coming. What she'd found most attractive about Mark Weymouth—his youthfulness—was released fully upon her when she filled him in on the general parameters of her condition: the missed period, the little plastic stick she'd turned bright pink when she peed on it. Since that first night they'd spoken on the phone most days, and he'd made return trips to the city each of the next three weekends, plus he met her for a middle-of-the-week happy hour thrown by Starland management as a reward for a better-than-usual month of screwing people. He was making an effort to be with her, but without being pushy or overbearing, signaling to Sydney the very real possibility—one that actually hadn't crossed her mind before—that Mark Weymouth truly *liked* her. Not as an idolizing co-ed, not as a one-time conquest, but as something else, something *beyond*. His one area of lingering self-consciousness was with her apartment: he'd only seen it once, and they never spent the night there when he was in town. He always got a hotel room. Sydney at first wondered if she should be offended, then worried that it was costing him too much (she'd noticed the quality of the hotels in which he'd stayed decreased with each visit; no more Gramercy). But she came to understand that, comfortable as he might have been with the idea of a relationship with Sydney, it would stand to reason that he'd be far less comfortable with flaunting that relationship around another former student, i.e., Karen, and crashing in that former student's tiny apartment, with all the unmuffled bedspring noises and bathroom sounds—though of course Karen didn't give a flying crap.

She waited for his next visit to tell him. An Indian summer evening, appetizers at a sidewalk café, since closed down, on Thompson Street.

"So..." he began, in a tone that implied a question was attached. But that question would have been, *Are you sure?* and it was clear from the information she'd just related that indeed she was. So he rearranged his silverware on the table and squeezed his bottom lip with thumb and forefinger. She felt bad for him; he looked like he'd been ambushed by the person he most trusted. "Hmm," he said. "Well..."

"I'm sorry," she said.

"No. No, no. It's just, I mean, what...How..."

He was an academic; it was all he knew. Of course he wanted answers, a rationale. He wanted things to be logical. He wanted to know how this could have happened. She told him it seemed pretty clear to her how it happened.

"No," he said, flustered, his voice slipping toward a panicky edge. "It's not...I mean, it can't..." He looked at her with drowning eyes.

What had she wanted from him? To fix everything? She would since come to accept that that had been impossible. He was older than her, yes, considerably older. But he was still a child: an unsure soul floundering through an accidental life, still aching for the respect of his parents.

Maybe the stigma of impregnating a (not-too) former student was something he just couldn't wrap his mind around. Maybe he couldn't face
his parents, admitting to them that he'd fallen victim to the most banal
cliché in all of academia, admitting that maybe he didn't know shit about
the real world after all.

When finally he got around to saying, "So…" again, the flesh beneath
his eye was twitching, and the color had drained from his cheeks. He
looked at her, hopeful, waiting, knowing that this was his moment to
say something that would make everything all right but at a complete
loss as to what that might be, just one way out flashing over and over in
his mind yet unable to voice *that* either. So she went ahead and offered
the solution she knew he was hoping for.

....

Carmelo had always been one of those *everything-happens-for-a-rea-
son* kind of guys. Sydney had always loved that about him. The old adage
was comforting, and surprisingly accurate. For instance: had she not
taken that ridiculous sham of a job with Starland Travel, she wouldn't
have had occasion to meet Brenda at Cerrano Realty, who took Sydney
on as a trainee and saw her through the licensing process, providing
a career she hadn't anticipated but rather enjoyed. Cerrano was not a
major player in luxury Manhattan real estate, not by any stretch, but Sydney did okay throughout the turn-of-the-century boom: her focus was
Brooklyn, a borough in the midst of a renaissance, and while she didn't
see the same windfall as most in her industry did, she considered herself
lucky to have been, to a certain extent, in the right place at the right time.

She was getting by. Isn't that the way life was for a New Yorker?

The regret she felt over the Mark Weymouth situation was without
focus, striking at odd moments and accompanied by a hazy sense of loss.
Over the next sixteen years she would be torn between forgiving the

frightened twenty-two-year-old who didn't know any better but should have, and cursing that same young woman for not being stronger, braver. The only thing that seemed clear to her was how fucking unfair it was that her one lousy, stinking horrible mistake could never be made right; it would always be with her, like an infected organ.

Somehow, though, for all those years, in the back of her mind, Sydney knew she'd make another colossal mistake, if only to blot out the first one. Is this what had happened with Bruce Lambert? And would her actions of that night, and the baby inside of her now, become Stuart's infected organ? Or had that next inevitable mistake *been* Stuart? Another college professor—or at least he *wanted* to be. But, unlike Mark Weymouth, Stuart had arrived at this profession, this career, over time, *organically*, as Mark might have said. He'd worked for it, struggled for it, was *still* struggling for it, because he loved it—literature—and, goddamn it, Sydney loved *him*. She did! A steely resolve filled her now as she stood behind Abigail: her sister-in-law leaned out over the curb, and Sydney held her gently by the shoulders to direct the steady streams of puke away from the truck. Oddly, an image of a swollen gray kidney floated just above the sidewalk, and Sydney blinked it away.

"I want to die," Abigail moaned.

Sydney took the ends of Abigail's hair in her fingers, to hold it away from her face, but it wasn't long enough anyway. So she patted Abigail on the back. *There, there.*

"*Oh-ohh…*" Another heave came.

"I'll get you home," said Sydney.

Abigail nodded. Hardly anything was coming up now, just stringy lines of spittle accompanied by lots of coughing.

"I feel a responsibility here," Andy Mooney said. He was standing on the sidewalk by the truck's front tire, hands stuffed in his pockets. When nobody responded he said, "Boilermakers. The hell was I thinking."

"Please," said Abigail weakly. "Don't…"

Celina dug around in her purse and took out a wad of Kleenex, walked over and handed it down to Abigail, who took it without looking. Celina then turned to Andy Mooney. "I'm thinking we'll skip our little field trip."

"Right," he said. "Sure." Though it was clear he was disappointed.

"No," said Abigail. "I'm fine. We can go. I can go." She coughed and then spat. "Oh, jeez."

"All right," said Celina, "that's enough. I'm putting an end to this. Mr. Mooney, thank you for the boilermakers and stories of seducing our mother-in-law, but we're *so* calling it a night now. I hope you understand."

"'Course," he said, then retroactively picked up on the *seducing* reference. "Wait—"

"No!" Abigail wailed. "I'm *not* going back yet. I *told* you—" her mouth opened like a fish's and she gagged, took two deep breaths—"I told you, we're . . . shit. I forgot what I said we were doing. But I'm *not* going back."

"Christ, Abigail, you're dry heaving."

"Celina—don't!"

Celina shook her head. "Fine. Whatever."

"Look," said Andy Mooney. "I don't want—"

"Except I can't drive," Abigail said. She had slumped down to a sitting position on the sidewalk and was shivering now, nearly convulsing. "Sydney, can you drive?"

Sydney nodded, then realized Abigail couldn't see this. "Yes."

"That's already been settled," Celina pointed out.

"Maybe I can drive," Abigail said.

"No, sweetie," Sydney said, "you can't."

"All right then. Help me up, you little bitch." She tried to smile but the expression looked more deranged than playful.

Sydney shifted her stomach out of the way and Abigail pulled herself up in stages, pawing at Sydney's hip, forearm, shoulder. Once upright, she swayed for a moment, steadied, and looked around proudly.

"Ha!" she said. "See? Okay, let's go."

Andy Mooney was parked around the corner on Ash, so Sydney was to wait for him to pull around with Celina, and then follow. Sydney loaded Abigail into the pickup, then got in and started it up, cranked the heater fan full blast. She had acquired a gentle tingling all over her skin, and she felt a weird energy radiating from the center of her chest; her breathing grew rapid, almost panting.

"I'm kind of embarrassed and kind of happy," Abigail said. "And kind of…something else. Ever feel that way?"

"I have, actually," said Sydney. "A few times."

"And, ohh man, and nauseous, too. Do you have any gum? A mint or something? Do I smell like vomit? Be honest."

"You kind of do, yeah. But it's fine."

"No more Joey O's pizza for *this* girl. Not until…for a longer while than…" Her voice trailed off. Sydney pulled the headlights knob a single click, so that the parking and dashboard lights flashed on. The cab of the truck took on an eerie yellow-gray quality, a hepatitis glow. The heater hummed; there was a slight rattle just beneath the sound, in the vents, like a man snoring. As the truck warmed, the baby woke and shifted, jammed a knee or an elbow into the underside of Sydney's lung. In profile, Abigail's cheek and neck looked creased with shadows; she was no longer shivering but her shoulders rose and fell rhythmically with each breath, and her eyes were focused on the floor. She might have fallen asleep. Outside, a thin wispy fog was collecting at street level; the buildings across the street looked two-dimensional, like a Hollywood replica of a small-town Main Street. The barber shop, the credit union, the shutdown Democratic headquarters—a guy named Boozer who apparently had run for Congress in the '06 midterms. Sydney wondered if he'd won.

Above it all, the sky looked menacingly orange: smoky clouds had moved in and were picking up a burnt-orange radiance seeping through from behind. It reminded Sydney of what it must look like inside the crater of an active volcano. She had a vision then, a satellite image taken from high above, from inside the orange clouds, an image of herself sitting in that idling pickup truck, in this little town out in the middle of mid-central Pennsylvania, a town most people had never heard of, the one person with her not even conscious, or half-conscious, and she was overtaken by a feeling of utter non-existence. Yet the sensation was not frightening; not at all. She felt empowered: In not existing she could do whatever she wanted, whatever felt right. No self-consciousness, no regret. There comes a time, she realized, when you have to stop waiting on the person you thought you'd become, and start being the person you want to be.

"Abigail," she said. "Abigail, are you awake?"

Abigail grunted, lifted her head. "Yeah. Yes," she said. "Where are those guys?"

"Abigail, this baby. This baby isn't Stuart's."

She turned in her seat, blinked at Sydney. For a moment her face was empty, absent of any trace of awareness, and then the shadows on her face shifted. "Oh. Sydney. Oh…Jeez."

"Yeah. It was—I just couldn't…I mean, Stuart was…" She put her hands on the steering wheel, ten and two, let them drop back down to her lap. "The whole thing, it's kind of cosmic payback for…for something else. Payback to *me*. And it's not fair to Stuart. Or to this…this baby. It's like, you do something, and nothing ever feels right after that. Everything's…a little restless inside of you. Your heart is restless. And you keep waiting for that to change, for that moment of, Oh, okay, that's over, I made it through, everything's okay now. But then it hits you: that's not ever going to happen, that nothing can ever change, things can't ever really be okay again. So you make another mistake. And, well, I thought I was ready to live with the consequences. I *had* to be. But now—" She twisted a quarter-turn in Abigail's direction, put her stomach right out there between them—"You and Nick, you have, like, a lawyer, right?"

Abigail's jaw did a little trembling thing. She squeezed her thighs, tightly, and held them. "Lawyer," she said. "Sydney. What..."

"I'm oh for two, Ab. And I'm done kidding myself. I probably won't get another chance. But that's no reason to keep piling on the pain. So whadda you say, Ab. I'm feeling really good right now." She felt herself smile.

"You..." Abigail cleared her throat; there was something croaky going on in there. "You don't *want* the baby?"

"I want to cut losses. Mine, yours, everyone's. I want to feel hopefulness."

"You don't think... I don't really hate you. I didn't mean that."

"I know. It's okay."

Abigail licked her lips, but it didn't help any; they were so chapped they looked plastic. "Are you say—"

A flash of light hit in the rear window and swept through the pickup. A moment later an eighties-vintage Jeep Wagoneer, complete with tan wood-grain, pulled up alongside, with Celina in the passenger seat. The window lowered; Sydney could tell Celina was rolling it down with the handle. Sydney rolled down her own window.

"Hi-ya, kids!" Celina said with exaggerated glee. "Wanna hang out?"

Sydney searched her mind for a witty response, but then just smiled.

"So we're goin' to the cemetery!" she said brightly. "How's *that* for late-night fun?"

"The cemetery."

"You bet'cha!"

"Um, okay. We'll follow you."

Celina's face dropped into a mask of seriousness. "You better."

Andy Mooney said something then, his voice a string of murmurings from the shadows. Celina turned to him and said, "Just go," and the Jeep pulled away through the intersection.

Sydney put the pickup into gear—you had to press down extra hard on the brake pedal for the transmission to slip into Drive. She was starting to wise up to the truck's eccentricities, beginning to think of it as *hers*. Andy Mooney's taillights faded into the darkness, but it was okay, Sydney knew the way to the cemetery, they'd just been there that very morning.

"So?" she said to Abigail. "What do you think?"

"You saw me vomit on the sidewalk," Abigail said. "And *spit*. You can't *ever* tell anyone about that."

Sydney took her foot off the brake, and the pickup lurched forward. "Deal."

....

What Andy Mooney had wanted to show them was a spot just behind Anne's headstone, where he'd buried his son's Purple Heart. "It's about a foot, foot and a half down," he said, one knee bent, flexed against the slight incline that cut through this section of the cemetery. A gust of wind snapped his pant leg. "Or it was, anyway. Maybe it sinks a bit over time, I don't know. Just keep digging, you'll find it." When no one replied he sniffled and added, "Grass come in nice around it, though."

Sydney couldn't tell. The orange-ish clouds had cleared and the moon was out now, casting some whitish light onto them. But the area behind Anne's headstone was all shadow, all blackness. Right next door, so to speak, Carmelo's plot had been filled in with fresh earth. This was a recent development—when they'd left this morning after the service the casket was still held in place by the winch, hovering above the open grave. The air here smelled of burning leaves.

Andy Mooney explained how he'd buried the medal a couple of days after Anne's funeral. It wasn't something they'd discussed, just something that had occurred to him to do, partly because of the friend she'd been in the aftermath of his son's death, partly because he couldn't stand looking at the goddamn thing in his house, partly because...well, he didn't exactly know why, but it had seemed right at the time, and he'd done it, and there it was. But lately he'd been thinking, it didn't seem right for the medal to stay there, behind Anne's headstone after he, Andy Mooney, dropped dead himself, which, let's face it, could be any time now. He'd put it there as a gesture from him to her, but he wanted to know if he could impose on these lovely ladies to see to it that the medal got moved once he passed on.

"Bury it by my grave," he suggested. "Or my son's. Or just toss it, for all I care. Or sell it. Must be worth a buck or two, though I have no idea really. While I'm still alive, that's different. Just wouldn't seem right, both of us dead, for the thing to be buried here with her—her husband right beside her, me off buried somewhere else, alongside my own wife and boy. It just...whatever sense it made when I buried the thing gets kind of...muddled, and what used to make perfect sense don't make *any* sense no more. You know?"

Sydney did. In nearly every conceivable way, Sydney had little to no idea of what Andy Mooney was talking about. Yet still she understood; it was like detecting a secret message by listening to a record album backwards.

"Yes," she said, "of course, Mr. Mooney. We'll make sure it's taken care of."

Celina looked at her across the packed dirt of Carmelo's grave.

"Just toss it," Mooney said. "I don't care. Just shouldn't be *here*."

"Don't you think," Celina offered, "that maybe you should *keep* it? Don't you think you owe it—" She cut herself off.

Andy Mooney stepped over and put his hand on Carmelo's gravestone. Though the sons had been presented with a flag at the funeral, the WWII flag and insignia had not yet been affixed to the stone itself. "You reach a certain age," he said, "and you get ready to meet your maker, the best you can hope for is to be able to say..." He brushed his fingers across the top of the stone, as if checking it for dust, then touched the tips together and stared at them. "You're gonna make a poor choice from time to time. I know that. I ain't dumb. Life's short, but that don't mean there isn't time enough to make a shit-ton of mistakes before you're done. You just hope when it's over you were able to make them right, somehow. Or to at least forgive yourself for not being able to." He glanced up, shifted his eyes from Celina to Abigail to Sydney. "I just can't ever look at that goddamn thing again."

"We'll be respectful," Sydney said. "I promise."

He nodded. "I just wish I could do something for you ladies, too. That I can't makes me feel like a worthless old man."

Abigail, who'd been swaying slightly on her feet, sat down gingerly in the grass and leaned her back up against Anne's headstone. She tucked her knees up into her chest and hugged them to her, closed her eyes. Her chest rose and fell a couple of times with her steady, contented breathing, and then she lifted her face to the moonlight.

14. Stuart

Stuart didn't feel so hot, though it wasn't clear to him if the ailment he perceived moving through him was entirely physical. When he tried to pinpoint the spot on his body that hurt, he found himself contemplating the possibilities. His head? Well, sort of. His stomach? Kind of, yeah, but not exactly. His throat? Yes and no. What he felt had more of a physiological edge. His "headache" was in fact more of a pulsing nausea behind his eyeballs. And he wasn't so much "dizzy" as vaguely aware of a structural imbalance in his equilibrium, a simulated vertigo, which in turn caused not exactly a "stomach ache" but a crampy whorl of queasiness floating around between his heart and his colon. If someone were to suddenly grab him by the collar and demand to know what was wrong with him, he'd end up babbling like an idiot, clueless. This bothered him.

Maybe he was just tired. His hands were shaking and his shoulder blades seemed to have minds of their own, releasing occasional odd jerks and shudders.

Maybe it was all in his head.

The spotlight was starting to get heavy, but at least he didn't have to carry one of the shotguns and risk shooting himself if he were to trip and fall, as he'd been known to do.

Not that it'd matter.

Nick and Lawrence walked a few paces ahead as they crossed the side yard toward Route 33. The beam bounced around out in front of Stuart, sometimes lighting up his brother's backs, sometimes waving across the grey-black grass of the side yard, reminding Stuart of those edgy independent films he used to tell himself he liked: A couple times a week he'd take the subway into Manhattan, to the Angelika on Houston, to see them. He loved the *look* of these movies, the grainy, twitchy, cement-block starkness of them. He admired how the filmmakers were able to somehow make black and white feel like primary colors, to achieve an atmosphere that was simultaneously rough and delicate: every image, every frame, so vivid and striking and precise. Yet, as brilliant as the image looked, Stuart always got the impression that if you pushed on any of it, even just a touch, it would shatter.

The fact that he was so much older than the filmmakers themselves was not lost on Stuart. Still, the anticipation of going to see these movies, especially if he were going with someone from his department, made him feel artistic—the fact that he truly did appreciate the visual aesthetics of the films somehow confirmed his intellectuality. To *whom*, he couldn't have said. To himself, he supposed. In any case, he kept going; when he was unable to dig up a companion on those occasional days when the sight of his insipid 400-square-foot apartment, and the idea of a fifty-year-old man living in it, made him sick with despair, he went alone and sat in the dark looking up at the flickering screen and sensing his blood tingle with the awareness.

Now, crossing the road towards the adjacent woods—his brothers up ahead of him, holding the stocks of their rifles right up to their faces as if unsure of what they held in their hands, trying to stay in the wavering beam of the spotlight—Stuart found himself finally admitting what he'd always unconsciously suspected: he was drawn to those movies because they were anti-Bentlee. Nobody he'd grown up with—not his parents, not his brothers, not his friends or even his teachers—would understand them had they been sitting in the empty theater seat next to Stuart. They wouldn't understand *him*. They'd blink at the screen, open-mouthed, thinking: *Stupid*, and then turn to Stuart and wonder who the hell he was. In this subconscious understanding there had been both great pleasure and sadness. He'd think: Man, if my dad could see me here, watching this movie, and *getting* it… But in the next instance it struck him that, *had* his father seen him there, he wouldn't have been impressed, he'd have wondered, The hell's *wrong* with that kid? Where did we go wrong?

All through graduate school, when Stuart visited for holidays, nobody asked him about his work—mostly because nobody saw it as "work": he was a middle-aged *student*. No matter that he was a graduate student, a *doctoral* candidate, and that he'd been awarded one of Rutgers' prized doctoral research fellowships. He never mentioned this. They wouldn't understand. And Nick would probably find some right-wing agenda in it anyway. ("They're *paying* you to go to *school*? Christ, what'll the liberal wackos think of next?")

Inevitably, Stuart felt it best to keep the news of whatever paper he was working on—a postmodernist examination of the domestic imagery in Richard Yates' fiction—to himself.

Even when he defended his dissertation (a hard-bound copy of which he presented to his parents and then watched, crestfallen, as their smiles froze and their brows scrunched into puzzled enthusiasm) and finished the degree, and even after B—— took him on full-time, he knew his family thought he didn't really *work*. Five classes a term? So, what is that—five hours a week? Plus summers off? Plus three weeks in January? Sheesh. Must be rough.

He was with Bruce Lambert, at a first-run showing of Vincent Gallo's *Buffalo 66*, the night he met Sydney. At the time, Bruce was Stuart's upstairs neighbor; he painted splotchy, eerie urban landscapes on huge canvases. Stuart thought they were cool, though he lacked the critical acumen and/or vocabulary to say precisely why. He just knew when he looked into them he detected a little echo in his heartbeat. But Stuart's critical shortcomings meant nothing to Bruce. In fact, he seemed to appreciate them. Once, early for a show after getting off the F from Brooklyn, they stopped in for a beer at Max Fish. Bruce was talking about one of the canvases he was working on, saying something about how the painting was turning out to be all backdrop and no foreground, and Stuart accidentally let his heartbeat-echo comment slip. He regretted it immediately—what a lame, pedestrian comment to make to an *artist*. But Bruce Lambert's eyebrows flicked upwards and stuck there; he held his beer bottle halfway to his mouth, considering. "Oh," he said. "Oh, *yeah*. An *echo* in the fuckin' *heart*beat. That's awesome, Stu. That's *it*. That's *exactly* what I'm going for. Every time." He elbowed Stuart in the ribs, like a big brother, though Stuart was older by ten years. "Wow, thanks, man."

Soon after that evening, Bruce Lambert abruptly quit painting—or anyway scaled way back on it—and moved to working primarily with sculpture—stone and metal—even as his reputation as a painter was beginning to take off locally. At the time, Stuart couldn't understand this move. Why would someone who'd managed, as a *young man*, to discover the thing he so clearly was good at, and that he loved doing, voluntarily give that thing up? Though the idea perplexed and frustrated him—even angered him a little—Stuart only brought the issue up to Bruce once (again at Max Fish, either by coincidence or because Stuart felt more comfortable, somehow more confident, there). He'd parsed the question delicately—*So why the switch?* or something like that, Stuart couldn't exactly remember—but even as the words were leaving his mouth, he suspected that he already knew the answer: Bruce was an artist, not by profession but by inherent truth of self, and as such had to go where the artistic impulses and challenges took him. How amazing, Stuart thought, not just to understand intellectually such an idea, but to believe in it. Bruce took a quick jerky swig from his beer bottle, rested his elbow on the bartop and propped his head up with a fist, and then gave Stuart nearly verbatim the explanation he'd just heard in his own head, all the while gazing at Stuart with the soft, squinty expression reserved for those who knew you best.

Which perhaps was why Bruce continued to suggest a couple of showings a week at the Angelika, and why Stuart, even though it was beginning to dawn on him that he didn't really *like* most of the movies that ran at the Angelika, kept going: Bruce treated Stuart like a fellow artist; or at least someone who shared Bruce's some inexplicable artistic sensibility. And in his presence, Stuart felt like an artist himself. For a time. An hour after he'd floated the *why-the-switch* line, as the movie started up, Stuart was aware of the usual warmth easing through him, the pleasure of feeling like another person, someone who went to films with artists and talked about them afterwards before going home to his apartment in Brooklyn and grading papers on *Tess of the D'Urbervilles*. The film's opening visual sequence (Stuart couldn't possibly recall the film's title now) consisted of a series of quick cuts, in muted gray scale, of what appeared to be the same field of tall swaying grass shot from varying angles. Stuart imagined that if there had been color the grass would have been tan. The wind whipped over the grass, folding it back and forth in several directions at once—the surface looked like a churning sea—so that dark shadows rolled across like rocks in a sack. Stuart felt a tingling just beneath his skin. The soundtrack playing with the images was all moaning organs and pedal-steel guitars, dirge-like, but with a soft, single-note whine sliding just beneath the surface, slowly rising in pitch and volume, creating, along with the choppy gray images, a squirmy combination of discomfort and giddy anticipation. Stuart could sense the white light from the screen flickering against his face. *This is who I am*, he thought. But then the opening sequence ended; the dirge faded and the camera swept over the field, as if from a low-flying helicopter, then rose above the trees and came down again in the middle of a archetypal small-town mainstreet; the camera continued on, as if strolling along the sidewalk for a block or so, then turned into what the viewer immediately identifies as a tavern. The men along the bar—four or so of them—turn in unison to inspect the new unseen arrival, faces blank as wet cement. Stuart felt a bolt come unhinged inside of him. He stood up, excused himself past Bruce Lambert's crossed legs, not meeting his eyes, and walked back through the outer lobby and out onto Houston Street.

The intensity of the world outside shocked him: the streetlights, the traffic lights, the headlights, the moonlight—light seemingly rising from the pavement, from the Earth itself. Stuart stood on the steps beneath the Angelika's marquee and blinked against the blazing night. *Where am I going?* he thought, *and how did I get here?* He'd just turned fifty. He'd spent his birthday alone: none of his handful of New York acquaintances even knew about it. He didn't *look* fifty, but facts were facts. He was fifty and single and had failed at two marriages. What was the point of pretending otherwise? It struck Stuart that at some point there comes a time when you have to quit hoping and start being the man you hoped you'd become.

Stuart always viewed it as fate that Sydney happened at that moment to step out of the café a half-block east. He was looking right at the door as it opened; his mind actually formed the words in his mind: *I wonder what's going to come out of there.* He had no idea what he might have been expecting. It was October. The air was dry and crisp and smelled faintly of aluminum. Was it possible that he'd fallen in love with Sydney the moment she stepped out onto the sidewalk? True, from that distance he couldn't see her too clearly. And he'd been in love twice before, at least, or *thought* he'd been. But the appearance of this young woman felt to Stuart acutely prophetic. She turned east, and he followed her.

....

He seemed to be adjusting to the chilly air; it felt as if he were submerged in water and his skin had acclimated itself to the water temperature, so that he couldn't tell where his body ended and the air began. Beyond the spotlight's beam, the trees and underbrush blended and overlapped, forming varying degrees of blackness. "Come on, Stu," said Nick from ten yards ahead, "that light doesn't do much good if you're *behind* us." And no sooner had the words left his mouth that Nick stumbled and went down headfirst into the shadows, rifle clacking along the path. Stuart caught up and directed the beam down onto him.

Nick rolled over onto his back, squeezed his eyes shut against the light. His golf shirt was littered with dried leaf residue and bits of briars. He sat up slowly, pulled one knee up toward his chest, and began rubbing his shin. "What was I thinking?" he said. "Christ, I need to... What's *wrong* with me?" He pressed both palms into his shin. "Let's head back, find the girls, put all this behind us." There was a note of defeat in his voice. "Before somebody really gets hurt. And get that goddamn light off of me, please, Stu."

Stuart swung the spotlight around and trained the beam on Lawrence, who stood stiff and apologetic off to the side of the path. He held the rifle down at his side by the strap, like you'd hold a suitcase. His other hand was touching his midsection, as if trying to determine where his appendix was located. "What?" he said. "What do you want from *me*?"

"I'm not ready," Nick said. "I'm not ready for this... for this next part."

Stuart felt something harden in his blood. His heart flexed and lifted. Something had to change. He thought: It's not what you're capable of doing in life; it's what you're willing to do.

He stepped over to Lawrence and held the spotlight out to him. "Here," he said. "Switch with me."

The beam pointed out into the woods, backlighting Lawrence's face. He said nothing.

"The rifle, Lawrence. Take the spot and give me the rifle."

"But...Nick said we're not doing this anymore. We're going home."

"No," said Stuart, "we're not. Here, take this. Come on."

"You can't shoot," Lawrence pointed out. It was not a criticism, not a challenge. Just a statement of fact. "You hate guns."

Stuart took the rifle from this brother's hand, pressed the spotlight into this chest until he took it. "I know," he said. "I know that, Lawrence. You're absolutely correct on both counts. Is the safety on?"

"Yeah," said Lawrence. Then, "Wait." He reached out and guided the forestock back towards him, held the bolt handle right up to his face, and squinted. "I think. Can't tell without my glasses."

"Doesn't matter," Stuart said.

Lawrence released the rifle and folded his arm around the spotlight, hugging it to his chest.

Stuart turned to Nick. It took a moment to re-find him, down there among the shadows. He wasn't moving, just sitting with his shoulders hunched and head hanging between his knees. He looked defeated and Stuart felt an abrupt pang of shame. *Everything*, at this moment, seemed to be his fault.

Is that what had kept him away from Bentlee for so long? Not that his parents ever expected him—any of them—to *stay* in Bentlee, but somewhere inside of him Stuart always knew that his parents were hurt by their—particularly *his*—seeming disdain for the life they led. It wasn't just that all three boys took off the moment they were able; Stuart mostly stayed away, even between his stints at various colleges. As time went on he told his family less and less about his affairs, his ambitions, his plans, went weeks without contact and when he finally did pick up the phone he found that he had no desire to fill them in on the minutia of his day-to-day life. During one phone call, when Stuart was in grad school in Scranton, he stood in the kitchenette of his apartment, listening as his mother told him he was breaking her heart. "Your father's, too," she added.

"What? Why? What are you talking about?" He'd tried to sound indignant, caught off-guard, but the truth was he'd been expecting this conversation, gone over possible responses in his head. Now that it was happening, though, his mind when blank.

"He thinks you're ashamed of him. Of our life."

"*I'm* ashamed of *you*?" he said. "That's a good one."

"What's that supposed to mean?"

"It means...nothing. Never mind."

This seemed to throw her off-track for a moment. Stuart could tell she was nervous; he wondered if this implication had been rehearsed.

"When you call—when you *do* call—you never ask about us."

"What are you *talk*ing about?" He felt like he had her now. "Of *course* I do. Just today—just now—I said, 'So how are you, Mom?'."

"Oh, that's not what I mean. I mean about our *lives*. You know, last week a man who's been working with your father at a job site in Latrobe—they're removing asbestos in a shopping plaza over there—this man got hit in the head by a scaffold. Jerry Pondo, his name is. They say he's going to have brain damage forever."

Stuart waited to see if there was more. He felt like he was missing something. "Well, jeez, Mom. That's...that's terrible. But what am I sup—"

"Your father was really shaken up. Still is. It happened right in front of him. And he likes this Jerry fellow."

"Well, I'm sorry to hear this, Mom. Really I am. Wasn't this guy wearing a hardhat or something? They're supposed to wear special suits for removing asbestos, aren't they? Masks and stuff? Was Dad wearing his?"

"That's just the point," she said, though Stuart wasn't sure which part she was referring to. He could hear cupboards opening and banging shut.

"He very much would have liked to share this event with his sons. He didn't say this to me, but I can tell. But none of them ever ask about his work. You're all ashamed of it. Especially you. And it breaks his heart. Mine, too."

Stuart squeezed the phone in his hand and was about to hang up when he recognized the warm awareness of embarrassment spreading through him: A grown man and being reprimanded by his mother. And *deserving* it. Pathetic. And the feeling would never, for the rest of his life, go away. He simply was embarrassed of himself. He felt the same way as he noticed his first gray hairs, when he got his first colonoscopy, his second colonoscopy, through all three of his marriages and two divorces. The original argument had seemed to be that Stuart, more so than his brothers apparently, considered himself to be somehow superior (intellectually? morally? Stuart was never quite sure) to anyone who lived in Bentlee and/or worked a job that hadn't required the acquisition of a Master's degree. And his distain, he was led to believe, was obvious.

Stuart had tried to be objective. *Had* he been projecting an air of superiority? He hadn't meant to, obviously, yet he couldn't deny the existence of a knot in his stomach—just above his stomach, actually, right underneath his heart; what would that be, his diaphragm?—that formed and tightened and hardened and twisted whenever the thought of his hometown entered his mind. Sometimes he would dream of still being there: forty years old and living in his boyhood house with his parents; waking at sunrise with his father and sitting with him at the kitchen table in the blue-gray light of ungodly early morning, silently tying their work boots while the coffee pot gurgles and hisses on the counter. And in the dream, within that moment, was the awareness of the life it entailed, and the possibility of one day having to return to it. Sometimes, in the dream, he can smell compost on the breeze drifting in through the open window above the sink. It clung inside his nose. To this day, the smell of compost made Stuart heartsick.

His response to his mother's accusations was simple: He began asking about them—about the job his father was currently working on, details of his garden each spring and updates on its progress throughout the summer, projects he was undertaking, camping or fishing trips they had planned, their health, even his mother's day-to-day routine around the house and in town. Stuart kept up this approach, even though his father's response to it was maddening—maddening because even in the face of Stuart's enthusiasm for details, his father would more often than not sidestep Stuart's inquiries in favor of some arbitrary occurrence: Electricity went out for nearly twelve hours the other day. Why can't the Township take care of that pothole over on 33? Soon it's going to spread and then they're gonna have a collapse on their hands, or worse. Nine and a half inches of rain last month, according to his own measurements. Raymond had two parties last week; I could hear them up there hootin' and hollerin' and blastin' music 'til all hours. Your mother's on me to get the patio furniture out for the season.

Still, Stuart pressed on with this approach. At some point, though, he began to notice, on his rare trips back to Bentlee, the appearance of new framed photographs, featuring his father decked out in requisite orange or camouflage, in the woods or a field somewhere, flanked by various (often unrecognizable to Stuart) young cohorts. In these photographs, his father was always smiling broadly, as were the other young men, as someone raised by the antlers the wobbly head of a just-now-bagged deer. Sometimes the details of these photographs varied—a duck instead of a deer; a marsh instead of a field—but the appearance of new ones was consistent. When Stuart would ask his father about a picture—where it was taken, who his fellow hunters were—his father would shrug it off, mumble a one- or two-word answer, and change the subject.

And now, as he located Nick in the shadows, Stuart admitted to himself what he'd always suspected: What broke his father's heart wasn't his sons' career choices, such as they were, or their haste to leave Bentlee, or even their seeming disinterest in his work; it was the way in which they all, aggressively, turned their backs on the thing he loved most—hunting—forcing him to live out his final years making memories with other men's sons.

"Our baby," Stuart said now, aiming his voice at a dark patch of fern. "This baby, mine and Sydney's. It's, well, it's not mine. Just Sydney's. And…"

Nick sniffled. "Huh? What're you *saying*, Stu?"

"I'm saying—" Stuart felt his chest heaving. He seemed to be taking in air when he should be breathing it out.

Lawrence swung the spotlight around, right onto Stuart—like a smack in the face—then quickly lowered it down at the ground. "Oh, jeez," he said. "Jesus, Stu. What did…When—"

"Tonight," said Stuart. "I just found out about it tonight. Or, rather, had it confirmed tonight." He lifted the rifle, snapped open the bolt to make sure there was a round in the chamber. There was. "So, Nick. What're we going after? Have either of you ever hunted at night before?"

Nick rose up onto his knees. "Let's head over toward Pymatuming Creek. Bound to be some coons around, or possum. There's a field right behind it, too. If we're lucky we could even spot a deer or two. Who has the extra shells?"

"Maybe a skunk," Stuart offered.

"Maybe, yeah."

"I'm not eating any *skunk*," Lawrence said.

"Yes," said Stuart. "Yes. That is exactly what I want to shoot tonight. A skunk."

Nick used the butt of his rifle to help push himself up to his feet. "Let's go see what we can find."

....

A lot had changed in Bentlee since Stuart took his first apartment away from home in 1971: The Red & White, which previously had been Mauch's Market, where his mother had worked, was gone; now everyone shopped at the Giant Eagle in New Bentlee or the Wal-Mart on the way to Greensburg. The high school, from which Stuart and his brothers had graduated, was remodeled in the late-seventies, added onto in '83 and combined with the junior high until the new middle school was completed in '86. There was a new little league complex, with an all-grass infield, out by the regional airport, which closed down a few years ago. Needles' Nursery closed down, too. So did Westmoreland Stone Monuments and the Bentlee Bakery. A few roads managed to get paved each year, though, and there actually was a combination coffeehouse and bookstore—a good one—on Lower Broad. Stuart couldn't remember the name; it was only open for two years, from '03 to '05.

But these twenty-some-square-miles of woods that began (or ended, depending on how you looked at it) just across Route 33 from his father's house, hadn't changed—not a tree, not a branch or jagger bush, not a blade of tamped-down grass along the path on which they now walked, appeared any different to Stuart. If he didn't know any better, he'd have sworn he was twelve years old. They didn't speak; the three of them progressed as if by instinct, like salmon in spring, or those tortoises that return to a certain island to die. They moved farther into the woods' interior, then gradually drifted northwestward. The forest began to open up, the trees spreading out a bit, the vine-tangled baby oaks replaced by patches of skunk cabbage. Stuart and Nick walked about five paces ahead of Lawrence; the wide beam thrown from the spotlight was disconcerting, stamping Stuart's and Nick's giant marching shadows onto the ground ahead of them, the images broken and skewed by intermittent saplings.

Stuart once had gotten lost in these woods. He was ten or so—the summer after he'd fallen off the roof. Nick and Lawrence had sent him off, claiming there was a treasure hidden in the hollowed-out trunk of a fallen tree, left there by Confederate soldiers during the Civil War—rare Confederate gold and silver coins. It was going to be the country's new currency, they'd thought, but the war was not going well so these soldiers had stashed a couple of giant sacks of it, not wanting to get caught with it should the South lose, and figuring they'd return for it if the South won. A couple of years later, once Stuart began reading in earnest, he looked into it and realized that the story Nick and Lawrence had concocted was impossible for a myriad of obvious reasons, yet he had to give them credit for its solid surface-level plausibility. Stuart entered the woods at the same spot they'd entered it tonight, followed Nick and Lawrence's mapped-out directions ("At the first big rock take a left; when you come to the place where two trees are growing like a V out of the same trunk, make a right…") for a while and then abruptly, like falling headlong into a dream, he realized he was lost. There was no build-up, no vague sense of disorientation that gradually intensified. Just *blam*—*lost*. So lost that Stuart had no earthly idea which direction his house was. He stood there thinking, every moment further confirmation of how thoroughly lost he really was. He heard the rhythmic knocking from a woodpecker, the *tick-tick-tick* of branches being blown against each other. He strained his brain, tried to flex his hearing muscles, if there was such a thing, to try to detect some kind of human noise. But there was nothing, just the sounds of emptiness and space, and he felt the panic rising in him. It was the first time he thought: *This is going to be how I die.*

For years afterward he would berate himself for not at least trying to find his way out of the woods. But he'd just sat down in a closet-sized clearing, too terrified to cry, and waited for someone to find him. Which, eventually, someone did—his father, as it turned out—the calls at first coming from so far off that they didn't seem audible to Stuart at all, but rather as if they were emanating from some trance-like place simultaneously deep inside and *out*side of him which he later came to think of as his soul. Even when it became clear to him that the voice was real, he still did not get up and try to head towards them. He stayed and waited, waited until his father's voice (calm, purposeful, powerful) was nearly on top of him.

Now, as Stuart strode through the same woods with his brothers, unafraid and with their own sense of purpose, he understood that he'd been lost ever since.

"For what it's worth," Nick said, his voice appearing as if from another dimension, like a voiceover in one of those arty movies, "I've always liked Sydney. We all do. Whatever bullshit you might hear thrown around about her age, or whatever, fact is she's a good person. There's got to be some explanation."

"Oh," said Stuart, "there is." He noticed his breathing was getting heavier; a faint wisp of steam had begun appearing and disintegrating in front of his mouth. "And, like most explanations, it all comes back to my fuck-ups."

"You've always been too hard on yourself, Stu."

They drifted a couple of degrees farther westward; Lawrence had become just a luminous presence behind them. Stuart's instincts told him that the field and creek they were headed to was not much farther.

"What's depressing is, even now, fifty-three years old, I don't know what's important to me. I don't know what I want. When I think about it, and I'm honest with myself, I've never known."

Nick tucked the rifle under his arms and blew warm air into his cupped hands.

"You know I got my Ph.D., right?"

"Of course I did, Stu. Why wouldn't I?

"Well, because I never told you."

"I know you didn't. Can't believe it either. Neither can Lawrence. We're not fools. It hurt that you didn't, I won't lie." He turned his chin over his shoulder. "Right, Lawrence?"

"Huh?"

"I guess…" After all this time of thinking it, Stuart knew what he was about to say was going to sound silly, juvenile. "Well, I guess I thought you'd think it was frivolous and pretentious. Part of the liberal academy and all that."

"Well, sure," said Nick. "It is that." He turned to Stuart and though his face was awash in white light, Stuart was sure he detected a subtle half-smile, maybe even a wink. "But you're my little brother. I was proud as hell. Mom and Dad were, too. Even if they never said so."

Stuart's throat stuck. "I'm probably going to lose my job. My wife and kid…And I think, maybe I don't care anymore."

He considered his own words. What was he saying exactly? That he was through with living? That maybe he was ready to pack it in? The questions did not frighten him.

"I know what you mean." Lawrence's voice, from behind. He'd closed the distance a bit. Stuart and Nick turned to look at him. He was nothing more than an ink-black silhouette behind the cone of light. Then they turned back around and kept walking.

"This is the kind of thing," he went on, "that you read about in the paper. 'Three brothers go out hunting in the middle of the night, and one of them gets accidentally shot.' Nobody ever knows how it happened. It just did."

Stuart could hear the creek up ahead now, a crinkly sound.

"Yeah, well, either way, we're shooting a skunk," Nick said. "For Stu. Maybe put down a deer, too. All three of our families are going to live off of our bounty for a year."

"I'm not suggesting anything," Lawrence said. "I'm just pointing out the facts. Sometimes one guy accidentally shoots another. Sometimes the guy shoots himself."

"Okay," Nick said. "We got it, thanks. Points taken."

"You've been wanting to shoot something since you were eighteen years old, haven't you, Nick. Why didn't you just go hunting with Dad more often?"

Nick took two more steps and then stopped and turned, waited for Lawrence to get to him. Lawrence kept the spotlight pointed straight ahead, right into Nick's face and beyond. Calmly, Nick took his hand and lowered the spot so that the beam pointed down at the trail. He blinked at Lawrence; it seemed to Stuart that once he'd negotiated this position, he was unclear of how to proceed.

"You don't know what it's been like," said Nick.

"What *what's* been like, Nick? Jesus. What *is* it with you? Your wife, who loves you, by the way, beats cancer—could've *died*, and beats it entirely, no looking back, flat-out clean bill of health—and instead of being grateful, you bitch and moan because some people have the audacity to question a bogus war and have to pay less taxes than you. I mean, you got a new chance at your life, and you…My God, Nick. Don't you understand how—how goddamn *shortsighted* that bullshit is? How unappreciative? When there are…when there are people who…Oh, Christ, just forget it. Never mind. Just turn around and shoulder your rifle and let's go let you shoot something while whistling the 'Star Spangled Banner.' Maybe then you can finally die happy. Go on, little brother. Go."

To Stuart's mind, it was the most authority Lawrence had ever spoken with, and he had to admit it gave him a little charge to hear his older, quieter brother speak with such conviction. He wanted to get on with things.

But Nick did not turn around. He did obey one instruction, though: he shouldered his rifle. "It's not that I want to shoot something," he said. "It's just that I don't know how—I mean, there doesn't seem like there's any way to fix, to find any relief, any…peace…" He closed his eyes and let his head fall back; it looked like he'd fallen asleep. The sound of the creek was now a constant hum that had seeped into the world, like the presence of fluorescent lighting. "I always thought that before Dad died I'd find a way to make things right."

"Right for *who*?" Lawrence wanted to know.

Nick lifted a shoulder and rubbed his ear with it.

Lawrence sighed audibly, a quick hearty exhale. There was resignation in it. He hefted the spotlight and aimed it toward the clearing up ahead. He touched his hip again. "All right. We've come this far, huh? If someone gets shot, someone gets shot. Some things you can't do anything about. What the hell—At the end of the day, the world's gonna do what the world's gonna do. Am I right?"

As they started on again, Stuart noticed a stifled squeak escape from the vicinity of Nick. Was he *crying*? Fighting not to cry? Stuart let it go. He had to admit that these newly realized struggles in his brothers' lives were making him feel better about his own. The reaction was weird, and a little cruel, he supposed, but it was real. Stuart felt beyond the point of even wanting to deny it.

The path widened and Stuart led them through the trees' overhanging canopy to the edge of the clearing. The sudden clarity of the world caught him off-guard; Lawrence stepped through to his left but the spotlight made little difference. The moon was that bright. The field lit up before him like a bare stage. It was roughly oval, about the size of a baseball diamond, exactly as he remembered it, except that in the moonglow the knee-high grass looked silver. Abruptly Stuart hoped there weren't any animals around—they'd see them immediately, vividly, and in this light even Stuart couldn't miss, unless he tried to.

"Well, we won't be able to see any small game," Nick said. "Grass's too high."

Good point, thought Stuart, though he suspected they'd easily be able to see the grass rustling if something were moving down below.

"Douse the light, Lawrence." Nick approximated a sort of half-crouch and shuffled a few steps to the right, rifle poised across both hands. "Let's check over by the creek," he said.

"I'm putting this down," said Lawrence. "I can't feel my arms."

They followed Nick in the direction of the water sounds. When they reached the bank, they saw that someone had built a stone wall along the inside edge, effectively eliminating the bank and creating a four-foot drop-off down to the water. It looked more like a canal than a creek.

"The hell…" said Nick.

But it hit Stuart immediately: "So animals can't drink from this part of the creek. People must've been coming out here and just sitting and waiting for them—like we are. This forces the animals go to some other part of the creek to drink, some more secluded area."

After a moment, Nick said, "Is this *legal*?"

Lawrence shrugged, bent and picked up the spotlight again. "Township property. It can do whatever it wants, I guess."

"Who says it was the Township that did it?"

"Dad built this," said Stuart, the connection striking him unexpectedly. "I think. Or, he helped anyway. The Township contracted out. I remember him talking about it."

"Sheesh." Nick said. "Okay, it's now official. *Everyone* outsources."

"I remember him mentioning this, but I can't remember what he said about it. When he'd talk about his jobs I just nodded and tuned out." Stuart closed his eyes; he felt himself sway a little. "Kind of despicable, when I think about it. Too wrapped up in my own shit, I guess."

Nick and Lawrence both grunted, and it occurred to Stuart then that he was never going to acquire a permanent place on B— College's faculty. Floyd Reese had his mind made up about him, and no one was going to challenge that opinion. It came to him that a person's actions, even his words, did not necessarily reveal what was in his heart. And so as a result, Stuart's choices were few and futile: He could make a stink, defend himself, gather some documentation and fight the charges. He could make a conscious effort to show that he is *not* what Floyd Reese has accused him of, show that he's turned things around; it would be an admission to Reese's accusations, but also would establish a context for improvement. Or he could do nothing, embrace his innocence and good intentions, hope that his true nature shows through to the other people who hold his professional life in his hands.

Or he could quit.

The thought terrified him—like jolting awake in the middle of the night to the sound of an intruder. But there was a faint release, too, a full-body unclenching that he didn't know was there, a psychological exhale. The department chairs, the senior professors, the deans and vice presidents, the contract renewal applications, classroom evaluations, the mandates to teach the right books in the right way, the petty jealousies and political backbiting: being a college professor had come to feel too much like being a student in high school, worrying about your report card. And he hated the idea of him getting older every year while the students he taught stayed the same age; when they graduated it was like they were departing for new adventures while there he was waving *buon viaggio*, still stuck on the dock.

What became clear to him now was that he possessed two worthwhile things in his life: his job, which he could now admit to himself, was going nowhere and never would; and he had Sydney.

Salvaging both was impossible. Stuart just didn't have it in him.

"I've made a de—" he began, and at that moment a sudden burst of fluttering and muffled thumping erupted from behind them. They swung around as one to find streaky spots of darkness rising from the tall grass twenty or so yards into the field. Without thinking Stuart raised his rifle and squeezed the trigger simultaneously with the cracking of

Nick's rifle on his right and another pop from his left. Lawrence trained the spotlight over the field just in time for them to see one of those black splotches falling in slow motion back down to the grass.

"Whoa," said Nick.

Stuart's mind felt heavy and frozen. Rifle still raised, he noticed Lawrence in his peripheral vision and turned his gaze just enough to see him holding the spotlight under one arm, while with his free hand he leveled a pistol toward the field. It was a tiny thing, the pistol, its barrel only stuck out a couple of inches from Lawrence's clenched hand, but Stuart could clearly make out a thin tail of smoke winding upwards from the muzzle. "What the..."

"Grouse?" Nick wondered. "Pheasant?"

Lawrence lowered the pistol to his side and held it there, pointed downward. "Too big for quail."

Stuart and Nick still had their rifles leveled and poised, cheeks to the stocks. They seemed to notice this together and lowered the guns to their waists.

"Lawrence," said Stu. "What *is* that? Where'd you *get* it?"

"Get what?" Nick asked.

Lawrence lifted the little gun flat in his hand and looked at it, like he was as surprised as anyone to find it there. "Oh. In the basement. Jesus Christ," he said. "I guess there was a bullet in the chamber." There was a measure of awe in his voice.

"A bullet in the chamber," Stuart repeated. "Meaning—meaning *what*, Lawrence?" Then it hit him. "Lawrence, what the fuck were you up to?"

"Wait. You're shitting me," said Nick. "You're shitting me, Lawrence. Right?"

Lawrence seemed to think this over. "I don't know." And it was clear from the sunken look on his face that he *didn't* know.

"Let me see that thing—" Nick stepped toward him, crossing in front of Stu, but Lawrence reared back and threw the gun toward the spot the birds had just risen from. Nick stopped and just stared at him, then turned to Stuart. "I've never seen that thing before," he said. It came out sounding like a denial.

"Me neither," Lawrence said.

"One bullet, huh?"

Nobody said anything. They just let the fact hover there for a second or two.

"Well," said Nick. He turned and regarded the black field. "We got one of them, huh?" He elbowed Stuart. "You or me?"

Stuart shrugged. "You, would be my guess." Then he added, "Could've been Lawrence."

"Yeah, I guess so," Nick said. "Lawrence?"

"From the angle of…" Lawrence began. "Ah, hell, I don't have a clue. You guys fired *exactly* together. I was a second after. Plus, who knows if this thing could even pierce the skin."

"It can," said Nick.

"I guess it doesn't matter," Stuart said, though for some reason he didn't believe his own words.

"So…" Lawrence waved the spotlight beam around the field. He seemed to have located a lost bank of optimism. Stuart closed his eyes and waited. Though a faint smell of cordite lingered on the air, it was difficult to believe anything had just happened here. "We go look around for it?"

"Damn straight," said Nick—overly brightly, Stuart thought. "That's breakfast for six is what that is."

Cautiously, they moved into the field, toward the area where the birds, whatever they were, had emerged. Lawrence led the way. The tall grass slapped their shins, and every few steps Stuart felt a slight tugging around his ankles. The sky had brightened to a deep denim blue; Stuart had no idea what time it was and wondered if it might be nearing sunrise.

Toward the center of the field, they separated and fell into ranks. Stuart moved in a tight serpentine, looking for matted-down pockets in the grass. Nick was off to his right doing the same thing, pulling aside thick tangles of grass with the muzzle of his shotgun, and Lawrence waved the spotlight beam around the area randomly. It reminded Stuart of a prison yard in the movies.

"It should be right here," Nick said. "Lawrence, anything?"

"Nada."

"I don't get it. The thing dropped like a stone."

"Actually," Stuart offered, "I thought it kind of...fluttered down."

"Nope. A stone. Right—" he chopped his rifle through the grass like a golf club—"*here*."

"Maybe we just winged it?" Lawrence said.

"But it still *fell*. We all saw it. There should still be..."

"Yeah. But there isn't."

Stuart continued circling; he felt his blood pushing through his veins, banging against the inner walls. Why did Lawrence have that gun? And what had its purpose been before he'd found it? He felt as if he was on the verge of a discovery that would only become clear if he found whatever it was that they'd shot. But as he began tracking through the same paths he'd already carved in the tall field grass, he understood that that was not going to happen—the thing they'd shot was gone. And he would have to accept that. They all would.

He took a breath, detected the balmy scent of morning dew.

"Come on," he said. "That's enough. Let's go."

"What're you *talking* about?" Nick nearly whined. He froze and glanced around, as if he couldn't fathom the idea that such a world as this existed.

"We did what we came out here to do," Stuart said gently. "It's over. Time to move on."

Nick broke open his shotgun and reached into his shorts pocket for another shell. "No," he said. "Huh-uh. Nope."

Stuart stepped over to him. He reached out and put his hand to his brother' cheek, and held it there. "Nick," he said. "Come on. We can do this."

"But . . . where did it *go*?"

"I don't know. It's just gone."

Nick cleared his throat, but the lump in it stayed, Stuart could hear it. He cleared it again. "What do *you* say about this, Lawrence?" Another throat-clearing; this one did the trick. "You have a vote here, too."

"I have to pee," Lawrence said flatly.

"Me, too," said Stuart. And he *did*, too; he couldn't remember the last time he'd gone. Sometime before his and Sydney's trek to Joey O's. Suddenly, the pressure in his hips was tremendous. He took his hand from Nick's cheek.

"Okay then," Nick said, blinking two, three, four times rapidly. He broke the shotgun open again and dumped the shells to the ground. His motions were sharp and abrupt. He had the air of someone who's made a decision that he didn't like, and the only way to get through it was to push his way through, quickly and without thinking. "Group pee it is."

"Yes!" Stuart said. The suggestion struck him as absolutely perfect. "Yes. Exactly."

"Wait. No." Lawrence took a step back. For some reason he shined the spotlight toward the far treeline. "That's . . . No, I don't like that idea."

"Why not?" Nick had set down his rifle and was unzipping his khaki shorts.

"Yeah." Stuart reached for his own zipper, found that it was already down. *How the hell did* that *happen*? "Why not, Lawrence?"

"Well…" Lawrence's expression drifted from horrified to puzzled, then seemed to steady itself. "I take a *really* long time, for one thing."

"That's okay." Nick sidled over closer to Stuart. "I'm in no hurry." He flicked his head at Lawrence: *Come on, over here.*

Lawrence waited a beat, then set the spotlight down—it disappeared beneath the high grass, lighting it from underneath—and stepped over to them. With Nick on his right and Lawrence on his left, all three of them with hands poised at the ready, Stuart felt his chest fill with something like hope.

"Okay," said Lawrence. "For those who are new, this is the part where we just stand here for a while and wait. So what do you want to talk about?"

But no one spoke. They just stood and listened to the breeze hum through the trees across the way, the soft rustling of the leaves, and watching the thin beam of light cutting through the grass at their feet.

....

The sun was rising behind them as they emerged from the woods along State Route 33 adjacent to their childhood house. The first thing Stuart noticed was that his father's pickup—well, *his* pickup now, his and Sydney's—was parked in the driveway. Inside the house dim lights flickered behind the widows. Stuart crossed the road with Nick and Lawrence and mounted the little rise into the side yard. Abruptly, Stuart felt exhaustion overtake him. He wanted to sleep and sleep.

They crossed to the back porch. They set their rifles and the spotlight against the vinyl siding by the door, and Nick pulled the door open. Stuart and Lawrence followed him inside.

The sound of voices hit him first—Sydney's and Abigail's—then the clattering of pans on the stove, sizzling noises, sounds of life. They turned the corner into the kitchen to find Sydney and Abigail sitting across from each other, knees almost touching, in two of the six remaining chairs, both giggling, seemingly, at once, while Celina busied herself with two pans—brand new, by the looks of them—on the stove. Eggs and bacon. Three candles in glass holders evenly spaced along the countertop threw wavering halos of light into the already brightening room. When the women turned to them and offered sympathetic smiles, Stuart inhaled the scent of the bacon, and all he could feel was gratitude: Thank God he and his brothers weren't returning victorious, dead and bloody grouse in hand.

Epilogue: Abigail

On the way back from the cemetery, they returned an emotionally exhausted Andy Mooney safely to his little house somewhere out in the Township, then Celina suggested a quick stop at the 24-hour Giant Eagle in New Bentlee. They picked up eggs, coffee, bacon, fat-free half-and-half, a day-old loaf of sliced Italian bread, two cheapo Teflon-coated skillets, a stove-top coffee pot, three scentless candles and a box of matches so they could see what they were doing, paper towels, paper plates, and a variety pack of plastic utensils, plus a bottle of Motrin, toothbrush, and travel size tube of Crest for Abigail. Celina used her credit card to pay for everything.

Back at the house, finally dropping down into one of the kitchen chairs, Abigail was able to confirm something that she'd suspected during the ride back: she was feeling remarkably chipper, considering. She couldn't remember the last time she'd been drunk—certainly it was well before the chemo—and, once she'd blown past the invisible line that separates inebriated from wasted, she would have expected her body to simply shut down. But it hadn't. In fact, she'd recovered like a seasoned drinker half her age.

Her muscles felt like pudding—soft and heavy, but pleasant.

Sydney disappeared to the upstairs bathroom and Celina began unpacking the groceries, spacing the candles along the counter and lighting them, then got the coffee going. When the pot began gurgling she took out one of the pans and held it up to her face. "Oh, shit," she said, setting the pan back down, rather calmly.

"What?"

"Forgot some, whatta-ya-call-it, dishwashing liquid."

"Eh…" Abigail shooed this dilemma away with a wave of her hand; she had regained her determination to not let anything get her down. "Just rinse it off."

"Yeah," Celina said, "okay, you're right," and she turned on the water. She rinsed off the pan, and then the other, dried them with a paper towel, and set them on the stove and began opening the package of bacon with her teeth. The sight of her sister-in-law busying herself around the kitchen was particularly comforting—even encouraging—to Abigail.

"I'm going to miss this place," she said.

Celina used a plastic knife to separate strips of bacon from the slab. "Yeah," she said. "I suppose I will, too."

The response was surprising, but no sooner had it registered with Abigail that an excited nervousness returned, filling her chest and causing a jittery sensation in her legs. She tried to stave it off, to think of something else, but she couldn't: Had Sydney been *serious* when she offered her baby to Abigail? Could a person just…*do* that? The words had been spoken, she was sure of that, but she also had had a lot to drink, had been nauseous and shivery and her brain had felt like soft tar. Maybe she'd misread the tone? Sydney could have been joking, speaking sarcastically, trying to prove some point that Abigail surely had missed. And what if Sydney *had* been serious? Would Abigail *actually* consider taking her up on such an offer? Would *Nick*? Well…she tried to shake the thought away; though she knew the answer, she couldn't let the words form in her mind.

"You were quite the little party girl tonight, missy," Celina said, her back to the room, still peeling off strips of bacon and placing them in the smaller of the two skillets. "Never saw that side of you before."

"Oh, I'm embarrassed." Though she really wasn't, not at all; it just seemed like something a responsible woman ought to say.

"When we get back to Maryland, I think I'm going to schedule one of those couple's spa treatments for Lawrence and me. Massages and facials and gooey wraps, the whole shebang. A whole day of it. We haven't been taking very good care of ourselves lately."

"It's important to take care of your health," Abigail agreed, perhaps the most obvious, unhelpful statement she'd ever uttered.

"I don't want the kids having to go through this stuff until they're at *least* as old as we are."

"I was only forty-five when my father went," Abigail said. "That was awful. But I can't say it's any easier now."

"No," Celina agreed. "I suppose it isn't." She folded the empty bacon wrapper into quarters and set it on the counter. Then she lit the burner underneath the skillet. "Just playing straight odds, Lawrence is next."

"Oh, Celina!"

"Hey, facts is facts. Plus—"

"Stop it."

"I haven't been the best . . . partner to him. Not for a while now."

"None of us are," Abigail said. "None of us *ever* are."

"Well . . . that has to change, I think." Celina slid the bread out of its paper bag. She stared at it for a moment. "I could make French toast. Or I could do those over-easy eggs? Inside the hole in the bread?"

"Mm." Abigail stood and adjusted the six kitchen chairs back into a loose oval, leaving enough room in the center for a table that no longer was there. Then she sat back down. "Once we all get back home, let's wait a month or two, put this behind us, then all meet somewhere for a long weekend. New York City. Or, I don't know, Vegas. Someplace fun like that. The only time we ever see each other it's . . . well, *here*. We need a new context, I think. With less stress."

"*You* set loose in Vegas? I don't think the world's ready for that."

"Well, I mean, it doesn't have to be Vegas. We could—"

"I'm joking, Ab." Celina smiled over her shoulder. "Too soon?"

The smell of bacon began to fill the kitchen. "Can I help?"

"Um . . . nah. Just relax."

The upstairs toilet flushed and the pipes began to hum and then Sydney came clomping down the stairs. She turned the corner and then stopped, as if catching Abigail and Celina in the act of something. She froze and flashed an impish smile. "Were you two talking about me?"

"Actually," said Celina, "we weren't."

"We should've got toilet paper. Oh my god, that smells awesome."

"Didn't think of toilet paper," Celina said. "It's like we're moving back *in*."

Sydney shuffled over and dropped into one of the chairs across from Abigail. "Pfew. You know, these days I've been sleeping at *least* ten hours a night. But, I don't know what it is, I feel kinda, *energized* right now."

"It's called delirium, dear," Celina said. She took an egg from the carton. "I forgot we didn't have bowls. It'll have to be eggs in the toast." She lit another burner.

"Maybe you're right; maybe I *am* delirious." Sydney turned to Abigail and gave a little giggle. She was beaming. "Oh my god, we're really going to do this, aren't we? I thought after it sat with me a while I'd . . . Hey, don't even *tell* me you're thinking of backing out on me, girl."

A hot flash struck Abigail. Her ears and neck tingled. "No. I'm all in."

"Backing out of what?" Celina asked. She cracked an egg against the counter.

"Abigail and Nick are going to adopt this baby." She pointed with both index fingers to her stomach.

Celina turned to them and stared dumbly. She blinked; blinked again. "Huh?"

The thought of having to explain this whole thing brought a wave of dread slamming down on Abigail, but Sydney spoke right up.

"Okay, here it is: The baby's not Stuart's. Terrible, horrible, regretful mistake of all mistakes. So Ab and Nick are going to adopt it. Him. Her. Whatever. Stuart didn't want to find out when we had the chance." She brought her hand to her mouth, a pensive gesture. "I probably should've figured out that he *knew* something wasn't right when he told the sonogram tech, 'No, that's okay, we're good, thanks. We'll pass on that particular information.' Wow. That's how blind *I* was, I guess."

"Wait. Just hold on one second here." Celina brandished a plastic fork in her fist, pointing the tines at them like a weapon. They didn't have a spatula and she'd been using the fork to turn the bacon. "So you're... good lord, Sydney. You're just gonna give up your *baby*, just like that? Because—because what? You're *embarrassed*? You don't wanna be *bothered*? Am I—am I hearing this right?"

"Oh, Celina." Sydney smiled sympathetically. "I'm not *giving up* anything. I'm saving my marriage. And maybe my husband's life."

"Stuart might surprise you, you know. Maybe he'll step up. Maybe he'll do what's best for you, and for..."

"That's just it. I *know* he will, Celina. I know he will. That's why I'm doing this. To spare him from having to. And Abigail needs this. Don't argue with me, Ab," though Abigail felt too numb to argue. "I've heard it in your voice these last few months; I've seen it in your eyes. You need this. Don't deny it." She turned and fixed her eyes on the window above the sink, on the now-brightening sky. "So they'll raise this baby, and I'll be able to still be in her life—Screw it, *her*. Her, her, her, her, her. Okay? I asked the technician after Stuart left the room."

Abigail's heart dropped in her chest, a sudden *thunk*, and had to double-time it to lift itself back to where it belonged, and when it did, her blood felt electric. She could hear the beating of her eardrums, all those little hammers and anvils.

"Please, Celina," Sydney said. "I'm begging you. *Please* don't let that bacon burn."

Celina stared them both down a moment then turned and began flipping the bacon with the fork; the steady sizzling sound crested like a wave and she pulled her hand away. "Damn it!" She shook her hand out. "Got me." She put the side of her wrist in her mouth and sucked it while looking Abigail straight in the eyes. She smiled. "Bentlee bacon," she said. "Extra grease."

Abigail and Sydney laughed and then the front door slammed open and the men came in stamping their feet as if to warm them—first Lawrence, then Nick, then Stuart behind, peering over their shoulders. They looked around, eyes wide, a sort of gleeful anxiety on their faces.

Finally Nick found his voice. "Well lookie here. What's this?"

"Breakfast," said Celina, an obvious answer but her voice was pleasant enough.

"Thought there wasn't any gas."

"No, it's just the electric that's been shut off. Gas still works."

"Oh, that's right." Nick stepped all the way into the kitchen. "Well…Wonderful."

It occurred to Abigail to ask where they've been, but she didn't; she waited for Celina or Sydney to ask, but they didn't either. They just let it go.

Nick pulled up a chair next to Abigail, and Lawrence took another. Stuart hung back, hovering, until Sydney patted the chair next to her and smiled a *please-sit-down-it's-okay* smile. Stuart shuffled over, pulled out the chair, and sat. Abigail noticed the way Stuart slid the chair out, then realized that they'd *all* done the same thing: slid the chair out, as if there was still a table there to squeeze between.

"What's the matter, honey?" Nick was leaning in; he framed her face in his hands.

For a moment, she was worried. "What?"

"You're crying."

"Oh." And the realization brought a titter to her stomach and she thought she might start laughing hysterically at the same time. "It's…it's nothing. I just wish we hadn't sold the table."

He used his thumbs to wipe away the tears.

Celina approached the ring of chairs. Behind her, on the countertop, she had the eggs in the hollowed-out Italian toast on one paper plate and the bacon on another, blotted with a paper towel. "Lawrence?" She placed her hands on his shoulders; he just sat there, didn't try to turn around to look at her. "Lawrence, come with me for a minute, would you, dear? I need to talk to you in the living room."

For five long seconds he didn't react. Then he slapped his thighs and stood. A quick pulse of fear stabbed through Abigail: What was she going to *say* to him? But as Celina followed her husband into the hallway she turned toward Abigail and subtly shook her head no: *Don't worry, it's not about that.*

And a wave of pure joy coursed through Abigail. She felt herself shudder. It was almost overwhelming, but beautifully so. In an effort at some sort of gratitude she tried to offer Celina a gesture of encouragement: She fixed her face into an expression she hoped conveyed this, but Celina wasn't looking.

When they were gone, Nick said, "So, should we eat? I hadn't realized I was hungry, but…man, I'm *hungry*."

"Me, too," Sydney said. "But that goes without saying, huh?" She placed her hand on Stuart's knee.

"Let's wait for them," Abigail suggested, meaning Lawrence and Celina.

"Yeah," Nick agreed. "We should."

"We have some things to talk about anyway," Sydney said.

Stuart's face pulled tight with something like horror, but Sydney was leaning toward him, gazing at him until he met her eyes. "It's okay, Stu," she said. "Look at me." He did. "It's okay."

His face relaxed.

"I'm so hungry," Abigail said quickly, brightly. "Let's talk later."

Sydney leaned back. "That's a good idea."

"Talk about what?" Nick said. "Hey, come on, guys, don't keep me in the dark. That's not playing fair." There was a playful whine in his voice.

Calm had settled over Abigail, and, suddenly dazed with sleepiness, she rested her head on her husband's shoulder.

"What's this thing we have to talk about?"

"After we eat," she managed.

Celina and then Lawrence came back into the kitchen. Lawrence moved with raised shoulders, as if a weight had been lifted. He slid out his chair and sat. "So what're we talking about?"

"Why didn't you guys get started?" Celina said. She shook her head as if she'd never in all her days come across such stubbornness. "Oh, well. I guess I have to do *every*thing around here, huh?

"That's why we keep you around, Leenie," Nick said.

Celina loaded up the paper plates and carried them two at a time over to the ring of chairs; she had to kind of fold the cheapo plates like a slice of New York pizza to keep them from collapsing onto the floor. When everybody had one, and a plastic fork, she went back for her own.

"Guess we don't need these anymore," she said, and one by one blew out the candles.

And she was right; they didn't: the sun had crested over the treeline across Route 33, and the kitchen now radiated in an opaque glaze of blue-white light. Abigail lowered her gaze to the floor, inside their circle of chairs, and saw four small squares of lighter linoleum where for all those years the legs to the table had been. Her breath caught and she held it.

When Celina had her own plate she settled into the one empty chair, between Nick and Lawrence. She smiled wearily. "So..."

For a moment all six sat with knees squeezed together, balancing the leaky paper plates on their laps, stalling, not wanting to take that first bite, not wanting to let the day begin.

Acknowledgments

Special thanks to my family—my parents, Carmen and Adele Torockio, Susan Mazzei, and Daniel Torockio.

Thanks also to Daniel Donaghy, Troy Fornof, and Jim Ritchie, and to Diane Goettel at Black Lawrence Press.

I am grateful to Eastern Connecticut State University for providing grants during the writing of this book.

Photo: Thomas Hurlbut

Christopher Torockio is the author of the novel *Floating Holidays*, and the story collections *The Truth at Daybreak* and *Presence*. His fiction has appeared in *Ploughshares, The Gettysburg Review, The Iowa Review, The Antioch Review, Willow Springs, Colorado Review, New Orleans Review*, and many other publications. A native of Pittsburgh, he now lives with his wife and son in Connecticut and teaches at Eastern Connecticut State University.